Unmade

The Lynburn Legacy

Book 3

SARAH REES BRENNAN

Random House New York

Text copyright © 2014 by Sarah Rees Brennan
Jacket art copyright © 2014 by Terry Bidgood/Trevillion Images
Map copyright © 2013 by Theo Black

"The Waking," copyright © 1953 by Theodore Roethke; from *Collected Poems* by Theodore Roethke. Used by permission of Doubleday, an imprint of the Knopf Doubleday Publishing Group, a division of Random House LLC. All rights reserved.

Visit us on the Web! randomhouse.com/teens
Educators and librarians, for a variety of teaching tools, visit us at
RHTeachersLibrarians.com

Library of Congress Cataloging-in-Publication Data
Brennan, Sarah Rees.
Unmade / Sarah Rees Brennan.—First edition.
pages cm.—(The Lynburn legacy ; book 3)
Summary: "Kami Glass and friends battle sorcerers in order to save the sleepy town of Sorry-in-the-Vale while Kami struggles with her own emotions, caught between Ash, the boy who loves her, and Jared, the boy she loves."—Provided by publisher.
ISBN 978-0-375-87043-9 (trade)—ISBN 978-0-375-97043-6 (lib. bdg.)—
ISBN 978-0-375-97996-5 (ebook)
[1. Magic—Fiction. 2. Magicians—Fiction. 3. Love—Fiction. 4. Family life—England—Fiction. 5. England—Fiction. 6. Horror stories.] I. Title.
PZ7.B751645Unm 2014 [Fic]—dc23 2013043640

Printed in the United States of America
10 9 8 7 6 5 4 3 2 1
First Edition

This is for Ashling and James, at the end of an era.
(February 2014)

In my mind, a true friend is someone who makes the world better, brighter, and more fun, and who is still there when the world sucks. Thank you both, for always doing both.

I hope your awesomeness will continue in this new era, and I have every confidence that it will. And in return for this excellent friendshipping, I wish to make you both these two promises.

1) I will always be on the other end of an email, and once I get the email, I'll find my phone.

2) I will never know anything about politics.

I know you guys will never be surprised.

Contents

PART V
SORROW AND SACRIFICE

PART VI
NO RESTING IN PEACE

PART VII
SORCERY IN THE VALE

EPILOGUE

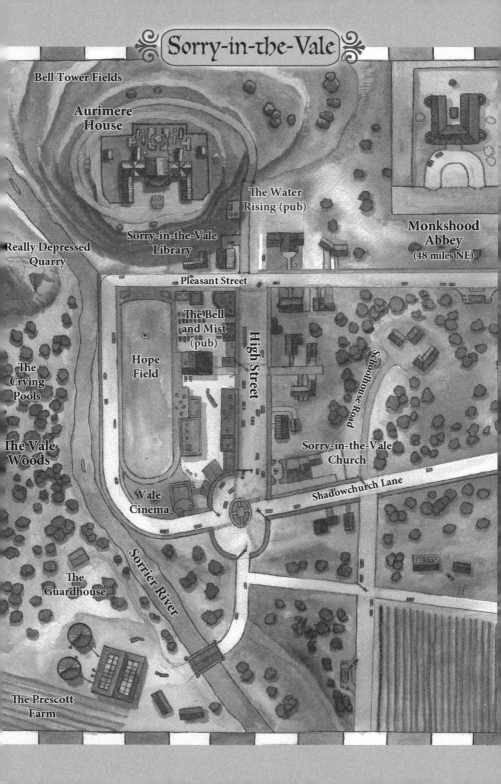

PART I
LOSS AND BLOOD

We are not now that strength which in old days
Moved earth and heaven; that which we are, we are;
One equal temper of heroic hearts,
Made weak by time and fate, but strong in will
To strive, to seek, to find, and not to yield.
—*Alfred, Lord Tennyson*

Chapter One
Desperate Times

Kami Glass was standing too close to the fire. The magical flames scorched her face, so hot that though her eyes stung and her vision swam, there was no possibility of tears.

Aurimere House, the golden manor from which the Lynburn sorcerers had ruled her town for centuries, was surrounded by a ring of fire that never spread too far or burned completely out. The flames ebbed and flowed like a wicked orange sea, separating her from the house.

There's nothing in there for you, said Ash Lynburn, one of the few good sorcerers left alive and the one sorcerer who was connected to her, mind to mind. *He's gone.*

You don't know that, Kami told him.

I do know that, said Ash. *And if you would admit it, you know it too. He's not in there. He's not anywhere. He's dead.*

Ash's emotions coursed through her, sinking into her every pore. The connection between them was like adding a drop of ink to a glass of water: everything that had been clear becoming distorted. There was no way to separate the two of them, no matter how different they were or how poorly they mixed.

No matter that Kami didn't want to be connected to

Ash, and he didn't want to be connected to her. They had linked because they had to, because as source and sorcerer together they had magical power that could be used to save their friends and protect their home.

They had been linked for over a month now. They were getting used to it, but it wasn't getting any easier.

Kami had always wanted to be in control of herself; she had never wanted anyone else to try to control her. Ash did not mean to, but his cautions and misgivings were constant obstacles in her path. She felt fenced in on every side.

Worse than that, she felt Ash's misery and despair, heavy as an anchor around her neck. He had no hope, and she did not have hope enough for both of them.

What was she supposed to say about Ash's half brother Jared, her first source, the one she had loved, the boy she had been linked to for so much of her life? "He's not dead! And we're still dating!"?

It was her own mother who had told her he was dead.

They had all known that something terrible must have happened.

Rob Lynburn and all the sorcerers on his side, the ones who wanted a return to the days when sorcerers sacrificed people for power, had beaten them in a battle and taken over the manor. Ash's mother Lillian, the only adult sorcerer left alive on their side, and Kami's little brother Ten had both been captured in Aurimere. Everyone had been trying to plan a rescue mission when Lillian, holding Ten's hand in a steely grip so he would not be able to get away from her, staggered in through the door of the inn. Lillian had always carried herself like the leader of the town before, but not then. She had seemed defeated, and instead of making a speech she had only made a proclamation, like a specter or a banshee calling out tidings of death, that Jared was lost.

Ten had stood mute, shaking in Dad's arms, but he had told his tale later, reluctantly, in small shuddering pieces through barely parted lips: how he had been held in a little room up in the attic, and the door had slammed open, and there Jared had been, ordering him to run. Rob had been there too; Ten could barely speak about it, but they knew Jared could not have escaped, that Jared would have had to stop Rob from going after the terrified fleeing child.

They knew no more until Kami's mother Claire, who was allowed entry into Aurimere House because she was a favored and submissive servant to the sorcerers, told Kami what she had found in that attic room.

Her mother had hardly spoken to Kami in weeks.

The silence between them was like the cold careful quiet that had fallen over their town since Rob had won the day and taken the manor. Nobody wanted to break the ice: the ice breaking meant dark waters might rush in and drown them all.

Kami had become used to the chilly absence where words and understanding had once been. She sat at the table, eating in silence as her mother made breakfast for the boys. It was a shock when her mother spoke.

"Please be careful today."

"Why?" Kami asked softly. When her mother did not

reply, she put down her spoon, watching her hands shake as she did so. She raised her voice, demanding an answer. *"Why?"*

Claire flinched, her shoulders hunched. "Rob demanded a sacrifice, and the town did not give him one."

"I remember," said Kami.

"Now he's the lord of the manor, and his word is law."

"Not to me," said Kami.

"To everyone," her mother snapped. "His word is law because to disobey him is death, do you understand me? He's been talking to the mayor, and the mayor promised him—he promised Rob would have the winter sacrifice today."

"Why would he promise that?" Kami whispered.

"The magic is greater if the sacrifice is willing," said Claire, making eggs and soldiers for Kami's brothers. She did not look up. "If the person who will be the sacrifice is willing, that is best of all, but failing that—if the town gives them up, there is more power in the sacrifice. That is the value of this town to its sorcerer. That is why Rob has always wanted us to cooperate, has given us time to understand that we must. We are going to cooperate. Cooperation is what will keep us alive. There is no choice."

"It can't happen! Nobody's going to just give up a person they know to be sacrificed!"

Kami's shout rang through the kitchen. Her own voice sounded desperate. It sounded like a lie. Her mother was silent.

"We cannot see evil and say nothing. We can't see people murdered and do nothing," Kami said savagely.

Claire turned then, wheeled around from the kitchen

counter, her back to its brightly painted egg cups and steaming coffee. She faced Kami.

"I can," said Claire. "I can and will do anything to keep my children safe. What was it that all your bravery won you, Kami? What came of your little rebellion? Your brother was taken up to Aurimere to be murdered with a golden knife. You dragged your family under the sorcerer's eye. You put your brothers in danger. You did that, and if Ten had died, you would have done that too."

It was something Kami had told herself all through this lonely winter, lying shivering in the dark, not able to get warm enough beneath her bedclothes to sleep. But she had not expected to hear it from her own mother, over a breakfast table in a room full of light. She stared mutely up into Claire's face, worn by terror and exhaustion but still beautiful, a face Kami had loved and trusted all her life.

Mum's shoulders sagged. She held on to the back of a chair as if she could not stand under the weight of all she feared.

"I don't want to say this, Kami," she whispered. "I know you meant it all for the best, but the only way we can be safe is not to fight. Fighting will win us nothing and cost us everything. Your Lynburn, I know what he did for Ten. I know he did it because of you. I know he went into that room and faced down his mother and his father for you."

Kami bowed her head. She didn't want to see her mother saying this. She did not want to hear her mother say it, did not want the knowledge, but she had always tried to face the truth and she could not run from it now.

"He saved Ten," Claire whispered. "But nobody has seen

him or Rosalind Lynburn for more than a month. I never wanted to tell you this, Kami, but I saw the room that Ten escaped from. I saw the blood on the floor and the walls. There was so much blood. Nobody could have lost that much blood and lived. Rob made me wash the boards on my hands and knees so I would have a tale to carry back to you. Nobody but Rob Lynburn left that room alive. He killed his own child. I will not let him kill mine. If evil is the price I have to pay for your lives, I will pay it."

"And I should pay it too," Kami said, her voice a whisper as dry as a dead winter leaf, ready to be blown away in the slightest wind. "I should close my eyes to everything going on in this town, because if I don't, someone I love will die, and it will be my fault."

"Someone's already dead." Claire looked at her hands as if there was blood still on them, scarlet embedded in her nails. Kami could almost see it, so vivid it was sickening, all that blood and her mother scrubbing it away, and not telling a soul until now. "Jared Lynburn is dead. Didn't you love him?"

Kami felt as if her mother had lifted one of those hands and hit her. "I thought the question was, did I kill him?"

"Didn't you kill him?" Mum asked. "Who else would he have died for?"

"Claire!"

Kami had not said that. She and her mother both turned, guilty as if they had been keeping secrets again, and saw her father at the door. His black eyes were narrowed.

"You don't talk to Kami like that," he said. "Not ever again." He paused. Kami knew she did not want to hear what he had to say next, when he was so angry and yet he still had to hesitate before he told her mother, "There's that flat over your restaurant. Why don't you go there for a while?"

They were both silent, caught in the stillness of utter shock. Dad had been sleeping in the office for weeks now, but Kami had not thought—she had not wanted to believe—he would do anything irrevocable.

"No," her mother said. She held on to the back of the chair with one hand and held the other out to him. Light outlined her hand, light filled her eyes, as if love was sorcery and she could make him change his mind.

Jon looked at her and, slowly, shook his head.

"You lied to me, you lied to Kami, you're acting like a sympathizer to murdering sorcerers, and you don't even seem to understand why what you're doing is wrong. I don't even recognize you anymore. I don't trust you with my children. I don't want you here."

Kami had not been able to bear it for a moment longer. She had stumbled out of their kitchen and down the crazy paving, through their gate and up the winding road to the rise where Aurimere House stood wreathed in flame. She walked too close to the fire and almost savored being blind to all the white blazing centers of the flame.

She could still hear her mother's voice saying, "There was so much blood. Nobody could have lost that much blood and lived."

She had not wanted to believe it. She still did not want to believe it. She wanted to hope, to believe that there was something she could do.

She wanted to believe that if Jared was dead, she would know. He had been so much a part of her all her life. Even if they had been separated, surely something would have told her that he was completely lost. It did not feel right that magic should be stronger than her own painfully stubborn, painfully clinging heart. She should *know*.

I knew, said Ash. *I knew my father would make Jared pay for defying him. We're Lynburns. We do not forgive. We never permit a second sin against us.*

She refused to surrender to despair, even in her own mind.

I'm getting a little tired of hearing all these mystical pronouncements about Lynburns, Kami said, and tried to show Ash nothing but determination. *"We are creatures of red and gold," "We do not forgive," "We do not need hearts," "Our family motto is 'Hot blond death . . .'"*

We don't say that last one, said Ash, both bemused and amused. The emotions ran through Kami, sweet but alien, more strange than pleasant.

I admit I may have made that last one up, Kami said. *But I stole the last piece of toast at breakfast yesterday, and you didn't say "Lynburns never permit a second sin" and stab me in the hand with a fork. Even Rob is not consistent all the time. We don't know what he did to Jared. We don't know anything. Jared could still be in there.*

And how would you suggest we get in there to find him? Ash asked.

Kami had been trying to think of a plan to do that for weeks, long before her mother's words had sent her running up to Aurimere as if she could plunge through the flame and rescue Jared, weeks too late.

All her plans had been ridiculous, the laughable imaginings of a panicking child. Or perhaps that was just how they appeared to Ash. Kami was slowly losing her grip on how to differentiate between her darkening view of the world and the shadow through which Ash saw things.

She felt Ash's regret, sympathetic but chilling, like a cold hand placed kindly on her shoulder. She tried to pull herself together the only way she knew how.

I have a plan to get in, she told him. *This is fire. We can go to our school and steal all the fire extinguishers there: we can put it out enough to get in.*

It's magical fire, said Ash. *That's why it never burns out and never spreads. Fire extinguishers aren't going to work.*

He had vetoed every one of her plans.

Lucky for you, I have another scheme. First I need a hundred ducks, but after that it will all be pretty simple.

What do you need the ducks for?

I'm going to put a whole bunch of them in a giant catapult and launch them over Aurimere, Kami said. *This will create a distraction. My message will be: Look at all the ducks I give.*

Ash's amusement sang through her body as a laugh would have sung through her ears: appreciative but humoring her too.

Jared would have said, *I'm in. What's our next move?*

Kami turned her face away from the fires around Aurimere and looked out on the town. She told herself the fire was too hot, and that was why her eyes were stinging; that the smoke had got into her throat, scorching it, and that was why it ached. She lied to herself because she did not know how she would put herself back together if she fell apart.

Sorry-in-the-Vale from this vantage point was all gold angles, roofs and spinning weathervanes under a sky pale and sick with long winter. She thought about Jared, his face that was all angles and harsh lines, one cheek marked with a long white scar and eyes the color of the sky above their town. He looked cruel until he smiled, and all his smiles were small and brief.

She had always thought that Jared looked like he fit into the town and the woods around it, maybe because he was one of the sorcerers this town had been created for and ruled by for so long. Maybe because she had always thought he looked like home.

"Didn't you love him?" her mother had asked. "Didn't you kill him?"

Ash, the constant unwanted guest in her heart, said, *You're not the only one who misses him. He was my brother. I barely got the chance to know him and now he's gone.*

She was not the only one who missed him, but she was the only one who could not accept his death.

Kami had tried to go on with her newspaper, had tried to cope with being linked to Ash and her mother being more and more under the sway of Aurimere. She had tried to carry on, and she had kept hoping.

Everybody was always telling her she was wrong: Angela and Holly with their quiet sympathy, Ash with the sharp grief that cut into every hope she had, and now her own mother in simple words, in the cold light of day.

Jared Lynburn is dead.

The crackling of the fire stuttered and hissed. Kami spun around to see the fire had parted, like water parting at a god's command to make a passage from the door of Aurimere House to the road that led into Sorry-in-the-Vale.

Kami watched Rob Lynburn come out of the great doors of Aurimere House, over which was written the legend YOU ARE NOT SAFE. He looked around with a smile, lord of all he surveyed.

Until his eyes fell on Kami. His genial beam flickered for an instant and then steadied. He simply smiled and let his gaze pass over her, as if she was a part of his town and thus a possession, something utterly insignificant over which he had absolute control.

His sorcerers followed him in a procession down the road to Sorry-in-the-Vale.

The last one was scarlet-haired Ruth Sherman, one of the sorcerous strangers Rob had called to enjoy the magical benefits of his town, the power that his sacrifices would offer. She was wearing her hair loose, trailing like a comet's tail, and in the wake of that scarlet trail, the circle of fire closed with a sound like a whisper in a hush.

Get everyone, Kami told Ash in her head. She felt his dread as well as her own, drowning out all courage. *Come quickly. I don't know if they killed Jared, but I think they are going to kill someone else.*

Kami followed where Rob and his sorcerers went, down the broad golden expanse of Sorry-in-the-Vale's High Street. Inn, sweet shop, grocer's, gift shop, the little café where they sold scones and lemonade, and just before the church, the town hall.

It was only a small building, though it was one of the oldest: four hundred years old, Cotswold stone. Kami remembered the details about it because one of the Somervilles, her mother's family, had built it. Under the eave of the low roof, almost hidden in shadow, were golden words: MUNDUS VULT DECIPI.

It meant: *The world wants to be deceived.*

The Somerville who had built this place had known about sorcerers, Kami thought. He had seen the town turning a blind eye and letting the victims be sacrificed.

There were people filing into the town hall.

Kami had not seen this many people in weeks. At the beginning of Rob's bid for power, everyone had pretended life would go on as normal. Everyone had talked a little more loudly and brightly than before, and continued determined on their course, thinking the sorcerers would sort it all out. Now that Rob had won, the streets were emptier, voices were fading into silence, and the shelves at the grocer's were half full and never restocked. When Kami passed by the windows of houses, she saw curtains moving and glimpsed scared faces hiding as soon as they were seen.

This was why Rob had waited. This was how Rob had got them to cooperate. He had known that people could not last long under the silent remorseless pressure of fear, that they would give up anything in hope that the fear would end.

This many people meant that Rob had called them here together.

The hall had a wide black-painted door, its handle twined with wrought-iron weeds, as though it had lain once at the bottom of a lake. Kami saw it fall shut behind the last of the crowd, and she ran up the steps and closed her hand around that wrought-iron handle.

Kami pushed open the door and saw a table, spread with white, saw the glow of light through stained-glass windows land on long golden knives. She saw the man, bound and gagged, on the altar.

Kami charged over the threshold. Ruth Sherman placed herself between Kami and the pale altar, her red brows raised.

"No sources allowed," she said, and knocked Kami back across the threshold, flat on the stone steps.

Kami had been able to fight sorcerers better once, before they had all fed their power with blood: when she had been linked to Jared, and the magic had flowed easily between them.

Now invisible blows and kicks rained down on her, as if the very air was assaulting her, telling her, "You are not welcome here."

Kami, we're coming, said Ash.

I have some advice for you, said Kami. *Come faster.*

She was curled up like a worm, so she turned, jackknifed on the stone, and grabbed Ruth's foot, pulling her weight out from under her. But the air that had hurt Kami caught Ruth and held her in place as if by invisible supporters.

Kami thought of standing outside Aurimere, watching the windows flicker orange and being unable to see inside. She thought of the bloodstained floor in the attic.

Ruth Sherman's hair burst into flame.

Kami shoved her into the street and ran inside the town hall.

It was too late. It had probably been too late by the time Ruth tossed Kami like a rag doll onto the stone steps.

Kami had seen this before with a slaughtered fox, seen the stained tablecloth and the candles. She had even seen what the knife could do to a person.

But she had never seen the whole ritual as it played out. She had never seen Rob Lynburn's golden head, limned by the stained-glass windows as if he was a saint, bent over his work. She had never seen the golden knife drowned in someone's lifeblood, running like a dark red river over the shining carved surface of the table.

She wrenched her gaze away from Rob. She looked at the white altar turning crimson, and into the slack face of the dead man.

Chris Fairchild, the mayor. Kami had seen him talking to Lillian once, and she had not appeared to be paying much attention, but at least she had been talking to him. Kami had never seen him do much, but he was their only symbol of leadership besides the sorcerers.

The magic is greater, her mother had said, if the sacrifice is willing.

Rob had talked to the mayor, and the mayor had promised him a sacrifice. He had given himself up for the town. Rob Lynburn had killed him, cut him open with his golden knives, and all the sorcerers' power was increased with his blood. The power came to Rob through the Lynburn blade, and then he would spread it to his followers like a king distributing largesse.

But not all these people were Rob's sorcerers. Kami looked at the faces of the people watching, and saw they looked sick but not surprised. Kami's guess had been right. Rob Lynburn must have summoned the people of Sorry-in-the-Vale to come see this.

Most of the town had not come. Most people must be hiding in their homes, turning their faces away. But enough people had obeyed. There were ordinary townspeople in the town hall, and they had just sat and watched this horror come to pass.

Kami scanned the faces of the audience, recognizing them, burning into her mind who had been there. She saw Sergeant Kenn, a policeman she would once have trusted to keep her town safe, standing in front of the altar and guarding his leader as he killed. She saw Amber and Ross, two kids from her class, sitting with the sorcerers and absorbing the power. She searched, with a fear that made her vision swim as if she could protect herself from seeing, for her mother's face in the crowd.

Claire was not there. She had not submitted to the sorcerers in this. It was the only mercy Kami could find on this cold morning.

Kami stood in the aisle between the half-full rows of seats, and looked once again at Rob Lynburn.

She concentrated, drawing together the magic she had but could not always command, and all around Rob the stained-glass windows exploded into glittering, sparkling fragments so tiny they looked like dust that shone. They fell all over the stone floor, and the chilly light of day illuminated starkly what Rob had done.

"Murderer," Kami called out. "That's what he is. That's what you all stood and *watched*. He won't stop. He won't stop unless we stop him."

Everyone turned to face her. Rob's gaze on her was steady. He looked amused.

Someone grasped Kami from behind, put a hand over her mouth, pulled her close and held her tight to his chest.

She knew who it was, knew it wasn't an enemy and didn't attack, because of the voice in her head.

Kami, please, please stop, Ash begged her.

She was a better fighter than Ash, but he'd caught her by surprise and was holding her locked to his chest, using his desperation to save her.

Over and above that, worse than anything, were his feelings pouring over her and crushing her: desperation to save her, yes, but despair too, utter lack of hope, consuming fear of his father, and the powerful, terrible urge to flee and hide. Kami tried to fight free of him, body and mind both, but it was so hard.

Rob came walking toward her down the stone aisle. Kami felt Ash tremble against her, felt his horror and fear and love for this man. He removed his hand from her mouth and put his other arm around her, less restraining her than clinging to her now.

She refused to tremble, even when Rob stopped in front of her and stroked her cheek, lightly, with his knife. She felt the hot smear of the blood and the sharp edge of the blade.

Kami raised her chin and glared at him.

"Don't kill her yet," said Rob in a casual voice to his followers. "She's got herself linked to another one of my sons. But I already cut one son loose from her, and I'll free the other. After that she will be beneath my notice, and you can do anything you want."

"Oh," said Ruth, magic turning her blackened hair red again, like a sea of blood drowning out ashes. "I will."

Rob turned away from Kami and Ash toward the townspeople sitting in the hall.

"A willing sacrifice has been given to me, and my power is stronger than ever. But you did not offer me a winter sacrifice on the day appointed," he said. "Your sacrifice was late. I hope that I have taught you all a lesson, and I will expect evidence that you have learned. I want you all to give me tokens to show that you have submitted. And at the spring equinox, I want you to choose me another sacrifice."

There was a murmur of dismay from the crowd, as if they had honestly thought that death would make them safe. Kami heard a sob, wild and loud, and saw Chris Fairchild's wife collapse into a neighbor's arms. Rob looked around, mouth curved as if smiling at a private joke.

"One more sacrifice. One more season. Then I promise you on my word as the Lynburn of Aurimere, there will be peace for Sorry-in-the-Vale."

Rob and his sorcerers left. Ash hung onto Kami, his heart beating a wild frantic rhythm against her back, even after they were gone.

Kami heard the whispers of the people around her, rising up to the low ceiling, slipping out of the broken windows, saying that they had no other choice, that everything would be all right, that there would be advantages, that the old ways were the best ways, that they could not be held responsible. She saw women taking their hair down, about to snip it off as a token for their sorcerous leader. Nobody was looking at the dead man on the altar.

She did not have to listen long, because finally the others arrived, all of them running, sunshine-haired Holly, tall, dark, and terminally idle Rusty, and Kami's best friend in all the world, Angela. Holly was trembling. Even Rusty did not look his usual unconcerned self.

Angela took one look at the altar and curled her scarlet lip.

"Goddamn sorcerers," she said. "It is the goddamn weekend."

A few people looked outraged by Angela's flippancy, but Holly smiled a tiny smile. Angela did not notice anyone's reactions, because she was busy making threats.

"Ash, let go of Kami this minute or I will punch you in the face."

Ash let go of Kami. Kami punched him in the arm.

"I didn't know that *all* my choices were punching," Ash said, rubbing his arm.

"Don't ever grab me like that again," Kami told him. "Or your whole life will be punching."

She crossed to the stone steps where Angela stood, and Rusty made room for her beside his sister, so she could lean into Angela a little. Angela glanced down at her face.

"What is it?" she asked. "Is it this, or is there something else as well?"

"My mother," Kami said quietly. "She told me something about Jared today."

Angela grasped Kami's hand and held it tight. That gesture, and the look on Holly's face, let Kami know that they had already expected to hear news of Jared's death. They were both utterly unsurprised.

She looked at Rusty. He was frowning slightly, biting his lip. He looked conflicted.

"Cambridge," he said, "can we go somewhere and talk?"

Kami followed Rusty down the steps and away from the building that bore the words that promised all men would welcome deceit, the building where people she'd thought she knew had watched a man die.

Rusty was moving fast, as Rusty, lazy as he was sweet, hardly ever did. Kami could barely keep up with him.

"What's this about?" Kami asked.

Rusty glanced over his shoulder at her. There was something apprehensive about his look, as if he was not quite sure she would still be there. Or as if he was not quite sure he wanted her to be.

"You're going to be angry," he predicted.

Chapter Two
Buried Alive

The last two times Rob Lynburn had opened the priest hole, Jared had tried to kill him.

The first time, Jared had tried to strangle Rob with his bare hands, and the second time he had used a weapon. There were not many weapons available when buried alive in a wall. The body of Edmund Prescott, twenty years dead, his fair hair turned white and brittle and hanging like spiderwebs in his gray sunken face, was all that Jared had.

Jared had shoved up Edmund's sleeve, rotten and disintegrating under his hand. Underneath his clothes, Edmund's body had shriveled to nothing but papery skin over bones. Jared tore the skin away and ripped a bone free out of the forearm.

He had spent some time—he did not know how long, time was hard to tell in this lightless trap—sharpening the bone against the stone wall of his prison. Hiding the bone in his sleeve, he waited.

Rob had lifted him out, and Jared had pretended to be more drugged than he was, head lolling, mumbling something about help and his mother. Rob had bent over him, almost seeming concerned.

Jared had whipped out his weapon and tried to plunge the bone into Rob's throat.

He had caught Rob unawares. Some of Rob's sorcerers had been with him and one had grabbed Jared's arm, pulling it back, so the wound was shallow instead of the gaping hole Jared had planned. The next minute, Jared had been pinned to the floor by the sorcerers as he struggled and lashed out under their hands, Rob's rage washing over him as magical pain.

Rob had taken hold of Jared's hair and banged his head, rhythmically and sickeningly hard, against the stone floor.

"Very resourceful, my boy," he'd said. "I'm impressed. Don't try it again."

They had left Edmund Prescott's body in the priest hole with him, but Jared had not tried it again. They would be expecting it now.

The food they gave him was drugged with something that made him drowsy and his magic not work. At first he did not eat it, but it became clear the choice was eat drugged food or starve to death, and the food let the days slip by faster, filled them full of dreams.

He was sitting with his head against the wall, dreaming, when the priest hole opened, a pale square of light on the wall above him. He felt himself being dragged up by magic, back against the wall, helpless as a puppet on Rob's string.

The light of day hurt his eyes: he squinted, dazzled, and in his blurry vision Rob's face almost looked kind.

"How are you today, Jared?" he asked gently. "Ready to be a dutiful son?"

Jared was lying on the ground. He knew he must look

pitiful, dirty from the grave below, not able to see or stand: he tried to raise himself on one elbow and could not quite manage it—the elbow kept slipping away from him.

"Yeah," he grated out. "I'll be a good boy. Don't put me back down there."

Sight and sound slipped out of his reach: the last thing he saw as his vision darkened was Rob's proud smile.

Jared woke up in his room in Aurimere. He remembered a time when he hadn't liked his bedroom, its high ceilings and the rich red velvet drapes, but now it was his, his yellowed old books piled in a corner, his weights kept under the bed, the whole room familiar as his aunt Lillian's voice in the hall. Just lying on his bed was a profound and amazing relief.

After lying there for some time, he crawled off the bed. It was pathetic how weak he was, his body cramped from the priest hole and feeling fragile somehow, as if he had become suddenly old. His limbs ached and his muscles burned as he made for the shower: he almost fell a few times but doggedly stumbled toward it, and did fall into the claw-footed bathtub.

He was finally under the spray of water, beating out some of the snarls in his shoulders. It hurt fiercely as well, like being under a rain of hot needles, but it was worth it.

He wanted to get the dirt and the smell of the priest hole off him, the old blood on his skin, the filth, the enclosed, built-up dust, and the drier dust smell that was Edmund. He scrubbed and when he didn't have the strength to scrub he continued to stand there under the water, leaning against the wall, until he realized that the water had been icy cold for some time.

He staggered out of the tub, shaved while avoiding looking at himself in the mirror, and chose random clothes in
his wardrobe that he pulled over his still-wet skin. They felt
clean and light, almost unbelievably luxurious. Now that he
was dressed, he could go to where the curtains were open,
each curtain held by a gilded rope. He undid the ropes and
the dazzling, painful sunlight was shut out.

Jared thought he could lie down again now. He went over
to the other side of the bed, since the pillow he'd been lying
on was gray, as if . . . well, as if someone had crawled out of a
tomb and left grave dirt everywhere he touched.

The door creaked open and Jared turned around, fast,
his hand clenching in the bedclothes. He felt so pathetically
weak, like a hunted, exhausted animal, hearing predators
close in.

At the door was Ross Phillips, a boy from Kami's year.
Jared found himself staring, unsure, when he would have
been wary of an adult sorcerer. This was a kid his own age,
no matter what magic he wielded or whose side he was on.

Ross stared back at him, and then bowed his head. It
was, Jared realized, a gesture of submission to his master's son.

He said, "It's good that you're up. Your father wants to
talk to you."

Climbing the stairs of the bell tower meant Jared had to
pause several times, sick and dizzy, to lean against the curv-
ing wall in the darkness. Every time, he had to take a deep
breath and will himself farther up the stairs.

When he dragged himself in at last, he saw Rob waiting

patiently in the space where the story said a great golden bell had once hung, before Jared's ancestor Elinor Lynburn had taken it and hidden it from soldiers in the Sorrier River, never to be discovered. Rob's hands were folded behind his back and he was turned away from Jared, apparently contemplating the view.

Sorry-in-the-Vale was laid out before him like a meal.

"Did you rest?" Rob asked him. He turned toward Jared, unhurriedly, as if it had not occurred to him that Jared could shove him right out of the tower.

It had occurred to Jared. He had used his magic to kill one father before, the first father, the man he had believed was his father before he knew about Sorry-in-the-Vale or magic or any of this. He had used magic to throw Dad down a flight of stairs and break his neck.

It would be different if he pushed Rob. Rob was a sorcerer. He could command the air to bear him up or carry him gently to the ground. So Jared nodded and smiled at him instead. He had been told his smiles were disquieting, and Rob did look briefly taken aback before giving him a fatherly smile in return.

He said, "We're going to keep drugging your food. I hope you understand that, my boy."

"Seems sensible," Jared observed.

"And we're going to have to restrict your movements to Aurimere itself," Rob continued. "It grieves me to say this when your agreement to join me has made me happy and proud. But let's face it, you weren't exactly eager, were you?"

"I was under a bit of duress," said Jared. "You make a

really compelling argument. Join me or get walled up alive with a corpse? You should be a politician."

Rob laughed, to all appearances amused by his son's sassy ways.

"I don't plan on taking any chances," he let Jared know. "I realize that you are complying with my wishes largely out of fear. But I do hope that will change as you realize that you have chosen the right side."

"The side that's going to win, you mean?"

"The side that's already won," Rob told him sympathetically, as if he was breaking the news to Jared that Santa Claus did not exist. "Aurimere is mine. The town is mine. All Lillian's sorcerers are dead. There is nobody left to fight me, and no hope for those who might wish to try."

"Good for you," said Jared, looking off into the distance. "I don't see what you need me for. What do you want me to do?"

"Be my son," said Rob. "Be at my side. Nothing more. You might think about what you want to do, though."

"Oh," Jared told him, "I am."

He focused his attention on Rob, cold and absolute, and saw Rob blink. But Rob quickly regrouped and clapped Jared on the shoulder, a hearty gesture that sent pain shooting through Jared's entire body. Jared gritted his teeth and bore it.

"I know you weren't raised as a sorcerer, and it will take you more time to be able to consider your position in the proper light. But surely there are already benefits to being on my side that you can appreciate. Here's one: If you fight against me, you cannot win. But if you are on my side, as my beloved son, then you can choose to spare the people you care for. I won't interfere."

"How interesting," Jared said.

"That Prescott girl, for instance," Rob commented. "Her parents are good people, loyal followers of mine. I have no doubt she could be brought into line. The Prescotts are a fine family."

"You seem very fond of them."

"Poor old Ed, do you mean?" Rob asked. "He was standing between me and what I wanted. It was nothing personal."

Edmund Prescott had been his aunt Lillian's boyfriend. Rob had killed him for that. Edmund's whole family believed that Edmund had run away. Holly had never even met her uncle. He had died long before she was born, and nobody but Jared knew.

Jared had been down in that hole for a long time, looking into that lost boy's face, before they sent down the drugged food and Rob opened the door again. He knew exactly how Edmund Prescott must have felt before he died.

"I'd hate to see what you'd do if it was personal," Jared said.

Rob laughed again, deep and fatherly, and put his arm around Jared's shoulders. Jared could remember a time when Rob had seemed like the father figure Jared had never had but had sometimes wished for, when Jared had desperately wanted this kind of affection and approval.

"You're right to be afraid," Rob told him, voice still warm with laughter. "I really do find that source girl very annoying."

Jared knew how to take a hit and not show he was hurt. He stared at Rob coldly. "You killed my mother for interfering with your plans. Don't ask me to believe you'd let Kami run around loose."

"I have no intention of doing so," said Rob. "She's enslaved both my sons at different times, and constantly tries to stir up trouble. But if you wanted to keep her, you could."

It was Jared's turn to laugh, a jagged sound that rang through the bell tower.

"Are you suggesting I wall her up with Edmund Prescott?"

"That would be my preference," said Rob. "But you can do whatever you like with her, as long as she's kept under control. So long as you don't put her in one of Aurimere's good bedrooms."

Rob wasn't stupid, Jared reflected, or perhaps it was just blazingly obvious what dark things Jared had thought about Kami: how he would have made any bargain to keep her.

He said nothing.

Rob squeezed his shoulder as they stood united, looking down at Sorry-in-the-Vale. The town lay in a valley, like something fragile and precious held in the hollow of a giant's hand. Able at any moment to be crushed, if the giant closed his fist.

"You don't know anything yet," Rob said. "You cannot even dream of what I have planned. So many people are going to die. But those you love will live. All you have to do is be the son I know you can be."

The son Ash could never have been, the son who could murder without hesitation or regret, kill and kill savagely.

"I think I can do that," Jared said slowly.

"That's my boy."

Jared had no choice. Maybe he could never have been anything else.

Rob walked with him down the tower stairs into the portrait gallery, patient with Jared's faltering pace. He walked him all over Aurimere, as if he had acquired a hyena and wanted to put it on a leash and parade his exotic new possession around in front of everyone.

There were a lot of mirrors in Aurimere, which Jared had hated once. The mirrors' reflective surfaces were golden instead of silvery, as if they were made out of gold, copper, or bronze. Their frames were made of wrought-iron river weeds and flowers, surrounded by towers and the profiles of drowned women. Actually, it was the same woman, drowning over and over again.

Jared saw image after image of what they looked like walking together, Rob the proud father and benevolent leader, with his hair like a crown. And the boy with the stark scar and the empty eyes beside him, face stony pale over his black shirt, but unmistakably his son. Jared didn't hate the mirrors of Aurimere anymore: they showed him exactly what he wanted to see.

He saw the same reflection in the eyes of a coppery-haired girl in Kami's English class, one of the sorcerers who sat with them at dinner. She looked at Jared and her eyes went wide with terror.

Jared lifted his glass and smiled slowly at her. He thought she was going to faint.

He leaned toward the head of the table where his father

sat, with Jared at his right-hand side, and said in Rob's ear, "She's very pretty."

"Amber?" Rob asked, loud enough so Jared was sure Amber heard. "She is, isn't she? And she's your own kind." He raised his voice even further. "I'm sure Amber would be delighted to instruct you in magic you have yet to learn. Wouldn't you, Amber?"

Amber nodded mutely. Ross Phillips, at the bottom of the table, glared at Jared. But if looks could kill, Jared would have murdered everyone in this room before Ross had the chance.

Rob pushed his chair back and stood, picking up the glass by his plate. "I hope you'll all lift a glass to welcome my son to Aurimere," he said, voice booming.

The ceiling in the dining hall was curved, with a hollow rising up in the center to form a cupola on the roof outside. A chandelier hung from the dome by a thick chain. When Rob's voice rang out, the tiny gold-leafed dagger shapes hanging from the chandelier jangled and made a sound like faraway bells.

Jared bowed his head in acknowledgment as all the dinner guests raised their glasses. Then he played a game with himself in which he glanced at every guest in turn and saw how many he could make look away.

All of them, it appeared. Not one of them wanted to meet his eyes.

Rob sat down and glanced at Jared's plate. Jared nodded and obediently started to eat, cutting his food up into small pieces and swallowing obviously, making not the slightest effort to avoid eating.

Rob smiled at him as if he was such a good boy.

"Eat up," he said. "You're looking a little under the weather. We wouldn't want you to be sick."

"I do feel a little peaky after the live burial," Jared admitted, and took a big drink of cranberry juice from the glass by his plate.

When he rose from the table, he wavered and caught the edge so he wouldn't fall. Rob put a hand on his shoulder, and Jared leaned into it.

"Come on," said Rob. "Let's get you to your room."

Jared let Rob loop Jared's arm around his neck, and allowed Rob to lead him out of the dining hall, through the entrance hall and up the stairs, along the corridor to Jared's room. Jared even hung on: he stumbled once, twice, three times on his way, and each time he held fast to his father.

So when the door closed behind them and Rob helped him toward the bed, it was simple for Jared to clench his fist in the material of Rob's shirt and punch Rob in the face as hard as he could.

Rob gave a shout, more exclamation than protest, and with his free hand Jared seized the gilded rope from the curtains that he'd hidden under his pillow and threw it around Rob's neck.

He only had an instant to cross the rope and pull it strangling-tight around Rob's neck. Rob grabbed at him, strong hands closing on his arms even as his face purpled, and Jared brought his knee up hard and, at the same time, knocked Rob's head against the shining walnut-wood headboard.

Jared had thought the fancy bed was ridiculous when he'd first seen it, but he was coming around.

He had Rob pinned underneath him: all he had to do was keep twisting the rope, tighter and tighter. Rob's eyes were wild and bloodshot, staring up at him in confusion.

"Wondering why your magic isn't working?" Jared asked, grinning savagely down at him. "I might've leaned toward you and commented about a pretty girl so I could switch our glasses. That's the problem with drugging the food and drink of someone sitting right next to you. Of course, Pops, I don't have any magic either, but that doesn't matter. I'm happy to kill you up close and personal."

Rob choked, his face almost purple now. Jared had wondered if he would feel any last hesitation, any regret, but instead he felt a wild exhilaration. He might not get out of this house, but Rob would be dead and she would be safe, the whole town would be safe. He'd *done* it.

Blackness came crashing down in front of his eyes. He tried to keep hold of the rope, but it was twisting and turning to water in his hands, and the blackness came in on him in another insistent wave.

Without knowing quite how he had got there, Jared was on the floor suddenly, gasping and sick, and everything had slipped out of his hands.

Rob was standing over him.

"A very good try, Jared," he said, and even as the blackness closed in, Jared took a cold satisfaction from the painful rasp of his voice. "But I didn't quite trust you enough to be alone with you without surveillance. What a shame for you. I'm afraid things are going to go badly for you, son. You have to learn."

Jared learned nothing right then, because the darkness swallowed him up in one hungry gulp.

When he woke up, he was back in the priest hole, high walls and shadows all around him. He was never going to get out of here again, and he had failed.

Instead of crying or screaming, he focused on Edmund Prescott's shrunken body, his pale, hanging head and gray profile.

"Hey, buddy," Jared croaked. "Miss me?"

The sound of his own voice scared him. He turned his face away from Edmund and laid it against the cool stone surface of the tomb. This didn't matter, he thought, squeezing his eyes shut, pressing his face so hard against the wall it felt like his own bones were grinding against the stone.

None of this mattered, and it would all be over soon. He wasn't going to last long in here. Rob would get tired of trying soon enough, and everyone outside Aurimere must already presume he was dead.

Everyone outside Aurimere would never learn any different now. He wished he could have killed Rob for her, though.

She was probably sorry he was dead, but she would obviously rather he died than her little brother. She had Ash now. She would be all right: she would be better than all right, and better off without him.

He had to concentrate on that. These last moments trapped in the dark, trapped with the dead, meant less than nothing. They weren't even real. They were happening to someone who was already dead. She was real, though, real somewhere out in the world and the light. If he could have wished for anything in his life, it would have been for her to be real, and she was. He had heard her laugh on the air and not in his head, that marvelous, marveling sound, and seen the tender, sacred curve of her face and her mouth. She would not end when he did. He had been granted his wish; he had been infinitely lucky. He could bear this: this did not compare to the gift he had been given.

This did not matter at all.

Jared woke up to the sound of a knife.

He blinked awake, muscles tensing, and realized he was held by magic strong as chains, unable to move no matter how much he strained and fought the inexorable pressure.

He was lying on a stone slab, and he recognized the dim arches and names carved on stone from the one time his aunt Lillian had dragged him down here before he'd excused himself on the grounds that it was all far too creepy.

He had been wrong, when he was searching for Kami's kidnapped brother in this house and thinking that Aurimere had no dungeons or dark secrets.

Now one of the carved slabs of the floor had been raised to make the table on which he was chained. Now he realized that all these slabs must have dark recesses beneath; that they could be moved to put Lynburn bones beneath the stone.

He had thought of this place as a little family chapel. It was nothing so innocent. It was the family crypt.

"Oh, I don't believe this," Jared said. "Am I being buried alive in a different location?"

"Shut up," murmured Amber, the copper-haired girl from dinner.

She was holding one of the Lynburn knives, he saw; its gold blade reflected tiny blurred points of candle flames. She had cut open his shirt.

"Uh, are you planning to violate my body?" Jared asked. "I request to be buried alive instead."

"I cannot believe that you never shut up," Amber said in a fraught whisper.

Jared lifted his head, which felt terribly heavy, and looked around the crypt properly. There were candles burning in several black wrought-iron candelabras, the flames refracting strangely in his vision, painting orange blurs on the stone and the names of his ancestors. There was a woman with scarlet hair standing against the wall watching him, and a man with Holly's green eyes.

At the door of the crypt stood Rob Lynburn. He had the other Lynburn knife in his belt.

It occurred to Jared that he was going to be sacrificed, that his blood might go to feed their power, and their power would be used to hurt those he loved, and that his last thought would be pain.

If that was their plan, there was nothing he could do about it. Here he was, laid out and helpless, the perfect sacrifice.

Jared turned his face away, toward the records of Lynburn deaths. REQUIESCAT IN PACE, he saw in a stream of candlelight: *Rest in peace,* like a promise, and beneath that a long epitaph for an Emily Lynburn who had died in the 1800s.

> *Shiver not as you pass by*
> *For as you are so once was I*
> *And as I am so you will be*
> *So be prepared to follow me.*

"I am not prepared," Jared muttered.

He had no other choice than to be prepared. Maybe they would lay him to rest here, afterward, not hide him away like Edmund Prescott. He was a Lynburn, after all.

He wondered where Rob had put his mother.

Low as the light flickering from grave to grave, a chant rose around Jared. He could not quite make out the words, though "gold" and "bound" were both in there, but he could make out the intent.

Rob had already let him know he was going to be punished.

"You have no idea what's coming," Rob told Jared, his voice the only clear one in the crypt. "No idea at all."

Shadows blotted out the pale candlelight as Rob drew in, and his followers drew in after him, a circle closing in all around Jared. Most of the faces surrounding him were familiar: the sergeant who had questioned him once in the police office, both of Holly's parents, Ross Phillips, and a man who worked at Crystal's gift shop. Jared had bought a notebook for Kami there once, and never had the nerve to give it to her.

Rob drew the golden knife from his belt and laid the point with tender care against Jared's bared shoulder. The cold point made him shiver, and pain followed.

Jared felt the chill slide of a blade against his stomach, tracing on and wavering against the skin. He tried to force himself not to look down, but he could not help a swift, horrified glance. The knives shimmered in the candlelight, and both pierced the place where they rested. Two thin trails of blood gleamed against his chest.

"Follow the pattern, Amber," said Rob. "You know what you have to do."

Amber knelt on the stone floor and looked up at Jared with wide imploring eyes. Softer than the sound of the candles burning, so softly that Jared almost thought he was imagining it, she whispered, "I'm sorry."

Rob touched the side of Jared's face, tried to cup it, but Jared jerked his chin savagely away.

"My boy," said Rob fondly. "You'll learn."

He nodded to Amber, and they both lifted their knives. The flares of candlelight dragged along the bright blades: Jared saw them blaze as they plunged toward him.

Agony ripped through him, two gouged pathways in his flesh. Jared roared like an animal, no sense left, only pain. Pain that both drowned out everything and burned through all that he tried to grasp.

It went on and on. He had nothing left but pain.

Chapter Three
Desperate Measures

"Rusty," Kami said. "Either you want to talk to me or you don't."

He, Kami, and Angela were in the Montgomerys' kitchen. Holly had slunk tactfully away, and Angela had forbidden Ash to enter her home.

"I do, I do." Rusty chewed his lower lip. "It's difficult to know how to put this. You have to break things to ladies gently if you are a proper gentleman."

What did Rusty have to tell her that would have to be broken gently? What else, but the thing everyone had been trying to tell her, the thing her mother had said this morning?

Jared Lynburn is dead.

Kami held on tight to the back of the stool; the loop of iron cut painfully into her palm.

"What is it?" she forced out between stiff, reluctant lips. She had to want the truth. She wasn't a coward: she wasn't going to hide from it, even now.

"Rusty!" Angela said, her voice sharp. "You are really upsetting her."

"Kami, no," said Rusty, and whirled away from the

smoothie machine and toward her. He clearly meant to take her in his arms, but she went stiff, rejecting comfort. Rusty took a gentle hold on her arms instead. "Kami," he said. "No. He's alive. He was alive last night."

The relief was so deep that Kami wanted to collapse, her knees going out from under her, but Rusty's hold on her suggested that was what he was expecting her to do. Kami had had enough of guys holding on to her for today: she was not going to fall apart.

"How do you know?"

Rusty hesitated, then looked down at her and said in a rush, "You remember that girl Amber Green, the sorceress?"

"The sorceress you have drinks with because you are a fraternizer with cute evil people," said Angela. "My own brother. A fraternizer. I can hardly bear the shame."

"Ah," said Rusty. "But I'm not, am I? I'm more like Mata Hari."

Kami was slowly beginning to regain feeling in her extremities. He was alive: she wanted to run to him, as fast as her legs could carry her, and scream at the sky in triumph.

Instead, she offered Rusty a faltering and hesitant smile. "So you go to the enemy and you do belly dances for them until they offer up information?"

"More or less," said Rusty. "Except instead of belly dances, what Amber needed was a sympathetic shoulder. The fact that it was an attractive masculine shoulder didn't hurt, I don't think."

"A sweetly humble shoulder too, I note," said Angela.

Rusty shrugged and smiled back at Kami, reassuring and obviously pleased that she was smiling. His voice was light, but his eyes were steady and kind. "Never since the days of King Arthur and Superman have such handsome and manly shoulders existed in the land. How could she resist? Made for weeping on and leaning against. If either of you ladies would like to try? Cambridge?"

"Pass."

"My hopes dashed, I'll continue with my tale," said Rusty. "Amber was slow to tell me anything about Jared, but she did tell me she thought Rosalind was dead, and she didn't say the same thing about Jared. I didn't want to push, which was why I was doing all of this solo. You are both charming ladies, but you are pushy. Charmingly pushy," he added hastily, when he was fixed with two identical glares.

"Your shoulders and your lack of push got you the goods; you were clearly the right man for the job," Kami told him. "I applaud your initiative, now just please tell me what's happened to Jared."

Rusty hesitated, and fear crawled through Kami's body, lacing her blood with ice. It felt, she thought wildly, stupidly, like someone was trying to make a margarita of dread in her veins. She grabbed Rusty's arms, just as he had grabbed on to hers, and held on.

Rusty took a deep breath and said, "Rob walled him up alive. He's been feeding him drugs to inhibit his magic and dragging him out occasionally, and yesterday he let Jared out for almost the whole day. That was what made Amber come to me."

Kami refused to deal with the horror of what Rusty had said. She could not be crushed by horror now. She had to concentrate on the fact that Rusty had said he was free.

"Amber came to you because Jared had been let out?" she asked, and heard her voice come out thin and furious, when she'd thought she was being so practical. "She has some sort of moral objection to people *not* being buried alive?"

"She said that Jared looked awful," Rusty told her, seeming to choose his words carefully. Kami wanted to snap, "That would probably be a result of the *being buried alive,*" but she knew she had to stay quiet and listen to what Rusty had learned. "Not only sick and pale, but that his eyes were—staring, that he looked half out of his head. He terrified all the other sorcerers. He tried to strangle Rob with a piece of rope from his curtains, and Rob put him back behind the wall."

The thought that Jared was not free, that he had been walled up somewhere by his own father and was still trapped, suffering and going slowly mad, was like a punch in the stomach. Kami tried to breathe through the blow and the sickness that followed.

"That's not all, Kami," Rusty said, so gently, as if she might need a minute.

"Go on," she ordered him.

"They took him out that night and tortured him," Rusty said in a hushed voice. "Rob got Amber to help, and gave her one of the Lynburn knives. Then he put Jared . . ."

"Let me guess," said Angela. "Back in the hole."

It was Rusty and Kami's turn to glare at Angela, but Kami stopped glaring as soon as she saw Angela's face. Angela was even paler than usual. She looked like she was going to be sick.

They all had their own ways of coping.

I should have known, Kami thought. I did know. I knew he wasn't dead, but I listened to everyone telling me he was, I listened to Ash, and all the time he was alive and he needed my help.

"Amber was so upset," Rusty said, and continued in his slow, steady voice, ignoring the scornful noise Kami could not suppress. "She was so upset that she called me and asked me to come to Aurimere. She brought me inside and we sat and talked in the garden. She was crying. She wasn't thinking straight. She took my hand, and because I was touching her—touching one of Rob's sorcerers—I could walk through the fire."

They had a way in.

Hope and horror were twisted and sharp as barbed wire in Kami's chest, but she could also feel Ash's soaring joy, when he had had no hope at all. She found herself smiling with clenched fists.

She looked at Rusty, who was regarding her with concern. He had not given up or surrendered to despair. He had kept following his one lead, getting this girl to talk to him, and it had paid off.

"Thank you for telling me," she told him. "Thank you for finding out. You are the best and handsomest man in all the world."

"Stop, you're embarrassing me," said Rusty. "Except by 'stop,' I mean 'please go on.'"

"Do you know what Amber's schedule is?" Kami asked, remembering talk of training young sorcerers that she had overheard once in Monkshood Abbey, Rob's childhood home. "She must get trained in Aurimere now. Do you know when she's due there next?"

"A couple of hours," said Rusty.

"Then I'll spend the next couple of hours getting some supplies and getting Ash," Kami said. She hesitated, reached out and set her hand on Rusty's arm. "Rusty, you're the one she trusts. I have to ask you to come with me."

Rusty smiled at her. "No, you don't, Cambridge. You never have to ask." She beamed up at him helplessly, so grateful, and he looked away and yawned with an almost-convincing air of lazy nonchalance. "I am going to spend the next couple of hours having a power nap before my next spy mission, though, and you can just run your errands all by yourself. What do you have to say to that?"

Kami stood on her tiptoes and kissed Rusty on the cheek. He started slightly and her lips caught mostly jaw and dark hair. "Sleep well, sweetheart," she told him. "Thank you. I mean it."

She did not say: I know you did this for me.

"I am also going to nap, but please do not demonstrate physical affection toward me," Angela announced. "I don't want to get feelings on this shirt."

Kami found herself hesitating again. A smaller group could be in and out faster—and she did not want to think about what would happen to the people without magic if they were discovered. "Angela, you and Holly don't have to come."

Angela rolled her eyes. "Holly is coming, and I am too," she said. "Don't be more stupid than you can help. I refuse to ever let you wander off like an idiot into danger without me. Who knows what could happen?"

"I know what's going to happen. We're going to Aurimere," Kami said, and felt her courage rise with every word she spoke. "We're going to rescue Jared."

"Kami, you have to wait," Ash implored.

"Nope, don't think so," said Kami.

Ash and Holly had come quickly, walking together toward them, blond heads bowed close as they talked, under the shadows of budding horse chestnut trees. Holly had heard Kami's story and glanced at Angela to confirm she was in, then nodded.

It was just the boys who were being wusses.

"We need to talk to my mother," said Ash.

"I won't," said Kami. "She might not think it's worth the risk. And I'm doing this today."

"I hate to say it, but I think maybe you should listen to Blondie," said Rusty. "You don't understand about Amber, Cambridge. She's so scared of the Lynburns. It took me so long to get her to trust me, and even then all I could get her to do was talk. She's not going to help us. She's terrified of Lillian, so she might help her."

"You don't understand about *me*," Kami said, sweeping both Ash and Rusty with a comprehensive glare. "Jared's being tortured in there. And Amber's going to help me. I'm not planning on giving her a choice."

Amber went to riding lessons at noon every day, according to Rusty, and then came back to Aurimere to learn magic and dance attendance on Rob. Torture at night, Kami thought, human sacrifice in the morning, healthy exercise at noon. What could possibly be on the schedule for the evening?

Kami thought she would pencil in a surprise.

Are you with me or not? she asked Ash.

I'm with you, said Ash. *For Jared.* He paused, and added, *It's nice to . . . feel you be happier.*

Ash felt happier too, and that made Kami feel guilty. Ash wasn't used to being linked to anybody, and though she tried to keep her thoughts separate from his, her every emotion came at him like a storm for someone used to a lifetime of calm weather. She hadn't been easy on him, and that had swayed him into a dark mood. Maybe it was her fault that they hadn't both been happier.

First things first, though, and the first thing on Kami's mind was the rescue mission. She could be kinder to Ash once Jared was safe.

For now, she and Ash were united, a pounding of anxiety and tension thrumming between them like a shared heartbeat. Holly was looking to Angela again, and Angela was waiting, her body tense to spring. She saw Kami's glance and gave her a nod.

"I'm with Kami," she said.

Kami nodded approvingly. "Because we are best friends forever."

"Also the longer we leave Jared there, the crazier he's going to get," Angela remarked. "Let's face it, he was not the mayor of Sanityville to start with."

She said it with a certain measured amount of fondness, and she had looked genuinely sickened by Rusty's story. Kami was glad: she had never been quite sure how Angela felt about Jared.

It was warm for the first day of February, or maybe it only seemed warm because Kami was sweating, her skin hot and clammy at once. The budding trees offered her no useful shade, and having her friends around her did not help. Maybe Angela would understand what she had to do. Nobody else would.

What are you planning to do? Ash asked.

Kami heard light footsteps coming up the path to the manor.

I'm sorry, she told Ash. *Don't stop me.*

Amber Green came into view, kicking up dust as she walked. She was still in her riding clothes, hair shining bright as a new penny in the sun under the black velvet of her hat.

Kami thought of the penny she had sent Jared when they were children, which he always wore around his neck. She thought of her mother, allowing terrible things to happen out of fear.

This girl had actually *done* terrible things; whether from fear or desire for power, Kami did not care. She had lost her claim to Kami's pity when she picked up the knife: Kami had someone to save, and she had to stop Amber and everyone else from hurting him.

Amber halted when she saw them all standing under the shadow of the trees. She had a riding crop and a purse in her hands, and she dropped both in the dust.

Maybe she was scared enough, or foolish enough, that she

did not think of the crop as a weapon. Maybe, as a sorcerer, she knew her best weapon was having her hands free.

"Hi," she said uncertainly, her eyes flicking uneasily from Ash's face to Kami's—the magical threats—and finally landing on Rusty, not in appeal but with the realization of betrayal and a promise of vengeance.

Kami recalled having no magic and being cut up and scared by this girl. Rusty had been brave to approach her, and clever to get her talking. Rusty didn't have any magic: Amber would have seen him as helpless.

But Rusty wasn't helpless, and he had led her to this moment.

"I'm going to give you a chance," said Kami, taking a step toward Amber. "I know that you hate all of this, and I know that you're scared. But you must see that Jared needs help. He's scared and alone and in pain, and that is partly because of you. We cannot cross the fire without one of Rob's sorcerers. You have a chance to save him. Will you take it?"

"Rob would kill me," said Amber, taking a step back.

Kami could feel her trying to call the wind to her aid. Kami quelled it with a thought, easy as blowing on the hot air rising from a cup of tea.

"We'll make it look like we forced you," she coaxed, being as sweet as she could, for Rusty's sake and Holly's sake and Ash's sake, and for her own sake too. She did not want to hurt Amber.

But she would if she had to. For Jared's sake.

The wheedling made Amber's eyes narrow, as if anyone who tried persuasion rather than force must be weak.

"I can't risk it," she said with sudden decisiveness. "Jared isn't my problem. And you'll be sorry that you tried to make him my problem," she added to Rusty.

Rusty met her narrowed eyes with a level gaze. "I don't think I will be sorry."

Amber looked at Ash, the Lynburn, again, and then took several steps forward, pushing past Kami.

Kami caught her wrist. "You're the one who's going to be sorry."

Amber tried to break Kami's hold on her wrist by yanking it away. Kami held on, and Amber looked down at her, both surprised and almost offended.

"I gave you a choice," said Kami. "Now I'm taking it away. If all you listen to is force and fear, you can be afraid of me. You're going to help Jared."

Amber made heat hit Kami's face in one fast stroke, as if Kami had been slapped by a fire.

"I'm not."

Kami's fingers bit into Amber's wrist so hard that Amber let out a soft cry of pain. And then Amber gave no more cries.

Her hair crackled as it began to slowly burn, the fire licking blue and scarlet in the winter sunshine. And from her lips issued a faint gurgling sound, the sound of water filling her lungs, bubbles forming on her mouth as flames surrounded her hair.

Kami, what are you doing? Kami, stop! said Ash, and Kami felt his horror course through her, saw it reflected on the faces of the friends she loved. Ash's horror met her own, horror built on horror until it was a towering nightmare feeling, but she refused to be stopped.

Amber hit out wildly at Kami with her free hand, and Kami grabbed that hand too, stepping in close with both Amber's wrists bound in her grasp.

"Which is it going to be, sorcerer?" Kami asked. "Drown or burn?"

Amber shook her head frantically, and Kami let the flames cool and the air filter into Amber's lungs so she could speak.

"Fine," Amber rasped. "Fine, I'll help you."

"Thank you very much," said Kami.

Chapter Four
The Lady of the Lake's Riddle

Passing through the flames and over the threshold of Aurimere at last did not feel like a victory. Kami was terrified for all of them as they stepped through the fire and she felt its heat on her skin, making the ends of her hair curl up, crisp and brittle.

She looked over at Angela, who seemed to be immune to sweating.

"How are you doing with the whole 'enveloped in fire' bit?"

"Basically how I feel every day when people ask me to do unreasonable things," said Angela. "Things such as get up early or talk to them in a civil manner."

"People are monsters," said Kami, and by then they were standing in the cool stone hall of Aurimere.

"Everyone's a monster," Amber said bitterly. "Given the incentive."

They had tied Amber's wrists with a skipping rope, all they had to restrain her. They did not seem like captors to be dreaded, Kami thought, but then she remembered the look of fear she had put in Amber's eyes and the cry of pain she

51

had wrung from her lips. She could not blame Amber, after all, for bitterness.

Aurimere was still austere and intimidating, with an arched stone ceiling like a church and windows with diamond panes alternating ice-white and blood-red. Kami had thought the place would be more altered, now that it was occupied and invaded by evil. She almost expected to see Lillian Lynburn come down the broad walnut flight of stairs, serene mistress of the house. Aurimere stood untouched, indifferent to good or evil. Aurimere would be the same when they were all gone.

They heard a step in the corridor on the floor above, and Amber looked as if she was going to die of terror.

"Which way?" Kami asked, keeping her voice calm.

"Not far now," whispered Holly, reassuring and sweet.

Kami's confidence and Holly's comfort together seemed to work: Amber squared her shoulders and marched across the floor. They all followed her, through the records room and along another corridor, going on until they were looking up at the flight of stairs leading up from the little hall beside the library.

The stairs were narrow, and gleaming with red from the room above. It felt as if they were ascending into hell.

There was a break in the stairs where they turned. The group paused there, and Kami felt Ash's unease in her mind, his memories of having run thoughtlessly up these stairs a thousand times.

There was a stretch of polished wooden floor, a light above that looked like a star caught in a golden net, and a wall that bore a black and white mural in mosaics.

The mural showed Aurimere, in the distance but unmistakable, and in the foreground it showed a woman standing by a lake. Even in black and white, the woman was obviously a Lynburn: she held her head like a queen, despite the hair tumbling long, heavy, and laden with river flowers down her back, and her face in profile was both disdainful and pitiless.

"He's there," Amber said in a low voice. "Rob put him behind that wall."

By magic, Kami assumed, but Kami had magic too. She could break him out. She envisioned the stones in the wall being moved around to suit her, as if they were Lego blocks.

Nothing happened. Her magic had absolutely no effect on the wall: it was as if she had tried punching the stone instead.

Ash, said Kami, like reaching out a hand, and with panic and fear that mirrored hers he reached back.

This wall's protected against magic, he said.

Then how does Rob open it? Kami demanded. *How are we going to?*

There was no answer from Ash, only desolation going through him, through them both, like a cold wind over a dead land. He stepped forward and laid his hand over the black tiles that formed the lake, as if he could reach through it to Jared. Kami understood the impulse: to hammer on the wall until it broke and gave Jared back, not caring how much noise they made or who they brought crashing down on them.

She had brought Angela, Rusty, and Holly into this. She could not risk them for nothing.

Instead she stood with the others in a hush of horror, and

she heard the sound of stone on stone, like the scrape of a pebble against a board.

"Wait," said Kami, recalling a scrap of history from her schoolbooks. "Did you hear that? This doesn't have to be a wall opened up by magic. This is an old house: there were a lot of reasons to build secret trapdoors and hideaways. This could be one of those. A lot of people had hiding places for Catholic priests in Elizabethan times. Somewhere convenient to pop your priest when the soldiers came by."

"A priest hole," said Ash. "I think Dad mentioned the house had one of those, once. Or . . . I think he said there was supposed to be one, but nobody knew where it was. He laughed about it."

Kami stared grimly at the wall. None of them were laughing. If this was not magical, there had to be some trick or some catch, some button to push or secret way to enter. She'd heard the shift of stone when Ash put his hand on the lake, but it hadn't opened.

"A priest hole covered with a picture," said Ash aloud. *The picture tells us nothing,* he said to Kami alone, because he could not hide bad news or fear from her. *A lake, a woman, a sword . . . there are symbols like this all over Aurimere.*

Kami knew it was true. She had seen the decorations of Aurimere, the outstretched sorcerous hands, the drowning woman, and the Lynburn crest with the motto beneath it reading in Latin, *We neither drown nor burn.*

"This isn't a picture."

"I don't want to contradict you," Holly said. "Obviously Jared being buried alive is stressful for everybody. But I'm pretty sure it *is* a picture."

Kami turned to her and beamed at her.

"No," she said. "It's a riddle."

Everybody looked confused.

"Think," said Kami. "The Lynburns as a family—egomaniacs to a man, am I right?"

"Personally, hey!" Ash Lynburn remarked. "But on the whole, your assessment's pretty fair."

"So if they had a system of which stones to press, and a picture on top of them," Kami said, "what else would it be but the Lynburn crest?"

The house, the woman, the lake, and the woods beyond. They were all in bright heraldic color on the Lynburn crest, and in shards of memory in Kami's mind's eye, the tentative green of the woods coming back to life, the shimmering green of the lakes the first time she had shown them to Jared, the golden house and the woman with golden river-bound hair.

Now they were black and white tile, all monochrome and simple as a chessboard, and all she had to do was know how to play.

House, woman, lake, and woods.

The wall did not move.

Kami tried it, with increasing desperation, in a variety of different combinations: woman, lake, woods, house. Lake, house, woods, and woman.

She realized after she had touched the stones in every order she could think of that everyone was staring at her as she randomly and frantically patted at the wall. They looked rather alarmed.

"I thought it might be the . . . the Lynburn family crest,"

Kami explained. It sounded like a wild idea when she said it. "The woods and the lake and the house and a woman, you know."

Holly frowned. "But the Lynburn crest has a sword on it?"

The crest did, though Kami had assumed the sword and its hilt only served as a creepy frame for the four pictures.

In any case, there was no sword in the mural on the wall.

Kami squinted at it, as if she could make a sword appear, and then she whirled and seized Holly in her arms.

"You are a genius!" she declared, and kissed her on both of Holly's suddenly blushing cheeks.

Kami let Holly go, stepped forward, and pressed the single large stone lying by the lakeside.

There was a grind of stone on heavy stone, the sound of a tomb opening. Slowly, the stones in the picture moved, so the pictured Aurimere was gone and the pictured woman was headless, until there was a gap into the dark about the size of a fireplace, halfway up the wall.

Jared, Kami thought, as if she could still speak to him like that. She did not let herself scream his name. He would be safe, soon, if she could only do this right.

"The Lynburns talked about King Arthur being a source and the Lady of the Lake a sorcerer," Kami said instead, almost in a whisper. "I thought they might have come up with an extra trick, to be clever. The sword in the stone."

"Arthur became king by pulling a sword out of a stone." Ash's voice was soft with wonder, soft as the feeling of his wonder wrapping around Kami like mist. Ash was the only one of the group who cared about stories as much as Kami did. He had been raised on stories told by sorcerers.

"The Lynburns, egomaniacs *and* tricky bastards," said Angela. "A riddle wrapped up in an enigma, wrapped up in a giant pain in the ass. Well done, Kami." She hesitated and added, "Well done, Holly."

Kami turned to Amber and began to unloop the skipping rope from around her wrists. It was not that she trusted Amber now. She needed the rope for something else. She glanced at Angela for support.

"I'm going down to get him," she told Angela. "I have to be the one. Okay?"

"Okay," said Angela. "Rusty and I will hold the rope."

"Holly, could you do something for me?" Kami asked, and Holly, blushing more than ever now that both Angela and Kami had praised her, nodded. "Creep down to the library and grab any books that look like they might be helpful— anything about the town, anything historical, especially anything about the 1480s. Be careful and come right back."

That was the time when Elinor Lynburn and Matthew Cooper the source had lived—the only source besides Kami that they knew of. That was as sensible as Kami could manage to be right now, with the prospect of rescuing Jared so close. Ash had to help her scramble up to the aperture in the wall, but once she was up she had hold of the rope, and it was being held firm.

She ducked her head so she would not bang it on the stone, and with the rope gripped tight in her hands she began to scale her way down the wall.

The wall felt dry and cold, rasping against her knuckles as the rope burned her palms. She trusted the people holding on to the rope, but her feet still felt as if they were dangling into a thousand fathoms of darkness.

But it wasn't so far down, nor so very dark. As Kami descended, her eyes became accustomed to the faint light provided by the opening in the wall above her head, where her friends waited for them.

The light painted the stones dark gray rather than black. She could see nothing but the stone wall before her.

She could smell old dust and fresh blood.

Kami told herself to just keep going, down and down, hand under hand and the soles of her shoes scraping against the wall. She went until her feet touched something else.

Kami let go of the rope when she realized she was standing on a corpse.

She did not scream, except in her head. She did not let herself panic. She ignored the feeling of bones crackling under her weight and simply stepped off the body onto a stained stone floor.

There was only a little light, but there was enough. She could see his pale hair, his face that barely looked human but still somehow looked young. She forced herself to stay in control. This was an old body, years old, and Jared had been alive yesterday.

Kami turned, carefully and gradually, in that terrible narrow space.

On the other side of that tomb was Jared. He was not lying down, because there was no room to lie down, but he was sitting in a lax, contorted way that did not look right.

Kami knelt down beside him, the black frills of her skirt falling over his legs. She looked up into his face: it was the same face she knew by heart, thinner but not irrevocably or terribly changed. She looked at him for one desperate hungry moment that had to count for all the moments she had not seen him; she took in the aristocratic Lynburn lines of his face, the starkness of his scar, the curling gold of his lashes—and the way something about his mouth softened when he slept and made him look as young as he was, as young as she was.

Kami reached out, touched his hand, and said his name. "Jared."

His hand was warm under hers, which eased a clawing wordless worry in her chest, but he did not stir. Kami slid her hand from his down to circle his wrist, as lightly as she could, hardly daring to move in case of what she would find. She let out a breath that came out stuttering like a sob when she felt the steady pulse of his heartbeat against her fingertips.

"Jared," she implored, and tightened her hand around his wrist. She could not reach out to him in her mind and she could not scream, but she had found him once in dark winter waters and she would find him now, no matter how lost he might be. "Jared," she said again, his name prayer and promise at once.

Jared's lashes flickered: his hand moved beneath hers, and his pulse quickened. He gave a shuddering gasp, and his eyes opened.

"Oh, thank God," said Kami.

Jared stared at her blankly for a moment, his eyes so dazed they seemed blind, and moved fast as a striking snake.

She did not recoil, and the next moment he had her other arm in his grasp. They had each other, held fast.

She did not mind until she saw what his movement had betrayed. The material of his shirt, which had looked closed in the dim lights, parted and she saw that the buttons had been cut away.

The skin beneath had been cut away too. Even in the dim light she could see the smears of blood against his skin, and the pattern the blade had cut into his skin beneath the darkness of that dried blood.

"What's the matter?" Jared asked, and his voice cracked as he spoke. "Don't—don't cry."

Kami shook her head mutely, and held on to his wrist. She was gripping on too tight, she thought, her fingernails probably biting into his skin. She should be careful with him.

She unloosed her grip, drawing her hand back.

"No," said Jared, voice suddenly urgent rather than lost. "No. Don't go away."

Kami shook her head again and reached out, fastening her fingers with care in the sleeve of his shirt. She could grip onto that and not hurt him.

He drew her closer to him, as if he didn't care if he was hurt. It was cramped and awkward in that living tomb, horror all around them. Kami knocked her elbow against the stone.

She got as close as she possibly could: she could feel his hot breath on her neck, and she knew he could feel her hot tears, falling onto his shoulder.

"Kami?" Jared whispered, her name soft as a kiss on her hair.

She tried to make her voice sound strong. "Yes?"

She felt the shape of his mouth against her hair and was amazed by how crazy he was: he was smiling. "Hey, Kami."

"Hey, Jared," Kami whispered back.

She held on to him, fists tight on the material of his shirt as if he was trying to get away. There was darkness and blood and the dust of the dead all around them, but they were all right. Everything would be all right, as long as she never, never let him go.

A yell split the air above them, echoing from wall to wall of the priest hole. Kami felt Ash's voice cut through the peace in her mind.

Ruth Sherman's seen us, he said. *We have to get out now.*

Chapter Five
Fire Burning Bold

"Right," said Kami aloud, in her normal voice. It sounded obscenely loud in that little space.

She scrambled away from Jared and to her feet, not letting go of his wrist. He looked up at her, eyes uncomprehending and hurt, wide as a child's.

"Come on," Kami said. "Get up. You're being rescued. I came here for you and I am not leaving without you. Get up."

"I'll try," Jared told her.

He did try. It broke her heart to see how difficult it was for him, leaning his weight heavily against her and against the wall. She could feel him shaking from head to foot, and she did her best to hold him up though he was so much taller than she was.

"You'd better try," she said fiercely into his shoulder. "This isn't a choice. I insist on rescuing you!"

"Well," Jared said. "If you insist."

Kami pushed him toward the rope, and tried to smile at him, though she was not sure that she succeeded or even if she did, if he could see it.

"Just hold on," she said, and gave the rope two quick

tugs. "Rusty and Angela will bring you up. Hold on. I'm with you."

He climbed as best he could, trying to haul himself up with the rope. She stood and watched his faltering progress: at the moment when she saw his hands slip, she willed him not to. She sent him with magic up along the stones, light as air, light as the rope, up to the outside world.

He looked down at her when he reached the opening. Kami made a gesture at him to go.

She stood there for another instant with the dead boy at her feet. If she had not come for him, if Rusty had not learned a sorcerer's secrets and Holly guessed a sorcerer's riddle, how long would it have been before Jared died? How long would the two dead boys have sat in each other's silent company, turning to dust?

"I'm so sorry nobody saved you," Kami whispered.

It was an absurd thing to say, but she said it in thanksgiving for the boy she had been able to save, in pity for this boy and those who must have loved but not saved him. She had been so terribly, frighteningly lucky.

The rope began to lower again, but Kami heard running footsteps on the stairs. It was no time to wait for ropes. It was time to help herself.

She set her fingers in the wall and told herself, *I will not fall. I am going to climb.*

It was not quite like climbing, or like falling either. It was like being lifted by both air and her own grip on stone, by the sheer force of her determination.

She reached the opening in the wall, one knee up on the stone, and saw Ruth Sherman throw a bolt of fire at Rusty.

Kami quenched it with a thought, lifted a hand, and sent Ruth tumbling down the stairs.

Angela and Jared—though Jared was not strong enough to really help—pulled her out of the space in the wall and set her on her feet. Ash was on the stairs above them, fighting with another one of Rob's sorcerers and Sergeant Kenn. Kami pulled away from Angela's and Jared's hands to run up the stairs and catch the sergeant's arm. She put the force of her rage into the touch and sent ice hurtling through his veins. She heard him gasp and stiffen, and Ash knocked him to one side and grabbed her hand, bringing her back down the stairs to the others.

"We've got to go, come on, now, now, now," Kami said.

"But we've only just got here," Rusty remarked as they charged down the stairs, a chaos of limbs because they were trying to keep as close together as they could and everyone was trying to give Jared a helping hand. "And I was having such a lovely time."

"Holly, you help Jared," Kami ordered.

Rusty and Angela could fight, and Ash and she could do magic. Holly was the only one who could be spared, and Kami could trust her to be gentle and not to leave him, not for any reason. They had always liked each other. Holly tucked the books she was carrying under one arm and put her shoulder under Jared's, her arm around his waist: made herself a crutch for him.

Amber yanked out of Rusty's grasp and made for the stairs, launching herself down after Ruth. Kami grabbed her back without touching her, as if Amber was a toy in one of the fairground machines that could be picked up and let go by a metal claw. Amber looked briefly stunned to be back at Rusty's side.

"You said you'd let me go!"

"Not until you help us to get *out*," said Kami. "It'll look like you came rushing to stop us, like the others, and we grabbed you. You'll be fine. Or they'll catch us all."

Amber's face went grim. She ran with the rest of them, like hunted animals through the grand rooms of Aurimere. Kami had to stop and fall behind when they passed Ruth, trying to get up. Ruth gestured and Kami fell hard on the floor, knocked down by nothing at all. She absorbed the impact on her hands and knees, and glared over at Ruth's scarlet head.

She filled Ruth's lungs with water, so Ruth gagged and collapsed again.

"Every one of you can burn and drown, for all I care," said Kami, and got up on unsteady legs to run after the others. Her legs and her lungs both hurt, she was running so hard, but up ahead she could see Holly and Jared, leaning close together, Holly helping him as much as she could and both of them going as fast as they were able.

Beyond them, beyond Amber and Rusty, she saw Ash and Angela lunge for the great doors of Aurimere and pull them wide open.

Kami ran to catch up and arrived a split second after Jared and Holly did, on the threshold of Aurimere.

"Everybody grab hold of Amber," Kami commanded. "Go now!"

Everybody did except Kami. Out of the corner of her eye, she saw movement: she whirled back into the hall of Aurimere and saw Rob Lynburn coming down the stairs.

She thought of the dead boy down in the hole, and turned the grand staircase to dust.

Rob was lost in the sudden carnage, a dust storm in Aurimere's great hall, and Kami turned back to see that the others had gone. The fire had leaped up after them with a ferocious snarl and leap of flame, like a tiger robbed of its prey.

She could see the others behind the fire, as if behind a scarlet veil. She could see Jared.

She had to go through, or he'd come back for her.

Kami took a deep breath of smoke: even that burned. She stepped into the fire.

Pain enveloped her, scorching and flaying: pain and fire blinded her. She crushed the impulse to use her magic to kill the fire. She held on to the shape of herself, whole and unhurt, made her skin impervious to flames, willed her blood to cool. She told herself she was not burning, and she stepped out of the fire iron cold.

As soon as she was out onto the grass, Angela seized her and shook her hard, though Jared tried to stop her. Angela brushed him off as if he was a fly.

"You crazy girl," Angela said. "Other people name their children after their best friends. I am going to name my ulcer after you! I am going to be forced to drink milk and take antacids and abstain from spicy food, and every time I want Indian takeout I will shake my fist at the sky and shout, 'Damn you, Kami.' Don't ever do that again."

"I promise not to walk through fire ever again, Angela."

Angela released her and gave her a sour look. "I know you're just saying that."

"Can I go now?" Amber asked, an edge of desperation in her voice.

Kami turned to look at her. She looked so terrified that she seemed utterly beyond the reach of being brave.

"Sure," Kami said. She had Jared back. She could afford to be generous. "Go. Be safe."

She did not say she was sorry for torturing Amber, and Amber did not say she was sorry for cutting Jared, but Amber glanced over to where Jared stood, still leaning on Holly, Ash beside him.

"I'm glad you're out," she said. "I wouldn't have let you go, but I am glad."

Jared raised an eyebrow. Out in the sunlight, he looked far worse than he had by darkness: there were more and deeper wounds on his chest than Kami had seen in the priest hole. He looked gaunt and his dark gold hair was dull, tarnished with dirt.

"That means so much," he said, his voice flat.

Amber nodded, her copper curls swaying, then disappeared behind the flames. Kami saw the door slam behind her in the rising smoke.

She turned away, back to Jared, and blinked for a moment in sheer astonishment.

Ash had turned to Jared and grabbed him, his arm tight around Jared's neck, his bright golden head on Jared's filthy shoulder. "I thought you were dead," he said in a low voice.

Jared stood for a moment with his arms spread wide as if he was being crucified and was very surprised about it. His eyes met Kami's over Ash's bowed head and he raised his eyebrows in silent frantic inquiry. Kami shrugged and made an encouraging motion.

After a moment, Jared let one hand drop and patted Ash's back tentatively.

"Um," he said. "There, there, buddy. I'm alive, but you don't need to take it so hard."

"You're not funny," Ash raged at him, and punched him, very carefully, on the shoulder. His arm tightened around Jared's neck, his body tense as a bow. Jared hesitated, then laid his other hand on the back of Ash's neck, fingers touching the ends of Ash's hair in a brief self-conscious caress.

"All right," Jared murmured. "All right."

"We have to go," said Kami, staring through the flames and dust. She could not see sorcerers coming, but that did not mean they were not.

They went down the path away from the great golden house on the hill, walking as fast as Jared could manage. Ash had hold of Jared on one side, having jealously taken the position as if someone else might seize it from him.

Heightwise, Kami supposed someone else should be on Jared's other side, but he looked for her: not raising his eyebrows or doing anything else to call her to his side, but concentrating on her as if the absolute force of his focus would bring her there.

He was right. She came to him, ducking her head and feeling absurdly shy, and then much less so when a good deal of his weight abruptly hit her shoulder.

Jared ducked his head and murmured in her ear, his breath warm against her skin: "What was that about?"

"Shush, you heartless monster," said Kami. "He's happy you're alive. I thought it was very sweet."

"I can hear you both," Ash grumbled from Jared's other side.

Kami couldn't see him, but she could feel how he was feeling, of course. It was the same way she felt, embarrassed but radiantly happy.

"Oh, Jared," said Rusty, mimicking Ash's voice. "I am sooooo overcome with joy that you are alive."

"Oh, Ash," said Angela. "The inbreeding has done such different things to us. You are so girlish and emotional, prone to swooning and embracing people, while I stand here with a face like a stone and eyes like a rabid squirrel's."

"All that stuff you're saying about your face is true, Jared," said Rusty. "But I still wish to clasp you to my bosom."

"I was buried alive five minutes ago," Jared muttered. "Already with the mockery?"

Kami glanced over her shoulder at Angela and Rusty, arm in arm and snickering with delight, and Holly on Angela's other side, smiling like a cheerfully wicked angel.

"That's how we roll," Kami said. "We live a mock-and-roll lifestyle."

She looked ahead to Sorry-in-the-Vale, and the curves of the streets and the spiky lines of the roofs looked as if the town was opening its arms to receive them.

Wonderfully and strangely, nobody followed them. They made their way slowly, because Jared could not go faster, and halted a few times when Kami had to make him stop and rest because his face had gone ashen, but finally they reached the High Street of Sorry-in-the-Vale.

Kami saw faces at the windows, peering out, and people on the street stopped and looked at them as they went past, curious but afraid. Many seemed taken aback to see a Lynburn as a stumbling wounded child, or maybe they were just surprised to see Jared alive at all.

Jared kept his head down and walked doggedly on. Kami held on to Jared's arm tight.

They were a few steps away from the Water Rising, the inn where Ash and his mother were staying, when they heard the sound of a commotion. It sounded like a few tables had gone flying into a few walls.

Kami tried to use her hold on Jared's sleeve to push him behind her, but he wouldn't move, and then the door of the inn opened and Lillian Lynburn came hurtling out, hair a loose golden sheet around her shoulders and her blood-red-painted mouth trembling.

She stopped like a bird that had hit a window, and stood on the step staring at Jared. He stood looking up at her, and Kami remembered that Lillian had his mother's face, and his mother was most likely dead.

"I'm sorry," Lillian said in a harsh, abrupt voice, more like Jared's own voice than Rosalind Lynburn's soft tones had ever been. She came tumbling off the step into Jared's arms. Kami felt Ash's surprise, greater than Kami's own, and shadowed with envy.

Jared had always dealt best with his aunt, perhaps because words and gestures of affection did not come easily to either of them. Lillian Lynburn had put Kami's brother in danger and Kami had not forgiven her for it, but she knew Lillian meant something to Jared. She was happy he had her.

He put his arms around Lillian, smoothed her tumbled hair, and laid his scarred cheek on top of her head.

"I'm sorry too," Jared murmured. "Aunt Lillian. Mom's dead. And Edmund Prescott didn't leave you. There's a priest hole behind the mural in Aurimere. Rob put me down there. Edmund's been dead for years."

Kami looked at Holly, whose whole family had been punished because her uncle had—as everyone thought— dared to leave a Lynburn. Holly had grabbed onto Angela's hand and was holding on tight, but there was no grief on her face: she'd never known the boy who died in the priest hole. She only looked tired.

When Kami's gaze returned to Lillian and Jared, Lillian had detached slightly from Jared but still had his face cupped in her hands.

"Maybe Edmund didn't mean to leave me," Lillian said. "It doesn't matter. What matters is that you're here, Jared. You're back."

She pressed his head down on her shoulder, and Jared shuddered slightly and then leaned against her. Kami thought he'd relaxed in his aunt's arms, before she realized that he had lost consciousness.

PART II
THE SWEET AND THE BITTER

There's blood between us, love, my love,
There's father's blood, there's brother's blood;
And blood's a bar I cannot pass.
—*Christina Rossetti*

Chapter Six
Call-Me-to-You

Jared had a fever for three days and two nights. Lillian led Ash and Kami in spells for healing, sending air to cool him and water to soothe him, and putting herbs under his pillow.

Eventually Martha Wright, who ran the Water Rising with her husband, mustered enough courage to stand up to a Lynburn and said that Jared was worn to a bone and needed rest, and completed this act of courage by shooing Lillian out of the room.

Lillian was admittedly not a very restful person. Even the way she smoothed Jared's sheets was peremptory, tugging at them in small irritable jerks as if she could tug health out of him that way.

On the second day, Martha Wright told Kami that Jared had woken up calling out with night terrors, and after that they took turns sitting with him. Holly and Angela were exempt because they had volunteered to go through the books from the Aurimere library, but Kami, Ash, and Rusty split their time.

Kami was uneasily aware that both Ash and Rusty were better nurses than she was. Kami suspected that she was only one step up from Lillian. Kami didn't like staying still for too long, while Rusty power-napped with one eye open. Kami was nervous about hurting rather than helping Jared, while both the boys had charming bedside manners.

Of course, Jared was not a particularly charming invalid.

Kami sat on the horsehair armchair that she and Rusty had carried up the dark stairs of the inn, curled up with a mystery novel in Jared's narrow, whitewashed room. Bright sunlight filtered through his single tall window in a thin yellow rectangle, half spilled on the wooden floor and half across his white linen bedsheets.

Kami wondered if she was a terrible girlfriend—if indeed she could be called a girlfriend, when it was basically a decision she'd come to entirely on her own—because she did not want to spend all her time gazing upon Jared as he slept.

He'd been sleeping a lot. Kami did like looking at him: every so often she peered over her book and checked on him, lying on his side in the tumbled sheets. He had one arm flung over the pillows as if he was reaching out for something, and the sun shone on his brown arm, on the slope of his back and the fresh-washed gold of his hair, curling soft against the pillow. She filled her eyes with him like taking a drink of cool water, and returned to what she was doing refreshed.

She couldn't help Jared. She couldn't quite banish Ash from her mind. She could not even see her mother: she had gone to Claire's restaurant and found it closed, with nobody answering the door no matter how insistently Kami knocked. What she needed right now was a mystery she could solve.

There was a mad butler hiding in the rafters of her book. It was very exciting. When she looked up from the pages the next time, she saw Jared was awake, his gray eyes shadow-dark and calm.

"I'm glad you're here," he said, his voice a sleepy rumble. "And I'm glad Ash is gone. He was just in here trying to force-feed me oatmeal."

Ash had been in there that morning, and the sunlight coming through the window was the mellow light of late afternoon. Kami did not mention that. It had been a while since Jared's eyes were clear and since he had talked to her rather than muttering, believing he was still trapped in the priest hole.

"Such an ungrateful brother," Kami murmured back, and smiled at him. "Oatmeal's good for you."

"I don't like it," Jared said crankily, and rubbed his eyes with the back of one hand. "What are you reading?"

"It's called *The Deadly Chandelier*," Kami said promptly and with satisfaction. "It's very good. What with everything that's been going on, I've really fallen behind on my reading. Want me to read it to you?"

"It's called *The Deadly Chandelier*?" Jared repeated in a skeptical tone. "Sounds like if you do I will never recover. Read to me one of the fine works of Mr. Charles Dickens."

"Shan't," said Kami. "Unless you want *The Mystery of Edwin Drood*, which Charles Dickens left unfinished when he died, thus accidentally creating the most epic mystery novel of all time. I'm warning you in advance, I will be making up a solution to the mystery of my own."

"Sounds good," Jared murmured, sounding half asleep. His lashes skimmed his cheekbones, but he opened them with an effort and reached out, this time with purpose though with no hope of actually getting to her, in her direction. "Will you," Jared began, and quietly, as if trying not to ask too much, "come here?"

"Sure," said Kami.

She felt a little awkward about it, but she didn't care: she scrambled out of the chair and sat on the bed, feeling it dip beneath her weight and the faint rasp of her flouncy cotton dress against the linen. Jared angled toward her slightly in the bed.

"You match the flowers," said Jared.

There was a small table at the end of Jared's bed with an earthenware vase on it, filled with wild pansies. Kami had always thought of them as love-lies-bleeding, but when Martha Wright had been arranging them she had called them call-me-to-you.

"They're from Martha," Kami told him, feeling a little embarrassed lest he thought she'd brought him flowers. Though she supposed she could have: maybe it would have been all right. "Your constant admirer."

"Very gratifying," Jared remarked. "But where are the posies from all my other callers?"

Kami laughed down at him and Jared smiled at her. He was touching her skirt, Kami saw with faint surprise, tracing the swirling yellow pattern on the dark purple material. His head was bowed, oddly intent, and all she could see was the fall of his lashes and the curve of his upper lip.

"I like the way you dress," he said quietly. "You're always—you look different from all the other girls."

"Thank you," Kami replied, uncertain, though she wanted Jared to like how she looked.

"What?" Jared asked. He was still lying down, but his eyes were open, more awake and concerned. "What did I say wrong?"

"Nothing. Go to sleep."

Kami aimed a punch at his pillow, which was meant to be fluffing it, but instead looked like random pillow violence. Jared had been tortured and buried alive. This did not matter.

"No," said Jared. "Don't—don't go. Tell me."

She hadn't even realized that she was edging away across the bed.

"Of course I look different from all the other girls," she said at last. "Anyone can see that. Half the town has suggested I date Raj Singh. Who's thirteen."

Because being part Japanese was the same thing as being Indian, and meant they didn't belong with anyone else.

It was something Kami noticed, that she couldn't help but notice: that she looked different from girls in pictures, girls on magazine covers, different from Angela and Holly and her own mother, who were all thin and pale and beautiful in what sometimes seemed to be the only right way. She noticed but tried not to mind, and didn't mostly—just because she noticed didn't mean she wanted to be someone else—but then she had met Jared and he hadn't ever seemed to want to touch her. It was hard sometimes, not to be self-conscious.

"Raj Singh can keep his hands off sexy older women," Jared said with conviction.

Kami smiled. "It's nothing," she said. "It's not about vanity or anything. Forget it."

"I'm awful at school," said Jared.

"You just need to apply yourself more," Kami told him sternly. "And speaking of applying, I don't see how that applies to anything."

"I hate school because I always want to be doing something more exciting than just sitting and staring at something or listening to someone," Jared continued. "But it's different with you. You do look different from all the other girls: I can always see you're doing something, thinking of something, laughing at something, or dreaming of something."

Kami found herself smiling even though she was blushing, and making a joke to cut him off even though she didn't want him to stop. "Are you saying that I'm, uh, interesting looking?"

"Yeah, something like that," said Jared, and she glanced over and saw the curl of his small smile. "Some synonyms come to mind. Fascinating. Captivating. I want to look at you all the time."

Kami was at this point too embarrassed to look at him at all. Embarrassed but pleased. She rolled over to where he lay, head on his arm and eyes half closed, and hid her face down by the pillow, her smile almost pressed against his throat. She had not forgotten anything about him, but memory had paled and thus lost the precise vividness of how intense he could be, how what he felt still seemed to go right through her.

Kami had felt cautious about it at first, about him in her real life, how out of control it could be, but now it made her happy. She could not control how she felt about him, and she did not want to.

"So what you're saying is that you're tormented by my beauty," she concluded. She felt him tense and touched his arm, in what was meant to be reassurance, but it only made him tense more. She looked up at him and said softly, "Don't worry. I'm tormented by your beauty too."

Kami was clearly terrible at reassurance. Jared was looking at her warily, his mouth twisted, as if he thought she was making fun of him.

He was obviously not quite coherent, saying all that he was thinking, fever bringing all his careful guards down. That made her think what he was saying was true, and that the few kisses and few words they had exchanged before he was taken meant what she wanted them to mean.

She looked up into his fever-flushed face, splashes of color on his high cheekbones, his mussed hair like old gold. Ash and Rusty were both objectively better-looking than he was; she remembered knowing that, even though it no longer felt true. The way he looked had more meaning to her than the way anybody else looked. She translated his face and ways to her town, to the woods, to fairy tales; she tried to guess at his moods by watching for the changing shades of gray in his eyes.

"I remember all the details of how you look, and I use them to tell myself stories about you," she said in a low voice. "I don't look at anyone else like that. I don't think about anyone else the way I think about you."

It was the most she had ever said to him about how she felt, and she did not know how to talk about it other than by talking about stories, and the way love changed hers.

Kami had not let go of his arm or looked away from him. She saw him bite his lip as if trying to hold back a smile, a slow-dawning one that moved through disbelief into happiness.

"I try—not to smile too much, or too wide," he said, as if he was reading her mind. "It makes the scar stretch. I always thought it looked weird—or scary, maybe. So I think I know how you feel, about being self-conscious about how you look. Not that . . . there's nothing wrong with anything about you. I like all the details of how you look." He paused, and looked suddenly worried. "Not that I have a fetish."

His almost-smile abruptly turned into concern. There was so much to trip over in a conversation like this, dragging all their lurking insecurities into the light, but she knew what he had meant: to share that there were things he felt self-conscious about too, even if they were not the same.

"I do," said Kami.

Jared blinked. "You do?"

"I have a fetish," Kami claimed. "For scars," she added, and Jared's mouth quirked. His smile still looked incredulous, but in a different way. "Obviously my first choice would be Mr. Stearn, who was in World War II and is by all reports absolutely covered in scars. Hot, am I right? But alas, our love can never be."

"That's tragic," said Jared.

"He's like a hundred years old, I'd kill him with my enthusiasm," said Kami. "I couldn't live with myself. He's a hero who fought for our country. You'll have to do."

"I'm a little reassured," Jared told her. He laughed, a slow, wonderful sound, warm as the line of his body against hers.

"But I'm mostly appalled. I had no idea of the massive age range my competition apparently fits into. Anyone from the age of thirteen to a hundred?"

Kami moved her hand with some daring. Every touch had such weight with them. She wanted, one day, to be able to touch him casually and have neither of them notice it as anything but a little everyday sweetness. Now, though, she could only draw in a deep breath as she drew her hand along his arm, to the swell of his shoulder, and be helplessly pleased that he tensed but did not move away.

She let her palm rest against the warm curve of his neck, and felt his throat move against her fingers as he took his own deep breath.

"You don't have any competition," she whispered. "And I love your smile."

She closed her eyes and let herself lean into him, head beside his on the pillow so she could press her lips lightly, shyly, against that smile. She felt the curve of that smile deepen, curling and sweet, against her own. The kiss ended, but their smiles did not. Kami curled in closer to him, and kept her fingers curled at his throat, feeling his pulse flicker against her hand, feeling him alive and safe here with her. She felt Jared hesitate, then slowly, as though she might stop him at any moment, drape an arm around her waist.

They were curved together like quotation marks with no words in between, and she was so warm.

She pushed Ash's thoughts, the cold insistent lap of an ocean against an unwilling and unwelcoming shore, to the back of her mind. She tried to ignore him, and almost could.

* * *

When Kami woke, it was still afternoon, but the day had mellowed, the sun brighter and lower in the window. The light pouring over their bed was the color of ripe pears.

Jared was already awake, leaning up on one elbow and looking at her. His eyes looked clearer now, and the fever-bright flush in his face had faded. Kami had heard the Lynburns called the creatures of red and gold before, but right now he looked like a creature of gold alone, all the blood washed away from the sleek bright lines of him, leaving him gleaming and happy in the sunlight.

"Watching me sleep?" Kami asked.

"Trying to work out a way to get to your book without waking you up," Jared returned, and grinned at her.

"I can tell when you're lying."

"That's because you're a very talented investigative reporter," said Jared, and leaned down toward her. He paused and checked himself as he did so, face hovering over hers, and Kami tried not to read too much into that hesitation.

She cupped the back of his neck, fingers threading through his hair, and brought his mouth to hers.

She was not expecting the shiver that went through her like light through water, the shock of urgent joy that had her surging up against him, her fingers clenching on his hair and her heart racing: she was so, so glad he was alive.

Jared's arm locked around her waist for a moment, hand warm at the small of her back, pressing her against him. Then they rolled together in the tangle of sunlight and white sheets so her head hit the pillow, and he was arched over her, obviously trying not to rest his weight on her. There was still weight on her, heavy muscle pressing her down into the sheets, but Kami liked it.

Everything was warm except for his mouth, which was hot on hers, slow and hungry and searching. Kami had to remind herself to be careful not to touch his chest, where despite everything Lillian had done there were new scars, but she slid her palms from his neck to the smooth planes of his collarbone, the coiled strength of his shoulders and his arms, mapping out all the skin she could reach.

She stretched underneath him, stretched up to where he was arched over her, and he made a small sound, half exhale and half gasp, into her open mouth.

"Kami," he said, voice low. He kissed her again, her mouth, her cheek and her chin, and then the side of her throat. She felt his lips curl, the smile pressed into her skin like a secret. "You once told me asking was sexy."

"Yes?" said Kami.

"So . . . ," Jared asked. "Can I?"

Kami looked at him inquiringly, her hand on his shoulder, fingers sweeping in a small continuous circle, a caress encouraging him to continue.

Jared kissed the hollow at the base of her throat, lips lingering on the spot. One of his hands left the mattress for the first time, to pull the side of her ruffled collar slightly open. He kissed the exposed skin and glanced up at her, a quick nervous glance through his sun-dusted lashes.

"Kami," he murmured, and his voice scraped in his throat. "Can I?"

All the breath left her in a dizzy rush. "Are you sure?"

She thought she should check: she had never seen him sure before, not about touching her, but one corner of his mouth lifted as if he found the idea of saying no laughable. "Yes," he said.

She was not sure what she felt: surprised and happy and curious and nervous all at once, but she did feel sure enough to smile.

"Yes," she said in return.

He surged up to kiss her again, his smile against hers, and as he kissed her he undid the top button of her dress with shaking hands, and dipped his head down to kiss the newly bared skin. Her skin felt different than it ever had before, prickling with cool air and a wash of sensation, made new piece by piece.

Jared glanced up again. "Can I?"

Smiling felt as irresistible and necessary as breathing. "Yes."

He undid another button, revealing bright pink pin-striped with darker pink and edged with a tiny line of purple lace, and kissed the curve just above where the lace rested.

"Can I?" he asked, and smiled against her skin again.

Kami looked down at his golden head, remembered her underwear did not match—it never did, not when it was important, it was one of life's great injustices that fate never lent a helping hand in the underwear department—and decided she did not care. "Yes."

He undid another button, asked for and received mur-mured permission to undo another and another, until all the buttons were undone. Kami's sleeves slid down to her elbows. Jared kissed the rise of her stomach, directly under her belly button, and looked up at her one more time.

Sunlight filled the bed, edge to edge, so the tumbled sheets were brimming with it, warming Kami all along her body. Jared's hands rested on the curve of her hips, fingertips brushing lace with intent, and the warmth rushing over her transformed into currents of anticipatory heat. Kami looked down her body at what she had found in the sunlight: at Jared, his broad golden shoulders and crazily ruffled golden hair, eyes bright and dazzled looking at her.

"Can I?" he asked, and she could see his smile now, sweet and shocked, as if happiness was newly discovered treasure he had never suspected was there.

"Yes," Kami murmured. Smiling was like breathing, utterly natural and impossible not to do. "Yes, yes."

The thundering rain of blows on the door made them both jolt.

"Guys," Ash said from behind the door, voice strangled. "I'm sorry, but *no*."

Kami clutched her dress together, doing up her buttons with fumbling fingers. Happiness felt chased away like a scared animal.

By the time her dress was done up and she looked for Jared, he was off the bed and pulling on the folded shirt Martha Wright had left on the chest of drawers. He was looking away from her, jaw set and gaze intent on the door.

Kami scrambled off the bed as Jared stalked to the door and swung it wide open. Ash stood in the doorway, face red and shoulders hunched. Jared didn't speak to him; he shoved past him and walked off down the corridor.

Kami expected certain terrible behaviors from Jared, and right now she felt let down.

If you wanted something done, she supposed, you just had to do it yourself, so she walked over to the doorway and punched Ash hard in the arm.

"That was not an okay thing to do," said Kami. "Ladies have needs!"

Ash hunched in farther, hands shoved deep in his pockets. He was really an impressive shade of scarlet: if he wasn't seventeen, Kami would have been worried about him having a heart attack.

She had been trying so hard to keep him warded off from her, to have that moment with Jared be a safe space. She was furious knowing that it had not quite been possible: that he had been there, like a cold stone in the bottom of a pool. Now that she had relaxed the vigilance of her bonds, she could feel what he felt bleeding through, feel the churning confusion of his emotions, embarrassment and humiliation and extreme discomfort among them. She could not blame him, even though she wanted to.

"I'm sorry," Ash said in a small voice, and added in her head: *It was very weird and I didn't know what to do—*

"Next time try humming," Kami suggested. "Think about kittens or gym teachers or large helpings of mashed potatoes, I don't care. Just don't do that again."

She was about to leave, but she looked at Ash's face again and remembered that she had promised herself to be kinder to him, when they got Jared back. He was her friend, and Jared's brother. Kami touched his arm, rubbing her fingers soothingly along the sleeve of his shirt. He looked at her, eyes very blue and very vulnerable, and she felt him reach out in her mind: she could not help sending comfort back to him.

It's all right, she told him. *I'm not really mad. I'm sorry for freaking you out. I know this is weird, but it's going to be all right.*

"Weird generally ends up working out for me," she added out loud, and went to find Jared, who could not have left the Water Rising, because he was in pajama bottoms and bare feet.

After searching the bar below, and the parlor, and the other guest rooms, Kami had to admit that if anyone was going to be lunatic enough to escape into the public streets in his pajamas, it would be Jared.

She checked again in the big bedroom where Lillian slept, in case he was hiding behind the four-poster or something.

He wasn't hiding behind or under the bed, but he was standing out on the little balcony, arms crossed over his chest. All you could see from the balcony was a brick wall and the gray square below where the Wrights kept their rubbish, but Jared seemed absorbed by the view. He didn't react when she came out to join him: he kept looking ahead, jaw tense.

It wasn't as sunny as it had seemed inside Jared's small room. February air slid into the thin material of Kami's dress like a sly pickpocket, warmth stolen before she knew it.

Anyone could go from seeming close to you to being distant, but it was always worse when it was Jared. She was so used to being close to him. He had been closer to her than if they slept cheek to cheek on the same pillow every night, closer than her own thoughts, for their whole lives.

Now was not an especially good time for Jared to seem so far away.

"Sorry," Jared bit out. His focus on the brick wall remained intent.

"Nothing to be sorry for," Kami said. "Awkward situation. I think Ash is off to rock back and forth in a corner and seriously wonder how his life got to be this way. He's a sensitive plant."

Jared nodded. "Might be better than stalking out to a balcony to wrap yourself in a cloak of bitterness and self-hatred like metaphorical Batman, though."

"Or trying to make light of a situation with constant awkward jokes," Kami agreed. "Whatever. Emotional health is for losers."

She put out her hand, but he went even stiffer and she put her hand on the balcony rail instead, cold fingers curled around the strip of cold steel, and stared at the brick wall as well. They must have looked as if they were at a museum, admiring the brick wall art.

"When Rob—when he had me, he said some things I think we all need to hear," Jared said. "We have to stop him. That's more important than anything else. I know that. You don't have to worry about me sulking over this or being a jerk to you or Ash."

"What did Rob say?" Kami demanded. "Wait, let me get a notebook. No, you're right, we need to have a meeting. Okay, do you think we can get everybody assembled in ten minutes, or is it too soon when you're only just out of bed? Is this why you're sulking even more than normal?"

She turned to look at Jared, who had his back up against the glass door of the balcony as if he was expecting an attack. She could tell nothing from his face: as if he had been an open book and now he was shut, simple as that, and she did not know how to make it so she could read him again.

"Look," he said. "I told you I was sorry. I didn't think about Ash, and how it was between the two of you now. I had other things to think about when I was at Aurimere with Rob, and then you came and—I guess I didn't want to think about it. But it's fine. I think it's going to work out for the best, in the end."

"Are you talking about the link?" Kami asked. "You said you understood why I made the link with Ash."

"I do understand." Jared still wouldn't look at her. "It's fine. It was the right thing to do. He's a good guy."

Ash was a good guy. Jared, however, was incomprehensible and impossible.

"It's fine," Kami repeated.

"Yes," Jared told her.

"You think it's going to work out for the best."

"Yes," Jared snapped.

Kami said, with slow-gathering fury, "But you're breaking up with me anyway."

Jared looked at her at last. His eyes were wide and cold, reminding Kami of ice over the gray waters of the Crying Pools.

He said, "Did you really think we were going out?"

Kami's hands clenched on the balcony rail, hard enough so that pain lanced through her, palm to elbow. Enough, she thought, enough, enough: nobody was allowed to make her this unhappy. She didn't have to stay around him, any more than she had to keep her hand in a fire.

Kami heard him say her name, but she turned and walked away. She went home.

Claire's hours at the bakery and restaurant had meant

she always left home early and stayed out late. Kami had not guessed how different it would be to know that her mother was not coming home at all. She realized that her mother's absence would fill the house, more noticeable than a presence. All four of them—Kami, her dad, and her brothers Ten and Tomo—were always looking to where she was not. Kami had no idea where Mum was, what she was doing, if she even still loved Kami at all.

Kami found her father sitting on the couch. He was not in his study, or even doing graphic design on his laptop: he was just sitting there, as if watching the blank black television. He looked helpless.

She curled up on the couch beside him, and laid her head on his shoulder. They sat and were heartbroken together for a little while.

Chapter Seven
Sharing Power

The next day, they were all finally assembled in the Water Rising. To Kami's surprise, her father said he was coming with her. Martha Wright, who loved children, had agreed to watch Ten and Tomo while they talked, since ten- and eight-year-olds were seldom brilliant at plotting against evil.

The four of them walked through the quiet streets of Sorry-in-the-Vale, hands linked as if they might be separated from each other in a rush of people who were not there.

Kami saw curtains moving as they passed. She saw one woman lingering in the doorway of her house, as if she was a ghost who could not leave the place where she had died. When she caught Kami looking, she closed the door and shut herself away.

Nobody was panicking. There was just this sense of persistent, lurking unease: the lives of all the people in town faded so that they could escape notice, and Kami felt it would not be long until they faded away completely.

Everyone was talking in whispers, and it made Kami want to scream.

By the time they walked in, the parlor was already

crammed with people. Angela and Rusty were on the sofa and looked prepared to defend it to the death.

Jared was sitting on the arm of Ash's chair, fully dressed. His eyes went to Kami when she walked in, but after one glance at him Kami looked away.

Lillian Lynburn, Ash's mother and Jared's aunt, the woman who still regarded herself as the Lynburn who should rule the town, was standing at the mantelpiece. She started slightly when she saw Kami's father; Kami was glad to see she still felt guilty about putting Ten in danger.

"Jon, Kami," she said, and sounded slightly proud that she remembered both their names.

"It's Lydia, isn't it?" Jon asked. "No, don't tell me, I'll get it. It's Laini, I'm almost positive." He went over to Angela and Rusty's sofa. "Move, you lazy brats," he said, and when they made room for him he patted Angela's shoulder.

Holly was standing at the window with Henry Thornton, the sorcerer newest to Sorry-in-the-Vale, the stranger from London who had come to help them for no reason other than that Kami had asked. He looked worried as usual, but he was leaning against her a little, and she was smiling—at him, at Kami when she came in, and all around. Looking at Holly's determinedly sunny smile made Kami feel stronger.

There was no place for Kami to sit, but she didn't want to sit. She walked over to stand at the mantelpiece beside Lillian.

Lillian gave her a faintly quizzical look, down Lillian's aristocratic nose since that seemed to be the only way Lillian knew how to look at people, but she did not object to Kami's presence.

"Here's the situation," said Jared. "Rob talked to me about his plans, and he said we had no idea what was coming."

"Did he get any more specific than that?" Angela asked skeptically.

"He said," Jared said, and hesitated, his voice changing. "He said, 'So many people are going to die.'"

There was a pause.

"I don't want to make jokes about people dying, since people actually are," said Rusty. "But doesn't it sound like a fairly standard evil overlord speech? 'Mwhahaha! You have no idea what you're dealing with, Mr. Bond! You have gravely underestimated me. You have no idea of the depth of my iniquity! Tremble, for you and all the puny forces of good will be utterly vanquished.' Et cetera, et cetera, megalomaniacal cackle optional. Does Rob have a cat to stroke?"

"He's not great with animals," said Jared, mouth curling up at one side. "I take your point. But he seemed so smug, so sure. He told me I didn't understand yet. I really believed that there was something else he knew and didn't want me to know, but couldn't resist crowing about. When he was torturing me—"

Kami felt Ash's distress flicker through her, like a scarlet fish through clear blue water. "You don't have to talk about that," Ash said.

"Wait," said Kami. She remembered how Jared had perceived the goodness in Holly before she had; if he thought there was something more to what Rob had done or said, she trusted his instincts. "Rob once said, to Jared, when we were linked—"

Jared flinched, and the sudden movement caught her eye. They looked at each other for a painful moment.

Kami swallowed and continued, "Rob said that enough magic could do a lot of things. He said that it could make you live forever."

Lillian raised her eyebrows.

"It can't," she said sharply. "Theoretically, magic could do that once, but the whole town could submit to Rob, he could demand sacrifices four times a year for ten years, and he would still not have enough power to make himself immortal. It's not a reasonable concern."

Lillian was the expert on magic, the sorcerer who had been trained to lead Sorry-in-the-Vale. Kami had only known that magic existed for a handful of months. She didn't know how to argue with Lillian, but she did know that she wanted to try.

"He asked for his first sacrifice on the winter solstice," Kami said slowly. "Now he's asking for one on the spring equinox. You guys, you set up shop hundreds of years ago in Sorry-in-the-Vale because the woods and the lakes power your magic—"

"We are not batteries!" protested Lillian, but Kami waved a hand at her dismissively.

"And you get sick in the autumn, when the year dies," Kami said. "It's all seasonal. He'll get more power if he does it on a certain day. He's willing to wait and wait until the right time. What's he waiting for? What does he want all that power for?"

"What do any of us want power for?" Lillian demanded. "To rule and to be feared, so your rule will be long."

"There's a campaign slogan," Jon muttered.

"But I am glad you assembled us all here nonetheless," said Lillian. "I wanted to talk about magical power, in fact, and who has the most power among us: namely, the source and her sorcerer."

She nodded to Kami and Ash. Kami met Lillian's eyes, regarding her dispassionately. She did not look over at Ash, though she could feel his flare of mingled worry and pride.

"What about us?" Kami asked, for both of them.

"Very few of our number can do magic now," Lillian said. "I have mentioned before that I shared power with Rob, once, so he could complete a magical ceremony. There are ways of setting up a magical bond, between one sorcerer and another. The bond is . . ." Lillian set her teeth. "It is uncomfortably intimate, though not to the same degree as that between a source and a sorcerer. Given the choice, I would not engage in the link again. But we have few choices and little hope left now."

Jon rubbed his forehead. "Please never become a motivational speaker, Lettice."

Lillian was dressed in one of Martha Wright's knitted cardigans, but she wore it with the air of a queen wearing a mantle. She drew it closed now with an air of offended dignity.

"I don't believe in telling children comforting lies," she said. "It lets them delay growing up. I wanted to lay all possible choices before my children, so they can decide what to do."

She directed her coolly demanding gaze to Ash and Jared. Jared looked badly startled.

"I get to decide what to do as well," said Kami. "Don't I?"

Lillian made a small face, as if she agreed that Kami got to decide but Lillian didn't have to like it. "It's Ash's decision."

"If I'm the source, and he's my sorcerer, wouldn't his being linked to someone else affect me too?"

Kami had never laid claim to Ash like that before, and she felt a ripple of his surprise go through her, but she wanted to be clear and she wanted them both to be safe.

"Maybe so," Lillian said. "All I know is, two sorcerers can share power, give each other power, and Ash has the most power of any sorcerer in Sorry-in-the-Vale right now. We need more power."

"So you want to link up Ash and Jared to create some sort of magic nuke," Dad said.

Rusty laughed. "Please come to all our meetings in future."

Lillian's eyes narrowed. "I wouldn't call it that, but essentially, yes. Though Ash could choose to share power with me, or Henry, if he wanted."

Henry and Holly looked about equally alarmed, but Holly got over it faster and patted Henry on the arm. Kami wondered how much Holly liked Henry, if she was scared for him and comforting him.

Kami did not have to look at Ash to know that he was the most alarmed person in the room.

"One of Rob's people told me," Kami said, and bit her lip and hoped she was not going to seem as if she was discussing kinky magic threesomes in front of her father. "She said that Matthew Cooper, the source who was married to Anne Lynburn, that he—was, um, attached to both Anne and Elinor Lynburn. Could she have meant that?"

Kami felt betrayed when her father and Lillian both gave her the same narrow-eyed doubtful look. Matthew Cooper, and Elinor and Anne Lynburn, had lived in the 1480s; Matthew and Anne had both died young.

Ever since Amber had mentioned them, Kami had been sure there was something more to their story.

"Perhaps," Lillian said eventually. "Matthew was Anne's source, and they both died. Elinor could have been using Anne's magic: she didn't die. She ruled in Aurimere for half a century. That's proof that one sorcerer sharing another sorcerer's magic will have no ill effects."

Kami was not surprised that suddenly her speculations about people long dead were "proof," now that they might get Lillian something she wanted.

"We have to think about it," Kami told Lillian.

"This may be our only hope," said Lillian. "Don't think too long."

Lillian turned and left, the baggy back of her cardigan seeming to sweep behind her like a cape.

"I wasn't kidding. Someone really has to talk to her about her motivational speaking," said Dad. "She's meant to be the town leader, isn't she?"

"She's the only adult sorcerer alive who isn't strictly evil," said Rusty. "So she wins the crown by default, I guess. Unless Henry wants it."

Kami supposed Henry was technically grown up, though he was only a couple of years older than Rusty.

"Your town seems very nice," said Henry, in the tones of one being very polite when offered a large unwanted present that was on fire. "But I only just got here. I don't feel qualified to lead."

"Okay," said Dad. "So she's all we've got to work with, as Ash and Jared are both so extremely and tragically seventeen. Fine. So what we need to do now is get the town behind her. Worse politicians have been elected every day."

"I don't think Lillian will be kissing any babies anytime soon," Holly said doubtfully.

"Since she probably hates babies. And kittens. And rainbows and sunshine," said Angela, who sounded like she had a certain amount of sympathy for Lillian's viewpoint.

"I'm going to have a talk with her," Jon said, and got up.

"You're so brave, Mr. Glass," Rusty told him soulfully. "You're everything I aspire to be when I grow up, in like ten to twenty years."

"You'll never have my dashing good looks, Russell," said Dad, and ruffled Rusty's hair before he went out.

Kami stood by the mantelpiece alone and watched everyone.

Holly was whispering to Henry, while Angela and Rusty whispered to each other. Kami knew that Holly and Henry were both living at Angela and Rusty's house, since Holly's family were on Rob's side and Henry was new to town, but she had not realized they were friends. She hoped for Angela's sake that they were nothing more than friends. Angela liked Holly so much; Kami was hoping Holly would not get a boyfriend until Angela was over her and maybe liked someone else.

Of course, Angela hardly ever liked anything or anyone, so that might take several years. Or a decade.

Kami felt a note of comfort, in the midst of the steady distress Ash was projecting to her. She looked over to see Jared clasp the back of Ash's neck. It would've been completely ordinary if it had been anyone else, but Jared did not touch people with casual affection often enough for this touch to be anything but noteworthy.

"You don't have to do anything you don't want to do," said Jared, low enough so that Kami wasn't sure if she was hearing it or understanding it through Ash. "Your mom's not the boss of you."

Ash smiled, rueful and charming. "My mom's kind of the boss of me."

"Nope," Jared said easily. "We time-share bossing you around, and it's my turn. I say do whatever you want."

Kami could not feel what Jared felt anymore, but she could feel what Ash felt, all right: warmth and trust and wanting to be closer. Ash inclined toward Jared, but Jared didn't notice and took his hand away.

She knew enough to know that the choice about who Ash would link with was made—that it had never been in doubt.

But no matter what Lillian said, Kami thought it was going to end up more complicated than Lillian imagined. Lillian, after all, was the one who had suggested that everyone perform the ceremony at the Crying Pools to get them more power. Jared had almost died. All the other sorcerers on Lillian's side *had* died.

Kami thought it might be a bad idea to be any more tangled up with Jared than she already was.

They weren't going to have a debate about it now. Kami made for the door. She was in the passage that led to the room with the pool table when she heard Jared say "Kami" urgently behind her. His tone suggested that if he was anyone else, he would have caught at her elbow and stopped her.

In this instance, Jared was right about not touching. Kami didn't want to be grabbed. She preferred to choose, so she chose to turn around.

"I'm sorry about yesterday," Jared said abruptly.

His hands were shoved into his jeans pockets; he was wearing ordinary clothes for the first time since they had taken him away from Rob, but he didn't look normal yet. His face was still thinner than it should be, strained in a way it had never been before. There were tiny new lines about his eyes, and there was something else about his eyes too: the haunted look of a child who had been hit and, worse, feared he would be hit again.

Kami found it harder to be angry when she was looking at him, so she wanted to stop looking at him as soon as possible.

"You said that yesterday."

She didn't want an apology for what was supposed to be a magical first time of taking wanton liberties with each other's persons. She just wanted him not to be a jerk, but apparently she could not have the things she wanted.

"About the last thing I said yesterday," Jared said. "I'm sorry, and I didn't mean to upset you. I was just surprised. I didn't realize you thought about it that way."

"Okay, thanks for that," said Kami, and began to walk determinedly down the passage away from him.

"Kami," Jared said behind her. "I'm—I'm honored that you did."

Which was not, Kami noted, "Let's be together, then." It was one of those nonsense things that people said, like "It's not you, it's me" and "You're too good for me." It meant, "I would like to very politely and very swiftly escape this relationship, like a Victorian gentleman in a rocket."

"Okay, brilliant," Kami told him. "All cleared up now! Please stop talking! I'm not mad! Let's forget it. We have more important things to think about."

She walked quickly away, past the pool table and into the bar. Her father and Lillian Lynburn were standing beside the bar itself, absorbed in a conversation that seemed to be ninety percent intense disagreement and ten percent keeping it civil for the kids. Her little brother Ten was at Dad's side, holding his hand and leaning heavily against him, staring up at Lillian with huge wary eyes.

Kami's brothers were dealing as well as anyone could ever have expected with the sorcerers, their mother leaving, and what had almost happened to Ten. To anyone who did not know them like she did, they were the same as they had ever been. Except now Ten was even quieter, his shyness transformed into a confirmed distrust of the world, and Tomo was even more boisterous, as if he could be loud enough to scare away his own fear.

They were so brave it broke her heart.

Tomo broke away from old Mr. Stearn and his bulldog, who were both apparently puzzled by Tomo's recommendation of lemonade over beer, and came rushing across the floor to Kami. She knelt down and he almost knocked her down, flying into her arms and knotting his arms around her neck.

"Hey, Kami," Tomo said brightly. "Did you have a good meeting? Is stuff fixed yet?"

Kami stroked the back of his head, and tried to keep her voice light too.

"Almost fixed," she told him. "I promise."

Lillian had not had to tell her. Kami knew how very little hope there was, and how very few choices they had left.

Kami went back to the parlor once it became clear that her dad and Lillian had a lot to say to each other and once she was sure via the link that Ash and Jared were long gone. She found Holly there alone, leaning against the window with a huge leather-bound book.

Holly glanced up. "You did say we should go through the books," she said, looking mildly abashed.

"I did," Kami said with conviction.

"I haven't found anything yet. I might be missing something, of course—"

"I'm sure you're not," said Kami. "But I can help you, if you like."

She went and leaned against the window beside Holly, lifting up a wedge of pages so she and Holly could read from different sections in the book. Holly leaned companionably into her side.

"So, there was a lot of intense glaring today," Holly said at length. "Did something happen between you and Jared?"

"Uh," Kami said, and kicked herself very suavely on the ankle. "Not exactly."

She hadn't told anybody much, but she knew Angela suspected something and she was pretty sure Holly did too. She looked around the room, at the mismatching chairs and sofas crammed in the tiny space. They were as safe here as they could be anywhere.

"We were kissing, a bit, before he was taken," she said. "And then yesterday we did a bit more than that, and then Ash interrupted and Jared seems to be of the opinion we were never going out. So I guess we weren't."

"Ah, the problem is that you didn't DTR," said Holly wisely.

Kami stared. "What?"

"D. T. R.," Holly spelled out, slowly and helpfully.

"Do try rollerblading?" Kami guessed. "Dump the recycling. Don't taste reptiles. No, that doesn't make any sense at all."

Holly wrinkled her nose. "Because the others made perfect sense?"

Kami shrugged, and Holly grinned.

"Determine the Relationship," Holly said. "That's when the two of you have been kissing a bunch and then you find yourself on a sofa or somewhere and someone's like, 'Oh, do you want to be my girlfriend?' or 'Is this an exclusive thing, then?' And then you say 'Yes' or 'No' and then you've either determined the relationship or determined that there isn't a relationship. You guys needed to DTR."

"Well, we have," Kami said. "We D'd the R, or rather he D'd that there wasn't an R, and now we're done."

Holly put out the hand that wasn't holding the book, and wiggled it noncommittally.

"I don't know," she said. "He—we talked about you, once."

"That one time you two made out?" Kami asked with a sinking feeling.

"Uh, I don't remember exactly when." Holly looked shifty.

"It was totally that time you made out, wasn't it?"

"Oh, come on," said Holly. "What's that thing you say? The past is another country. You make out with different people there."

"That's not how it goes but I admire your creative weaseling," said Kami. "You are the most promising reporter on my newspaper staff."

It gave Kami a pang to mention her newspaper. She was still writing it and putting it out, but so few people were coming to school these days. She didn't know if anyone was still reading it.

Holly blushed. "Oh no, Angie's really smart." She changed the subject back quickly, always so surprised when she was praised, almost as uncomfortable as she was pleased. "But when Jared talked about you—"

"Did he say he wanted us to go steady and he was planning to offer me his pin and/or letter jacket?"

Kami crossed the fingers of her free hand, mouthing "Please say yes," and Holly grinned and batted at them. "I may not remember exactly when this conversation took place, but I'm pretty sure it wasn't in the 1950s, Kami."

"I don't understand why magic can be real and time travel can't," said Kami. "I want to go back in time and meet Jane Austen and Dorothy Parker and bet on the horse races."

Holly leaned against Kami a bit more heavily this time, as if she was nudging her with her entire body.

"Try not to make a joke for maybe five minutes. Or, like, three. You know he cares about you, and if he was messing around with you, it wasn't because he didn't take it seriously. He takes you seriously. You matter to him in a way no one else does. That's obvious."

Kami leaned her head back against the window. She wondered if she could just not talk for three minutes until she was allowed to make jokes again. She suspected not.

"That's obvious," she repeated. "But I don't know if it's because of the link we used to have, and because he had nobody else for his whole life. He can have messed-up feelings about me, and not—not those feelings."

He can love me, and not want me to be his girlfriend, Kami thought, but she didn't know how to talk about love.

She'd always thought she was sensible about romance: she hadn't ever wanted any sort of wild destructive passion that would interfere with college applications. She had thought love would change the story she told about herself too much, that love would make her story less smart or less meaningful. She'd had Jared in her head all the time, though. She'd had love already. Only those who already had love could afford to dismiss it.

"He might," Holly said. "I don't know. But if he only backed off after Ash interrupted, that could mean something."

"You think he's in love with Ash?" Kami asked. "I mean, could be. It'd explain why he's so grouchy all the time."

"That was only two minutes without a joke," Holly told her sadly. "I believed in you."

"I have no idea why," Kami told her. "No, I think I get you. So, we need to Determine the Relationship, where you both get to talk over what the relationship actually is, because discussion's a two-way street. Unless of course one side of the street is being an idiot about psychic bonds, at which point it's okay to make decisions without him."

"I don't think that's quite what I said," said Holly.

"Thanks, Holly, you've been a big help, I have a plan now and I feel much better," Kami told her.

Holly still looked alarmed, but she also looked as if something had occurred to her. "If I have helped," she said tentatively, "and I don't think I have, and I don't know what you're planning but I'm mildly scared about it—"

"You'll see," Kami told her. "You'll see the plan."

"Not feeling any better," said Holly. "But if I have helped, I was wondering, could you help me? With, uh. With romantic stuff."

"Oh no, who are you interested in?" Kami wailed, then remembered what a great friend Holly was and instantly regretted it. "No, I'm sorry, that was not supportive. Let me try again. Oh wow, who are you interested in?"

Holly laughed at Kami's fake chipper voice and then blushed. "Well," she said, and ducked her head, examining the book's pages with sudden enormous intentness.

Kami turned her own page, which was focused on spells about maintaining the health of a sheep flock.

"Is it someone you're currently living in the same house with?"

"Well," Holly said again, and nodded tentatively.

"Oh my God," said Kami.

Holly peeped out at Kami from behind her falling clusters of golden hair. Kami had never seen Holly Prescott, Sorry-in-the-Vale's good-time girl, acting shy about anything to do with romance.

Kami didn't know Henry well, but he had come to this town to fight for strangers, for no other reason than that it was the right thing to do. She patted Holly's arm with perhaps more force than necessary.

"You're great and smart and beautiful and amazing," she announced. "If he doesn't like you, he's an idiot."

Holly blinked. "He?" she asked, and shook the hair back from her face.

Kami blinked back. They sat blinking at each other, like a pair of bemused owls.

"Is it . . . ," Kami said very slowly. "Is it . . . not a he?"

Holly's hands clenched on the book. For a long moment, Kami thought she had got this absolutely wrong, but then, even more slowly than Kami had spoken, Holly nodded.

Kami launched herself at Holly, trying to hug her and hit her on the arm and let out a triumphant war cry all at once. She almost punched Holly in the chest but stopped herself at the last moment.

"Kami, watch the book," Holly warned, laughing and breathless.

Kami kept one arm around Holly's neck.

"I shan't watch anything, I'm too happy," she declared. "Ahhh! I'm so happy! This is so great!"

"Yeah?" Holly asked, shy again. "You think so?"

"Uh, you are two of my favorite people in the world, so yes, I do," Kami declared. "Oh, wait, okay, you need my help. What do you need? Do you need practice kissing girls? That's totally fine. I can do that. Come here, I'll kiss you right now."

The creak of the door made Kami look away from Holly and Holly look up from the book.

Ash looked as if he seriously wondered why it was always him. "Ah, don't stop on my account," he said. "Please go on."

"Get out right now, we're talking," Kami commanded. "Come back in a few minutes."

"There's no need—" Holly protested.

"Yes, there is," said Kami. "Out! Get out! We don't like your face and we don't want to see it around these parts."

No, seriously, I mean it, I need a few minutes, Kami warned, and sent the need for privacy at him. They were both sending that message to each other all the time, and Ash didn't need to know that it was Holly's privacy Kami was concerned with right now. He would still be able to feel what Kami felt, but he would not know exactly what was going on.

"Okaaaaaaay," said Ash, and backed out.

"You didn't have to do that," Holly said, blushing.

"Yes, I did," Kami informed her. "What can I do to help? I'll do anything. I'm serious about the kissing."

"Please don't kiss me," Holly said, with conviction.

"Hurtful," Kami commented. "But all right. What else can I do?"

Holly stared fixedly at a drawing of a sorcerer's hand, limned with light. "I know Angie used to—like me," she said in a low voice. "But I heard her say to you that—that she didn't anymore. I wondered if you could find out if she does or not."

"Absolutely," Kami said. "I'm sure she does, but I'm happy to do it. Holly, I'm so happy for you guys."

"I'm—I'm a bit scared," said Holly, and Kami took her hand, held it tight in Kami's own. Holly took a deep breath, seeming encouraged, and went on: "I'm scared of everything, what people will think, and of not doing things right, and what it means about me, but when we were all fighting Rob in the square I realized that of all the things that scare me, the one that scares me most is losing her, without her ever knowing how I feel. I'm trying to get up my nerve to tell her. I'd like to be brave enough to try."

Kami pressed Holly's hand. "You're brave enough for anything."

"Kami," said Holly, seeming stricken with a sudden terrible thought. "Please be subtle."

"Totally," said Kami. "You can rely on me absolutely. I will have the stealth of a lioness stalking the grasslands. In this metaphor Angela is an antelope, and she'll never know what hit her."

Holly did not look reassured.

"I promise you, Holly, 'Subtle' would be my middle name, except I'm too subtle to have a middle name that's such a giveaway. You don't have to worry about a thing."

There was a knock on the door.

"Is it safe to come in?" Ash's voice asked. In Kami's

mind, he asked with a certain amount of excitement, *Are you guys kissing?*

"Yes," Holly called out.

When the door opened, it was suddenly clear that Ash had brought reinforcements. Jared's face was relatively unmoved, so Kami presumed that Ash hadn't told him about any potential ladies kissing.

You'll never know, sucker, she told Ash.

"Hi, Ash," she said out loud. "Hi, darling."

Jared's face looked slightly less unmoved.

"One moment. Holly, please keep my place in the book," Kami said, and rose from her position leaning against the window to make her way purposefully across the room.

Ash got out of the way very quickly. In fact, he went to stand behind a chair, as if there was about to be an explosion and he wanted protection from the blast.

Jared stayed where he was, leaning against the doorframe and watching her. His hands were in his pockets, which Kami thought was excellent because it meant he couldn't defend himself when she caught him off guard.

"I just wanted to make something clear, cupcake," she told him, and his eyes widened fractionally as she grabbed him by the collar of his T-shirt, stood on her tiptoes, and pulled him down into a kiss.

His mouth was warm against hers: amazingly, he did not flinch or try to pull away. Of course, he might simply have been stunned, but Kami chose to enjoy the moment anyway, his body bowed down toward hers and hers arched up toward his, forming an easy natural curve.

For a moment things were sweet and simple, and then

Kami leaned back and looked into Jared's eyes. "I'm Deter-mining the Relationship," she told him in a low voice. "We're going out. I refuse to be broken up with."

She didn't give him a chance to respond. She patted Jared on the shoulder, ignored Ash's startled face and his startled feelings coursing through her, and walked back to the other side of the room, to Holly and the book. Holly's face was the picture of dismay.

"That was very subtle," she said, in a low voice. "And I—I think I found something here, about the spell for shar-ing power."

Kami forgot that she was carefully not looking at Jared and devoted all her attention to the book, abandoning her page and laying it flat so Ash and Jared could see the spell and the picture.

"It says here it's temporary," said Ash. "We can cut it off any time we like. And there shouldn't be any hearing each other's thoughts, just—an emotional connection, which honestly is a lot less invasive than what we're already dealing with."

You flatterer, said Kami.

I can't help being honest with you now, Ash said. *I'm afraid it's not that charming.*

It wasn't all that charming, Kami reflected, all confusion and distress, his every uncertainty and imperfection rained down on her with none of the guards she and Jared had built up between them and none of the way she and Jared had formed their faults around each other, their jagged edges fit-ting up against each other. Before they were linked, Ash's enormous surface charm had been able to smooth out every interaction they had, made her forgive more easily or think of him as a safer, more attractive option when she was trying to make choices. Charm had made everything a lot easier, but this insight was probably better, if they were going to be real friends.

It's a nice change, said Kami, and let him feel that she meant it. *Do you want to make the link with Jared?*

The spell looked simple enough to do. It was the pictures that shocked and frightened Kami: the knife, and the rope.

You're not surprised, she said to Ash.

She could feel his calm resolve. He wanted to do the spell, and his comfort with all the weird wild world of magic seeped through her, stilling her own fears even as it made her slightly uneasy somewhere in the back of her mind where Ash had not yet invaded.

I expected it, Ash told her, so peaceful. *A spell is like a promise. All words work best sealed with blood.*

Chapter Eight
Visited upon the Sons a Thousandfold

They did the spell that night.

It was better this way, Kami told herself. They had come to a decision, and there was no point wasting time worrying. They would do it, and deal with the consequences, whatever those consequences might be.

You are not being very soothing, said Ash.

It was as if they had changed places. She could feel his resentment of her fears, and she could feel his resolve. Ash wanted to be useful, to be wanted and loved, wanted it with such passion she could see why he might become a tool in anyone's hand. She tried not to come too close to that need of his, as if it was a black hole that might swallow her. They tried to avoid the dark unlovable corners of each other's hearts.

I know this is our best option, said Kami, which was all the comfort she could give.

She stood at the door with her father and looked inside at the room. Lillian's bedroom was dim, tall candles creating tiny islands of light in a murky sea. Ash was sitting on the bed, which was draped with white sheets, and Jared sat on a low stool at the opposite side of the room.

Kami's soul shriveled slightly at the idea of taking romantic action in front of her father, but she was determined to determine this relationship, so she left the doorway and walked over to where Jared was sitting. When he lifted his face to look up at her, she leaned down and kissed him.

"Hi there, dream canoe," she said. She got hold of his arm and sat on his lap, drawing his arm around her—which he allowed, although she supposed the lack of resistance could mean he was in shock—so she had her back to whatever expression he made.

Sadly, she could still see the expression her father was making.

"Do you have any tattoos?" Dad asked Jared suspiciously.

"No!" said Jared, and added hastily, "Sir."

Her father looked like he had further questions for Jared, and Kami did not have high hopes about the answers—history of violence, check; poor academics, check; leather jacket, check; motorcycle, check; despoiling his innocent daughter, no check but not for lack of trying—but then everyone's attention turned to Lillian Lynburn, standing at the door to her balcony. Moonlight streamed in on her long fair hair and the long sharp knife in her hand, surrounding them both with a silvery halo.

Kami pressed her back into the warm solid line of Jared's chest.

"It's a pity that Rob has our Lynburn knives," Lillian said. "But any knife can be cursed or blessed."

"Right, but can any knife be disinfected?" asked Jon. "Specifically, was this one?"

Lillian smiled thinly, holding her knife up to the moonlight so the metal glittered. She looked ready to use it, and Kami presumed she was.

Nobody else was coming. When asked if they wanted to see the Lynburn boys cut up and tied up, Holly had weakly claimed that she was absorbed in studying, Angela had said a flat no, and Rusty had assured them all that he would be washing his hair.

"You want to come downstairs with me, Henry?" Jon asked sympathetically.

Henry Thornton was standing in one corner of the room and looking pale, but he shook his head. "I've never seen this kind of spell performed before. I'm very interested to watch."

Jon lifted his eyebrows. "Okay. Note to self: sorcerers are freaks every day of the week. Are you sure you want to stay, sweetheart? Or do you want me to stay with you?"

Kami looked up at her father. Dad looked back, his gaze steady: she knew he would stay if she wanted, and hold her if anything went wrong. And she knew that magic was new and strange, more terrifying to him than her.

"Nah, Dad, I'm good. Please leave me in this hotel bedroom with my handsome boyfriend. And several of his relatives, and a very sharp weapon."

"Clearly I went badly wrong somewhere when raising you," said Dad. "Well, best to go down before Tomo gets into the vodka."

He pulled a lock of Kami's hair gently, then fixed Jared

with a deeply suspicious stare, which he maintained until he had backed out of the room.

The door closing softly behind him seemed to be the cue for the sorcerers to act. Lillian drew the knife up to her face, leaning the sharp edge against her forehead and her lips as she murmured. Ash got up, his nerves fraying the edges of Kami's nerves, like two exposed wires sparking together. Kami tried to be calm and spread calm to Ash, and she felt Jared tense slightly more against her body.

"Good luck with your horrifying blood-and-knives spell, pumpkin blossom," Kami said, unlooping his arm from around her waist and standing up so he could. She dropped a kiss on the side of his mouth as she did so.

Jared paused and then said, "Thanks."

That was almost encouragement, Kami thought. She didn't even know where the dumb terms of endearment had come from, except from her inherent terror of being serious about anything, but they appeared to have the effect of a stun gun on Jared. They worked when nothing else had worked, and she had to use what she had.

Kami wondered if she should count it as a victory that he did not seem to be actively attempting to foil her plan of going out with him. Of course, he wasn't actively participating in it either, so maybe it was a draw.

Lillian ran her blood-red nails along the shining surface of the knife.

"Kneel down," she told her boys, "and bare your arms."

"Good thing I wore a wifebeater," said Jared, looking back to exchange a brief smile with Kami. "Because there is no way I'm doing this shirtless."

Ash undid the button of his shirt cuff, rolling it up well past his elbow. Jared went over to the table beside the door and picked up the small coil lying there, unwinding the thin rough length of rope quickly between his hands.

"Be careful not to cut along the artery," Lillian commanded. She walked over to the end of the bed, where Ash sat, and handed him the knife.

Ash looked up at her, face naked and unguarded in the moonlight, obviously seeking reassurance. Lillian met his gaze for an instant, her face calm and still as a statue's, touched by moonlight but not emotion. She turned and walked back toward the balcony door, where she stood outlined, an impassive silver silhouette against the glass.

Ash knelt slowly on the rug at the foot of the bed, in the circle of lamplight. Kami could sense how alone he felt, as though the circle of light was an island far away from anyone, because nobody cared enough to cross the floor and go over to him.

Compassion flooded Kami, so overwhelming and warm it felt for a moment like passion. Ash's face and heart both turned to her, as toward the sun. He looked like a young poet with his gilded hair and rumpled shirt, and his eyes bright with hope.

Kami lost sight of Ash for an instant as Jared walked across the bedroom rug toward him, casting a shadow on Ash's face. She looked at Jared and saw him looking back at her, just a glimpse of his cool eyes for a brief instant before he glanced back at Ash, and she knew with a sinking feeling that he was putting the way Kami had leaned forward and Ash's uplifted expression together. He towered over the kneeling Ash.

"You all right?" he asked Ash, voice gruff with discomfort at evincing any evidence of concern.

Kami found herself smiling at the same time as feeling a pang. It felt viscerally wrong, being in this position, slightly intimidated by Jared from the outside when she should not be outside at all. She should never be surprised by his lurking secret kindness, because she should always be wrapped in it.

It had been months since she had linked with Ash: months and months since she had broken the link with Jared. It should be something she was used to by now.

But she could feel Ash's fondness for Jared too. She smiled at Jared's back, then saw the knife in Ash's hand and stopped smiling.

Ash swallowed and said, "I'm all right. I'm only worried I'm going to forget the lines."

"It is not the words that matter," said Lillian. "It is the intent. And the blood, of course."

"Thank you, Aunt Lillian," said Jared dryly. "You always know just what to say."

A faint smile crossed Ash's face. He offered Jared the knife.

Jared knelt down, rope wrapped around his fist, and took the knife in his free hand. Ash took a deep breath in the hush and offered up his arm, veins long twining lines of pale blue under his skin, so white it was almost glowing in the low light.

Jared turned the knife with a flick of his wrist that looked disturbingly expert, laid the point against Ash's arm, and drew the keen edge along his skin. The skin parted, simple and easy, and for a moment the blood was beads of red against white.

Until the gleaming drops turned into a stream, then a river, of red.

Kami felt the pain strike through Ash, saw his expression contort and heard the low sound of pain he made, before he buried his face in Jared's shoulder. Kami saw the shudders run through his kneeling body.

Jared's hand, the one holding the rope and the knife, hovered over Ash's hair in an unfulfilled gesture of comfort.

He spoke instead, intoning the words of the spell in a steady voice.

> "Pain buys power, power pain
> Mine to you and back again."

Ash breathed in again, released his hold on Jared's shirt and straightened up. He was even paler, sweat beading on his face as blood had on his arm, but he looked at Jared and saw something there that made him square his shoulders. Jared pressed the knife into Ash's palm and held out his arm: the underside was as pale as Ash's and looked unexpectedly vulnerable.

Kami's hands formed into tight fists, fingernails biting into her palms. She didn't want Ash to touch him.

The only thing that helped was Ash's expression, and the feeling coursing toward her beneath his pain: he didn't want to hurt Jared either, not at all.

The knife came down, and Kami had to set her teeth as

she saw how Ash flinched and slipped, the hesitation surely causing Jared more pain, the slash on his arm jagged.

Ash's voice was shaking too, but the words of the spell rang out clear.

"That which was whole, now make it part
That which was hidden, show the heart."

No sooner was he finished speaking than Jared took hold of Ash's injured arm and pressed the insides of their wounded forearms together, each of their hands clasped around the other's elbow. Their labored breathing was coming in sync, the blood dripping between their locked arms, dappling the rug where the knife lay now.

Jared wound the rope around their arms. As he did so the moonlight crept in through the glass door and wound around them in shining tendrils: shimmering around their sealed arms, moving like the lines of light cast on water along their backs and circling their fair heads, bowed together so their bodies formed an arch.

They spoke together, and Ash's voice was no longer trembling, and Jared's was a little less rough.

"Blood to blood and breath to breath,
Until spell's breaking or our death."

The rays of moonlight shivered and rippled around them. Kami felt a strange sensation, as if what was happening with the moonlight was happening inside her. As if the light that lit the world within her was changing, expanding and luminescent, and on the edge of darkness but moving into the light was a loved one she had not seen in too long.

Kami leaned forward on the chair even farther. Jared turned to look at her.

Their eyes met, and Kami felt the spark between them turn into leaping flame, recognition and yearning twisting together at the same time. She could feel Jared's familiar feelings, brushing at her consciousness. She could not be mistaken: she knew the exact edge of his anger, the rush of his surprise, the taste of his grief, and the enveloping warmth of his affection. Nobody else felt the same.

Ash had not been able to fill the space Jared had carved out in her heart: he could not fit the place made by someone else, and it hurt to have him there.

But now Jared was almost back, where he had been before.

Ash was there too, a rush of feeling like a channel separating her and Jared, but she could almost reach Jared, as if they both had hands outstretched and there was only an inch between the very tips of their fingers.

And then Kami found herself drawing back in her mind, in alarm that she did not for a moment understand.

It was like seeing a loved one coming toward you, and seeing a shadow behind him, having your joyous desire turn to fear even before you realized that the shadow was an avalanche.

Kami threw up the mental walls she had spent so much time constructing with Jared, had used so often with Ash, trying to protect herself. She concentrated on shielding the small bright place in her mind that she used when she was writing, which she thought of when she tried to do her magic. She could still feel them, but more distantly, as if she had taken a hasty step back.

The rays of moonlight wrapping around Jared and Ash were turning darker, from ribbons of smoke to what looked like trails of ink, circling them in, binding them tighter and tighter.

Until they disappeared, leaving only a faint grayness in the air like traces of ash.

Jared was still looking at Kami, but his expression was wary.

"Did it work?" Ash asked, his voice hoarse.

Jared unwound the rope from around their arms. "I don't know."

Lillian moved from her place at the door and strode toward them, stepping over the fallen knife and spilled blood until she was by Ash's side, her fingers hovering over his wounded arm.

That was something Kami could do, at least. She jumped up and hurried over to Jared, kneeling down beside him and taking hold of his wrist as gently and carefully as she could. He'd been hurt too much, by too many people: she did not want to be one of them.

She shut her eyes and concentrated. It took more of an effort than she had thought, but she had healed someone only once before.

When she opened her eyes, she saw that Jared was breathing more easily, and when she touched the blood on his arm it came away on her fingers, showing whole skin beneath the stain.

"If you want to know if it worked, do a spell," Lillian suggested. "Test your new power."

Ash glanced from Lillian to Jared, and got up, stumbling as if he had forgotten how to walk, uncertain on his legs as a newborn foal. He lifted a hand and gestured at the balcony door.

Kami could feel it even behind her walls, the strange void where once there had been something that surged.

She did not know what Ash had been trying to do. Nothing happened.

"I don't understand," Ash said, his voice rising with panic. "What's going on?"

"You can't do the spell?" Lillian inquired sharply. "You don't have the power?"

Ash shook his head. The light through the glass door of the balcony illumined his face: he looked lost. "I can't do anything. I don't have any power."

"That's impossible!" Lillian snapped.

"Is it?" Kami asked.

Nobody answered her. Kami looked at Jared. She didn't want to say this, didn't want to seem as if she blamed him when none of this was his fault, but she had to speak.

"The night before we saved you," Kami said. She held on fast to his wrist, tried to hold her eyes with his. "When Rob was torturing you, when he and Amber hurt you, he was using the Lynburn knives. Wasn't he?"

Jared nodded.

Lillian wheeled on him. "Have you done any magic since you were taken from Aurimere?"

"No," Jared said. "Rob was drugging me, I got used to

not using it. Also, you may have noticed I've been delirious most of the time."

His voice was sarcastic, but it was obvious he understood the horror of what had happened as well as any of them.

They could all see the edges of the scars Rob had left on Jared's skin, not quite hidden beneath the material of his shirt.

"I see he's learned some new tricks from his strange sorcerers," Lillian said at last. Her voice was vicious. "Rob used the Lynburn knives and your Lynburn blood to taint your power, to twist it so you could not use it again. Rob poisoned your magic, and now you've poisoned my son's."

"Yes, Lillian, this was all Jared's idea," Kami said sharply.

Lillian looked at Kami as if Kami was mad. "I am not blaming Jared. I am simply stating the facts. Try to use magic, Jared, if you can."

Jared looked at the mirror hung above Lillian's dresser. Nothing happened: his reflection stared balefully back at him.

Kami looked at it and it broke, splitting clear across, so he would not have to look at himself anymore.

"I can still do magic," she said. "I put up a block between us, between me and Ash . . . and Jared, I think. While the spell was happening. It protected me."

Lillian did not look greatly relieved at the news that Kami had been spared.

Kami could not blame her for despairing. Kami could not even blame Lillian for suggesting this spell, not really, no matter how it had turned out. They had all agreed to do it: none of them had thought it would work out like this.

They'd all known they were badly outnumbered before, and now the two Lynburn boys were powerless and helpless.

They had been desperate, and now they were more desperate still.

Kami was too tired to even despair. And from the look of Jared, he was more tired still: bleeding all over the floor could not be good for him.

"You need to go to bed," Kami decided, and hauled him away and out of Lillian's room. "Come on. Everything will still be ruined in the morning."

It was a brief walk down the narrow hall to Jared's little room. They did not speak until they were at his door.

"Can you believe that we screwed up everything about twice as much in the space of a couple hours?" Kami asked.

"I can," said Jared. "But only because I truly believe in us, the utter depths of our incompetence, and that it must inevitably lead us to our ultimate epic failure."

"Aw, sugar flower," Kami told him. "You always know just what to say."

"And just how to poison my brother," said Jared.

She looked up at him, leaning against the doorway with his white shirt stained with blood and sweat, his too-thin face sick and weary of the world. She'd known he would take that to heart. Kami grabbed a handful of Jared's shirt and stood on tiptoe so she could press their foreheads together. She closed her eyes and did not try to kiss him, because insisting on determining a relationship all by yourself was hard work and she didn't, couldn't, know if he wanted her to.

"I once told you I was always on your side," she murmured.

"I will always be on your side, even in times of ultimate epic failure. I'll see you in the morning and I'll be glad to see you, even on a ruined morning. Good night."

Jared did not kiss her, but he leaned his forehead against hers and let out a long weary breath, as if he had reached a refuge where it was safe to rest and breathe for a moment.

"Night," he said, and after a moment: "Thanks."

She walked home through the night with her father, the boys walking between them. Her father had seen her face and not asked any questions.

The night was dark and deep: the stars seemed lost somewhere. The sound of their steps seemed like the only sound in the world, or at least in the still quiet of the town that was now at once both home and prison.

None of them looked at Aurimere on the horizon.

"I propose that we just stop letting Lillian 'Bad Idea' Lynburn make plans," Jon said. "I know she means well, but this is a lady who seems to never have had a good idea in her life."

"She was the one caught off guard, not Rob. She didn't know that the people she loved and trusted would betray her, or that her home would be taken away from her. She's doing the best she can, and it's all turning to dust in her hands." Kami did not like the too-perceptive way her father was looking at her, and added, "She is basically the most insensitive person who ever lived, though, and she and her plans can keep the hell away from my brothers."

Tomo looked up at them anxiously and said, "I want to help."

"You are helping by being awesome," Kami told him.

Tomo nodded thoughtfully. "That's true."

Ten said nothing. His hand was cold in Kami's, but when she looked down at him all she could see was the glitter of his glasses and his solemn, unreadable face.

There was a clatter and the sound of glass breaking near them. Dad spun both the boys behind him and Kami stepped forward, hands uplifted. They saw a man stepping out of the grocery store, carrying paper bags full of food. Under the hood of his coat, Kami recognized Timothy Cartwright, one of Dad's friends.

He started when he saw them, stared at them for a guilty moment, then mumbled, "I left the money in there."

Timothy slipped away down the street, until he was nothing more than a shadow among shadows. They were all shadows, crouched in the shadow of Aurimere, making useless plans and slinking around afraid to be seen.

They were a town under siege. The people of Sorry-in-the-Vale were going to give up, to give in and do what Rob wanted, under the pressure of sheer fear.

When they were home and Tomo and Ten were in bed, Kami and her dad sat down on the sofa together. Kami curled against his side.

"When Jared was sleeping and Rusty was watching him," Kami said in a small voice against his chest, "I went to see Mum, at Claire's, but it was shut up. She wasn't there."

Dad said nothing for a long time. Kami waited.

"The word is, your mum is up in Aurimere," Jon said at last. "She's cooking for them, seeing to the sorcerers' needs, being a good little villager and the example that every citizen of Sorry-in-the-Vale should copy. So I hear."

Kami did not know what to say to that. But she knew she did not have to speak; her father felt the same desolation.

"Are the Lynburn kids all right?" Dad asked, after another pause. "I know they had to hurt themselves, for that spell."

"They're okay," Kami said. "I can feel Ash sleeping. I'm a bit worried about Jared. He shouldn't even have done this spell when he's still sick, and now he's going to feel like this is all his fault, and he—he tries so hard."

Once again the way her father was looking at her was too perceptive, saw too much of her that she hadn't meant to betray. Kami put her head down onto his shoulder, hiding her face, and he sighed and stroked her hair.

"None of you should have to do any of this," Jon murmured. "You're all far too young."

Kami woke up alone on the sofa, a soft woven blanket pulled up to her chin and a soft sound in her ears that for a moment she did not recognize.

Until she sat upright on the sofa, scrambled off it, and ran to her window. She saw her father swinging open their gate and realized that the noise that had woken her had been the door shut stealthily behind him.

Ash! she screamed in her head, wrenching him out of sleep. *You have to come watch the boys. I have to go after my father.*

Chapter Nine
A Glass Heart

Kami could intuit where her father was going: down the road by the woods and up the hill to Aurimere, but she didn't know what his plan was. To see her mother—to beg her to come home? What if she didn't? What if she did, and Rob Lynburn didn't like it?

She did not know what her father intended, or what she should do. She didn't try to stop him, but she did follow him so she could try to protect him.

It was a clear spring morning, bright as if the sun was a lamp whose brilliance had been turned up a few notches, white rays stretching out across a sky lucent as glass. Kami had had to stop to find her shoes and her coat, and she was trying to be subtle as she hurried, so her father was well ahead of her on the path. No matter how clear the morning, she could barely keep him in sight.

There was no way her father could pass through the flames around Aurimere.

But she was only a little way up the hill when she saw her father reach Aurimere, a small dark figure outlined against the fire, and the living leaping walls of fire flickered and parted like a red sea. Jon passed through the flame. The sorcerers at Aurimere had let him in, and Kami did not know why, and she could not see him at all.

Kami charged up the hill, racing as if she could stop him though he was already gone. She mentally apologized to Angela and did not stop as she ran straight into the fire.

The sorcerers must have strengthened their spells since Jared escaped. It hurt, as it had not hurt last time, and as she felt tears roll down from her smarting eyes to her scorched cheeks and smelled the smoky scent that was the ends of her hair burning.

Maybe you should wait, Ash told her, and she could feel the wash of his nervousness against her walls.

Maybe you should shut up, Kami suggested. *That's my dad.*

Lillian had told Kami about the magical ways to hide yourself, how to wrap yourself in shadows and fade into stone. There were not many shadows on a morning like this, but as Kami pushed open the door and walked into the vast hall she found a few. She took the darkness lurking in the alcoves where marble busts stood, the shadows in the corners of the high ceiling and the dark stairs, and wound them around herself.

She did not think it would stand up long to a sorcerer's scrutiny, but she went running through the hall toward the sound of voices anyway. If they were distracted, they might not notice, and her father had no magical protection at all.

The voices were not her mother's and father's. This was no private meeting between them.

Rob Lynburn had been redecorating Aurimere, Kami saw, to be more appropriate for his evil-masterminding needs. In the parlor there was only one of the red sofas left, pushed up against the farthest wall, where the windows were tall, curved at the top like church windows. There was stained glass, too, like a church, but instead of saints and angels the windows showed a blue glass river, a girl's face, and vivid green leaves in the drowned girl's sun-yellow hair.

Rob was sitting on the red sofa, talking to other sorcerers, who were standing. Kami recognized Hugh Prescott, Holly's father, who was laughing at something Rob was saying.

They all stopped laughing when they noticed Ruth Sherman at the door, holding Jon Glass's arm.

"He came to the house and asked to be let in," said Ruth. "He asked to serve you."

Rob leaned forward in the same instant Kami hurried forward, through the door, hardly caring if she shoved into a sorcerer or if they all saw through her cloak of shadows.

Nobody did. They were all focused on her father, who was standing in a puffy black jacket, his black hair ruffled by the wind outside, and giving Rob Lynburn a little crooked smile.

"Did you?" Rob asked.

Jon nodded.

"How interesting," Rob said. "Tell me more."

Rob did not even bother to climb to his feet. He was a big guy, bigger than either of his sons and a lot bigger than Kami's dad. His shoulders strained against the material of his checked shirt, his smile was genial, and he looked like a perfect down-to-earth example of English manhood. All except for the cold gleam of contempt in his blue eyes.

"I'm not an idiot. There's no point fighting you," Jon said. "I want my wife back, and my kids to live happy and safe. You seem a reasonable man. Your family looked after mine once, didn't they? I'm willing to offer my services as a source. I'm willing to do whatever you want."

Kami didn't know what her father thought he was doing. Lillian had already examined him: it might run in the Glass bloodline, but he wasn't a potential source for any sorcerer. Kami and her brothers were.

Of course, Lillian and Rob were not exactly on speaking terms right now, and maybe Ruth Sherman did not know how to read the signs that identified a source.

"Come here," said Rob, which meant Kami was right but also that Jon's bluff was being instantly called.

Dad did not look dismayed. He kept smiling—like a small black terrier stepping up to face a golden retriever, recklessly confident that he could handle the situation— and walked over to the very edge of the sofa. Rob leaned back farther into the sofa cushions, hair gilded in the light of the stained-glass windows, looking up at Jon. For a long moment, blue eyes focused on black, and held.

At last, Rob said softly, "You're no source. Did you think you could trick me? What were you hoping to do?"

Jon Glass's smile spread into a grin.

"I was hoping to get close enough to do this," he said, and Kami's father—the graphic designer with funny T-shirts, the man who always laughed at farmers and their guns and made jokes about getting one that nobody took seriously— produced a gun from under his puffy jacket. He took aim in one smooth expert motion, moving quicker than anyone in the room, and shot Rob Lynburn.

He jerked the gun down at the last moment and hit Rob

in the leg. Kami's breath exploded from her lungs in shock, as if she had been punched.

Her gentle father, who carried his kids up to bed, who made dumb jokes and played computer games and who she was sure had never aimed a gun at a person before. Dad might have hesitated at the last second and missed killing Rob, but now Rob had fallen from the sofa on his hands and knees, making a guttural noise of rage and pain as he scrabbled to rise from the stone floor where blood was pooling. His leg was a mess.

Jon stood over him, sucked in a deep breath, and aimed the gun again. This time at Rob's head.

Hugh Prescott rushed forward, both hands outstretched. Kami abandoned shadows and all hope of hiding and threw herself bodily at him, knocking him and his spell off course.

All the stained-glass windows blew outward, glass shards vanishing into the sunlight.

Ruth Sherman raised her hand, and Jon's gun spun out of his grip.

"Grab them," Rob said thickly. "Girl, you break the bond between yourself and my son right now, or I will kill your father before your eyes."

"I can't!" Kami shouted, and thought fast as Ruth aimed her hand at her dad. "I can't, I truly can't," she said, her words stumbling over each other. "You outwitted Lillian . . . you tricked us all, when you did the blood spell to mess with Jared's magic. Ash and Jared did the ceremony to share power, and now none of us have any magic! Not me, not Ash, not Jared. I can't cut the link between me and Ash. I don't have any magic to do it."

She stayed kneeling on the floor and hardly daring to even hope that Rob would be deceived. It was just possible that Kami had followed her father without magic, and Lillian hadn't expected Kami to keep her magic when Ash lost his. Nobody had expected Kami to be able to walk through the sorcerous fire. None of them knew anything, really, about sources. The Lynburns had not had a source for five hundred years.

She knew Rob would always underestimate her, and thought Rob's vanity would make him want to believe.

"Sir," said Alison Prescott humbly—Holly's mother. "You're bleeding, we have to help you—you could bleed to death, and I don't even know if magic can do anything for the bone—"

"Shut up!" bellowed Rob, with rage and pain and what Kami thought might even be fear, beneath it all, that someone whom Rob considered so beneath him could walk into his home and very nearly blot him out. He tried to rise again, on his shattered leg, and cried out. "Take them away," he said eventually, through his teeth. "Keep them safe. I'm going to break the bond between that girl and my son, and then I'm going to punish them."

Ruth and Alison raised their hands in unison: Jon jerked around, as if the very currents of air around him had turned into puppet strings.

Hugh Prescott clambered up, one hand clamped hard around Kami's arm. As he dragged her out of the room, he made sure to bang Kami's hip hard enough on the doorframe so that the pain resounded down to the bone. It was such a spiteful, bullying little gesture that Kami refused to give him the satisfaction of showing she was hurt. She bared her teeth at him instead.

"Careful, Hugh," Alison said, to Kami's surprise. "She's Holly's friend."

"And where do you think our girl got the idea to mess with the Lynburns, you stupid woman?" Hugh demanded. "Not out of her own fluffy little head."

"Why not? Holly's smart," Kami said, and got banged against the wall of the stairwell for her trouble.

"Like father, like daughter, I suppose," said Ruth as they pulled them both down the stairwell and into an underground stone hall. Hugh pushed at one of the walls to reveal—oh God, Kami thought, were the Lynburns competing for some sort of title in creepiness?—what seemed to be a family crypt.

"Thank you," said Kami.

She looked at her father. He didn't seem to have heard Ruth. He had been looking at her, in love and horror, and at no one else, since she had revealed herself.

They threw Dad down on the stone floor, and Kami wrenched out of Hugh's arms so she could go to him.

"By that I mean you're both stupid," Ruth told them. She closed the door with the heavy scraping sound of stone on stone. Her red hair, the last light Kami could see, was lost. "And doomed."

It was dark in the crypt. Kami did not mind, honestly, since what she had seen of it—engraved stone tablets and the faces of the dead rendered in stone—had not made her want to see more. She was not a fan of crypt décor.

Dad had his arm around her, tight and warm.

"Don't worry, Dad," Kami whispered. "They don't know I still have magic. We just need to wait a little, until they're not suspicious, and then I can break us both out."

She spoke to Ash in her head, saying the same thing, at the same time as she spoke to her father. Ash was frantic to do something, to tell someone.

No, said Kami. *It will only worry Jared and Angela and the others. I can get myself out of this. Nobody needs to know. Nobody needs to do anything stupid. Are you with the boys?*

Yeah, Ash said. *Ten took one look at me and shut himself up in his room, but he's okay. I'm playing Scrabble with Tomo, but, Kami, I have to do something besides playing Scrabble.*

You'd better watch out, Kami warned. *Tomo cheats.*

"Ash is with Ten and Tomo," Kami told her father. "They'll be okay."

Dad's arm tightened even closer around her. "I thought you'd all be okay," he said, in her ear. "If I'd just managed not to mess up, you would all be safe now."

"You didn't mess up," Kami said, curling up small, but not letting her voice be anything but fierce. "Not being ready to kill someone isn't screwing up."

"Isn't it?" Dad asked softly. He rocked her a little, almost absently.

"I don't even know where you got a gun," Kami whispered.

"I took it out of your room," Dad said.

"Oh," said Kami. "I took it from Henry Thornton once. I never shot it. I didn't know what I was doing with it."

"I barely knew what I was doing," Dad whispered back to

her. "I just wanted to make things right for you. When you have a kid, you think, Oh my God, I'm not grown up enough for this. I'm going to mess this up."

"Because you and Mum were really young when you had me," Kami said, hesitating.

"No," said Jon. "I don't think anyone ever feels grown up enough. But who is there left, to be a grown-up?"

He was silent for a minute in the dark with the Lynburn dead, and Kami thought of who there had been, once: Kami's grandmother and her dad's mother, the woman who had died last summer and whom Kami had always wanted to be like.

A few years ago, Kami had tried to learn all about Japan and would come rushing to tell her all about *The Tale of Genji* or *kintsugi,* the art of repairing pottery.

"I suppose you know this already, Obaachan," she'd said to her, crestfallen.

"No, why would I?" asked her grandmother calmly. "Do you know everything about England?"

"Did you know that pottery can be repaired with gold?" Kami asked. "Then it's meant to be stronger than before, and more beautiful. Which is awesome, though it seems expensive."

Her grandmother had nodded. "Makes sense to me," she said. "Why be broken when you can be gold?"

Kami clung to her father. She could not answer him. There was nobody left to fix anything.

"I'm sorry," Dad whispered. "I always wanted to be able to solve all your problems and keep you safe forever. I couldn't do it."

"I wouldn't want you to, even if you could," Kami whispered back.

"Oh well," Dad said. "I also always knew that I would let you down, but I hoped that if I loved you enough and you were amazing enough, you would forgive me. And I loved you more than I knew I could, and you, well, you turned out all right, considering."

Kami laughed and punched him in the chest. "You know I'm the greatest achievement of your life."

"Nope," said Jon. "That would be this wicked cool home page I made for this sports star once. Later I saw it painted on a van."

Kami laughed again and her father put his other arm around her, hugged her in close.

"I didn't achieve you. You are the greatest achievement of your own life. And you are great beyond my imagination."

Kami laid her cheek against her father's chest, held on to the material of his T-shirt, and stayed there a long while. Dad didn't talk like this. He was always the cool dad, always easygoing and joking and hardly ever making rules because he never wanted to be angry with his kids for breaking them.

She knew why he was saying these things now. He understood as well as she did how furious Rob would be at this humiliation, at almost being bested by someone who had no magic at all. Rob had a reason to keep Kami alive: because if Kami died linked to Ash, Ash died too. But Rob was going to be intent on crushing her father now, and Kami did not know how to stop him.

She tried not to think about it. She held on to her father, measuring her breathing to the rhythm of his. She was able to sleep for a while, even in the heart of Aurimere, in the stone crypt, because she was in his arms.

The sound of that heavy stone door slowly moving inward made Kami let go of Dad and jump to her feet, putting herself and her magic in front of him. There was only a faint pale slice of light, but Kami stood facing it, watching the slice widen and the light pour over the gray stone of the room. Kami blinked, and then she could make out the face of the person standing outlined in the doorway.

It was her mother.

"Mum?" Kami gasped.

Her mother looked utterly out of place in the Lynburn crypt in her flannel shirt and worn jeans, her golden-brown hair piled up on top of her head. Her beautiful face looked a little distracted, a line of worry etched into her smooth brow.

"Come on quickly, you two," she said. "I've just poisoned all the sorcerers."

"What?" Kami exclaimed. "I mean—what? Are they all dead?

Claire blinked. "Well, no," she said. "No, I just gave them all food poisoning."

Apparently neither of Kami's parents was any good at assassination. Kami took a step toward her mother, and somehow she could not stop, it became a run at her mother and into her mother's soft arms. It seemed like a miracle to have this back, the everyday feeling of her mother holding her, her mother's voice in her ear and her mother's love certain. Kami felt foolish for ever doubting it, felt like a child who had believed a star was gone because it had disappeared behind a cloud.

"I heard they had you, and I had to do something," Mum said, into her neck. "It didn't matter that I was scared: all that mattered was what I had to do. Is this how you feel all the time?"

"Is Rob Lynburn actually getting sick in a toilet right this minute?" Kami asked delightedly.

Mum said, "I'll take that as a yes."

Kami wondered what she should do, how quickly sorcerers could heal themselves from food poisoning, and how angry food poisoning might make them. She wasn't sure how to take advantage of the situation.

She was holding on to her mother, and now that the shock had passed for both of them she registered the fine trembling running through her mother's body. No matter what great act her mother had done, she had not done it lightly; a lifetime of fear could not be washed away in an instant.

"Let's go," Claire said in her ear, and smoothed Kami's hair back. Kami suspected the gesture was just as soothing to her mother as it was to Kami. "Quickly."

Kami held on tighter to her mother for a second. "Whatever you want."

Her mother let her go, brisk and efficient now that she felt certain of her course, and led the way out of the crypt.

Dad made sure Kami went through, and as they went up the steps Kami got out in front. Just in case there were any sorcerers to be dealt with, any magic to be done.

Kami looked back and saw her father looking up at her mother. Dad was always shorter than Mum, but especially now that he was standing on a lower step. His smile at her was the best thing Kami had seen all day.

"Claire," he said, just her name, only that. He said it the same way he always said it, simply, with love.

"Jon," she answered, and smiled back.

Kami took the next steps two at a time, smiling to herself. They all walked together through the hall of Aurimere, its red and white windows blazing sunrise colors by the light of a setting sun.

The fire that circled the house had gone out. The sorcerers must be feeling pretty bad. Kami was already thinking of the mocking editorial she planned to write in her newspaper, which was now produced out of Angela and Rusty's absent parents' home office.

There might not be many people at school anymore, but Kami had found that leaving piles of *The Nosy Parker* around in the grocery shop meant that they would all be gone within the day. She had to hope people were reading them and not throwing them away.

Kami walked between her mother and father, holding their hands as they went down the hill.

Kami knew that the sorcerers would not be out of commission for long. She calculated that they would have to work out where to hide from the sorcerers' revenge tomorrow, but for now they left Aurimere behind them and went home together.

Chapter Ten

I May Burn

"Jared! Jared, wake up!" There were hands on him, shaking him, rough and impatient, and Jared lunged out of the winding embrace of blankets and bedsheets, lashing out.

He almost succeeded in hitting his aunt Lillian in the face. She caught his wrist a hair's breadth from cracking across her cheekbone.

Jared scrambled away from her, his back hitting the headboard with a thump.

"I'm sorry," he gasped, the remnants of his nightmare clinging to him like tattered clothes around old bones. "I'm sorry, I'm so—"

Aunt Lillian kept hold of his wrist. "There's nothing to be sorry for," she said in her crisp voice.

Jared tried to pull his hand away. She did not let it go, and her mouth thinned and her eyes narrowed as if she was extremely unimpressed that he had made the attempt.

"I didn't mean to—" Jared began, but she cut him off.

"You didn't hit me," said Aunt Lillian. "You were having a nightmare. I was the one who put myself in the way of your flailing arms. I knew what I was getting into. I have dealt with children having nightmares before."

"Oh my God, Aunt Lillian," said Jared, and she let him have his hand back so he could scrub it exasperatedly over his face. "You probably *give* children nightmares," he added accusingly.

Aunt Lillian shrugged, as if conceding that she might have given a few children a nightmare or two in her time.

She was wearing one of Martha Wright's voluminous white flannel nightgowns, hanging on her like a slightly fuzzy tent. Her long blond hair fell down her back like a waterfall, too baby-fine to tangle, and she should have looked like his mother. But her face was too composed for that, her mouth always firm and never vulnerable, her back held straight as if she was balancing an invisible book on her head, and her eyes met Jared's eyes steady as a soldier's hand holding a weapon. His mother was dead. Aunt Lillian had never been much like her.

"What were you dreaming?"

"About your husband burying me alive," Jared said grouchily.

He felt sick a moment later, thinking of who he had been buried with, the boy Aunt Lillian had loved.

"I'm sorry," he said again, too quickly.

"Don't be sorry," Aunt Lillian said. "I don't like it when you hang your head like a whipped animal. You didn't hit me, and you never will hit me. You would never have hit her, either."

Jared flinched. "Her?"

"Rosalind," Aunt Lillian said, and Jared flinched again, couldn't stop himself even though he could hear his aunt's voice in his ears—*like a whipped animal*—and see her disapproving face. "Other people hurt her," Aunt Lillian said. "And other people hurt you. And you were both angry, and maybe you were both scared, but no matter what dark thoughts you have you didn't hurt her. Someone else hurt her. Don't waste time blaming yourself when you can spend time planning how to destroy our enemies."

"Can we get that last thing embroidered on a cushion, Aunt Lillian?" Jared asked.

Aunt Lillian flicked up an eyebrow. "You can make as many bad jokes as you want, Jared. I really do not care. But stop being so ridiculous about yourself."

She reached out and touched his face, the line of her cool hand against his scar. He had his back to the headboard already; he wasn't sure how to get away from her without making it obvious.

"I think you believe that you might destroy anything you touch," Aunt Lillian said. "Give yourself more credit. You're a Lynburn. I believe that you will only destroy that which you mean to destroy."

Rob was a Lynburn too. His mother had been a Lynburn, and she had known what rage and hate he was capable of.

"I get—really angry," said Jared, and swallowed.

"So do I," said Lillian. "I would kill anyone who hurt what is mine to protect. I would kill anyone who hurt you. You don't have to be like Rob, or like the man you thought was your father. You can be like me."

Jared paused. "Okay, Aunt Lillian," he said in a low voice. He swallowed and let his cheek rest for an instant against her palm, then looked up at her. "Except that you're terrible."

Aunt Lillian put her arm around his neck and used her

hold on him to pull herself across the bed, then sat on the pillow beside him.

"So you will be terrible. But that does not mean you have to be unloved, or unforgiven."

Aunt Lillian had killed her own sorcerers without meaning to. Aunt Lillian was as much of a destructive force as Rob. Jared didn't want to tell her that, though, and not only because he did not want to hurt her. His mother had made him believe that being a Lynburn, he was born to destroy and never to be loved. Aunt Lillian was telling him that he could be loved, even if he was the hurricane his mother had said he was born to be. He wanted to hear that more than he wanted to hear anything else. That probably meant he was terrible.

She leaned her fair head against Jared's shoulder. Jared had no idea what he was supposed to do about that. When he put his arm around her, her shoulders felt terribly thin, but she leaned against him, so perhaps he had not got it too wrong.

"I love you," said Aunt Lillian. "And I'm sorry you were buried alive. I hope you get over it quickly."

She patted his arm. The door opened, the very creak of the hinges apologetic.

"I'm sorry if I'm disturbing you. I could . . . ," Ash said tentatively. "I could feel that you were upset."

"You kids and your psychic bonds," Aunt Lillian scoffed. "I had to hear him shrieking in his sleep."

Jared would have objected to her phrasing but was aware that would earn him the patented Aunt Lillian stare, combining indifference and arrogance in the way mostly only cats could. Instead he looked at Ash, shyly edging his way into the room, the lamplight hitting his bowed golden head. He was holding on to his arm; Jared felt guilty that he'd hurt him, even though he'd seen Lillian healing him.

Jared felt other stuff too, feelings that were not his own: Ash's swirl of confused emotion, and beyond that—beyond that a glimmer, perhaps, of someone else. Maybe it was only that he wanted to feel it so much.

It was not anything like that other link. He couldn't talk to Ash in his head, and he was honestly deeply uncomfortable with getting Ash's feelings all over his: it seemed as undesirable as ketchup getting mixed up with his eggs.

But he could feel how Ash felt about him. He had assumed, though he knew Ash was trying to make things between them go more smoothly, that some of the distrust and fear and anger he could sense swirling darkly in Ash like blood in water would be directed at him. But it wasn't.

How Ash felt about him was surprisingly nice.

Jared did not know if he and Ash were really brothers. Rob and Lillian both thought Rob was Jared's father. Jared's mother had not been quite sure. There was no way to tell, now.

Jared supposed they could be brothers, if they both wanted to be.

"Are you all right?" Ash asked now, sidling closer to the bed. He had been meandering around it until he was on the other side. Now he sat down tentatively.

"Yeah, I'm okay," said Jared, and jerked his head in what Ash could take as an invitation if he wanted.

Ash clambered onto the bed, which was not quite big enough for two and definitely too small for three. He sank his head down on the pillows instead of sitting against the headboard, and Aunt Lillian laid her hand on his blue-pajama-clad shoulder.

"You're both perfectly all right," she informed them. "And we will get Aurimere back, and our magic back, and our town back, and then we will have everything we need."

"We have some important stuff already," Ash offered tentatively.

Lillian frowned. "What do you mean?"

Jared surrendered himself to the strangeness of this situation, sank back onto the pillows himself with his head near Lillian's hip, and sighed heavily to attract his aunt's attention. "He wants to know you love him more than that stupid house."

"It is a very nice house," Aunt Lillian said, sounding offended. "Your ancestors are buried in the crypt of that house."

"Sure. Okay. We'll get our lovely creepy house back. When they bury me in that crypt, I want 'Jared, very inbred, deeply uncomfortable about it' on my tombstone."

Lillian transferred her frown to Jared, but on the other side of her he heard Ash's soft laugh, and felt the wash of feeling: comfort, relief, affection. He could recognize them all, but they were different from his own feeling of the same thing, like seeing different shades of the same color or a different garment made out of the same material.

Ash felt things in a better way than he did, he thought, but it was hard to resent him for that. Jared knew what was bound to happen between Kami and Ash. He wanted the best for her and—feeling what Ash felt for him—Jared could not find it even in his ugly heart to wish Ash ill.

Jared didn't want to hurt Ash. In fact, he felt the urge to protect him more than he felt anything else.

He tried to project that feeling of protectiveness over to Ash, tried to soothe him enough so that Ash could sleep.

Jared levered himself up on one elbow and looked beyond Lillian, who was stroking Ash's hair with a faintly perplexed air, as if she was not quite sure how she had come to be in this position. Ash had his face tucked against the pillow, hair a golden curve over his brow and eyes almost completely shut.

Jared could not help but wonder: Did I do that?

"Sometimes I worry you two do not have enough respect for your heritage," Lillian said. "Your father may have betrayed us, but Aurimere is ours by right. Power has been wielded and passed down from Lynburn to Lynburn for hundreds of years. You should honor that legacy."

Jared thought it was amazing she could say this kind of thing with a straight face. He was tired, so tired he felt almost dizzy. Aunt Lillian was unbelievable, and so was Ash, and so was the big stupid house and their big stupid legacy, and yet somehow he'd surrendered to it. He had found somewhere he did not fit but could belong anyway, and thought perhaps that meant family.

"Aunt Lillian," said Jared. "I'll tell you what I honor. I love you even though you are terrible, and even though I am too. Ash, I love you even though that puzzles me even more than loving Aunt Lillian, and I will probably never have anything in common with you. I'm not learning how to use the right forks or whatever, you both still annoy me, and I will always be there for you when you need me and I will never betray you. Now let me sleep."

Jared put his head decidedly down on the pillow and shut his eyes. One of them would have to hit him with something to make him move or talk any more about his emotions.

He felt instead Ash's happiness and Aunt Lillian's hand, lighter than a breath of wind, touching his hair. She had touched his hair like that once before, he thought. And she might again, and again, until demonstrations of affection became something he did not notice so painfully much. It was strange and wonderful to think that one day he might even take it for granted.

He had the chance to doze for a few minutes before Ash bolted upright in bed, and Ash's fear ran through him cold and sharp as a sword.

"Kami," said Ash.

"Again?" asked Aunt Lillian, but neither Jared nor Ash paid her any attention.

"What's happened?" Jared said, and tried not to sound angry that Ash knew something about her Jared did not. She was in danger and that he could only know, only help her, through Ash.

"I don't understand," Ash said, stumbling over his words, so they came even more slowly and Jared was even more maddened. "I thought she was safe now—"

"Safe now?" Jared repeated. "She was in trouble before?"

Ash stared at him, speechless with dismay.

"She was in trouble, and you knew, and you didn't tell me."

Fear and regret were dulling the edge of Ash's panic, and that made Jared remember there was something to panic about. His stupid jealousy, the way he felt as if he had a right to her mind and her heart when he did not, when he had no right at all—that couldn't matter. If he let himself demand any answer from Ash but one, then his selfishness was greater than any feeling he had for her.

Jared took a deep breath. "Ash," he said, "what's happening to Kami right now?"

It was late, and Holly felt like a complete creeper.

She'd been on the other end of this with boys, of course, where they delayed making their move and thus made her stay out later and later. Said boys never seemed to understand that hooking up—which seemed like a fun idea at eleven at night—seemed like the least appealing thing in the world at four in the morning.

She had a little more sympathy with those boys now.

Holly and Angela had been studying alone together all evening. Even though Kami hadn't reported back on whether Angela might like-like her, it seemed the ideal time to make a move.

She'd always thought of herself as awesome at making moves, in the way girls made moves, smiling significantly and sitting close and leaning in. Actually trying to initiate a hookup was much more difficult than she had suspected. Especially if there were feelings involved, which tangled her tongue and made her shy, when at least with all other hookups she had been fairly confident about what was going on and able to at least make basic conversation.

"So nice it is for Henry to stay," she said, a sentence that came out way more garbled than it had sounded in her head.

The more important it was to get something right, Holly suspected, the more sure she, Holly Prescott, was to mess that thing up.

Angela had agreed to stay in the Water Rising and study Aurimere books with Holly, but Holly was sure that Angie had not thought this process would last long into the night. Angie rested her elbows on the table and regarded the world with a pissed-off stare, as if she hated the night, tables, and air generally.

"What?" she asked flatly.

"Uh," said Holly. "It's really nice of you—and Rusty, of course; I like Rusty, who doesn't like Rusty, he's so likable—to let Henry stay with you. And to let me stay with you. I really appreciate it. And so does Henry. I'm sure."

"Okay," Angela said.

"I mean, it's not just staying with you, of course. This is a tough time, and—and I bet Henry is grateful for the support. And of course Henry really enjoys your company."

Angela made a slight face. Holly couldn't interpret it, other than knowing it meant things were not going well. It was possible that Angie hated appreciation, Henry, the very sound of Holly's voice, or all of the above.

"Okay," Angela repeated.

She got back to turning the pages of her book. Holly felt more and more like a creeper, the kind of guy who didn't say suggestive stuff but did insist on having a conversation, who hassled beautiful girls who obviously wanted to be left alone.

She only knew one way to do things. She didn't know how girls were supposed to go after other girls.

And yet Angie had fancied Holly once before, and Holly hadn't even meant to do that. Maybe the problem was that Holly was being too subtle.

"You look tired," was Holly's next venture.

She knew that was not the smoothest possible thing to say, but she had a plan.

"Almost constantly," Angela replied, staring at her book and resting her fingers against her temples. "I am tired of asshole sorcerers, I am tired of having my life threatened, and I am tired in the sense that I want a nap. Yes. And your point would be?"

The temptation to say "Never mind," and also hide behind the sofa because Angie was terrifying, was almost irresistible.

But Holly wanted to be brave, and she wanted to have this. Guys were often really persistent, and it worked: she didn't want Angela to think Holly wasn't trying hard enough because she didn't like her enough.

Holly braced herself and jumped to her feet.

"Oh, I was just thinking," she said with forced and perhaps slightly manic brightness. "You must be super tense! How about a massage?"

Before she finished speaking, she had her hands on Angela's shoulders, so much narrower than a boy's shoulders and almost fragile-feeling, even though she knew Angie was strong. She felt for an instant a sense of accomplishment.

Angela's shoulders moved under her hands in a shudder of indignant recoil, like a scandalized maiden snake whose Victorian sensibilities had been deeply offended.

The movement was enough: Holly had her hands off

Angela and up in surrender, but Angela spun around in her chair and wheeled on her anyway.

"What," said Angela, and the ice in her voice chilled Holly, "do you think you are *doing*?"

"Sorry," Holly muttered. "I'm really sorry. I didn't mean to upset you."

"It was right out of order, Holly," Angela said.

She was not even standing up, but she was a tower of outrage. Angie might go around traumatizing people, but she always knew exactly what she was doing.

Holly didn't know how to behave, had never quite known how to be friends, let alone anything more. She was the fluffy idiot her parents had always believed, the girl the other girls didn't want to be around, not someone who knew the magic trick of being taken seriously. She was so, so stupid.

Holly knew she was blushing and was afraid she was going to cry, which would be even more humiliating.

"I was just trying to—" she got out.

"What?" Angela demanded. "What were you trying to do?"

"Never mind," said Holly. She turned her face away and looked at the door, just before it burst open to reveal Ash Lynburn, in a T-shirt and shoes but also blue pajama bottoms.

"Come quickly," he said. "It's Kami."

That was when it occurred to Holly, horribly and for the first time, that now that Ash and Jared had no magic she was one of only three sorcerers left on their side.

"I can help," she told Ash. "I can do magic."

Holly pushed past him. She did not want to see the hope lighting his face. She had to act, since there was nobody else to do it, but she was so scared. If she messed up, people she loved could die. And the one thing Holly was sure of about herself was that she would mess up.

Kami had gone to sleep warm and happy, Tomo sharing her pillow because she wanted to be sure he wouldn't disturb their parents. She woke up with a combination of shouting in her head and the sound of glass breaking.

She sat up, bewildered and sick, still warm but coughing now. Her nose stung with smoke. Her vision swam and coalesced into the sight of Ash crouched on her bedroom floor, glass shards around his feet and glinting in his hair.

Kami opened her mouth to ask what was going on, and burst into another fit of painful coughing.

What's going on? she asked, her hands moving almost of their own volition until they found Tomo's silky hair and narrow back. Her palm flattened against the worn, much-washed material of his favorite pajamas, the one with the pattern of trains on them. Someone had broken through her bedroom window, and her little brother hadn't even stirred.

Ash did not answer her, in her head or out loud. He staggered forward, through the broken glass and the general debris of Kami's room, made for her bedroom door and flung it open, saying, "Ja—"

A roar answered him. An inferno waited beyond. What had been Kami's familiar old corridor, the floorboard that squeaked, the wall that bore a painting of Kami's that her mother had framed and hung up against her father's wishes— because, he said, he loved her but it was truly terrible—the corridor where Tomo had kicked off his shoes today and which she had called good nights and good mornings down all her life, had become the dark hole for a glowing, growling monster. All Kami could see were shadows and consuming flames—the fire seemed to leap at Ash, and he slammed the door again.

Kami was coughing with her eyes smarting because of the smoke. She shook Tomo frantically, ignoring his groggy protests, and looked at the door. She could see the fire now, see the burning orange light around the edges of the frame, smell the smoke as it hit the door.

She had been so stupid to count on the sorcerers not recovering quickly, to believe that they would not strike back right away.

This was what came of standing against Rob: this was the retribution of the Aurimere sorcerers.

Her house was on fire, with her family inside it.

PART III
THE STORY OF THE FIRST SOURCE

This shaking keeps me steady. I should know.
What falls away is always. And is near.
I wake to sleep, and take my waking slow.
I learn by going where I have to go
—*Theodore Roethke*

Chapter Eleven
Those in Glass Houses

"Okay, Tomo, don't panic, don't panic, you're fine," said Kami, patting him frantically.

Tomo peered at her, eyes still sleepy. "You seem like you're panicking," he said in a small, smoke-cracked voice.

"Well, that's all you know, because I'm not!" Kami exclaimed.

She climbed out of bed, and tried to pull Tomo with her, but he resisted, fighting her, his whole small body locked in a panicked spasm: he clearly did not want to get any closer to the surge and hiss of the fire.

Ash walked over to where Kami stood, then sat on the bed.

"Come here," he said, his voice still clear, and always charming. He held out a hand to Tomo, eyes on him. He had a compelling gaze, Ash, blue and sweet and shamelessly utilized. "I'll keep you safe," he promised.

Tomo obviously found his argument persuasive.

"Okay," he said, tumbling promptly into Ash's arms.

Kami was the one who would have to save him. She had magic, and Ash did not. Ash was as vulnerable as Tomo. She would have to save them both.

She ran over to the closed door. The floorboards already felt hot under her bare feet, almost scorching her, on the point of kindling.

Throwing open the door again, she threw her magic at the fire, willing it down with all her might. It only surged at her again with a sound that was almost furious, erupting into her room and making her jump back.

She could not only see and hear and taste the fire raging into her room, choking their air away: she could feel what had created the fire, the spell that was pushing her magic back. This fire was Rob's devouring fury, his rage and pain channeled into nature and intent on destruction.

Ash stood up, still holding Tomo, who was clinging around his neck. He was looking to Kami anxiously.

"Ash, how did you get in here?" she demanded.

"My mom floated me up," Ash said. "You can make the air light around someone, but—I don't know how to do it, and Mom went to get your father."

"I can't put out the fire," Kami shouted, above the crackle and thunder of fire bringing down her home. "I can't even hold it back, there's so much magic behind it. We have to find some other way out."

She stopped and shoved her feet into black backless mules with silver and black sequins, shoes she'd planned to wear when summer finally came, before she ran over the shards of glass to her broken window.

It was not so very far down, but it was far enough. Ash joined her at the window, moving toward the cool air and away from the fire.

"You could try to float me down!" he yelled.

"I'd take that risk with you," she said, "but not with my baby brother."

Oh well, Ash said. *Thanks very much.*

She felt a hint of amusement from him, as well as panic, and it was reassuring in the same way that having Tomo laugh had been. It calmed her too.

Her room was a burning trap. Kami looked out of her bedroom window at her familiar view. Her little garden and the wild woods beyond, the woods that made magic stronger. She tried to block out the hiss of the fire and listen for the whisper of the woods.

She gripped the windowsill tight, grains of glass prickling into her palms as if she had grasped thorns, and saw the silver-tipped tops of the trees in the woods all sway and incline toward her like a crowd of courtiers at the sight of a queen.

In the moonlit square of grass that was her garden, the laburnum tree that stood against the fence stirred, shook leaves suddenly bursting with vivid yellow splashes of color, and woke to life.

Kami pushed magic into the tree with such determined force that she could almost feel her magic, as if it was blood coursing into new limbs. As if she was bearing the heavy weight of leaves, stretching her tall trunk, pulling her long roots out of the clinging earth.

"Mum says I'm not allowed to climb," Tomo remarked, watching the slow progress of the tree across the garden.

"That's okay, buddy, I'm old enough," said Ash.

"Anyway, you never listen to Mum," said Kami, who knew her brother and did not believe in coddling children like Ash was doing.

They could all feel the fire, hot at their backs. It was easier to breathe at the window, but the whole house felt like it was being split apart into splinters by a fiery giant. Kami refused to let the knot of panic in her throat rise. She stared out at the tree, and it came closer and closer, creeping across the ground leaving broken twigs and fallen leaves in its path, until its branches hit the windowsill outside.

"Ash," said Kami, "take Tomo and go."

Ash hesitated. *You'll come right after us, won't you?*

Kami hesitated in turn, and Ash read her anxious love as clearly as she had been able to read his fear.

He reached out with his free hand and touched her face.

We came for your whole family, he said. *I promise they'll all be safe. Come out right after us. There's nothing you can do, and I can't bear the idea of something happening to you.*

"Get my brother out of here," Kami said. "Now."

Ash gave her one desperate look, and then he was climbing out of the window, the knee of his pajamas tearing on the glass still scattered on the sill. He caught the top of the window frame in his free hand for balance, then leaned and grabbed one of the branches hanging up above where she could see, and swung himself and Tomo into the tree.

Kami let herself look back over her shoulder.

Her room was a ruin. Fire had swallowed her bed, the ruffled pillows and bedspread embroidered with flowers and bees replaced by a living blanket of flame. Her wicker bookcase was lying on the floor, burning. Her piles of books and her notebooks were ash. Her wardrobe door stood open, and where there had been rows of colorful dresses there was greedily licking flame. In the smoke-tarnished mirror, she saw herself, small and disheveled, wearing black pajamas with glittery red hearts, and almost lost.

She didn't know what to do. She didn't know how she could even make her way into that enveloping fire. She was scared and already hurting as sparks hit her bare arms, as the tears ran down her face but her cheeks were scorched dry. But she was the one who could do magic. Her family was helpless and she was responsible.

I promise, Ash thought at her, and she could feel the strain of his worry as well as the strain of physical exertion he was feeling, carrying Tomo's weight and his own. *I promise they're all safe.*

Kami looked down from her window to the laburnum tree leaning against it, and the top of Ash's head glinting in the moonlight. She looked just in time to see the branch Ash was holding break. There was only air to catch them, and then, because Kami wanted it, the air did.

Ash and Tomo were safely deposited a foot down, on the soft grass. Kami saw a shower of sparks hit the grass at the same time they did; she looked at the branches resting against the sill and saw how fire was turning the brown bark, the tender emerald of new leaves, and the yellow bloom of new flowers all black and dead.

Ash had said her family was safe. Her room and home were both gone, and this tree would not last long.

When Kami scrambled out onto the stone of the outer sill, she cut her hands on the broken glass. She reached out into the dark and grabbed at a branch that was not burning. Pulling herself out of her room, she felt another blast of fire hot against her back.

She swung from the furious heat and the shriek of flame and thunder of falling beams into the calm darkness of the tree. She gripped one branch and then another with her bleeding hands, cautiously at first, then as she smelled smoke and burning sap, climbing down faster and faster.

Kami felt a rain of sparks landing on her head, the tiny points of pain shooting through her scalp and the smell of her own burning hair. Her pajama pants got tangled in the branches and she wriggled to get them free, and was still wriggling when pain blazed at her back.

She lost her grip and plummeted into the grass, landing on the ground so hard she was jarred all over. Before she could recover, she felt Ash's hands on her, urgent and ungentle, rolling her back and forth on the grass until her nose was as full of the smell of wet grass as of smoke.

She sat up spluttering.

"I'm so sorry, you were on fire," Ash blurted.

"Obviously, I didn't think you were rolling me around on the grass for fun," said Kami. "Um. Or something that sounds less saucy than that, sorry."

She leaned her face in her hands, damp from the grass, and concentrated on healing herself, the burns on her back that she could feel but not see. She looked up after an instant, pain not spelled away but forgotten, to see Tomo hovering anxiously by Ash's side. He was holding Ash's hand.

"Don't worry, kiddo," Kami said. "I'm all right."

"You're bad at climbing trees," Tomo whispered.

"I'm bad at climbing trees when I'm on fire, yes," Kami said. "Not my sport."

Ash made a choked sound, and knelt on the grass where Kami sat. "You're all right."

His feelings seemed terribly close to her suddenly, close as the fire that had set her clothes alight. Kami felt almost scared by their warm intensity, and yet she could not help catching alight, just the same.

She reached out, touched his free hand, and met his eyes.

"Thanks to you," she said, and looked at him for an instant longer, an instant too long, when she saw her father over his shoulder.

Kami scrambled to her feet and dashed to her father. Jon was wearing his Star Wars T-shirt and sweatpants and fighting Lillian Lynburn's grip on his arm. Ten was standing by their father but warily away from Lillian, a sooty black mark covering his cheek and one of the lenses of his glasses, and Kami had to stop and touch his face and his frail squared shoulders, feel him safe and whole under her hands.

"Ten, you all right?"

Ten shook his head mutely.

"Dad—" Kami began, and looked around the dark garden. "Dad—where's Mum?"

"That's what I want to know!" Dad snapped. He tried to lunge forward again, but Lillian's thin pale fingers were tight and magic-strong around his bicep. "I was sleeping in the office and then this one broke in and dragged me outside and she wouldn't let me back in!"

"You were on the sofa in your office?" Kami asked. "Why?"

"Because sometimes adult relationships are complicated," Dad said. "And sometimes adults don't want to talk about that when their houses are burning down!"

Kami had never been unaware of their house burning, but seeing her father and her brother's face had pushed the knowledge to the back of her mind for a moment. Now she looked back at the collapsing shape of what had been a house, the thatched roof that was a seething mass of flame, and the orange shimmer against the black sky. The night was painted glowing colors by the destruction of her home.

"She's still in there," Kami whispered.

"Jared came for me," Ten offered unexpectedly. "Like he did before. He went back to get her."

They were both in there, and both of them were helpless.

The roof fell in then, with a groan and a crash and long streaks of orange light stretched across the night sky, like the marks left by a burning witch's fingers.

Kami let go of Ten. Jon lunged for the house. Lillian held him firm.

"Let me go!"

"I will not," said Lillian, with furious calm. "What good will it do for you to die too, for your children to be orphans? Do you think this is how I want things to be? Do you think I value the life of this wretched woman over the life of my boy?"

"Do you even know her name?" Jon demanded.

"Do I care?" Lillian demanded in return. "Possibly I would have learned it if she had not been so busy making profiteroles for the traitors in Aurimere!"

Kami heard their arguing, but did not pay attention. She was walking toward the burning house, concentrating on wrapping the deep dark of the night, the bite of the air, the dew of the grass, and her own determination around her as some sort of shield. She could not stop the fire, and she did not know if she could protect herself, but she was going to try.

The door of her house was standing open. It didn't even look like her house anymore, not her door with the little watering can hanging beside it. It was just a burning wreck that she had to walk into even though she was hurt and scared. It was an ugly trap with people she loved inside it.

She crossed the burning threshold, into her burning kitchen. There was a flaming beam in the chaos of shadows and heat and twisting fire, in her way as if someone had set it there as a barrier to forbid her entry.

Fire was a fiercely burning veil over her eyes and her face, settling in a hot weight over her hair. She reached out and took hold of the beam, thought of Lillian holding back her father when she shouldn't have been able to, and told herself that she was strong, that she would neither burn nor yield, that she was marble.

She could magic herself, but not the fire. The fire was still there, and still so terribly hot. Kami was keenly aware of that: she could feel the heat even though she was not burned. It was as if her magic was material covering her, and she knew that only the thinnest layer of magic in the world separated her from agony.

She threw the beam into a burning wall and stumbled through the curling smoke and the raging fire, almost putting her feet through the collapsing floor, not even sure of where to go, when she saw movement in the hallway at the bottom of the stairs.

Kami ran toward the sight of her mother and Jared, their arms around each other's hunched shoulders. The fire cast their faces in white, red, and shadow in quick succession—it was like seeing people she loved in hell.

Neither of them ran to her. Neither of them could run, that much was obvious. She got hold of her mother's hand, soft and clinging, the only thing in this house Kami could touch and feel safe, and began to usher them out.

They were almost in sight of the front door when part of the wall fell in. Kami put her arms around her mother and Jared both, spun them away from the shower of white-hot sparks. She put herself between them, thought only of protecting them, and felt as if the material of her magic was tearing and fraying all over. If it failed, they would burn together.

The brick wall was burning coals around their feet. Kami, Claire, and Jared dragged themselves over it, through the furnace of fire and finally, finally out the door.

The light of the burning Glass house shone through the black thornbushes like a star in a spiked cage. When the wind blew in the wrong direction, Holly could feel a blast of heat as if she had passed by the open door of a furnace.

She wanted to run to Kami and help her. But someone had to stand guard between the Glass house and Aurimere, had to stop the sorcerers from coming down to pick off any survivors. Holly peered into the darkness and saw a familiar face coming toward her.

"Hi, Holly."

Ross Phillips. He'd been Amber Green's boyfriend for years and years, for as long as Holly could remember. Holly had made out with him once, when they were both drunk, sitting outside in a field at one of those parties that were mostly boys and Holly, because nice girls didn't go to that sort of party. Holly had always thought it was sort of a self-fulfilling prophecy—the nice girls weren't asked, because the boys respected them. The boys chose who they respected and who they did not, and then condemned the girls for going along with their choices.

Ross had told her, that night, that he really loved his girlfriend, and even though Holly didn't love him and hadn't wanted him to love her, she'd known he was really telling her that she was unlovable—not someone to be taken seriously, one of the grubby Prescotts, desperate and scrambling and out of favor with the Lynburns in the manor.

"Stay back," Holly called. "I'm a sorcerer, just as much as you. I'll hurt you if you come any closer."

"I doubt that," said Ross, and took several steps closer without even hesitating.

She didn't even mean to do it. She felt indignation rise, wanting to make a scathing comment and not knowing quite how to: the feeling burned in her chest. Fire shot from Holly's fingertips and almost took Ross's eyebrows off. He stumbled backward in a hurry.

"You mean you doubt me," Holly said, breathing hard and trying not to show how shocked she was. "You really shouldn't."

"Come on, Holly," said Ross, gently scornful despite his singed eyebrows. "I think we both know—"

Ross collapsed. Holly stared at her own hands in disbelief for a moment, then glanced up and saw Angela with a large branch.

"That you're an asshole?" Angie asked Ross's prone body. "Yeah, we're pretty clear on the subject."

She's so mean, Nicola Prendergast had once whispered to Holly, and Holly had nodded because she wanted Nicola to like her. *Angela Montgomery doesn't have to be so rude all the time. It wouldn't cost her anything to be nice.*

Holly didn't know about that. She'd felt like being nice cost her something, even if it was just feeling a little bit lesser, every time she smiled without meaning to. Angie was smart and rude, no second thoughts tripping her tongue, able to make anyone be sorry they ever crossed her path and refusing to feel sorry about it. She could even deliver cutting repartee to an unconscious body. She was so mean, and it always made Holly smile.

Holly was a bit concerned about Ross's physical well-being, though. "Uh, I heard head trauma is actually kind of a serious thing to happen to someone. It's not like in the movies. It can cause permanent damage."

"I heard that about burning people's houses down as well," Angela spat, as if she was a fire herself, throwing out sparks.

Holly knew it was hard for Angie, not being able to go to Kami and help her. Lillian Lynburn had sailed in with her boys behind her, assuming she would lead, and someone had to guard the perimeter. But that didn't mean Holly wanted to kill anybody, or to let Angie kill anybody either.

She was silent, thinking of how to phrase this. She didn't

know what showed on her face, but Angie drawled, "Oh, all right," and knelt down to check Ross's pulse.

"He's alive," she said in a voice that sounded so bored Holly might've been imagining the thread of relief running through it. "That's the best I can do for him. His evil sorcerer buds can heal him or take him to the hospital and bring him an evil magic fruit basket for all I care."

Holly barely had time to feel relief herself, just the beginnings of it, like beginning to take a breath and then being hit again. She saw in the darkness something darker moving. She saw her parents were coming toward her.

Holly felt dumb. She should have known Rob Lynburn would send more people than Ross to do his work.

She had run between her father and Angie once before, at the great battle in the town square. Her father had backed away, lifted his hands as if in surrender, and then turned them on another of Lillian Lynburn's sorcerers, who died later that night. Holly didn't even remember who it had been. All she remembered was kneeling down beside Angie on cobblestones that were iced by night but warm with blood, and being so thankful that Angela was all right and that her father did not put his loyalty to Rob Lynburn above his daughter.

She was the baby of the family, the youngest girl; nobody had particularly wanted her when she was born, and she had no reason to think that since she was born she had impressed anybody enough to make them change their minds. About the only thing her parents had ever said positively about her was that she was pretty, and they had been clear that being pretty did not matter.

It was so strange and horrible that now, with the night wind rushing through her hair and her blood pounding in her ears, her parents were looking at her as if they loved her. Now when she was afraid that she was going to hurt them to stop them from hurting her or those she loved, now when love was nothing but a double-edged weapon that would hurt them all worse than they already were.

"We don't want to hurt you, baby," said Holly's mum, speaking as if she could read her mind.

"Holly, you never were that bright, but this is the outside of enough," her dad snapped. "Do you think you have a hope of standing against Rob Lynburn and Aurimere? It's not for us to decide what the best course of action is. We know the bargain. We have all known the bargain, generation after generation."

"So you're ready to burn down houses with children inside them because Rob Lynburn tells you what to do now, and you've decided never to think for yourselves again," Angela shouted back. "How dare you call her stupid because she doesn't want to be herded like a sheep?"

"She's not a sorcerer," Holly's mum whispered. "We can go through her, if Holly would just stand down—"

Angela lifted her branch, and Holly's dad lifted his hand.

Angela looked down at her branch. It was burning but not quite enough to burn her—not yet. She pursed her mouth and shrugged.

"Thanks," she said, and lunged at Holly's dad.

Flames would devour the branch in a moment, but in this moment it was a weapon. There was the sudden sharp smell of burning fabric as Hugh Prescott's shirt caught on fire. Holly's mother darted in toward Angie, but Holly got in front of her. She was standing in front of Angie, facing down both her parents, before Angie had to drop the branch.

"I won't stand down!" Holly shouted. "*You* stand down! You have to surrender, because *I won't*!"

She saw her father's face twist in anger, as it did when any of them stepped too far out of line, gave him too much lip. She saw his arm rise and braced herself, stupidly again, as if she was about to be felled with a physical blow.

A blast of wind knocked Holly off her feet, sent her spinning through the air. Holly landed hard on the ground and rolled, jolted and sick, helpless as a doll sent tumbling down a hill.

She gasped, blood but no air in her mouth, and watched his big, heavy boots move toward her across the earth, every footfall a thunderclap. She remembered being woken by the sound of those boots on their stone floor when it was still dark. She remembered raw, cold mornings, with her dad already in the fields, hearing her mother say that her father was out there working for them, only for them.

"Hugh, no, no!" her mother screamed, and threw herself between them, blocking Holly's view of those dirt-streaked boots. "Not my little girl!"

Angela hesitated. She had dropped the branch, but Holly knew she would have gone after him with her bare hands— except now they were all waiting, and listening. Even Holly's father seemed to be listening.

"Listen to me," her mother said rapidly. "If we take young Ross and say that we felt we had to get him to safety, that they were ready for us—well, that's true, isn't it? What if we just left, eh? We don't need to hurt Holly. Leave it to someone else. Come on now, do."

Holly lifted herself painfully, a long streak of pain aching across her ribs, her palms dug into the cold earth. She called through a mouthful of blood, "He killed Edmund!"

There was a pause that Holly thought might be a heedless silence, but then she heard her father say, gruff and grudging, "What?"

Holly did not lift herself up again. She spoke with her eyes turned to the ground, bitter earth between her lips. "Rob Lynburn killed Uncle Edmund. He didn't run away, he didn't want to leave Lillian, he didn't want to leave you. Rob shut up Jared with—with all that was left of him. You hated your brother for leaving you to suffer, but he didn't. He suffered. He died. Rob Lynburn killed him. He never left Sorry-in-the-Vale. He died when he was seventeen."

"It's a lie," her father said hoarsely.

Holly thought for a moment that she might have made a mistake: her father, when presented with what he did not want to hear or could not understand, became baffled and enraged at once. She didn't want to be hurt again, and she wouldn't let Angie be hurt. She began to lift herself up again.

She saw her mother physically turning her big husband, small hands firm on his shoulders.

"Hugh, Hugh, it doesn't matter. You never knew her to lie, did you? Holly's not a liar. She believes it if she said it. Maybe someone lied to her and—and maybe they didn't, but we can't get anything else from her. We agreed to go, didn't we? Let's go."

A lot of family fights had ended this way, with her mother

leading her father away, patting and coaxing and ending the whole scene. It was so normal, and that made it seem bizarre and awful on this burning magic night.

Holly watched their pale backs receding from her until Angie blocked the sight, her dark eyes wide with concern.

"Holly," she said, and knelt down, pulling Holly into her lap. "Are you okay? Are you hurt?"

Holly did not know if Angie's carefully gentle hands meant what she wanted them to mean, or if it was just what she had thought for so long was all that was between them, simply friendship, as if she and Angela had exchanged feelings as simply as swapping each other's jewelry.

If Holly had to feel all the pain and longing, she would take the comfort. She closed her eyes and whispered, "Can someone see about a magical fruit basket?" and heard Angie yelp with bright sudden laughter. She laughed too, even though it hurt.

Chapter Twelve
Stone Marks the Spot

The night air was so different from the air inside that stifling house that it felt like plunging into deep cool water. Kami gasped with relief even as she turned to her mother and sank her hands into her mother's burning hair, putting the fire out, turning the trails of sparks back into long smooth tresses. Kami stroked her mother's hair lightly, before she let Claire go. She thought she understood why parents stroked hair so much: it was a gesture that said, Here you are, lovely and alive and entire. *I* did that.

"Mum!" said Ten, and Claire turned to the sound of his voice. Kami's hand dropped from her hair, and her mother caught that hand in hers and pressed it, then let go to lean down and scoop Ten into her arms as he ran to her.

"Claire," said Dad, with the softness of deep relief.

"Jared, thank goodness you're all right," Lillian said pointedly. "And well done for saving What's-her-name, I suppose. I would have been devastated if anything happened to her."

Kami looked at Jared. She hadn't been able to look at him, not properly, when he was on the other side of her mother, when she'd had to think of protecting and saving them. All she'd known was that he was whole, and now he was safe. They were all safe.

She was smiling, which was probably wildly inappropriate, but he nodded at her. "You did it," he said.

"I didn't do it alone," said Kami. "Thanks for saving my mum."

The corner of Jared's mouth twisted up a little, in the small smile she felt he was always trying to sneak past people without noticing. "You're welcome."

The firelight cast his face half in light and half in shadow. There was a dark smudge along the side of his eye, across his temple: Kami had thought it was soot, but now she could see the raised skin and recognized a bruise.

She hastily lifted a hand to the spot. Jared flinched back, but she grabbed his wrist and held him still so she could heal him, and tried not to mind.

"What happened?"

"Well," said Jared. "Your mother threw her bedside lamp at me."

Kami looked over at her mother, who looked apologetic. She could picture the whole scene: her mother waking to fire and chaos, and finding a Lynburn's face framed against the nightmare. She was quite proud of her mother for fighting back.

"That's what happens when you insist on going around wearing a leather jacket and riding a motorcycle," she remarked. "When you start dating a girl, parents are going to have strong words. Deliver lectures. Set curfews. Hurl projectiles."

Jared shrugged. "About how I always expected it would go, yeah."

The bruise was fading under her fingers, like invisible ink disappearing into a page. Unexpectedly, Kami felt her knees go out from under her.

It was in no way a romantic feeling. It reminded her of having the flu, her body simply shutting down and forcing her to fall. Distantly, she heard Jared's hoarse shout of alarm and felt his arms go around her, holding her close to his chest and keeping her on her feet.

"What's wrong with her?" he demanded.

"She doesn't have as much magic as she used to, now her sorcerer's magic has been poisoned," Lillian's voice said dispassionately, from somewhere up in the air. "She pushed herself past her limits."

"What if Rob's sorcerers come?" Kami asked, trying to fight back dizziness with the urgency of that thought.

"There were only a couple of them left, hanging back maintaining the fire," Ash said. "Holly and Angela dealt with them."

"What amazing ladies," said Kami, her voice distant in her own ears. "I am so lucky to have them in my life. The guys in my life are okay too, I guess."

"Could be better," Jared contributed.

Kami nodded. "Tell Angela and Holly I'm going to need to borrow some clothes."

All her clothes. It was stupid to feel a pang thinking of them when her whole house had burned down, but she did. She had spent a long time building her wardrobe, begging her dad to let her use his credit card and buy things from the Internet, spending a lot of time in secondhand shops. She hadn't wanted to dress like anybody else. When she was wearing one of the outfits she'd chosen, she would find herself looking in the mirror, both recognizing and approving of what she saw.

"Come on," said Mum. "The kids need sleep. We can all go to the flat over Claire's."

She did not add "where I've been staying since your father kicked me out." Dad looked a little uneasy, Kami thought, but they had nowhere else to go. They should have gone before now: they had been fools to believe Rob's sorcerers would be out of commission, even for a night.

They all made their way out of the garden, down the crazy paving path and out the gate. Kami looked back over her shoulder as she went, and saw the black frame of the house, wrapped in devouring scarlet. The tree she had leaned against the window was also on fire, part of the house and thus part of its destruction. Around the house the grass stretched black as if their little house stood in the center of a black lake. Nothing was burning except their home.

Kami looked at it for a long moment, then looked away at the moonlit road ahead.

"Do you want my jacket?" Jared asked. He was taking it off as he spoke, a little awkwardly as he still had to hang onto her.

"Yes," said Kami instantly. He drew it close around her shoulders. "Also your pin and your class ring. That's how you do dating in America, isn't it? You see, I know the ways of your people."

"I don't really know how dating works," Jared told her.

"High school for me was mostly musical numbers. That's how it is in the States, you've seen the movies. Every time someone had an emotional dilemma or epiphany, they would burst into song, and we would all have to break out into perfectly choreographed dance sequences. It took a lot of intensive training. So many jazz squares, no time for love."

Kami laughed, and the laughter was alchemy, a sound that disappeared in the air and yet changed the whole world. He didn't change the world for her, but he offered her the opportunity to see the world differently and she chose to take it. It had to be both of them: they could choose to change the world together.

"That's a real shame."

"It's possible I can make up for lost time. I hear girls like bad boys. I hope that's true," Jared said. "Because, baby, I'm bad at practically everything."

Kami laughed enough that, still unsteady, she might have fallen if Jared had not been there to hold her up.

"I'd make a joke about falling for you," she said. "But that's cheesy and terrible, and I've decided I don't believe in falling. I believe in something else."

"What's that?" asked Jared.

"The opposite of falling," Kami said, after a long time. "I did not fall. I climbed, to a place high enough that I could see clearly. Once I saw, I was certain."

Jared did not seem to know what to say, but he walked along with her, his arm still warm around her shoulders. She told herself that it was enough.

Dad and Ten and Mum all converged on each other, Lillian seeming disgruntled to be part of the group but walking with them nonetheless.

Tomo did not join them. Kami saw that he had taken one of his violent fancies to Ash, the way he had taken to lemonade, Mr. Stearn's bulldog, and his favorite toy race car that had burned with everything else in their house. He walked happily alongside Ash, holding on to his hand, and clearly wished for nothing more.

Ash seemed alarmed to have been so firmly taken possession of by an eight-year-old. He and Tomo fell back a little, until they were walking with Jared and Kami.

"I am so sad about my underwear," Kami announced, and Ash looked as if he regretted all of his life decisions.

"Not in front of the little boy!" he said reproachfully. "Anyway, you were saying that you would borrow clothes from Holly and Angela."

"I'm the third tallest in my class," Tomo informed him, with the air of one out to impress. "And I know all about underwear."

"You heard the man," said Kami. "Besides which, no. I cannot possibly borrow underclothes from Holly and Angela. Bras especially."

"I know," said Jared.

"Oh, you do, do you?" Kami inquired. "And how do you know, may I ask?"

There was a slight flush along the lines of Jared's cheekbones. "Observation."

It was probably sad that this cheered Kami up, but Jared usually seemed so wary about her body, the physical fact of it, that the simple knowledge that he had been looking did please her. She leaned back infinitesimally closer into the warm line of his arm around her shoulders, the warm line of his body against her side.

"Kami, would you maybe stop mentioning your unmentionables," Ash said, spoiling the moment.

"I shall not," Kami told him. "It's a serious problem. I am, and I mean this absolutely literally, in need of support."

I'd suspect you of going funny in the head from smoke inhalation, said Ash, *but you always talk like this.*

Kami laughed, and felt Jared's arm go tense around her shoulders, but he said nothing. Ash must have felt something, from one of them—and it was so weird, that Ash was the link between them, that Ash was between them at all— because he fell silent too, and after a little while he let Tomo drag him forward and away.

When they approached the town square, Kami's mother fell back, coming toward them over the cobbles. The stones under her feet were as dark as the stones lying underwater in a riverbed, and the shadows were combing her bronze hair. She gave Jared a look that was not hostile—Claire had never dared be openly hostile to any of the Lynburns—but wary, and more than a little afraid.

"I'll go," said Jared, and quieter, to Kami, "If you'll be all right?"

"Always am," Kami told him. She looked searchingly at her mother's face, then glanced up at Jared. "See you in a few, sunshine puppy," she told him, and lifted up on the tips of her toes and pressed a kiss on his mouth. She only caught the side, a little clumsily, but felt the curl of his small smile against her lips.

"Sunshine puppy?" he asked. "You're not even trying anymore."

"I am trying very hard," Kami informed him. "To be ridiculous."

She smiled at him. He didn't smile back and she didn't know why, but her mother had hold of her other hand, so she leaned into her mother and let him go.

She and her mother were quiet for a moment, leaning against each other, walking very slowly.

"I was really proud of myself earlier," Claire said at last.

Kami leaned her head down against her mother's shoulder. "I'm really proud of you now."

"I'm glad about that," Mum said. "I don't know how I feel now, but I'm glad." She stopped walking and was silent for a moment. "I loved our home," she said very softly.

"The Lynburns gave us that house so we would serve them," Kami said. "I loved it too, but it wasn't ours. I wasn't willing to pay the price for it, and neither were you, Mum. Not really. Not in the end."

Mum curled her fingers around Kami's wrist, under the sleeve of Jared's leather jacket. "No. But I was willing to pay the price for you," she said. "For you and your brothers. I would make any bargain to keep you safe."

"I don't want to be safe," Kami said.

"My fearless girl," said Mum. "I always wanted to be braver. Sometimes I think that was another bargain I made, that I would be twice as afraid but you never would be."

"I'm not brave," Kami whispered. "I'm so afraid some-times."

"I'm always so afraid," Mum whispered back.

Kami looked away from her mother's face when she heard a soft sound.

Down the narrow black street by the church, something was moving that wasn't human. The streetlamps touched brindled fur, striking silver off the ends, and lit watchful yel-low eyes. Kami and her mother stood holding on to each other and watching the wolf pad toward them. It gave them a baleful look and passed by Kami, so close she could feel the thick fur brush the thin cotton material of her pajamas. The creature could have clamped its jaws down on her leg. It could have leaped at her, knocked her down, and torn out her throat.

It continued to trot steadily on, and they turned to keep it in sight. The animal crossed the stretch of cobbles to where its master stood. He was standing beneath one of the street-lights. His hair glowed the same fierce yellow as the wolf's eyes.

"You're right to be afraid, Claire," said Rob Lynburn.

Kami summoned every drop of magic she might possibly still have left. It was like drawing down a bucket into a dry well, hearing it scrape the sides and clatter in the dust at the bot-tom. Her mother's fingers bit into her arm, the sharp sudden pain drawing her attention.

"Don't scream," Mum murmured.

Kami understood. Jared and Ash had no magic; only Lillian had power, and she was not strong enough to stand against Rob with any certainty. Everyone else was helpless, and everyone else included Dad and, worse than that, Tomo and Ten. They could not put the boys at risk.

She could already feel Ash's alarm, beating at her fragile calm like a battering ram into doors of glass.

Don't come, she said. *Don't tell anyone, don't help us. Keep going, say we're fine. Make them keep going until you have my brothers somewhere safe.*

"You didn't think the house would be enough to pay for what you did?"

It appeared to be a rhetorical question. Rob did not have the air of someone looking for answers. He took a step toward them and Kami saw the new stiffness of the motion, the wince as he set down his bad foot. A smile curled Kami's mouth without her mind giving permission, and Rob's face darkened.

He walked forward, his leg dragging, shoe stuttering over the uneven cobbles. Kami knew it would do no good to run, and her mother was shaking too hard to do it anyway. Rob came closer and closer, and Claire's grip on Kami grew tighter and tighter.

"Run," Mum whispered.

"No," Kami whispered back, and louder: "No. What do you want, Rob? You want everybody in this town to submit to you, to give you their tokens of obedience and your sacrifice. You thought my mother was one of the people who would do it, who lived to serve you. But she is more than you thought she was. Everybody in this town is more than you think. Nobody in Sorry-in-the-Vale will live or die to serve you anymore."

Rob smirked at her. "I don't want servants. But you're right, I don't want Claire's ill-advised actions to give anybody ideas."

He reached out a hand to them. Kami felt her mother flinch violently, her grip on Kami only getting tighter.

Kami shoved herself at her mother, directly into the path of Rob's hand. She grabbed at his wrist, moved forward and past him, twisting his hand behind his back. She heard his shout of pain and the wolf launched itself at her. Her head cracked against the cobbles and her world was a nightmare of darkness and teeth and Ash screaming in her head.

She could feel the moment his resolve broke and he began to run back. She knotted her fingers into the rough fur at the wolf's ruff and held it back for an instant, forced the snapping jaws and hot panting breath an inch away from her face, so she could twist her head and look across at her mother.

Rob was stalking through the light of the streetlamp, and Claire was shrinking into the shadow cast by the statue of Matthew Cooper: her husband's ancestor, the man who'd been the source for a Lynburn, whose family had been left the house that Rob had burned down tonight.

Rob reached out and touched Claire's hair. He lifted his hand, one long tress curled in the center of his palm. It fluttered in the night breeze, a bronze ribbon, and the light struck it so it shone white.

"You were always so pretty, Claire," Rob said. The only sound besides his voice was Claire's breathing, fast and harsh with fear. "Maybe you thought I'd spare you for that. But I have only ever loved one woman in my life." He paused, and added, with an almost gentle finality, "And it certainly wasn't you."

The world exploded into noise and fragments. The wolf's snarl and running footsteps echoed and Kami's eyes were blinded by dust. She heard Ash's voice in her head, calling her name over and over, and felt his hands on her arms, dragging her backward. The cobbles scraped roughly against her back, protected only by Jared's leather jacket.

She heard the wolf make a choked-off sound and blinked until her vision cleared and she saw Jared with his fist actually in the wolf's mouth.

They had both come back for her.

Jared clearly thought this was a very efficient way of making sure the wolf did not bite anybody else: did not bite her. He was breathing hard, strained, his chest heaving against the wolf's back, but the wolf did not try to savage him. It twisted around in his grip and ended up staring at Jared, its pointed muzzle close to his face, its yellow eyes on his eyes. They were alike for a moment, these snarling sorcerous creatures of Rob Lynburn. They stared at each other until the wolf turned tail and disappeared into the dark.

Kami looked around at the white shards scattered all around the town square, and thought for one sick, terrible moment that they were bone. But when she moved her foot, her shoe struck against one shard and it was like kicking a pot—the shards were heavy, dense stone.

Rob had shattered the statue of Matthew Cooper. Kami had no idea why he would do that, and at this moment she did not care, as long as her mother was safe and whole.

She turned to Claire.

Rob was gone and Claire was on her feet, looking at the spot where Rob had been with eyes that were turning blind. Kami's whole body went cold. Her eyes refused to register what they were seeing. Claire's clear gray eyes had a milky sheen to them, and her hair was slowly turning white, from her crown downward. While the bronze locks of her hair were ruffled in the night wind, the white of her hair shone perfectly smooth in the moonlight. There was a gleam to her high cheekbones, and a new carved look to her lips.

Kami had always thought that her mother was so lovely she looked like art, but now she saw the difference between what was alive and what was only beautiful.

Her mother tried to move. Kami saw it, saw the slow gradual movement, what had been natural to her becoming impossible. Claire lifted a hand, moving as jerkily and slowly as a puppet held in inexpert hands. Her searching, turning-to-pearl eyes fixed on Kami.

Her pale lips parted.

"You are always brave," her mother whispered, her voice soft as the wind coming through a chink in stone, "and I am always proud."

Kami scrambled up, hands in the dust and fragments, until she was on her knees and able to grasp at her mother's hand. But they did not truly touch: it was no longer truly her mother.

Kami's hand met cold stone.

Matthew Cooper's statue, made in memory of a time when their town had once been endangered and then saved, put up in honor of a hero, was in shattered pieces. And her mother stood a pale and silent witness to the fact that nobody in their town was safe. Her hand was outreached, but Kami could not hold it and she could not help her. Love could not reach her now.

Kami sank back down onto the cold stones, and was enveloped in warm arms. More than arms—there was comfort, all around her, concern and hope and misery for her, about her. For an instant it felt like love.

Shhh, said Ash, *shhh,* though Kami was not speaking. *It can be undone. This can be undone.*

Who can undo it? Who has enough power? Kami demanded, but she knew the answer before she asked.

The same man who had done it. Rob had woken the woods enough so he could bring forth the creatures of his imagination from it, could bring wolves running to his call. He could turn a living woman from flesh to stone, and from stone to flesh again. Rob Lynburn was the only one who had enough power.

And he would never do it.

Kami thumped her fist on the cobblestones as if she could kill him, as if she could force him to do what she wanted. A sharp sudden pain went through her hand, the feeling of her skin being cut by something jagged rather than bruised or torn by stone. She swallowed, her throat dry and tight, and her fingers closed on what had hurt her.

She lifted her hand to her face and opened it. In her dusty, filthy palm lay a small metal object.

It was a key. Someone had hidden a key in Matthew Cooper's statue.

Kami remembered old words, written in an old book.

Their memories lie under Matthew Cooper's stone and wrapped in Anne Lynburn's silk.

She had thought it was about their bodies, but this was a key. A hidden key meant there was a lock somewhere, an important lock.

Kami knew that, but though she held fast onto the key she could not make any plan for what to do or how to find that lock. She could not envision anything but her mother's face, frozen forever.

Kami knew she was shaking, because Ash knew she was shaking. She felt so distant from herself that Ash seemed closer. His distress and affection was a comfort. This was how she had been comforted all her life. Every hurt in childhood, every secret pain, had been washed away by someone who could reach inside her and feel all she felt. She put her head down on his shoulder, and shook until she was still.

She did not even remember that Jared was there until she finally lifted her head and saw him standing and watching her and Ash. He did not say a word. She did not know what to say. She hardly knew how to feel. It was as though she had been turned to stone as well.

Chapter Thirteen
Your Secret Heart

Kami's family still went to the flat above Claire's restaurant. Even if their mother was lost, the boys still needed sleep.

Her father tucked them into the bed Kami's mother had been sleeping in, and he slept on the floor beside them and insisted Kami sleep on the sofa in the little sitting room. The flat was only three rooms, four if you counted the small bathroom. There were memories of her mother everywhere that Kami looked. A hairbrush with her glinting light hair in it, a book that she had left open and would never finish, a smudged mirror. Kami wandered the house for most of that night laying her hands on each object, as if she could somehow get one last touch from her mother, passed on through these last small things she had handled. But they remained lifeless and meaningless in her hands. Love was not magic: it could not transform anything.

Kami crawled back onto the sofa when the sky was pale gray, like white stained so badly that no matter how many times it was washed it would never be clean again. She went to sleep holding Matthew Cooper's key tightly.

When she woke up, new light striking the old metal in her hand was the first thing she saw, and the key seemed like a talisman. She could not allow herself to think of anything else. She had a mystery to solve, and so she could get up.

She had to go somewhere, but she did not want to go alone. So she fished her phone out of her pocket and called her first choice for company.

"Hey, Angela," she said. "Want to come with me to the graveyard?"

"I absolutely do not," Angela told her. "But I'll see you in ten minutes."

Angela met her outside Claire's. Kami sneaked down the dark narrow stairs as quietly as she could. She tried not to look at the quiet restaurant her mother had been so proud of, but she had it memorized: the swinging doors that hid the kitchen, the little colorful paintings, the one big blank white wall that her mother had always wanted Dad to paint a mural on, the tables with their white circular tabletops and curling iron table legs.

When Angela opened the door and handed in a dress and a bra, the large glass front of Claire's immediately became a problem.

"I think this might fit," Angela said. "And this is my sports bra. Obviously, as I have never participated in any sport, it has never been worn."

"Thank you! Be my lookout, okay?"

"Sure," said Angela. "If somebody comes by, I'm happy to say 'Kami, you're changing your clothes in front of a giant window on the main street of town, someone is going to see you naked, and I'm going to laugh.'"

"Your unfailing support means the world to me!" Kami

said, pulling off her pajama top, which was basically charred rags at the back.

It turned out that Angela being so much taller meant that there was extra fabric to go over all of Kami's extra flesh. The dress fit: it did not matter that it was black and plain and spoke to Kami of nothing so much as beautifully tailored boredom.

When Kami emerged, Angela looked at her for a considering moment.

Kami spread her hands in a self-deprecating gesture. "Not really me, is it?"

"You're always you," said Angela, and linked her arm with Kami's, something she would not have done on any other day. "And you're all right. For a lunatic nudist."

Kami tucked her cheek against Angela's shoulder and walked leaning against her as they went into the town square. It must have rained sometime after Kami had fallen asleep: the air had a fresh, damp springtime feel to it, and all the dust on the cobblestones had washed away. The fragments of Matthew Cooper's statue were still there, washed clean and scattered like unearthed bones on an archaeological dig.

Kami saw the gleaming statue that was her mother out of the corner of her eye, but she did not dare look at it head on. She could not betray her mother by shaking and weeping and doing nothing else, by despairing and losing her mother's only chance to survive. She had to carry on, so she did, walking fast and leaning against Angela until they were past the square and turning up Shadowchurch Lane. Angela supported Kami's weight and let Kami set the pace.

"So what are we searching for?" Angela asked as Kami

unlinked their arms and stepped under the stone horseshoe arch into the churchyard and round to the graveyard.

"Anne Lynburn's grave," Kami answered. "We have to dig it up."

Angela blinked. "Oh, great," she said slowly. "I was definitely hoping you were going to suggest grave robbery. I would have been disappointed if it had been anything else."

"There was a key hidden in Matthew Cooper's statue, and there was a note in the books that said their memories lay in Matthew's stone and Anne Lynburn's silk. I think they used silk for her shroud. I think whatever this key opens will be with Anne."

Kami drew the key out of Angela's exercise bra, which just about fit with some brimming involved and yet was where she had to keep things because Angela's dumb dress had no pockets. She showed the key to Angela.

Angela sighed. "All right, Nancy Drew, let's go grave-digging. Should be jolly larks."

"The book said it would be along the farthest wall," Kami said, and they both moved toward the wall encircling the little graveyard, where the oldest stones were leaning, as if away from the wind of time.

While Kami was searching, she remembered a promise she had made.

"So . . . how are you and Holly getting on?" she asked tentatively, skirting around a gravestone.

Trying to decipher a name almost worn away on a lichen-covered stone, Kami traced it with her fingers. She was fairly certain it said either *Elizabeth* or *Hepzibah*. For the dead lady's sake, she hoped it was Elizabeth.

"Fine," Angela said.

"Really," Kami said encouragingly.

"Fine, and that's final," Angela snapped. "You may have decided this is the perfect time to be worrying about romance, but some of us actually have our priorities in order."

Kami was silent.

"I'm sorry. I didn't mean that," Angela said, after a pause. "It's a sore subject with me, but I'm glad you have someone. I am."

"I have a lot more than just one person," Kami told her, and patted her arm. "I'm sorry too," she added. "I should know better than to talk to you about feelings before noon."

"Nothing's happening," Angela said. "I don't want anything to happen. And I don't want to talk about it."

"Okay," said Kami.

There was a skull and crossbones on one of the graves. Kami hoped that meant there was a pirate buried here. She hoped even more that one of the last remaining stones would be Anne Lynburn's.

"How are things going with young what's-his-face?" Angela asked, in what for Angela was conciliatory fashion, which of course meant not very conciliatory at all. "You know the one. Blond. Scowly. Bad attitude, which I have some sympathy for. Sloppy dresser, which I have no sympathy for at all."

"Also a terrible driver," Kami said. "Wild about the eyes. Daddy issues so numerous the issues may be compiled into a book called *Who's the Daddy? Both Options Are Evil.*" She sighed and touched another gravestone, which was for someone cursed with the name of Edgar Featherstonehaugh.

"Well, I'm pressuring him into having a relationship with me, and I don't know how into it he is, and there are even worse problems than that, but apart from that, it's okay."

"Anyone would be lucky to be emotionally blackmailed or physically forced into romance with you, friend," said Angela. "What a jerk."

"Thanks," said Kami. "Anne Lynburn's grave isn't here."

"It sure isn't. What a pity, I was really looking forward to my first experience violating a resting place."

Kami punched her in the arm.

"It must be in the Lynburn crypt," she said.

"Which is located in the evil lair of evil?" Angela asked. "Terrific."

"Let's go get Holly," Kami proposed.

"She'll be in the Water Rising, going through the books as usual," said Angela.

Angela sounded a little resigned, maybe upset that she wasn't seeing more of Holly—Kami couldn't quite put her finger on it, but there was an emotion there that was not annoyance or anger, and with Angela that was unusual enough to be remarkable.

Kami said nothing, though, besides a mild "I think it's awesome she's become a blond bombshell research ninja. Her powers have multiplied!"

She rested her head against Angela's shoulder again as they passed her mother, and again they said nothing.

"So you're going to walk through fire again?" Holly asked, looking dismayed.

Holly and Kami were alone in the back room of the Water Rising, but everyone else—including Kami's father and the boys—had congregated at the inn as well. Kami was pleased that Angela had stopped to talk to Ash, because otherwise she felt like they would gang up on her with their judgment of her lifestyle choices.

"Probably," said Kami. "I hear you're a sorcerer who held off Rob's people when they burned our house and came after me and my family. I think that's terrific. Want to come with me?"

Holly swallowed. "I'll come, but I'm not very good."

"I trust you. And I want to tell you something real quick before Angela comes in," Kami said.

"We don't have to talk about anything like that now," Holly said, looking at Kami with soft, sympathetic eyes.

Kami turned her face away. "Sure we do," she said, insistently chipper. "I tried to talk to her but she stonewalled me. The thing about Angela is that she's really private and really straightforward at the same time, so, and I totally understand if you don't want to do this, but I think the only move might be—"

"Telling her," Holly filled in.

"That move," Kami said. "Yes."

Holly nodded, her curls bobbing and the face framed by those curls resolved. "It's my fault she thinks I don't like her. I'll do it."

Kami got up, ostensibly to look at the book Holly was studying; she hung over her shoulder and got hold of her hand.

"It's not your fault," she murmured. "You went at a different speed from someone else emotionally. That's not your fault or their fault."

"On that topic, how are things going with Jared?" Holly inquired.

"I want to interfere horribly in my friends' love lives and keep my own embarrassing and pathetic one private, is that so much to ask?"

"Mmm," said Holly, and gave Kami a grin that reminded Kami of when Holly had been the sunny confident school goddess she had barely known and envied a little. "Now that you know that I'm not at all interested in Jared, is it inappropriate to say that I did get the impression that he might channel all those simmering repressed emotions in a useful way? I mean being explosively good in bed."

"Viking tiger in the sack, I have no doubt," Kami said lightly, and felt a blush stage a hostile takeover of her neck and march up to claim the territory of her face.

Holly stopped grinning and added in a low voice, "Kami, I can see you don't want to talk about it, but I can't just joke around. I have to tell you, I'm so sorry about—"

Kami wanted to say that she appreciated it but did not want to talk about her mother, but feared even trying to say that would make her throat tighten up too much for her to speak. Instead, she looked at the drawing on the page Holly's book was open to. "I know you are. How's the research going?"

Holly was tactful enough to stop talking, and disconsolate enough to sigh. "I keep wishing that there could be a movie montage. And I could put on a pair of glasses and flip pages at appropriate moments, until the music gets dramatic and I spot the crucial thing and I say 'Voilà!' "

"I used to think that there was an awesome investigator lady called Viola, and when people made a discovery they would shout 'Viola' in her honor," Kami said reminiscently. She turned a page and frowned at the sketch of a wall. "Is this about architecture?"

"It's about the changes made to Aurimere over the years," Holly said. "Basically a whole lot of 'then we added essential drowned-lady décor' and 'then we turned the farthest wall into a rockery' and 'then—' "

"Oh," Kami said.

"What?" Holly asked, somewhat apprehensively.

Anne was drowned and lost, the book had said, and Lynburns since then had filled their house with images of drowning women. The graveyard and the Lynburns' crypt were both sacred ground, and Anne had died in a time when that mattered. She stared at the drawing of the wall, and remembered the wall she had knelt beside once, with Jared on the other side of it. She remembered the flowers strewn over the ground.

Kami felt her smile spread and warmth spread within her, the sudden sweet joy of discovering the truth. "Viola."

The first thing to do was slip away from her father, who might have questions about why she kept insisting on going back to the lair of ultimate evil. Kami saw why so many teenagers who had adventures in books were interestingly tragic orphans. Parents were a real buzzkill, adventure-wise.

She would take fewer adventures, though. She would pay

any price, she thought, if she could only find a way to free her mother from Rob Lynburn's spell.

She thought she was getting out of the Water Rising clean, because she didn't see her father anywhere around: there was only Ash and Lillian sitting at a table, and a few other patrons at as much of a distance from Ash and Lillian as they could get. She made for the door, at which point Lillian caught her arm.

"Where are you going?"

"Uh," said Kami, eyeballing her wildly. "I'm going to buy some drugs."

Lillian stared. "I beg your pardon?"

"This is a really stressful time for everyone," said Kami. "So I thought maybe I could buy a little weed, take the edge off. I might be a while. This is a very clean-living town, apart from all the murders, so I don't actually know any drug dealers. I realize Jared kind of looks like one, but he's not, which is a shame because I think the drug dealer's girlfriend gets her drugs free."

"I realize you are attempting to be humorous," said Lillian, after a pause during which she stared some more. "I don't understand it."

"Hey, you're not the only family with a legacy. 'Glass' rhymes with 'sass.' Have you met my dad?"

"I have had that dubious pleasure," said Lillian. "He is, in fact, meant to be meeting me in order to, and I quote, 'teach me to integrate better with society, display leadership skills, win over the populace, and stop acting like a robot princess from space.' I admit that the humor in his humor escapes me as well." She paused and suddenly looked determined. "I'm going to start without him."

She climbed off the stool and headed toward the group of people in the corner. Kami and Ash watched as they collectively shrank away.

"Come on, quick," said Kami, and as if summoned by some spirit warning him of his child's intended reckless behavior, her dad appeared through the inn doors.

He looked distracted. "Where's Lillian?"

Kami checked over her shoulder. "Appears to be trying to wrest a screaming baby from the arms of her frightened mother in order to kiss it."

"Oh no no no," murmured Jon, and raised his voice as he made his way over. "Libba, we've talked about this!"

"The good news is the grown-ups are distracted by politics," said Kami.

You mean that your poor father is distracted by my awful mother, said Ash, who was far too polite to say such a thing out loud and looked vaguely embarrassed to be thinking it.

Kami grinned. "Why quibble when we have the results we want!"

I wish I could ask you what you're planning, but I know what you're planning, said Ash. *Lucky me. I know this is important information, but going to Aurimere at all is a huge risk.*

"See, the thing is, if I ran a business it would probably be called Risky Business," said Kami, and smiled at him. She felt affection radiating from Ash, so strong that she was startled.

He was right, though. The risks they were taking were worse now. Kami's mother was lost. Jared had been tortured.

She didn't know how to do anything than take greater risks in the face of greater danger, and hope that somehow they could all be saved.

As they walked out of the pub, Jared fell in with them. Kami let herself be weak and grasped for his hand. Jared linked his fingers with hers and matched her steps.

"We're going to—" Kami began.

"I know," said Jared. "Ash told me while it was happening. I was just grabbing my jacket."

Kami felt wariness and something close to guilt pass between herself and Ash, as if Ash had been telling secrets about the things they both wished they had not done. She felt the urge to exchange a glance with him over her shoulder, but stopped herself from doing so because she didn't want Jared to see the look, and then felt bad about that.

"You two are getting on well these days," she said lightly instead.

"Bros before hoes," said Jared. "By which of course I mean gardening tools, because I hold all the fine ladies of Sorry-in-the-Vale in the highest regard."

Kami glanced up in time to catch the end of one of his shy, almost-not-there smiles. She smiled back at him, held on to his hand, and wished they were alone together.

But they were not alone together. They could never really be alone together.

"I don't know how to take you guys through the fire," she said. "But I think I have enough power. Rob always underestimates what a source can do. I can go through, and I think Holly can too, if I help her. We have to walk through alone, and you all have to wait outside. Is—is that all right?"

"It's not all right, but I will try to stand outside of and radiate moral support."

"Like a true gentleman should," said Kami, patting his arm.

"You don't have to come with me," said Kami.

Holly had not wanted everyone to know that she was a sorcerer. It had not escaped Kami's attention that only Angela had not seemed surprised.

Kami was very much in favor of their great love, and she had tried not to be hurt that she had been left out of the sorcerous information loop. She was not entitled to know everything just because she wanted to know everything . . . and take detailed notes and ask personal follow-up questions.

She knew she was a pushy person, but that didn't mean she wanted to push Holly too far. She did not want to make Holly do anything she did not want to do.

Holly stood with her hand in Kami's. The firelight gilded her curls, turning them from sunshine to real gold.

"I also realize that I could have brought this up before dragging you all the way here," Kami said. "Sometimes I get too caught up in charging."

"I like seeing you charge," said Holly, and grinned. "And I want to do this."

Her voice was firm, but her hand in Kami's was trembling slightly. Kami got a firmer grip on it.

"It's okay if you're scared."

Holly lifted her chin. "I'm trying not to be."

"You don't have to try. I mean, you're still awesome if

you're scared. You can do it anyway. Being scared is okay, because it won't stop you."

Holly looked at Kami out of the corner of her eye, a little shy and a little doubtful, as Holly was when complimented on the things she believed were her faults.

They walked into the fire together. Kami felt the heat of it, like lifting her face up to the sun on a hot day and feeling its warmth spill onto her face, its light beat against her eyelids.

She heard Holly's shocked, scared gasp before she felt the pain slice through her own body. It was a new pain, one that seemed both numbing and profoundly more agonizing than the burning that had come before. Every atom of her body seemed turned to crystal and stabbed with knives.

Rob had learned from their two escapes. He had determined he would not be made a fool of a third time.

Within the ring of fire, they had laid a ring of ice.

She was so cold she felt she was burning inside in reaction to it: her blood boiling to nothing, her bones turning to lightning.

All Kami could do was cling to the thought that Rob had so much vanity, and no experience with sources. He had underestimated her, had underestimated her power, over and over. She had to believe he was still doing it. Kami held on tight to Holly's hand, stopped her retreating back into the fire that waited for them both. Fire hissed behind them, ice tore at them, the pain stretched on, and Kami thought for a moment that she had killed Holly by keeping her captive in this dual ring of pain.

Then suddenly it was over. The cessation of pain was as

stunning as the bright wave of agony had been. She opened her eyes and they were standing on the cool grass.

Kami did not hesitate. Every moment was a moment that Rob Lynburn could discover them. She dashed around the back of the house and heard Holly's footsteps flying after her.

She wanted to slow down as she entered the garden, remembering its late-summer splendor when she had walked into it once before. She had had her first real conversation with Jared here. But she couldn't let herself be delayed by sentiment, shouldn't even be thinking of something so silly.

The colors of the budding spring flowers at night were nothing but a blur until she was on her knees by the crumbled stone wall, at the very end of the wall where she had knelt once, where the wall stopped in the center of the garden rather than meeting another wall. Loose stones and flowers were all around her, like a sweet-smelling sea lapping at her knees, and she said, "Here, I think."

There was no time for spades and shovels, for the childish joy of digging up buried treasure. Kami sent her power into the earth, made it break into a tiny localized earthquake. She found herself sinking in swelling soil, and she scrabbled in the hole she had made, sent her thoughts down into the earth until she found something that was not earth, and then she followed her power with her fingers until her fingers found it too.

A little box, far too small for a coffin, the wood under Kami's palms slick with a patina of slime. There was a symbol carved on the top of the box, but she could no longer make it out. She tried to undo the rusty catch: it broke off in her hand. When she opened the top of the box by force, it came off in pieces: Kami discarded the lid and looked at what lay at the bottom of the chest in her hands.

It was a pool of shimmering material. Kami remembered reading a book in Aurimere, listing the gifts given to the sorcerers. She remembered one item on the list now, very clearly: *silk for Anne Lynburn's shroud.* But if Anne Lynburn had drowned in the river where her sister's bells had been sunk, never to be seen again, her body had never been found. Her shroud had been used for another purpose.

The spelled silk was like finding a pearl in the heart of the oyster, glowing in the muck and silt of the bottom of the sea. It looked fresh and new as if it was a second away from being laid on a bride's shining hair.

Kami wondered at the love and loss that had been put into this enchantment, to keep it shining after centuries buried in the dark. She touched it, and something rustled under her hand. She drew back a layer of material, and she heard Holly let out a soft sound near her ear: surprise as much as triumph.

Lying in the pool of cool white silk at the bottom of the rotted ancient box was a letter. The paper was yellow as old bones and the ink was faded as brown as old blood, but it was written by Elinor Lynburn, and it told Kami everything she had been aching to know.

To the Lynburn who discovereth this last relic of Anne Lynburn, I leave a story and a warning.

Our need was dire. Our good king Richard was dead, to the great heaviness of the town. The soldiers of the usurper king marched themselves upon the town we had taken a holy oath to protect. Through mist and enchantment the soldiers came marching, and ere they reached us we acted to keep our vows.

Whereupon under the moon in springtime, before the start of the new year, we went down to the pools. They are made twain, for a sorcerer to go in each. I can scarcely bear to write what was decreed by fate to happen next.

The three of us went down to the Crying Pools and performed the ceremony together. There is a way for sorcerers to help each other during the ceremony of the Crying Pools, and Anne and I shared power so we could do so. There is a way for a source to help a sorcerer complete the ceremony of the Crying Pools. Matthew helped Anne, and then reached through the bond between Anne and me to help me too. Matthew was Anne's source. Matthew came to be my source. Anne belonged to me and I to her. We married two enchantments, and came away with power in abundance not to be described.

Great power comes with such joining. No soul can bear being so joined. They were doomed to die from the moment that we cast the enchantment. They emerged from the pools cursed to madness and ruin. They did not live to see another dawn.

Remember Matthew and Anne, loving souls and passing well beloved. Farewell sister, farewell love. I live on alone and am called fortunate by fools.

To go three into the lakes is to go into a charnel house.

I pray you do not take this course. Do not do this unless there is no other choice. If you want to live, do not do it. If you want those you love to live, do not do it.

Yet I know that those in their last extremity will do what they must.

When the bells ring, when the first moon of the new year

shines, when the cost of keeping your word is breaking your heart, you will go down to the lakes, down, down, down, to your great sorrow.

Elinor Lynburn
In the year of our Lord 1485

Kami looked up from the paper and into Holly's eyes, wide open with shock, green as the Crying Pools in summertime.

But Holly did not say a word about the letter; instead she said, "Watch out."

And she grabbed hold of Kami's arm and hauled her upright, turned her around, so that they were both facing Holly's mother. Alison Prescott was standing with her feet buried in yellow flowers and her hands shimmering with magic. She was wearing an old, worn green dress, the faded green the same color as her eyes.

Rob had not only put in another circle to cross. He had posted a lookout.

"I won't let you hurt her," said Holly, her voice and hands both firm now. She tried to push Kami behind her, but Kami dug her heels in.

Alison hesitated. "I don't want to hurt either of you."

"Terrific!" said Kami. "Then we'll just be going."

"You know I can't let you leave with that, dear," said Alison Prescott, and bent her gaze on Elinor's letter.

The letter seemed fine for a moment, then one end turned into dead black and warm violet, blurring into flame. For a moment the words "your great sorrow" were lit and highlighted in the waking flame. They became written in shadow against a burning light.

The paper was ashes, crumbling away into charred flakes and soot, leaving Kami with nothing but soiled hands.

Kami could not help but feel a pang. It had been a last relic of Elinor Lynburn, the keeper of all the old secrets Kami had been working so hard to discover ever since the Lynburns returned. They were all lost now, the three who had gone down to the lakes. Matthew Cooper's statue was dust, and Anne Lynburn had disappeared under water and from all memory. It didn't matter, Kami told herself. She knew the secret. She could remember it. She could write it down again.

"Come on," said Holly in her ear. "We were lucky it wasn't someone else."

But Kami felt like there had been someone else. Kami still felt watched. Kami looked up, and behind glinting glass she saw the flash of fox fire that was Amber Green's hair.

In spite of Elinor's letter, in spite of Holly's anxious shepherding away, Kami found herself smiling a tiny smile. There was a guard at the window and a guard at the gate, but neither guard had raised the alarm. Two of Rob's people had let them go.

Kami grasped Holly's arm as they stepped into the fire. She whispered, softer than the hissing flames, low enough so that nobody on the other side of the fire could hear them: "Don't tell Jared what the letter said."

PART IV
SING ME NO MORE LOVE SONGS

The face of all the world is changed, I think,
Since first I heard the footsteps of thy soul. . . .
—*Elizabeth Barrett Browning*

Chapter Fourteen
Lies and Other Love Tales

Holly did not tell. Kami was the one who led the way into the Water Rising, and collected up everyone she could. They all ended up sitting in the parlor: Holly, Ash, Jared, Rusty, Lillian, and Jon. Even Kami's brothers were there, sitting on the floor.

Even Martha Wright was there.

Kami had stopped at the bar and asked if she wanted to come hear something new. "I wish you would," Kami had added.

Martha Wright had hesitated, and Kami had been briefly sure she would not do it. Then she had said, with sudden decision, "I'll come and listen, at least," and called for her husband to come work behind the bar.

The inn was empty, anyway. There was no sound of customers, no sound in the streets outside the windows. Kami repeated all that she could remember from the letter: all of the parts she had decided would be useful.

She told them that if a source and two sorcerers went to the Crying Pools, and the sorcerers were linked, and one source and sorcerer were linked, a link could be made between all three of them. She told them the conditions that

Elinor Lynburn had outlined. She told them of how much power they could gain: perhaps enough to defeat Rob Lynburn, enough to save the town.

Enough to save her mother.

She did not tell them of the death and ruin Elinor Lynburn had warned would follow.

"Wait a second," said Ash. "How is there a 'moon in *springtime* before the start of the new year'? I think it's a riddle. It makes no sense."

"Yes, it does," said Jared. "The new year was in March in England until the 1700s, when the pope introduced a new calendar."

Everyone stared at him. Jared flushed slightly, scar thrown into relief, and muttered, "I read a lot of old books."

"Well done," said Jon. "See where learning gets you, lads? So much better than messing around with girls or playing those video games which one hears are full of violence."

Kami, as a witness to many of her father's video game marathons, gave him a long judgmental stare. "You total hypocrite."

"Hypocrisy is what being a parent is all about," Jon said. "Well done for cracking the books, Jared and Holly. You see how it pays off."

Holly smiled and the light of her smile seemed to spill all over the room, reflections of light refracted all over everywhere.

"It's true reading is a wonderful thing," Rusty observed. "I read a *Cosmo* a year ago, and I still remember how to keep my nails in perfect condition and also ten top tips on how to dress to accentuate my ass."

Now everybody was staring at Rusty. Unlike Jared, he did not blush.

"Those tips are working," he said. "Don't pretend you haven't all noticed. I know the truth."

Kami rolled up a magazine on the table—sadly, for the sake of dramatic irony, not a *Cosmo*—and hit Rusty over the head with it. "Does anybody have anything else to say—I can't stress this enough—*specifically* about Elinor Lynburn and medieval New Year?"

"Want to know what it was called? You'll like this," Jared added, and he looked at Kami. It was a simple glance from his gray eyes, but it felt like being put in a room that was just the two of them. "Lady Day."

Kami beamed at him. "You know what I like, sugar-prune. So . . . Elinor Lynburn, Anne Lynburn, and Matthew Cooper went down to the lakes at night, sometime in March. That means the spring equinox, doesn't it? That's what it has to mean."

"Those dates have power," said Lillian. "That's why Rob wants to sacrifice someone at or near the spring equinox: why he asked for the sacrifice he did not receive at the winter solstice."

"He already sacrificed the mayor," Rusty said. "And I never wanted to live in a world where I had to say that sentence, so thank you for that, Rob Lynburn. Can't he be done with death for the year? He's already got the house and the town has pledged their allegiance. What does he want all this power for?"

Lillian shrugged. "Why do we have to keep having this discussion?"

"Because something's not right," said Kami. "The way he's behaving makes no sense."

"It makes perfect sense. What do people want love for? Why do people want more money than they could ever spend? Power becomes the measure of you, and you always want more. He wants to rule over the town, and for his rule to be unbreakable. He wants a death to be volunteered and not simply accepted. He wants the extra power that comes with a sacrifice done at one of the turnings of the year."

There was a long pause.

"But what," said Jared, "if that's not true?"

Lillian looked frustrated enough to be angry. "I don't understand."

"Let him talk a minute," said Martha Wright. Unbelievably, Lillian glanced at her and visibly checked herself.

"Rob said," Jared said slowly, "before he put me down with Edmund Prescott, that I didn't understand what he was really doing yet. And okay, I know Rusty's right and it sounds just like the standard evil overlord speech, but I was talking to Rob in the garden once. He said that he never wanted to come back to this town."

Jared glanced at Kami. She saw what he meant so clearly that it was like having the link back, having perfect understanding pass between them, for an instant.

"What if we got his plan wrong all along? What if he doesn't want to rule Sorry-in-the-Vale?" Kami asked.

"Then *what* has he been doing all this time?" Lillian demanded, breaking silence with a violence that showed what an effort not speaking before had been.

Kami spoke quietly. "What if he wants to do a lot more

to the town than rule it? What if he wants to make everyone his slaves—not just have people not saying no, but people not *able* to say no? Turning everybody into statues or trees, or . . . I don't know . . ."

"You're saying he wants to kill someone on the spring equinox so he can do something specific," said Holly. She sounded convinced.

"So he can use that magic to exert his power over everybody. You guys—" Kami nodded to Lillian and Ash. "You taught us that if you have somebody's possession, you can do a spell on them. That's how we defend ourselves from the sorcerers. Rob insisted on his tokens of submission, and he got them. I saw people cutting locks of hair to give him myself. What could Rob do with tokens from the whole town, if he had the power from his equinox sacrifice as well?"

"I don't know," said Ash.

At the same time, Jared said grimly, "Nothing good."

"So we have even more reason to go down to the lakes," said Kami. "We have to perform the ceremony. Whatever Rob is planning, we have to stop him."

She felt Ash in her mind suddenly, his curiosity like a friendly cat brushing up against her to see what she was doing.

"I can tell you how to do the ceremony," said Lillian. "Rob and I did it together, when we were bound as Jared and Ash are now. It does make sense that if a source was there, the source could help. I suppose it even makes sense that the source's power would be multiplied, and that would mean a source would have enough power to reforge a link that was broken—" Her eyes traveled from Kami to Jared.

"And enough power to bind two sorcerers to her. Enough power to overcome the spell on Ash and Jared. Doing the ceremony when only Kami has any magic is going to be very risky, of course."

There was a small line between Lillian Lynburn's eyebrows. She wanted the plan to succeed, she wanted her town back safe and in her hands, but Lillian knew how magic worked. Kami could see the wheels in her mind turning, trying to see the catch.

There was a price for magic: it was taken from somewhere, life and death, earth and air. This was magic that involved their minds: this was magic so great that it might save the town, but Elinor Lynburn had said it would break their minds and kill them.

Elinor Lynburn had seen it happen. Elinor Lynburn knew what she was talking about.

"So we're all agreed," said Ash. "We're going to do it."

Kami felt a rush of gratitude toward him. He was the one person she couldn't hide anything from, and she hadn't asked him to keep her secret, the way she had asked Holly. He knew all that Elinor Lynburn had written, knew all that Kami knew. He didn't have Kami's motivation: his mother was not the one who needed saving. He felt her feelings, her fear and her determination, and she could feel his own fear, so different from hers that they hardly seemed like the same emotion. Ash's fear often paralyzed him, but not this time. He wasn't even hesitating.

They both wanted the same thing, wanted it enough so it felt like her own emotion was being mirrored back to her— they wanted to protect Jared.

Kami's dad looked unhappy, a twist to his mouth as if he wanted to argue but was not sure how. Even now, Kami knew, he still didn't understand how magic worked. He had a hard time believing a spell and the pools in the woods could actually be a threat to his daughter's life. And he wanted Mum back as much as she did.

"So if I understand it, the plan is to lie in wait until the spring equinox," he said. "And to make Rob Lynburn think that we've accepted that his way is the way things are going to be from now on. How do we do that?"

"Well . . . ," Martha Wright said hesitantly. She glanced at Jared, who was leaning forward and bending an attentive look upon her, and took heart. "We always hold a Christmas party at the Water Rising. We didn't this year, on account of all the troubles. We could do it now, invite everyone. That might be a good signal to show people what they want to see: that we've all given up fighting and life's going to be more normal from now on."

Dad looked pleased. "Also a good time for Lenore to show people that she's a better option than Rob."

Lillian looked appalled at the thought of more socializing. Angela looked as if she agreed with Lillian but would rather develop insomnia than ever say she agreed with Lillian about anything. Martha looked delighted at how well her suggestion had been received. They all got up, the meeting over by silent consensus, the talk of magic dropped and the arrangements for a party on. It seemed like everybody had the same response that Martha had suggested the town would have: they were all delighted at the thought of some normalcy to talk about. Kami pushed her chair back, prepared to follow Angela and talk about party decorations, but before she reached the door, she heard her name, spoken quite softly.

She looked around at the only other person left in the room, and her hand fell away from the door handle.

"Whatever it is that you're hiding from me," said Jared, "you have to tell me now."

He was standing with his back to the wall, and Kami knew that was how he stood when he wanted to feel safe, when he wanted to remove himself from the world. She had the impulse to go to him, slide an arm around his waist, kiss him, and not have this fight.

She moved, but not to cross the floor to be with him. Instead, she simply moved away from the door and placed one hand flat on the little coffee table. It shook because its legs were unbalanced, not because she was shaking.

"I'm not . . . ," she said. "I don't want to hide anything from you."

"Then don't do it," Jared said, and swallowed on the words, as if he was in pain. "I know I'm not—smart like you, but don't lie to me just because you can do it now."

"What?" Kami said, stricken. "Jared. Come on. You're smart. You know I think you're smart. I've told you that I think you're smart."

"Oh, sure," said Jared. "Held back a year in school. Can't do the simplest things that you and Ash and Angela can do. Can't do anything but snap and snarl at people. I know you don't think badly of me, but you do things like simplifying stuff for me when you tell me what you want to do at Cambridge."

"What?" Kami asked, baffled, and then remembered telling Jared once that she wanted to study journalism at Cambridge, rather than explain taking literature and extra courses. "Because you're American, and getting into the intricacies of my English college plans didn't seem like the most fun conversation ever for you. Not because I think you're stupid."

"It doesn't matter," said Jared. "What matters is that I can tell you're hiding something from me now."

"Okay," said Kami. "You're right. I didn't want to say in front of my dad and your aunt Lillian, but this spell has a really good chance of killing us, or at least some of us. But we've all risked our lives to stop these people before. It's not any different because it's magic we're doing to ourselves instead of facing other sorcerers. You've done it, time and again. Rob could have killed you when you went after Ten. I thought he had. Any of us could have been killed in the battle before that. And I need to have enough power to save my mother. I won't let anybody stop me."

She gripped the edge of the table and looked at Jared. He was looking back at her, his head tipped back against the wall, his peculiar pale eyes full of light and her image.

"No," he said. "You're not . . . You're still lying to me, and I don't know why, but don't," Jared ground out, and it was almost a sound of anguish. "Please don't."

"It's the truth," Kami told him unsteadily.

"It's not the whole truth," Jared said. "I can tell. You know I can sense what Ash is feeling. I can't read his thoughts but I can feel how he agrees with you, how you both want to—to shield me from something. I don't want to be shielded. We might die, and that means we have to be honest with each other. This isn't fair. If you thought I was protecting you by lying to you or stopping you from making your own decisions, you'd kill me. Don't make me ask again, Kami. What are you hiding from me?"

It was the first time, Kami thought, that he'd acted like his feelings might be as important as hers, instead of lashing out when he was hurt because he could not think of any other way to say he was in pain and could not imagine his pain would matter to anyone. But his pain had always mattered to her and she *did* want to spare him. This felt too horrible to share, too heavy a burden to lay on him.

Only he was right. She would want the truth, no matter how terrible. She owed him the same respect she demanded from him.

"The spell killed Matthew Cooper and Anne Lynburn," Kami confessed. "It killed . . ."

Jared stopped leaning against the wall. She usually found him hard to read, but she saw what he was thinking now so clearly. She felt his horror, like a shadow on her own heart.

"It killed the source, and his original sorcerer," he finished for her. "The second sorcerer lived."

He was suddenly in motion, but not toward her. He crossed the floor to the mantelpiece and leaned one elbow on it. Kami stared at the arch of his back, the way his every muscle was strained. She saw his face only in the mirror, and she did not want to see even that much.

"You and Ash die," Jared said hoarsely. "I live."

"We don't know that's what will happen," Kami said.

"We only know it's what Elinor Lynburn said would happen."

"We might all live," Kami said, and lower: "We might all die."

"And you didn't want to tell me, because you knew there was no chance in hell I would agree to anything like that," Jared said. "There is no reward that could make that risk worthwhile."

"We could be talking about the whole town," said Kami. "We are talking about my mother."

"This is your *life*!" Jared shouted.

"That's right!" Kami shouted back at him. "It's *my* life! I get to decide what to do with it! Don't you dare act like my life means more to you than it does to me!"

She expected him to shout again, but he turned to face her. What little color there had been in his face was all drained away.

"I see you and Ash have already decided," Jared said. "You'll do the ceremony, with or without me. It could still kill you both, and unless I do it, it won't save the town. That leaves me to be a monster or let you both be martyrs. I'd be a monster if I could stop you. I'd be glad to be a monster, if you were saved, but I don't have a choice. I have to do it, and all I can hope is that I die too, that I don't have to go on like Elinor Lynburn did with the town saved and nothing but death and silence in her head for the rest of her life."

"I don't want you to die," Kami whispered.

It would be a comfort to think Jared would go on even if she did not, but she couldn't trust him not to despair or do something desperate, wreck it all because he did not value himself or understand why anyone else would value him. It turned everything that should have been comfort into fear.

But he had seen quickly that she and Ash were determined, had worked it out from Ash's feelings and her face. Maybe she could trust him, to try to survive even if he did not want to and he would have to do it without them. Maybe she should not have kept it from him. Maybe it would be all right.

"I can't do this," Jared said abruptly.

He left the mantelpiece now and came toward her. She took that as an encouraging sign. She watched him, and tried to make a bargain with herself: if he took four steps to her, she could go to him.

Or even three.

"We all have to do it," Kami told him. "I know it's hard, but I really think that it's the only way."

"No," said Jared. "I don't mean that. I mean this. I mean us."

Kami looked at him. He looked back: he looked serious, as if one thing had something to do with the other, as if that made sense to him. As if the thought they could all die soon meant he could not bear the idea of being with her in the time they had left.

"What?" Kami said at last, and heard her voice come out weak in her own ears. "You're punishing me for making my own decision, is that it?"

"I'm not *punishing* you," said Jared. "It's not like I'm any kind of prize. The whole idea was ridiculous and pathetic anyway. I never agreed to it. You decided it all."

That was true, but she had never expected him to say it. It was all the secret uncertainties she had ever had, all the insecurities she had told herself were stupid. But maybe she'd been the one who was stupid. She swallowed and looked at him. He looked back at her, his gray eyes serious and intent. He didn't even look angry. He wasn't trying to hurt her, like he had once before. He was just telling the truth.

"When someone else will always know everything about you, when someone else will share your feelings and know your secrets in a way I never will, we can't be together."

"We could try," Kami argued, and she wanted to argue more but found her mouth, for once, empty of all words.

She had been trying not to think about it, because when she did think about it—about Ash begging them to stop and about the way she found herself always sharing secrets and smiling with Ash—she knew Jared was right. She had known all along that it was impossible, but she had hoped and she had wanted and tried, and she had thought that if he did too, there might somehow still be hope.

"If you want to be with me . . . ," Kami said, and hesitated. If a miracle happened, if they all survived and she and Ash broke the link, then what? But she didn't think they were going to survive.

And she had never been sure of exactly what she meant to Jared, beyond the link and his memory of the link. She didn't want to hear that her link with Ash meant Jared wouldn't want her, ever. She was going to die. She didn't want to have the memory of asking him to be with her, and having him say no.

But he said it just the same.

"Kami," Jared told her, and he sounded sad. "I can't keep pretending. I don't want to."

"Right," Kami said. She'd thought her voice would be faint but it came out strong then and furiously, irrationally angry. "Fine. Forget it. But we're doing the ceremony."

She banged the door as she walked out. She felt sick with how unfair this was, as unfair as the choice she had had to make and the spell they would have to cast. She had never wanted love, the kind of love her childhood group of girlfriends had dreamed of, something that would cause her life to make sense. Her life had made sense already. It had seemed silly, all the clichés of being completed, of wild despair or transcendent joy, love at first sight or ever after, certainties when she had never been certain about anything but how much he mattered. It still seemed so far removed from the desolate pain she was feeling now. She had wanted university, and journalism. She'd thought that she was smart about life and about love.

She'd had Jared already, had him all along and wanted no one else. She'd had him and she'd lost him, and she had spent all this time scrambling to convince herself that she had not lost him, not really.

Nobody could tell a love story by themselves: people told love stories to each other, and Jared had refused to tell her what she had been hoping to hear.

Jared was right. Now when they might be about to die, it was time to be honest, time to admit the stark truth to herself. He didn't want her. She had lost him.

Chapter Fifteen
The One I Love Best

The days passed, in spite of heartbreak and fear of what was to come, and Kami tried to keep busy. She kept living above her mother's restaurant, wearing borrowed clothes. She kept living without her mother. She kept telling herself that if she did everything right, she could save her.

On the day of the party, she helped Martha Wright string red and white ribbons from the rafters of the Water Rising, standing on chairs and her tiptoes to do so, even though the shortest person on the team was probably not the best qualified for ribbon-hanging maneuvers.

"At least you won't bump your head on one of the beams," said Martha, the fourth time that Kami fell off a chair.

"I like your attitude," said Kami. "Always think positive!"

A girl who fell off chairs and kept laughing at dumb jokes and messing up party decorations didn't fit in with any idea Kami had ever had of heartbreak. Maybe if she just kept doing what she could, and acting like she did, it wouldn't hurt as much.

She looked down at Martha, who was behind the bar making orange peel into delicate spiraling shapes.

"You've been such a big help. You've been so kind to us,

and I don't even know why. I hope you don't mind my asking," said Kami. "And I really hope you don't say 'Wow, now that I come to think of it, I don't know why I'm doing this and it seems kind of risky, maybe I'll stop.' I'm a big fan of you helping us. I just wondered, since almost nobody else is helping us, since everybody is too scared of Rob Lynburn to even help themselves, I wondered what made you decide to help."

Kami hoped that she was not coming off as asking why Martha dared to help, when she had no magic. She hadn't had magic, in the time between breaking the link with Jared and forming one with Ash. She'd still fought. She refused to act like the Lynburns did, as if magic was the only power someone could ever have.

But Martha Wright had been raised in the time of Lillian's parents, when the Lynburns had still held sway over the entire valley. When people had been glad to have the Lynburns' power and, more than that, had been used to them. Habit could be stronger than happiness. So many of the people Kami had thought she knew had bowed their heads and let Rob Lynburn do what he liked. They had acted as if they simply could not see any other path to take.

She looked over at Martha again, her gray head bent over the bright orange shapes.

"You remember how Jared left his home for a spell, left his aunt and his cousin and came to live with us, just him," said Martha slowly.

"I do, I do remember when he ran away to live in a bar. It was like the adult version of when I ran away to live in my friend's tree house, but Jared lasted longer."

Lillian had made Jared an offer he felt he couldn't accept, and he'd thought that meant he should leave. Maybe he'd thought it meant he had to leave. She knew that Jared understood what a home was: he'd always known what hers meant to her. But he had never understood, perhaps, that "home" could be a word that applied to him, or describe something that could belong to him.

Martha didn't seem to be listening. Kami understood: sometimes people responded like that when Kami talked.

"It was raining the night he came," she said, and her voice was warm. "It was very late. The bar was shut up, and John and I were in our bed listening to the sound of the rain trying to take off the roof tiles. Then there was a hammering at the door. We knew the Lynburns were back, we knew that the sacrifices were being made again. We didn't—we grew up with it, grew up in the days of red and gold. People were talking about it a little. Not a lot, everybody has always been too scared to talk too much about the Lynburns, lest spies carry word back to them or the very leaves on the trees whisper news to them. The old stories say that the sorcerers see your reflection in their mirrors, that they can look at you through the knotholes in wood. Some were saying that things had always been this way, that it might be better. Some were as scared as we were, but they knew as well as we did there was nothing to be done against sorcery. I was scared. Maybe I was being silly, but the noise sounded to me like the summons for Judgment Day. I held on to John and I wanted to say, 'Don't you go down there.' But the Lynburns don't like to be kept waiting, and they can never be ignored. The only thing worse than the thought of John going down was the thought of waiting there cowering in bed, and having him not come back up. So we went down together."

If it hadn't been for Martha's tone, Kami would have thought that she was telling a story to frighten children. That was what the Lynburns had always been to Sorry-in-the-Vale, she supposed. Masters and monsters, as if one word meant the other.

"Young Jared was standing at the door and he was wet to the skin. He has a look about him sometimes, like a stray dog that has been kicked too many times and has gone all the way past snarling and biting until all it does is shiver, waiting for the next kick. They're almost patient about their misery, creatures like that, and they look at you with such eyes, beseeching you to make it all stop but not—not hoping that you will. It's like they know you won't, that the world isn't going to be kind to them. Do you know what I mean?"

"I know," said Kami.

"I'd heard people whispering about him, Rosalind Lynburn's son, that she'd gone mad out there in America and that he wasn't right either, that he might kill for sport and not sacrifice. I didn't believe it, exactly. I didn't know what to believe and what not to believe about those up there on the hill. I'd seen him on his bike, driving like a bat coming out of hell and about to hit a fence, and I'd seen him on the streets a few times. I'd thought he had funny eyes: they go right through you. I didn't like the look of him at first. But he came into my bar one night with his cousin and young Rusty, and he was a bit different from how I thought. Some boys ask for a drink, and honestly sometimes I give it to them, if they're boys I know won't get stupid with it.

Some boys don't dare ask. But he said 'I don't drink' in this straightforward kind of way, as if he'd thought about it and he wasn't going to do it when he grew up either. I've been in the business a long time. There was something about the way he said it that made me wonder about his dad: not Rob Lynburn, but that American Rosalind ran off with. He smiled at me and it looks odd, you know, with the scar. I didn't quite make it out at the time, whether he was trying to scare me or not, but later I thought he might be shy. And then there he was on a wild winter night."

Why hadn't he come to her, Kami thought: why had he preferred to throw himself on the mercy of strangers? She tried to swallow past the prickling knot in her throat, which felt as if she had swallowed a bit of holly bush. She tried to smile and look attentive as Martha continued her story.

"He asked if he could spend the night in one of the inn rooms. I was the one who stepped aside from the door. John thought I was mad for doing it. I don't know if I would've let another Lynburn in. If I had, it would've been only that I was scared not to. And I was scared, don't mistake me about that. I didn't sleep all the rest of that night for fear of what he might do to us while we slept. But it wasn't the only reason I let him in. Even if he was a Lynburn, he was a boy, and I couldn't leave that boy out in the winter cold. The next morning, he looked as tired as I was, as if he hadn't slept either, but he had it all thought out, that he would stay and earn his keep. We said yes because we didn't know what else to do, what he might do if we said no—but he did the work. He's a big brawny lad, and a good worker," said Martha, with an unmistakable note of pride in her voice, the words simple and casual as if she was talking about a favored nephew. "He always takes the time to help about the place, even now. He noticed right off that John has a bad back and he made sure he was on hand to do all the heavy lifting when boxes or casks needed hauling up from and down to the cellar. I kept waiting for him to do magic. I used to think about it at night and feel a choking in my throat, I'd think what a fool I was, that I knew what they were. And then I did see him do magic, and it wasn't so bad. He kept the other sorcerers from our door. Even after he went back to Aurimere, back to *her*—" and Kami understood then from Martha's tone of voice, something she hadn't known before, that Martha did not like Lillian. "He'd come down, make sure we were safe from them."

Kami thought of how Jared had lashed out when Rob's man Sergeant Kenn went after her, how he'd threatened to bury Kenn alive at her garden gate if he touched her again. She did not doubt that he would do everything in his power to keep safe whatever he cared for.

"But it wasn't like he was our guard dog," Martha said anxiously. "That wasn't how I thought of him, not at all. And it wasn't that he'd come down like the stories of old lady Lynburn's mother, with her charity basket on her arm and magic in her hands. He took care that he'd be here on the days when we bring boxes up from and down to the cellar. He'd do all the heavy lifting. He didn't forget."

Martha had not forgotten, either. She had taken him in not once but twice. She had harbored Lillian and Ash Lynburn, whom Kami knew she was frightened of, for months while Jared was immured in Aurimere and they had all believed him dead. She had arranged flowers at the bottom of his bed when he had a fever.

"He's a good lad," said Martha. "That's all. He does his best and I want to do my best to help."

Kami looked out at the narrow streets of her town, at the winds rippling through the woods, at Aurimere and its circle of fire against the sky. There was something burning in this woman, brighter than the red and gold. Jared had not forgotten, Martha had not, and Kami did not want to forget this reminder: there was hope for the town. There was something stronger than fear in the world.

By the time darkness was lapping up against their windows, the inn was full of light and noise. People who had not come at Lillian's battle cry would turn up for a party.

Kami tried not to blame them. She tried to be glad that they were there: that was what Kami and her friends had all wanted, to make it seem as if they accepted that Rob ruled now, that this was the new normal and they could all live with it. She saw that, in people's faces—saw they believed in Rob's promises and were willing to make Rob's bargain, or at least thought there was no other choice than to make Rob's bargain.

As if it didn't matter that Rob had asked for a spring sacrifice. As if they were going to do it, choose a death, or at least turn a blind eye like they had with Chris Fairchild. His wife and his little boy had not come to the party.

Dorothy the librarian was there, though, wearing a festive

red cardigan instead of her usual pink one. Amber Green was there, though her boyfriend, Ross, was not. Henry Thornton went shyly over and asked her to dance. One of Holly's brothers and her sister had shown up, tentative, as if they were not quite sure of their welcome, but Holly had gone over to talk to them and it looked like the talk was going well.

Dad was giving Lillian very firm instructions on how to ask after people's health, and ask how life was treating them, and how their jobs were going and their children were getting on.

"I fail to see the point of all these questions," Lillian told him in acid tones.

"These questions are going to show that you have basic consideration for others, Lilliput. Such a thing will come as a surprise to many, but with luck it will be a nice surprise."

"If I show consideration for others," Lillian Lynburn said grumpily, "will you tell me again about how you shot my husband?"

Jon rolled his eyes. "Yes, Leigh, if you manage to approximate human behavior for half an hour, I will tell you your favorite story again."

Lillian propped her chin on her hand, looked smug, and bestowed a smile on old Roger Stearn as he went past. He looked briefly dazzled, but that might have been his cataracts.

More and more people kept coming: Alan Hope, who had inherited the Hope farm now that his cousins were dead in Lillian's service, but who had not inherited any sorcerous powers. Terry Cholmondeley, who seemed to have brought two dates to the party and thus to be engaged in a complicated game that Kami could not imagine would end well. Some people had brought their kids. Alan Hope had brought his fiddle, and he struck up a tune. More people began to dance, whirling about or going slower. Roger Stearn took a gradual creaky turn with Dorothy across the floor.

Rusty looked at Kami, a laughing dark-eyed inquiry, and in response she started to dance. Rusty also began to dance, in a way.

Rusty was significantly more graceful than Kami but also could never resist a joke.

"It's cool that you've been practicing your self-defense, but I am trying to dance here?" Rusty said, ducking theatrically from one of Kami's enthusiastic gestures. Kami danced up on him and Rusty backed away in mock terror.

The people around them laughed. Kami waved and Rusty had to duck for real.

"Save your loving brother!" Rusty appealed to Angela, who was sitting on a bar stool and smirking at them.

"Take that insulting ruffian away," Kami ordered, giggling, and shoved him toward her.

Rusty led Angela out onto the dance floor: they danced beautifully for about ten minutes and then sat down and refused to get back up again for an hour.

It should have been fun.

Everybody was mad to pretend that life could be happy again, could be something close to what it had been before. Kami could understand the impulse to forget, even if she could not do it.

She felt Ash's infectious happiness before she saw him.

Ash loved to see people enjoying themselves around him. He was so conscientious, felt so responsible for the happiness of others.

His smile made her smile, before she even saw it.

"Hey, Kami. I was wondering if I could get a dance with the best-looking girl in the room."

"Sure," Kami said. "Go ask Angela. Take your life in your hands. I'll miss you and all, but I'm going to give her an alibi for the murder, because that's what best friends do."

Ash laughed and put his hand over hers, which was resting on the bar. He linked his fingers with hers and used his hold on her to tug her gently off the stool.

"You look great," he said.

She was wearing a black silk dress of Angela's, tailored to flow, because anything of Angela's that was tailored to cling would not fit. It did fit, though the silk clung to her short legs and strained slightly at her bust. She might even look simple and elegant. She hadn't seen anything wrong with her image in the mirror before the party, except that it was not an image she would ever have chosen. Kami knew Ash could feel how uncomfortable she was with how she looked. He was trying to make her feel better: it wasn't his fault that this was not the way to do it.

She could feel his concern for her, though, and the sincerity of the compliment. She let both course through her, as the music was coursing through the air, and she let him pull her all the way off the stool and into the middle of the floor.

Ash spun her into the center of the dancing couples, and moved smoothly to catch her when she stumbled. The glittering lights and the music became a whirl, like being wrapped in a bright gentle storm. When the dance was over, Kami was blinking the dazzle out of her eyes, briefly blind and laughing.

People were clapping, happy to see people enjoy themselves, with a certain amount of indulgence for the young people even if one of the young people was a Lynburn.

Jared was gone. He did not come back. When Kami asked Martha, she said she thought that he'd gone up to his room.

"—glad to see they've decided to accept things," Kami heard Alan Hope say as she shoved past him.

Kami was glad he was fooled, but she had not accepted anything. She did not even know how.

Kami told herself that she should definitely not go after Jared, even as she was climbing the stairs.

Jared was not in his room. Kami checked Lillian's room and Ash's, and she opened the door a chink and checked the spare guest bedroom where they had put Tomo and Ten. After the appropriate time of knocking, calling out a polite inquiry, and waiting, she checked all the bathrooms. She considered that evildoers might have kidnapped him, and then she noted the open window in his room.

Kami leaned as far forward out of the window as she could manage, squinting at the difference between the brilliant enclosed lights of the party downstairs and the wide, dark expanse of the sky outside.

"Hi, Jared," she said, leaning out of the window. "Are you brooding?"

He was leaning back on the roof, looking up at the sky,

at the gray clouds spiraling as if to make steps to climb up to the silver hook that was the moon. His hands were linked behind his head, his body one long lean line.

"No, I was about to strip off all my clothes, stand on the edge of the roof, and shout, 'I'm a golden god,'" Jared said. "That's the cool thing to do at parties; I saw it in a movie. Except I'm afraid that in this town, considering I'm a Lynburn and the worst family trait we have besides the constant murdering is our crushing arrogance, people would take it seriously." He paused. "Just kidding, I was brooding. Brooding's my favorite."

"I know the ambiance isn't as good as a starry night overlooking your shadowed town, but might you consider coming down and brooding on a bar stool?"

"What was I going to do in there? I can't dance."

Kami wanted to protest that she didn't care, but before she could open her mouth she told herself she was a fool. Jared had not said anything about dancing with her.

She recalled a couple of little digs Ash had made about Jared's table manners or being held back a year at school. She remembered Jared feeling self-conscious about it, though he would never have shown anyone what he felt. She wondered if he wished he could dance in the same way he wished he could do a lot of things Ash did so easily, with grace so perfectly trained it looked natural. There was Jared's aunt Lillian, and there was Martha Wright: they adored him and would be pleased if he took them for a turn around the room. They wouldn't care if he didn't dance as well as Ash, any more than Kami did.

She didn't think that he wanted to dance with a specific

other girl. Maybe one day he would, but not yet. At least that was something to hold on to, poor comfort though it was. She wasn't worried about him having a real girlfriend, one that he wanted, one that he'd asked. Not yet.

"Nobody expects you to be able to do everything Ash can do."

"I'm aware," said Jared.

She put her knee on the windowsill and hauled herself up and then out, walking on her knees for a moment. It wasn't graceful. Probably a tall, skinny girl could have slid from the window and onto the roof like Jared's dream come true, but Kami was focused on not showing her underwear in this dress.

She eventually scrambled to her feet and almost over-balanced because of the slope of the roof. Jared leaped up, but didn't catch her arm: he hovered around her while she steadied herself. He would've caught her if she'd fallen, she knew, but it was another reminder of the way he did not touch her unless he absolutely had to.

"You looked like you were having a good time in there," said Jared.

"Sure, I was," said Kami. "But I'd be having a better time if you were in there. We're—we're still friends, right?"

"Course," said Jared.

"And parties are a time for being with your friends," said Kami. "Not brooding alone up on a roof. That's basic party etiquette. Come on, it's not like I'm any good at dancing. You know this about me."

"You looked like you were doing fine."

He didn't say it with any rancor. It might've made Kami feel a little better if he had seemed at all jealous, but at the same time she appreciated that he wasn't trying to make her feel bad. He'd been the one who broke up with her. He had no right to make her feel lousy.

"All an illusion," Kami told him cheerfully. "Ash is able to mask my many failings."

She began to dance as an illustration of this fact. Jared ducked out of the way of one of her flailing hands, and she caught the edge of his little smile, in the light cast by the sliver of a moon.

Ash could smooth anything over, make anyone look good, but Kami liked to figure things out for herself. Encouraged by the smile, she caught hold of Jared's jacket and pulled him in a little closer to her. He started to dance with her, and promptly kicked her on the ankle.

"Sorry," said Jared. "Sorry, sorry—I'm really bad."

Kami tucked her smiling mouth, her silent laugh, into the collar of his T-shirt. "Me too."

Jared wasn't good. He was too awkward and she was too enthusiastic, and she kicked him in return, once lightly on purpose and then quite hard by accident. He let out a short shocked gasp and she hung onto his jacket and grinned up at him. Combined terrible dancing made them lurch, and Kami grabbed hold of Jared tight in panic that they were going to topple right off the roof. He let her stay there, tucked up against him, even when they had steadied themselves and started dancing again, in extremely poor rhythm to music almost too far away to hear. Hope flickered in her chest, a sweet small flame curling warm under her breastbone, and Kami thought, Maybe.

"Come on," Jared said against her hair. "We can't."

He said *We can't,* but Kami remembered what he had said before. She didn't have to be able to read his mind to know that he was saying it again.

I don't want to.

Kami came in from the cold, rubbing her hands. They felt numb. Jared walked in behind her, but he did not stay with her for long. He walked over to Martha Wright behind the bar, lifted a box of fresh glasses from over her head, and chased her off to dance with her husband. Martha hesitated about going, and Jared put his hand near hers, testing, waiting in case she flinched, braced to yank himself away. But Martha didn't flinch, of course. She tipped her head back, her white hair limned with light so it looked butter-yellow, and said something to Jared Kami didn't catch. Kami did catch the fond note in her voice, and Jared caught Martha's hand and twirled her, a little awkwardly and looking self-conscious about doing so, until she was out from behind the bar.

Martha beamed at him. She was still smiling as she danced with her husband. Kami's dad was making the rounds with Lillian, whisking her away before she could say anything too awful, and people were actually relaxing enough to talk to her. People were chatting with Lillian Lynburn. Kami's dad was a miracle worker.

It was all going so well. Kami felt tired.

She excused herself and went into the parlor, where she expected to find some much-wanted solitude.

Instead she saw Ash, sitting in the deep armchair with his head bowed over the book in his lap. He looked lost in thought.

I wanted to be alone, said Ash.

She was surprised: Ash had always seemed to her like exactly the kind of person who never wanted to be alone, but she could feel how much he meant it. He felt sad, in a heavy way that company could not soothe or pierce. He felt like she did.

"I can go," Kami offered.

No, said Ash. *Stay.*

Kami supposed they could be alone together. She went and leaned against the window, opened a book and leafed through it, though she felt impatient with reading history books now she'd learned Elinor's secret. She had already done the research and wanted to get to the action. Kami wanted to be done feeling helpless and not able to do anything she wanted to do.

The fierce restlessness of Ash's thoughts was infecting hers. Investigating his feelings seemed like putting a hand between the cage bars a tiger was prowling behind.

Kami could hear the sound of the party going on, through the little corridor, through two doors. Eventually the noise died down, the creak of the heavy inn door swinging back and forth becoming the most frequent sound, but the party winding down did nothing to ease the cold knot under her breastbone. Kami shut her book and leaned her head back against the window with a small sigh. She felt the hair at the back of her head stick to the condensation on the glass and stared up at the low, wooden-beamed ceiling for a long moment.

There was a sudden touch at her wrist and Kami dropped

the book in her hand. It thumped against the wooden floor and the sound echoed. Ash was standing in front of her, his blue eyes darkened with the feeling she had sensed in him before, the feeling she had shared.

His hand was circling both her wrists. He closed his fingers, bringing her wrists together and over her head in one smooth movement. It brought her body forward, brought it against his. She felt the cool slick glass against the back of her hands at the same time as she felt the warmth of his mouth close over hers. He set his free hand on her hip, and she felt the heat and greed of his fingers sliding over the loose silk of Angela's black dress. He was pressing her hips against the glass and making her back arch away from it, while his warm lips searched hers.

She was wearing someone else's clothes, feeling someone else's feelings. She could feel his rapt intentness, so focused on her that it felt as if it was piercing through her, but the piercing was sweet. She turned her face up, kissing him back as he was kissing her, feeling his fingers clench around her wrists and in the material of the dress. She did not want to feel the way she was feeling any longer, and she did not have to—she could feel other emotions sweeping through her like fire, destroying everything that was hers.

"Kami," Ash whispered against her mouth, "don't you know that I love you? I love you. I'm so in love with you."

Kami's eyes snapped open.

"What?" she whispered. Ash kissed her again, and she turned her face away, tested his grip on her wrists. He didn't let her go. She felt his harsh breath against her cheek, felt his hot mouth catch the edge of hers, and she almost turned back, surrendered to the scorching rush of urgency and lack of all thought.

Almost. Not quite.

A lightbulb, set in an old-fashioned iron sconce in the wall, flickered as if it was a candle's flame, wavering and almost going out. Kami thought for a moment that it was Ash doing it. Then she remembered that she was the only person in the room who could do magic.

"Stop," said Kami, and pulled away decisively.

She infused extra strength into her muscles with magic, but she didn't have to use it. Ash let her go when he registered she was really trying. She felt the echo of his dismay as he realized she was serious, that she was bent on getting away, felt the desolate soreness of rejection. She knew how that felt.

"I'm sorry," she said instantly, and caught at his hands, wanting to comfort him and wipe away all the pain churning inside them both. If she could make him feel better, she would feel better herself.

She retreated but he followed her, keeping the hold on her hands she had given him. She sank down into the chair that he had vacated, his book—*Melmoth the Wanderer,* Kami noticed, and did not know why she was noticing except that everything seemed so strange and fragmented, and it did not seem like Ash's type of book—was shut and placed on the arm. Kami almost knocked it off.

She thought Ash, leaning down with her hands still in his, was going to sit at her feet, that his lips were parted so he could speak to her. But instead his lips pressed against hers, desperate and imploring. He let go of her hands to cup the back of her head, and for an instant Kami let her mouth open against his, let sparks of heat and pleasure travel from him to her.

Everything was tangled up and confused. She didn't want to say yes just to please him. It wasn't the same as pleasing herself, even if it felt like it was. She pushed him back, just a little.

"I'm going to have to repeat myself," said Kami. "Stop. What—what did you say?"

"I love you."

"Ash," said Kami. "Please don't be hurt or take this the wrong way—but have you gone completely off your head?"

Ash blinked. At least he had stopped trying to kiss her. Kami supposed it was a highly inappropriate thing to say to a gorgeous guy professing eternal devotion. She should probably either be professing it back or rejecting him with passionate tears at seeing a good man's heart wasted on such an unworthy creature as herself, who could not give hers in return.

"Sorry," she said, and squeezed Ash's hands. "I don't mean to be flippant. I'm just so surprised. You love me?"

Ash squeezed her hands back, and did not release them. "Yes."

"Uh," said Kami. "Since when?"

"Uh," said Ash, helpless in his turn. "I don't—it isn't something I made a note of on my calendar. I didn't plan on falling in love with you. I didn't even realize I had until I was already gone."

"Do you think," Kami said, and paused. "Do you think it might be about the link? That can create feelings, or intensify them, in this particular way, but that doesn't mean you truly do feel this way. Once the link is broken, you might feel entirely differently."

She thought about Rob Lynburn, of all people, telling her, *The emotions that come with the connection are not real. Not entirely real. How could they be? A connection like this would make anyone feel close to anyone.*

She had a lot of reasons to doubt Rob, but nothing she had ever learned about the link had made her doubt what he had said.

"No!" said Ash. "I don't think the link is romantic at all. I didn't feel that way about you when we were first linked. When we were first linked, I thought I'd never be able to feel anything for you romantically, ever again, but, Kami, I was so wrong. I've never felt like this about anyone in my whole life. I didn't know I could feel this way about anyone. I think about you all the time, it doesn't stop, it's relentless, it's like being invaded by the thought of you. It—it hurts. If you could just try to feel the same way about me, I would do anything to please you. I'd do anything to make your feelings for me grow."

"It's not that I don't have feelings for you," Kami said. "Of course I do. But it's a bad idea."

She was shocked by how tempted she was. She'd thought she'd been tempted by Ash before, allured by the way he liked her, how normal and safe and painless a relationship with him might be comparatively. But that had been a bloodless sort of feeling compared to this, to the pounding in his veins that she could feel echoed in hers, to the certainty of being so desired.

"I can read your thoughts," Ash said eagerly. "I can see that you like me. I can see that you want to—"

She turned her face away. Her own doubts and desires were betraying her, and she was mad at them.

"It's not fair to bring my thoughts into this," Kami told him. "It's not about what I think. It's about what I choose."

"I wouldn't ask for anything that you do not have to give," said Ash. "The link means that we understand each other. I could be patient, I'd be so happy to wait. I can value you, as nobody else in the world seems to. You don't know how terrible I feel, all the time: it's like I have a hungry wolf living inside me, clawing at me. If you could just try, all this restless longing in me could be quiet. I could have some peace. You are the only person in the world who can bring me peace. Doesn't that mean anything?"

"You can read my thoughts," Kami said miserably. "You can see why it wouldn't work."

"That's right, I can read your thoughts. I can see how much you need this. You need it as much as I do."

Had she done it? Kami wondered suddenly. Had her desperate, pathetic longing to be wanted traveled to Ash through the link, and convinced him that he did want her? She might have. She couldn't be sure of anything.

She put her face in her hands, and would not look into his beautiful pleading face, into his eyes that offered her almost everything that she wanted.

"Come on, Ash," Kami said. "Don't make me say it. Don't. You know why I can't. You know."

PART V
SORROW AND SACRIFICE

Childhood is the kingdom where nobody dies.
—*Edna St. Vincent Millay*

Chapter Sixteen
Nowhere Safe

Kami left the parlor with her party mood even more ruined than when she had entered it. Ash followed her, silent and somber, and she dreaded a painful and awkward scene in the next room.

She was not prepared, however, for what she found.

The lights were dimmed, the party over, the floor scattered with festive debris. Jared was clearing the bar, his golden head bowed in the dim light, and Amber Green was sitting on a bar stool.

"Well," said Amber, raising her eyebrows. "Pretty clear what you two were up to."

"So what?" Jared asked abruptly.

He looked up from the bar for a moment, eyes pale in the dark light. His face was shadowed and set, but he didn't look unhappy.

"Did you know all along?" Ash asked, his voice sharp with indignation. He took a step forward and stopped when Jared turned his shining, strange gaze on him.

"I knew," Jared said very softly. "So what?"

"That's right," Kami snapped, glaring at Amber. "He dumped me. I'm a free agent. And you're an evil sorceress who participates in murder and torture, so your commentary on my social life is not appreciated or necessary."

This was awkwardness and pain on a level she had not anticipated. Kami felt like if there was a higher power looking down on her from above, that higher power was sniggering wildly.

"Fine," said Amber. "If you don't want my help, I don't have to give it."

"I want your help," said Kami. "Yes, please, thank you, help us. Have I done enough buttering up the informant, will you give us some information now?"

Amber sighed. "I came here to warn you." She twisted her hands in her lap. "It's messed up, that's all. It's so messed up."

Kami was alarmed to see that Amber was trembling. She was even more alarmed to see Amber was edging toward the door. She was sure Rusty did better at buttering up informants than this. She wished that either Rusty or Angela was here, but of course they had both gone home early to rest and recover from the exertion of their ten-minute dance.

She should have asked them to stay. Either one of them, or Holly, would have stayed with her all night, if she had only asked.

They were gone. It was up to Kami.

"What's messed up?" Kami asked, and tried to keep her voice gentle.

"Just look out for them," Amber said, and made a grab for the door handle. "He's coming."

She was out the door before any of them could stop her. Kami looked wildly around at Jared and Ash, and then dashed headlong out the door and into the street after Amber.

"Are you kidding, did you really just give me a cryptic warning?" Kami demanded. "I hate cryptic warnings! You know where they lead, it's nothing but confusion until the disaster the cryptic warning was about comes to pass and then you think, 'Oh, so *that* was what the cryptic warning meant, well gee, I wish it had been more clear.' Stop right now and explain yourself!"

Amber turned and said, "I'm sorry," even as she disappeared, becoming transparent so that the twinkling lights of the town and the darkness of the night bled through her body, turning her into a shadow and a sigh.

"Amber said that Rob Lynburn is after us?" was Angela's verdict. "I hope she also wowed you with some radical statements about water being wet and oranges being orange-colored."

They had all got together in the parlor the day after the party to discuss Amber's warning. Kami was thinking of rechristening the parlor as "the council room" or possibly as "the chamber of justice."

"It's clear what the girl meant," said Lillian. "She meant a specific 'them.' She meant my boys. Of course Rob wants to lure my boys onto his side. They have to be protected—they can't do magic and are utterly helpless and vulnerable."

"That's so true," said Jared, folding his arms so the sleeves of his T-shirt strained and fluttering his eyelashes. "Please save me, Aunt Lillian."

"I realize you are making another effort to be humorous," said Lillian, patting his arm, "and I wish you would stop. But of course I will save you."

"It's probably me and Angela," said Rusty, sounding

distinctly worried for Angela but managing to grin. "Since Amber likes me. I'm not sure why. It's either my sterling worth of character or the fact I am super handsome, but which?"

Kami didn't know what she thought, but she knew how she felt: cold, as if the shadow of the coming disaster had already fallen on her. She looked over at the sound of the door opening and saw Ten slipping out with a book tucked under his skinny arm.

She started to get up, but Henry Thornton touched her shoulder lightly. Kami looked up into his thin, kind face.

"You should stay. I'll go after him. I never have much to say at these talks, and I wouldn't mind a quiet read somewhere."

"It's not like *I* have much to say at this talk," Kami murmured.

"I did notice that," said Henry. "It's very unlike you. Are you sure you feel quite all right?"

She saw the twinkle in his eyes behind his glasses and beamed at him in a sudden surge of fondness. He smiled back and left the room unnoticed by everyone else as Rusty was talking.

"Not that I'm not all torn up inside with worry about Sulky and Blondie," said Rusty, "but isn't it all the same thing in the end? If Rob Lynburn comes after them, he comes after us. If he comes after us, he comes after them. If he takes a break from evil to catch up on his TV shows, we'll all be relieved but nobody is expecting it. The plan is still to lay low, be ready for him to act, and wait until the spring equinox."

Tomo ambled off upstairs, heading either for an escape

from the tedium of adult conversation or for a bathroom. Kami found herself not wanting to let both her brothers out of her sight, and went up the stairs after him. "Hey, kiddo. Stick around."

"Will you play a game with me?" asked Tomo, who was a shrewd bargainer. He rattled the contents of his pocket. Kami realized the brat had come prepared with one of those little magnetic travel-sized board games, which Kami personally believed were of the devil.

"Fine."

She was about to sit down on the floor and submit to another round of Tomo's vicious Monopoly playing or his Scrabble playing full of wanton lies and made-up words, when Lillian Lynburn's voice made her turn her head.

Lillian was climbing the staircase. "I wished to have a word with you."

Kami turned to Tomo. "Set the game up," she said. "Give me a minute."

Lillian reached the top of the stairs and stood there looking mildly uncomfortable. "We are the two women in this town with the greatest power," Lillian said, formally but with a nod to her, and Kami realized this was Lillian trying to be nice. "That means it is our duty to stand ready and to protect the others. I want to give you something."

She took Kami's wrist and turned it so that her hand lay palm up. In it she placed a curved shell. Kami felt the ridges of the shell's surface against her skin and glimpsed the pearlescent curling cave within.

"You can hear the sound of the sea in these shells," said Lillian. "So you can hear the sound of a sorcerer's voice. If I need you, I can call to you through the shell. If you need me, do the same."

"Okay," Kami said slowly. "Thanks very much for this artifact of wondrous magic. I have a small suggestion, though. I'd like you to give me what my people call a 'phone number.' And I will give you mine in exchange. You can also have my dad's and Angela's and Rusty's."

"I do not want anybody's phone number," said Lillian, flushing slightly.

She turned and went back downstairs, toward the sound of Dad's and Martha Wright's voices. Kami slipped the shell in her pocket.

"That lady is a weirdo," Tomo observed.

"You're an astute judge of character, Tomo," said Kami. "Okay, get ready, because I'm coming for your snakes and your ladders."

She knelt down on the floor, about to lie down on her stomach and commence the game, when she heard the front door open below. The Wrights ran an inn and customers were always going in and out, the door constantly swinging open and closed. If it wasn't for her current state of hyper-vigilance, she would never have noticed that the creak of the hinges was softer than usual, as if someone was trying to be stealthy.

Kami looked across the colorful little square of the board game and into her brother's small face. She put a finger to her lips. Tomo wasn't dumb. He gazed back at her, eyes liquid and steady, and nodded. Kami raised herself from a kneel to a crouch and grabbed Tomo by the shoulders. The pieces of the game scattered across the floorboards as Kami pulled him quietly into Jared's room.

She heard Lillian's scream of rage from below, like an outraged pterodactyl. She couldn't pay any attention to that, not when she had her little brother with her. She opened Jared's window and pushed Tomo out of the windowsill and onto the roof. She scrambled out behind him, closing the window as well as she could, and followed him.

The roof seemed different in daytime. She did not feel above the town, but in the midst of it. The rooftops seemed like streets, both familiar and strange, their golden slopes like hills and their weathervanes like street signs. But Kami did not start jumping from rooftop to rooftop. She made for the big brick chimney at the side of the roof, and sat there, as hidden as she could be. She drew Tomo's small sturdy body into the curve of her own and felt him tremble against her.

She reached out, as she always did in times like this, for Jared. She'd been without him long enough to know what to do now when she found nothing instead of support, like leaping for a missing step and feeling her stomach plummet before the rest of her fell. She just had to grab onto something—she just had to act as if the courage was still there.

The window scraped open. Kami tensed and clung to Tomo with one hand, feeling the hammer of his heart against her chest, listening to the sound of shoes scraping on the roof tiles, coming around the chimney and toward her and her brother. She freed her other hand.

"Just give us one of them," said Sergeant Kenn, and reached out for her.

A blast of wind knocked him off his feet and off the roof. Kami heard him hit the cobbled street below and the long low groan that told her he was still alive. She stayed curled up on the roof tiles, clutching her little brother tightly, waiting for Sergeant Kenn to come back or one of the other sorcerers.

She was actually grateful to Amber Green for her annoying, unclear warning, for frightening Kami enough that she had watched her family. If it hadn't been for that warning, Kami would not have been on high alert—they would have been caught off guard.

She could not believe she had not realized it before. Of course Rob Lynburn wanted a source to sacrifice—he wanted the most power and the most revenge he could get. He didn't want Kami, because killing Kami meant killing Ash. What he wanted was worse.

Rob Lynburn wanted her brothers.

He had asked the town for a sacrifice, and Kami had assumed that meant the sacrifice would at least be someone grown up. If she had ever dreamed of something as evil as this, she would have thought the town would rise up against Rob.

But maybe it wouldn't. Maybe nobody in town cared, so long as it was not them, so long as their own families were spared.

Kami held on to Tomo and felt him crying, his hot tears slipping down her neck. He did not make a sound.

Sergeant Kenn did not come back. No other sorcerers came, and Kami felt Ash pushing reassurance at her, telling her it was safe to come out. She and Tomo left the shelter of the chimney, and Ash put his head out the window.

"Is Ten all right?" Kami demanded.

"I don't know. I haven't seen him. Jared went after Henry," said Ash. "He said he thought they'd gone into the woods."

"We'll go after them," Kami said with resolution.

It was a comfort to have a next step, even though everything ahead was darkness. They could go into the woods, but Rob's people had come to find them here at the Water Rising, and they would be bound to search for them at Claire's, and at Rusty and Angela's. She did not know where they could possibly go next. Nowhere would be safe.

Jared ran into the woods with a wild wind chasing him. A flurry of wet leaves slapped him in the face. He only realized that sharp twigs had left scratches on his skin when he felt them stinging as he ran on.

Rob had made enough sacrifices, and now the wood was waking for him, as it had woken once for Jared and Kami. The world was being shaped by Rob's thoughts, according to his design.

Jared was not afraid the wood would hurt him, not one of Rob's sons. Rob had had many chances to kill him, and was welcome to try. Ten was a different matter.

He ran up the sloping ground toward the quarry, the place where he remembered Kami playing when she was a kid, and hoped that Ten might have felt drawn there.

The air smelled of damp earth and crushed greenery, with a faint bitter edge as of faraway smoke. Roots kept catching at his boots, like malicious imps trying to trip him. He saw the glint of golden stone among the trees and heard the splashing of the Sorrier River. His footing on the slope was suddenly snatched away from him, mud sliding and dry grains of earth crumbling away like old cake. He ended up flat on his back, winded and staring at green leaves pinwheeling against a blue sky, and a hoarse scream echoing in his ears.

He scrambled up, snatched a fallen branch off the ground, and launched himself back up the slope, refusing to let the woods stop him any more than he would've let Rob himself stop him.

When he reached the clearing, Jared paused and his breath shuddered hard out of his chest. It was a half circle surrounded by trees, like a horseshoe, with one side broken by the side of the quarry.

Ross Phillips, Amber's boyfriend, was standing in the long grass above the quarry. He was holding on to Ten's arm, though Ten was struggling like a trapped wild animal. Henry Thornton lay in the middle of the clearing. His face was black, as if he had been strangled. His glasses had been knocked off and his eyes were open, staring blindly up at the clear blue sky.

Jared wrenched his eyes away from Henry and toward Ten. Jared had saved him once. It had seemed worth dying for to save him then—and now.

"You don't have to do this, Jared," said Ross.

Jared didn't look at him. He kept advancing, eyes still on Ten's small tear-wet face. "Yes, I do."

"You think this is brave?" Ross snapped. "It's just stupid. You're my leader's son. I don't want to hurt you, but I can. You can't do a thing to stop me. *You don't have any magic*!"

Jared came closer. Ross hesitated, either too frightened to hurt his boss's son or too sure that someone with no magic must be no threat. It didn't much matter to Jared, because it let Jared get just close enough. He didn't lift the branch to hit Ross; instead, he kept it low and scythed Ross's legs out from under him, the way Rusty had taught him to unbalance someone.

Ross toppled back into the quarry and Jared lunged, snatching Ten out of Ross's hands and hurling him to safety. Jared was only just able to catch himself from falling into the quarry after Ross by grabbing hold of a tree. He stood on the very lip of the stone, and looked down at Ross, who lay pale and stunned on the stone.

Jared was pretty sure Ross had broken bones. He grinned down at him.

"Abracadabra, moron."

Ross rolled painfully onto his front with a grunt and a stifled cry of pain, and then disappeared the way Kami had said Amber had disappeared—there one moment and nothing but dissolving shadow the next.

Jared looked over at Ten. "Are you all right?"

Ten was sitting at the base of a tree, curled up in the roots as if he was a fox cub seeking shelter. His arms were locked tight around his legs, and he was shaking. He stared back at Jared, and Jared got the impression that Ten would have looked at anything, just so that he could avoid looking at Henry.

"I hate sorcerers," he said. "I hate them."

The woods were quiet as evening fell and they buried Henry Thornton. Lillian chose the spot, a birch tree pale as a gravestone, and they laid him among the roots and earth and covered him over.

"The woods will always take us back again," Lillian murmured, and laid her hand on the smooth bark of the trunk.

Kami looked at the heap of turned earth at the base of the tree. She could not escape the feeling that this was all her fault. She had been the one who asked Henry to come from his safe home in London, to help them for no other reason than that it was the right thing to do. He had died for her brother. He had been so kind to her always.

And Kami could not mourn him as he deserved, because she was so overcome with fear for her brothers.

Angela touched her wrist.

"We can go to my house, if you want."

"They'll look for us there," said Rusty.

Ten was clinging to Dad, and Tomo to Ten, but Tomo was also holding on to Rusty's jeans, so Dad and Rusty were bookending the boys, keeping them safe. It was clear to Kami how desperate the situation was if Tomo wanted to be with Rusty, who had babysat and shared naps with him a thousand times, rather than Ash, his shiny new favorite. It was even more clear because Rusty's expression, for once, was somber. This was the first thing Rusty had said since they found Henry.

"I have an idea," Holly volunteered. "We could go to my house. My sister Mary said none of my family are living there now. And Rob thinks of them as on his side."

There seemed nothing else to do. They could not live in the quarry. The boys were already cold and tired.

As they began the long walk to the farmhouse, the night drew in closer, like an old woman drawing a black cloak tight against the cold. With the night came reminders of Rob Lynburn's power, the woods waking at his touch and looking at them with dark eyes.

Kami watched the silent silvery shapes of Rob's wolves when they appeared: saw the leaves of the trees cluster above them, blocking out the light of the moon. There were small dark faces surmounted by blood-red caps, peeping out at them from behind boughs. She was certain she was not imagining it. She and Jared had woken the woods once, and she had not been able to see through the eyes of any of the creatures who had stirred from her mind into life: she did not think Rob could use the wood as his spies. But it was bad enough to be reminded that this town was Rob Lynburn's little world now.

Turning her head at a sudden light, she thought for a moment that it was the moon, but it was not. It was a light warmer and closer than that.

The others turned toward the surrounding woods, and Kami saw brief flashes of light reflected on their faces. Racing among the trees, fewer than the wolves but faster, were lithe bright shapes glowing like campfires, their sharp noses held up to the hidden moon.

"*Kitsunebi,*" Ten whispered.

"Fox fire," Tomo translated helpfully, with a look at Ash as if he wanted him to be impressed.

Did we do that? Ash asked her in the privacy of their minds, and she felt his wonder travel to her, his awed happiness that they had been able to accomplish such a thing together.

"I remember these," said Angela. "Kami's Sobo told us a story about them once, and Kami was obsessed with painting foxes with luminescent paint for months."

They still had a Hiroshige print that showed golden glowing foxes assembled at the base of a tree. Foxes were a symbol of bad luck, sometimes, and sometimes good. Kami had liked how they were mysterious. She wished she could take them as a sign of good luck now, but they hadn't had much good luck lately.

"Was that what painting Mrs. Singh's cat blue was all about?" Dad asked.

"Obviously," said Kami. "It was a celebration of my cultural heritage and everyone was extremely and unnecessarily harsh about it."

She walked on, her path illuminated by strange lights.

Henry was dead, and the woods belonged to Rob Lynburn. But Kami found the gentle candlelight flicker of the foxes woke a flicker of hope in her own heart. The woods might belong to Rob Lynburn, but they were not wholly his. He thought he had all the power, and he was wrong.

Rob Lynburn might want her brothers, but he was not going to have them.

If only she could think of how to save them.

Chapter Seventeen
Remember You're My Sweetheart

It was dark in Holly's house, with spoiled food in the fridge and the kind of heavy cold that settled in after too long without the heating. Even after they turned the lights on and huddled together on the stone flagstones of the kitchen, they were somehow colder than they had been outside. It was clear nobody had been home in weeks. Holly's whole family was living in Aurimere.

"It's not much," said Holly.

"It's so great," said Kami. "Thank you so much."

She meant it. Having a refuge of any sort was a huge relief. But Kami could not help hugging herself against the cold when Holly went out, intent on checking on the animals. This remote farmhouse seemed like the last bolt-hole for their little band of soldiers. Rob Lynburn was not going to stop, when it was a couple of days before the spring equinox and Rob had decided who his sacrifice was going to be. Rob might well think to look for them here, but Kami could not think of where else to go.

She did not know who else in town might have agreed that Kami's brothers should be the sacrifice.

Jared, apparently brainwashed by his time working in an inn, had insisted that he would make up all the beds. Ash and Lillian had been sent out into the woods to take the first watch, and Kami's dad was putting the boys to bed in one room for security.

Kami gave up standing alone in the kitchen worrying and waiting and went to find Angela and Rusty in the small sitting room down the hall. Angela was curled up against Rusty's chest, sleeping on the sofa like a cat who had found a lap and needed nothing more in the world. Rusty was rubbing her back, rocking her a little in the circle of his arm, as if she was a child. Kami recognized the old ingrained habits of love, thought it was for his own comfort as much as hers.

She was comforted, just being with them.

"Hey," she said softly. She crossed the carpeted floor, which had been blue but had white tracks worn on it, and looked out the window.

She could feel Ash's anxious thoughts as he patrolled the woods with his mother, but he seemed very far away. Across the fields and woods, an ocean of indistinguishable darkness in the night, the faint lights of Sorry-in-the-Vale seemed far away too.

"Tell me," said Rusty, and Kami glanced around to see him extricating himself gently from Angela. He laid a blanket gently over his sister, and his voice was gentle too. "If the Lynburns had never come to town at all, if none of this magic war had ever happened, do you think you and I could have made it work?"

Kami hesitated. "Do you mean romantically?"

"No, I meant as a pair of professional race car drivers," Rusty said. "Or ballroom dancers."

Kami had thought this was settled. Well, she'd thought that she had brushed the matter off with a joke, and he had let her do it, and she wished that happy state of affairs could have continued.

"So romantically, then," she said.

Rusty seldom acted, seldom wanted to. Kami did not know how to do anything but act, to be consumed by an ambition for action. Her whole life was dreaming of acting and then doing it. She did not want to hurt him, but she did not see any world in which they would not have driven each other past the point of frustration.

"There was always Jared," she said. "Before he ever came, before I ever met him. I don't know what I would be without him. It's like wondering who I would be if I grew up in a totally different place, or if I'd had a different grandmother, but it's more than that. Every thought I ever had, for years, I shared with him, and they were different from the thoughts I would have had on my own. He shaped the way I think, and the way I think is who I am. Maybe you wouldn't have liked me if I was someone else."

She'd lost her first best friend when she was twelve because of her strange imaginary friend, and that had made Kami reach out to the new girl in town. She didn't know if she would have tried so hard to befriend someone as aggressively unfriendly as twelve-year-old Angela if she'd had other company. She could have missed out on so much.

"I like you pretty okay as you are," Rusty conceded. "I

remember when you were just Angie's friend who I vaguely thought might be high on cough syrup all the time. But then I saw how you were with Angela, and what you meant to her. I saw your home, the warmth of it, how different it was from mine, how much I wanted a home like that for Angela. I loved you, and the thought of all that came with you. I wanted to make that love mean something. For the first time in my life, I wanted to do something, and I wanted what I did to matter. I wanted to take what I felt for you and build something beautiful."

Kami glanced nervously up at his face.

"That's, um, that means a lot to me, but you have to know I'm not looking to settle down and build a home with anyone until my mid-thirties, if ever, because I am going to be pursuing my career as a hard-hitting reporter."

Rusty smacked her lightly on the top of her head. "You were a beautiful dream to me, you brat; please cease inserting your unpleasant and hurtful reality into my dream. It was the kind of dream that's not supposed to come true. It was the kind of dream that does something else. It taught me who I wanted to be."

It was so different from what she had expected to hear that it surprised a laugh out of Kami. She laughed, and was so tired she swayed, and Rusty caught her. They wrapped their arms around each other and held on.

"Thank you," said Kami.

"No, thank you, Cambridge," Rusty murmured. "But, sweetheart—and I say this with love—I really think it might be time to get off the cough syrup."

"This cruelty about my addiction is why I won't drive race cars around England with you," Kami murmured back.

She felt him rocking her, in that infinitesimal way he'd rocked Angela, felt his hands stroking her hair.

"Promise me you and Angela will stick together, okay?"

Kami peeped over Rusty's shoulder at Angela, curled up with her high-heeled boots under her and her hair spread out like a black silk fan on the cushions.

Rob might want to sacrifice a source, but it was clear his main motivation was to punish Kami. He could try to take any one of them. Angela didn't have magic to defend herself. Rusty didn't either, of course, but naturally Angela was the one he was worried about. He knew how focused they all had to be on protecting her brothers. But he also wanted to keep what was his safe.

Kami understood how he must feel.

"She's like my sister," she promised Rusty. "Nothing will hurt her. Nobody will part us."

"That's good," Rusty said. His arms were warm and strong. "That's all I wanted. No matter what happens, you two are always my girls."

Kami laughed. "We're always going to be your girls."

Rusty did not laugh with her, which surprised Kami since Rusty always laughed with her. Instead he spoke, and his voice was steady and kind. He sounded sure.

"Then this will have been enough," he said. "Enough and more than enough. I'll always be grateful."

Kami rested her cheek against his chest. She knew why he was talking like this: just in case they never had another chance to talk. They all knew that death was waiting for them: that it could be so near. All they could do was take this brief moment to be warm.

Jared was able to feel how Ash felt as he and Aunt Lillian walked through the woods together, his worry coursing through Jared's body like chills before a cold set in. He knew Aunt Lillian and Ash were as safe from Rob's wrath as anyone in Sorry-in-the-Vale could be. But they were his family. He was relieved when it was his and Rusty's turn to serve as guards, and went out into the night gladly.

The forest at night was a dark glittering thing, wrapped around them. The air had a heavier quality, as if the leaves lent it weight. Light refracted in the corners of Jared's vision. He glimpsed cool glints of moonshine on water, like the light touching diamonds on a woman's fingers.

He saw one light he recognized for certain: the glow of one of Kami's foxes. He was angry, and nerved for an attack, but that didn't mean he felt bad. Adrenaline was thrumming through him. He had a purpose, he was in his woods, and they were influenced by her thoughts.

He glanced over at Rusty, who was being unusually quiet. He was not looking out at the night, but leaning up against a tree. His head was bowed. Jared was worried for a moment, but then Rusty looked up, met his eyes, and grinned, the shards of moonlight filtered through the leaves waking green in his hazel eyes. Jared had always been a little jealous of how he looked. Rusty's face was not a façade like Ash's: it was just the face of someone good, someone with no malice in his soul or in his past. Rusty's face was open and easily good-humored, as it had ever been, and Jared had to repress the urge to sneer, the impulse to lash out at what he could never be. Rusty didn't deserve that.

"What's up, sulky bear?"

"I was appreciating the beauty of nature," Jared said. "In a sulky way."

"You might have noticed me giving you odd looks occasionally in the past."

"I assumed you were thinking, 'Three fairies clearly attended that guy's christening, and all three gave him the gift of chiseled,'" said Jared. "Why, were you thinking something else?"

"When I first met you, I thought you were a creep with serious behavioral and emotional issues."

"But once you really got to know me," Jared suggested, "you realized I was a creep with behavioral and emotional issues that were quite funny?"

"And then you made Kami unhappy, so I was too mad at you to process any of the magical stuff that might be a reason for some of your extreme weirdness and some of hers."

"Hey!" Jared snapped.

"I say 'extreme weirdness' with love," said Rusty. "Kami said that for years that every thought she had was shared with you, shaped by you, and every thought was different because of you."

Jared looked away into the woods, the moon caught in a cage of branches. One long black thorn cut across it, seeming to pierce its heart.

Rusty kept talking. "I figured she thought something like that, before she said it. Once I was less mad, I watched you to see if you were more like her than I'd thought. She thinks a lot more of you than you deserve."

"I know."

Jared was not surprised by Rusty's conclusion. There was brightness to her, and it had been shed on him. He still remembered its warmth and the clarity it had lent to the world. But there had always been too much darkness in him. He could not give light of his own. Jared knew that to be like her was nothing he could hope for.

"You're alike in some ways," said Rusty, as if he had no idea what a ridiculous and amazing compliment he was bestowing. "Even though it's hard to see at first. The same things matter to you, and you're both always acting. I don't understand it, myself. I suppose some were born acting, some achieve action, and some have action thrust upon while they wail feebly 'Dear God, no, let me sleep in.' I'm only acting once, and then never again."

"You don't have to act at all. It's the Lynburns' fault all this is happening. It's our place to act," said Jared. "Not that I'm saying you can't handle yourself. Clearly, you can. You kicked my ass once and I'm sure you could do it again."

"Anytime, day or night," said Rusty. "Call me."

"But you don't have magic," said Jared. "Once Kami, Ash, and I do the ceremony, we should all have magic again. We should have enough magic to protect you all. This is our responsibility."

They would have so much power for a little while, until they died. He could not bear to think of it. Even less could he bear to think of living on without them.

"That's if we can get to the spring equinox," said Rusty, and his voice was uncharacteristically serious. "They'd be fools to let us. That's why we're out here, isn't it? Because they are going to come after the kids."

"It's only one more night," said Jared. "They might not know about Elinor Lynburn's Crying Pools ceremony for three."

"We can't count on evil to be stupid, which is a sad disappointment to me because I was hoping that Rob Lynburn would helpfully install a big red self-destruct button in Aurimere. They don't have to know our plan. They only need to know their own. They need a death."

They needed a death, and they wanted one of Kami's brothers. Jared remembered feeling Kami's love for them, had felt it himself in a strange secondhand fashion. He'd sometimes been sorry that he knew what it felt like, having a real family.

"They're not getting one," Jared said sharply.

"Kami's brothers," Rusty said, his voice slow and unaffected by Jared's sharpness. "What would you do for them? Would you do anything to save them, if you could?"

Jared would have thought that was obvious. From the way Rusty was looking at him, careful, a little wary, as if he was testing him, he supposed it was not. He figured that it was reasonable enough for Rusty to doubt him.

"Anyone who is Kami's is mine," Jared said, trying to explain, trying to convince him. "I felt . . . a shadow of what she felt, sometimes, but that shadow was the best thing in my life. Everyone she cares about, I care about. It's not for you, or even for her. It's because you all gave me a gift, without even knowing you did. She taught me love could be a clean thing, by loving you. I'll die to protect any one of you."

"Oh," Rusty returned.

He sounded pensive. Jared did not know if he believed him or not.

After a moment, Rusty said, "I think I heard something."

Jared had been listening carefully to all the nighttime sounds. He had heard nothing, but he trusted Rusty. And he believed that if things could get worse, they would.

He looked around the wood, and saw a place where someone might be hiding.

Framed by branches and curling leaves was a roughly built shed. He had come here with Kami, once. Kami had come here before, alone, before he ever met her. She had seen blood and death here, and he had been so afraid for her.

The door to the shed stood open. As they watched, they saw a few leaves stray onto the floor on a sigh of night air.

Rusty pitched his voice very low. "The noise came from inside."

Jared strained his ears for what Rusty was so sure he was hearing, and moved in front of Rusty, arm outstretched. He might not have magic but he had meant what he said: Rusty was Kami's. Rusty was Sorry-in-the-Vale's. And Jared was a Lynburn. Aunt Lillian would say it was his responsibility. Jared would do anything he could to protect him.

He was totally unprepared for the blow that hit square between his shoulder blades, sending him crashing onto his hands and knees on the rough wooden floor. He scrabbled on dirt and leaves, flipped himself over and launched himself at the door, but it was already shut and bolted.

"I thought you might help me," said Rusty, from outside the door. "But I understand why you won't. Take care of them, okay, Sulky?"

"What?" Jared demanded. He hated the way his voice sounded, like a distraught abandoned child's. "What are you talking about? What are you doing?"

Rusty's voice was so kind. It had always been kind under the put-on detachment and drawl, Jared thought numbly, but it had never seemed as kind as it did now. "Take care of yourself too, if you can manage it."

It was only then that Jared understood.

He threw himself at the door, hard enough so his whole side ached, and then he threw his aching side at the door again. He smashed his fists against the door and saw the bloody streaks on the wood before he felt the pain of the skin splitting. There was a window, but it was too small to break out of, even though he smashed the glass with his elbow. That was another shock of pain but he ignored it.

He was trapped—again—and this time he was trapped knowing he hadn't been able to save anybody. He couldn't get out, and he knew what Rusty was planning to do.

Chapter Eighteen
Blood of the Innocent

Kami woke to the sound of a door opening. She jerked upright on the sofa. She had not gone to sleep in any of the beds Jared had made up. Instead, she had curled up on the other end of the sofa from a sleeping Angela, taking comfort in the fact that they were close even if Angela was very unconscious.

Her neck hurt, and her tucked-up legs were cramping, and none of it mattered, because Ash was at the door, pulling his jeans on, his T-shirt sleep-rumpled and his hair going in all directions, the light behind him reflecting from his flying locks like a shattered halo.

"Something bad is happening to Jared," Ash said. His voice was panicked and Kami felt his panic spiking through her. "I don't know what. It's not like with you—he can't tell me anything—but I can feel what he feels and it is horrible. We need to find him. We need to go to him now."

Kami glanced at Angela. She was already awake, uncurling from under her blanket, blinking sleep from her eyes. She looked vulnerable for a moment, in the brief confusion between waking and sleeping.

Kami did not know which of them should go and which should stay. She wanted to help Jared, but she could not abandon her father and her brothers when her brothers were being hunted, when they were so entirely vulnerable. She was almost certain none of Rob's men would kill Jared.

Almost certain was not entirely certain.

She sat there, fists clenched and body frozen, and they heard a slamming of fists against the door. Kami jumped at the sound, echoing through the house, and Ash hurtled from the doorway down the hall. Kami and Angela ran into the hall as Ash flung the front door open and Jared burst in. He was bloodstained and wrecked, a shining thread of red leading down from his temple. His shirt was torn and bloody as well, with a large rip in the back, and one of his elbows was as raw as the skin on his knuckles.

"Jared, what happened to—" Kami began, but Jared cut her off.

"It doesn't matter," he said. He didn't even look at her, and that sent prickles of unease down her spine. She saw his eyes were fixed on Angela, and it was suddenly hard to breathe through the fear. "We have to go now."

Ash was the only one who looked confused, still worried about Jared. "Why are you—"

"Ash," Jared interrupted. "What is the one thing that would bring your father the most power?"

Ash went white as he answered: "A willing sacrifice."

Holly volunteered to stay behind. The Lynburns all had to go, the ones who Rob would not kill, and Kami had to go because she had the most magic. They could not leave the boys unprotected, though. They had to leave a sorcerer to guard them.

Kami saw the look Holly gave Angela, knew how much it cost her not to insist on going too. There was nothing Kami could do about it. There was nothing Kami could do at all, except try to get to Rusty as fast as possible.

There were no glowing foxes in the woods in the early morning. The sky was dark and slowly lightening, like ink being gradually diluted with water. They had run through these woods before, but never so silently, never so desperately.

The trees were whispering wildly, boughs crackling above them, the winds running as fast as the wolves. The woods were in turmoil, and Kami felt the buffeting wind and tumult of leaves as if they were at sea.

A loud clear call sounded once, and then again, like thunder coming from the earth rather than the sky. Except, Kami realized, that the sound was not coming from the earth. It was coming from the river.

From river to sky the peals echoed. It was a toll, warning and despairing. It was the sound of Elinor Lynburn's bells, sunk beyond finding five hundred years ago.

Then it all stopped.

It was as though the whole world had shifted a degree. The air pressed down heavier, the shadows flattened the landscape, and nothing in all the once-wild woods moved. Light had been streaking across the sky but now it was dull. In no more than a moment, their town had become a still and silent land: no longer really their town at all.

Kami did not stop running. She could not bear to stop

running. They all ran up the road to Aurimere and around the bend until they reached the manor house.

The fire was not raging around the manor. It was a soft peaceful day now, clouds muffling the sun. The whole sky was muted.

They had taken the stone slab that Jared had been tortured on when his magic was bound in the crypt of Aurimere, in the very heart of the house. They had brought the slab out and laid it before the golden manor, on the highest part of the hill overlooking their town.

Jared's blood was still on the stone, mingled with older blood that had sunk in, the stain part of the very stone. There was fresh blood shining on it now, the only bright thing in a gray world.

Rusty's face was turned toward them. His eyes were shut as if he was just resting quietly, having one of his naps. As if it was an ordinary day. There were marks of pain on his face, but no anger and no fear. He looked a little sad.

She could see the rest of what they had done to him, the evil fools. They had tied his hands, Rusty who could fight better than anyone in town, who had carefully taught her to defend herself from anything. Nobody's face was marked with bruises, nobody was limping or otherwise hurt. He had let them do it. He had been an irresistible offering, a willing sacrifice. He hadn't fought them, and they hadn't needed to tie his hands, but they had done it because they could.

There were other people standing there, Rob's sorcerers and a handful of townsfolk. Kami looked at their scared, sick faces. Alison Prescott, Holly's mother, was crying. So was Amber.

Rob Lynburn was standing before the stone slab, with his brown muscular arms bared and the great golden Lynburn knife coated with scarlet in his hands. In this moment, all masks were off. Rusty looked like what he had always been, and Rob looked like what he was too. His face was rapt with evil delight.

"This is the inevitable end of all struggles against a greater power. This comes every turn of the year, every season, if the sorcerer chooses," Rob said. "Every breath you take is by my mercy, a sign of your lord's graciousness. I took my death, in recompense for the winter price this sorry town failed to offer me. I was given this death at the year's awakening, as is my due. Finally, all has been set right."

Angela threw herself at Rob like a dagger flying for his throat.

The air itself slowed, held Angela like a dragonfly suspended in amber. Rob strolled forward casually and laid his knife against her throat. The blood from the knife smeared on Angela's skin, as if it was jam on a butter knife.

"Don't move, little source," said Rob. "Or she dies with her brother."

Kami froze.

"Nobody else has to die today," said Rob. He turned around, arms up, as if he was expecting a cheer to rise from the crowd. The bloody knife was still in his hand. All he received was a great rush of silence. "But you came here to interfere with the sacrifice offered to me. There is a price to be paid for that."

Kami spoke through stiff lips. There did not seem enough air left in the world to breathe, let alone speak. "What price?"

Rob must know that she had lied before. He would ask her to break the link with Ash, and that would mean the ceremony of the pools would not work. Their last hope would be gone.

Kami did not feel panic at the thought. She felt empty, desolate as the gray sky, quiet past the point of misery. It seemed almost reasonable that hope would die too.

"What would any man want, with the world at his feet, but someone to share it with? I want my wife."

"No," snapped Jared, and took a furious step forward. Ash said nothing, but Kami felt the flare of determination behind the walls in her mind. He stepped up too, standing at Jared's shoulder, having his back.

Rob's eyes traveled contemptuously past Jared, over his shoulder, and fixed on his wife's face.

"Lillian," he said. "Will you come?"

"If I do, you will let every one of them go?" asked Lillian, staring ferociously at Rob. Kami knew Lillian well enough by now to know that she was deliberately not looking at anyone, unwilling to betray that she had weaknesses.

"Lillian," said Kami's dad. "You don't have to."

Kami saw the look on Rob's face when he heard that. She had a single terrible moment when she thought she would have to act, would have to choose whether to save Angela or her father.

"Shut your mouth." Lillian's voice was more cutting than Kami had ever heard it, like a whip handled in expert hands. It was either a Lynburn's scornful outrage or a desperate plea for him to *be quiet*. "I am so tired of hearing you babble to your betters on subjects you know nothing about."

Rob's tensed muscles visibly eased, and a smug smile spread across his face.

Lillian turned her salt-white face to her husband. "I assume I do have to, if I want them to live?"

"I would prefer to think of it as you seeing the cleverest and most reasonable course of action to take. You are my lady. You should be second in this town only to me, and all should bow their insolent heads to you."

"All *should* bow their insolent heads to me," said Lillian. "That's true."

Rob wasn't stupid. He saw what Lillian was implying. But he laughed, gently. It seemed bizarre and grotesque, seeing the two Lynburns bicker over a body. But Kami saw Lillian's hand clenching into a fist at her side, knuckles whiter than her face. She had to trust that Lillian was playing for all of their lives.

"I always admire your spirit, Lillian," Rob said. "Even though I find the display of your spirit often so stupid. Are you going to be smarter now?"

"Are you going to let them all go?"

"Go, go," said Rob, and waved a benevolent hand. "All of you can go about your business now. All of you can rest easy in your beds. Order has been restored to Sorry-in-the-Vale. You may depart, safe in the certainty of a true sorcerer's peace."

He waved a hand negligently at Angela, who sagged, gasping, as if she was a fish held on an invisible hook. Jon Glass stepped up to Angela and took her hand, caressed it and would not let it go. He held her back and drew her away, not letting her lunge again or stumble as she went.

Rob did not deign to notice what any of his defeated foes were doing. He held out a hand to Lillian, a gesture less of affection than command.

Lillian reached out and took it.

They walked, the golden pair, the lord and lady followed by their retinue, into Aurimere.

Enough of Rob's people stayed behind so that Kami knew they had to go, and go quickly. Any one of them could be a victim of Rob's malice, even if he had already taken his sacrifice.

She could not go, though, not quite yet.

She stepped up to the stone dais. She refused to look at the ruin that was Rusty's body. She looked only at him.

Kami used the edge of her sleeve to clean the blood from his dear face, until it was untouched, until she could tell herself he looked as if he was only sleeping, as if he might wake soon. She smoothed back his hair with a tender hand, light as though she could wake him, and bent down and kissed his cold brow.

"Sleep well, sweetheart," she whispered.

She hated to abandon him there on that cold stone, but she did it. She turned and walked the long road down.

PART VI

NO RESTING IN PEACE

All the words that I utter,
And all the words that I write,
Must spread out their wings untiring,
And never rest in their flight. . . .
—*William Butler Yeats*

Chapter Nineteen
The Boundless Deep

They went back to the Prescotts' farmhouse. Kami had thought Angela might not go, but she came back with them, walking silently. It made sense. How could she return to the place where she and Rusty had lived? Angela had never gone away to be alone before, not really. She had always had someone to go home to.

Angela did not speak to any of them, all the long walk home. She did not even let Kami walk near her, outstripping Kami effortlessly when Kami tried. She had let Kami's dad keep her hand, for a little while, but then tore it from his grasp as if his sympathy burned her.

Once they were at the house, Angela headed for the bedroom farthest away from the others, as far away from everyone as she could get. But she had still chosen to go home with them. Kami hesitated and then followed after her in a rush, shutting the door behind her hastily.

"I understand if you want to be alone," Kami said quickly. "I just want you to know that you don't have to be, that you never have to be. I want you to know how much I want to be here for you and oh, God, how sorry I am."

Angela stood across the room, by the bed. Her eyes were like holes burned in a sheet.

"I'm sure you are sorry," Angela said slowly. "You should be sorry. Would any of this ever have happened if you hadn't had the burning urge to know every damn thing that wasn't your business, if you hadn't decided that you were on some kind of stupid crusade? Everyone told you to stop, but you wouldn't listen. You were so sure you knew best."

"Was I wrong?" Kami whispered.

"I don't care if you were wrong or right. I don't care about good and evil. You're the one who made all this some kind of story, and it never has to be real for you. Your Lynburns will protect you. But they didn't protect him. You wanted to have your stupid adventure, and you got him killed. All I care about is that my brother is dead and it's your fault!"

Angela stopped speaking, panting. She looked despairing and exhilarated at once, looked as if she'd needed to punch someone in the face and done this instead.

Kami felt lashed by the words. She opened her mouth to shout that she had suffered too, that her mother was gone, beyond all real chance of recovery. But there was that faint hope, the thread that Kami was clinging to. She didn't know what would happen, what she would do, if that thread broke and she fell. She didn't know how Angela felt, and she could not stop fearing that she would.

She didn't shout. She didn't want to hurt Angela any more than she was already hurt.

"We could stop, if that's how you feel about it," she said in a low voice. "Rob Lynburn can do what he wants. He doesn't need us anymore. He's not going after my . . . he might leave us alone. He doesn't have any of our tokens. He could rule or destroy the whole town, and we could—let him. We could run away. He might not try to stop us. He might just let us go. We could go far away from here, and never know what happens next to anyone in Sorry-in-the-Vale. We could stop fighting and forget it all."

She looked up at the end of the speech to see Angela arrested, somehow, caught in a startled moment with her mouth open and her tear-wet eyes wide. She looked at a loss with her anger taken from her, even briefly. She looked young and terrified of feeling anything else.

"You're lying," she said in a hard, sullen voice. "You won't stop. You never do."

"That's right. That's who I am. I won't stop for anybody . . . but I will for you," said Kami. She wasn't sure if it was right, or okay to say, but nothing was right anymore. She told the truth. "You're my sister."

"I'm nobody's sister anymore!"

Angela screamed the words. It made Kami think of the way the wind had howled, the sound of a world being torn to pieces.

Kami could do nothing but throw clumsy words at all of Angela's pain, move forward with her hands held out, knowing that words and arms were so little comfort it was almost laughable.

"You don't have to be my sister, and I know it doesn't make up for anything, but I'm yours, I'm yours. I love you and I won't stop loving you even if you hate me, I won't leave you, I won't want to, nothing you ever do or say will ever make me turn away from you. And that's family, it is, it has to be."

Angela could not back away any further. Kami had always been the one who took the extra steps, acted and dragged Angela in her wake, from the time that they were both twelve, when Angela was the new girl who hated everyone and Kami had refused to be hated and insisted on friendship.

Kami hesitated now. She didn't know if she would be welcome. If what Angela wanted was for her to be different, to give up, then Kami did not know what a different person would do for Angela. She tried to imagine being a better person, who could be better for her friend.

She was here, and she loved Angela. She did not know how to be any better than that, be the person who loved Angela, as hard as she could.

Kami took a step toward Angela, and then another. Angela sat on the bed, in the corner, with her head bowed. She did not make a move in Kami's direction or away from her. When Kami took Angela's hands in hers, they were cold.

Angela's hands were limp in Kami's for a moment, and then they clutched far too tight. Her grip was icy and strong, like the grip of a hand in a nightmare, breaking through a grave. Kami tried to chafe some warmth into her fingers, and Angela slipped free and clutched at her sleeves, at her shirt, got a handful of her hair. She grabbed at her like someone drowning, and as she did, she began to sob.

"I'm sorry," Kami whispered. "I'm sorry, it's so bad, there's nothing I can do to make it right. But I love you and I'm here."

"And we give up if I say?" Angela's voice was choked with tears, like a river choked with leaves.

"We give up."

"And if I say we go after them, we kill them all, we wipe them out? If I tell you that we have to make them pay for what they did?"

"Then we will do that together," Kami said, into Angela's tumbled hair. "I swear."

Angela let out a wail, a terrible sound torn out of her throat, one that made Kami's own throat ache in sympathy. It was true what she had said, there was no action she could take, no way to make this right. The only thing she could do, in all the world, was be there.

Angela's arms went slowly around her waist, and they sat locked together, until Angela's wild sobbing was muffled, finally, against Kami's shoulder.

Angela collapsed with exhaustion at last, after the storm of tears. Kami staggered out of the room feeling as if she had been in a fight, her body aching as though she had been beaten, but not feeling as if she could ever collapse. She hated the thought of even closing her eyes. She had to do something. She found a little room where she thought Hugh Prescott had done his accounts, with a kitchen chair and a workbench that he seemed to have used as a table, with paper and pens on it. Some of the paper had sums scratched on it, some of them crossed out, as if Holly's dad had not been able to make the numbers work the way he wanted them to.

Kami sat on the kitchen chair: parts of the yellow wood were blistered, and patches of it were worn white. She stared at the blank page in front of her until it seemed like a doorway into oblivion, until her eyes were so strained they burned, and she could not think of a thing to write or anything else she could do. She could not think of anything but Rusty, and how she had not valued him enough.

Rusty. She had known he was sweet, known he was loyal, known he was loving. But he had been so familiar to her, for so many years. She had not thought of her lazy, goofy Rusty, her best friend's big brother, as a hero.

She had not told him she loved him too. She had not told him that she was grateful to know him as well. She had always prided herself on her way with words, but she had not told him how much he meant to her when she had the chance. He was gone and she would never have the chance again. He would never hear another word she said, would never say another word to her. He was lost to profound silence that no words could ever break. No words of hers could ever matter to him now.

She had almost wanted to give up, when she had told Angela she would. She did not know how to keep hoping and keep acting, how to say that she would not surrender at any cost, when now she knew what real cost was.

She had seen death before his. She had seen her old friend Nicola die at Rob Lynburn's hand. She had seen the sorcerers on Lillian Lynburn's side, people she had known all her life, dead because they had followed Lillian's command, dead for nothing. But she had loved Rusty. And they had murdered him.

There was a light knock on the door. Kami flinched and looked up.

"What do you want?"

Jared stood in the doorway, one hand still raised and curled against the door as if he was going to knock again. "I wanted to see how you were doing."

"I'm fine," said Kami. She felt short of breath, but flattered herself that her voice sounded normal. "I'm fine."

Her love had not been able to save Rusty. She'd thought she knew that those she loved were in danger before, but she realized now that she had been a child, thinking everything would work out, thinking that love was magic and it would form a protective spell.

She had been so blithely arrogant, so happily stupid. Beloved people died every day. Her love was not special, and her wishes would not order the universe.

"You're not fine," Jared said.

"I'm not—I'm not happy," said Kami, and pressed her hand against her mouth to stop the sob, as if she was stifling a hiccup. She did not even know how to react, when everything seemed like a ghastly, obscene version of itself. "I thought I had to always be in control, and then I thought maybe it wouldn't be that bad if I wasn't—but it's so bad, and I'm so miserable. He's gone and I have to . . . I have to do what he would have wanted, but I don't know what I can do. He's gone and there's nothing I can do about it."

She scrubbed at her face with the back of her hand. She wished Jared would go away, that she could go back to looking at the blank page and trying to think of something to do. Feeling numb and hopeless was better than this. She did not know how to deal with this.

"He's not gone," said Jared.

"Oh, and how do you figure that?" Kami demanded. "He seems pretty gone to me."

"When my dad died . . . ," said Jared. Kami stared at the blank page and the workbench instead of watching him come toward her. "Not Rob, but my real dad, the one I grew up with," Jared continued. "When he died, he wasn't gone. My mom and I could never be what we might have been without him. He stayed like a shadow in every corner of our home, stayed a stain on our hearts. I felt it. I can't believe that good will leave us when evil remains. I will not. I do not."

Jared knelt down, crouched at her feet so that she could not help looking at him, at his eyes filled with the light of the battered old lamp. He looked like he believed every word he was saying. He took hold of her wrists, his grip light but warm, touching her as if he always did it, as if he found it easy to do. She watched her tears fall on his hands like drops of rain.

"The way he made you feel, the way he felt about you— they can't wipe it away. They can't take away all he was to you. It was too much. They don't have the power. Nothing can take that from you."

His hands on her wrists were the only thing she could really feel, the only anchor when the rest of her body was so numb she almost felt like she was floating, about to come apart. She was held together, was able to remain whole and herself, because of his grasp on her.

"Whenever I thought about dying, I always thought that you would remember me," said Jared. "I thought about living on in your mind. I knew I would be safe there, that I would be good there, remembered as better than I had been. I know all you have lost, I know everything is changed, but when I thought of death I didn't think of going away. I always thought of it as still being with you."

Kami knew she was crying, but had not realized how hard she was crying until she tried to talk and could hardly speak. "That's because you're kind of crazy," she said, sobbing and tender, and it seemed strange and miraculous that tenderness could survive when she was in such pain, that she loved him through even this.

"Be crazy with me, then," said Jared. "You're always good at that. Believe me when no one else would believe me. You have faith in him, and I have faith in you. He didn't want to leave you and Angela, and I don't believe anyone could make him. They could change him, but they couldn't change what was between you. They can't make him leave you. He will not fade from the world. You would never let that happen."

Jared's voice sank as he spoke to her and looked up at her, as if he was murmuring in the hush of a church. Kami trembled looking at him and could not look away. She thought that she knew now why the words "scared" and "sacred" had the same letters, almost made up the same word. And she realized that she still wanted Jared when all thoughts of passion were dead, when other consolation seemed like a cruel joke—that she wanted to be with him when the thought of being with anyone else was unbearable, when the thought of someone else touching her made her want to scream.

"Do you think you could believe me?"

"I think I could," Kami whispered, her throat clogged with tears and aching. "Since it's you."

Kami moved closer, rested her weight against the solid

warmth of his body. She closed her eyes and laid a hand on his chest, felt his heartbeat until her own heartbeat gradually fell into rhythm with his, so her heart felt like his heart, so they were as close as they could be.

She had not realized before that she had thought that there must be another way, that she would find some alternate route to victory. She knew now that there was no other way, that she was going to have to do the ceremony, go down into the lakes and down into the darkness of death afterward.

Rusty had known what a willing sacrifice meant. He had guessed that if he went to Aurimere, if he offered himself up—not one of the Lynburns, not a sorcerer or a source, but one of the group of rebels that Rob hated—Rob would think it was close enough to the equinox, and that a willing and certain sacrifice would make his triumph certain as well. Rusty had done it to save Kami's brothers. He had done it to make sure that nobody else died defending them, so that Kami, Ash, and Jared would be alive to do the ceremony and save the town.

Rusty had taken such a terrible chance; he had gambled and known his life would be the price no matter if he won or lost. The price was paid. Kami could not fail him now. He had trusted her with all he had.

Kami laid her head down on Jared's shoulder, rested her cheek against the worn leather of his jacket. She rested in the circle of his arms and cried and cried, for Rusty, for Angela, for herself, for everything that they had lost. She wept for love and wept for the new dark strangeness of the world.

Chapter Twenty
Turn Again Home

Holly opened the door of her brother Ben's room to check in on Angie. She kept doing it, like a nervous cook checking on dinner in the oven.

The creak of the door seemed terribly loud in her ears. Holly didn't know what else she had expected, but she was alarmed when the light from the hallway fell across the white sheets, the swell of a pillow, and Angela's open eyes.

They stared at each other for a little while.

"I'm sorry if I disturbed you," Holly said in a meek voice. "I just wanted to be here if there was anything you wanted. If there was anything I could do."

It sounded feeble and stupid to her, but Angela looked at her for a long time, then nodded and made an obvious attempt to smile. The smile trembled on her lips and then slipped away, but the effort was real. Holly let go of the door handle and crossed the floor, went and sat down tentatively at the foot of the bed.

"Thank you," Angela said slowly. "You're a good friend."

She disentangled herself from the clinging sheets and crawled to the end of the bed. Even bowed down by misery, Angie had a certain inherent grace.

Holly thought, *What if I wanted to be more than your friend?* On one hand, this was not the time for thoughts like that. But on the other, there might never be any more time. They were only a day and night away from the equinox. Angela might want to know now. Angela deserved to know, at a time like this, that there was someone who cared about her more than anybody.

Holly risked a look over at Angela. Angela looked tired and worn, softer than she usually did, as if she needed to be cared for. Holly let her hand creep across the covers and touch Angie's hand. Angela glanced at their hands touching, and laced her fingers with Holly's. Holly caught her breath and determined to act.

She leaned forward, and Angela knocked her back, so hard that Holly's shoulder caught a glancing blow off a bedpost. Holly nursed her pain-dead arm and stared, bewildered, at Angela's cold face.

"Don't you ever try that again," said Angela. "I don't want you like that. Do you think you could possibly make me feel better? Your ego is out of control, and your pity is insulting."

"I didn't mean to—I never meant to insult you."

"I don't care what you meant," said Angela. "All I want from you is for you to get out."

Holly went out.

Mr. Glass was in the hallway, looking uncertain about which way to go—Kami in one direction, the boys in another, and Angie behind her door. Holly was amazed that he had feeling left to spare when his dark eyes lit on her and softened. She suspected that she just looked that pathetic.

"Oh, kiddo," he said.

Holly flung up an arm as if he was attacking her instead of consoling her. "I don't want you to feel sorry for me," she said in a whisper. "I don't need any help. Angela is the one who needs help. And I don't know how to help her."

"Nobody knows how to help at a time like this," Jon Glass said. "Nobody even knows how to go on. Yet somehow we do. We always do."

Holly shook her head mutely.

"Would you do me a favor?" asked Mr. Glass. Holly blinked, stunned, and he went on, "Would you watch the boys for me? Let me sit with Angela for a bit."

He looked at her the way kind teachers had sometimes looked at Holly, when she had given them a piece of homework she thought she had done all right with and was waiting around to maybe hear them say so. Holly felt pathetic again—she was seventeen years old, someone had died, and she was still hanging around hoping for an adult to call her a good girl.

"You're a brave girl," said Mr. Glass instead, and Holly would have done anything he wanted.

They had put two beds into the storage room. The little room had no windows. It was intended to keep the boys safe, to keep everyone else out, but when Holly walked in she felt like she was walking into a prison with white walls.

Tomo was sitting on a chair with a comic book on his knee. He smiled when the door opened, and though there were tears on his cheeks he seemed honestly all right, uncomplicatedly and cheerfully pleased to see her.

Ten was different. Ten was sitting on the edge of his bed,

and the curve of his back was like the curve of a bowstring so taut it might snap. Holly hadn't ever thought of herself as good with kids, she wasn't comfortable with them, but she found herself rushing over to put her arms around him.

Or rather, she tried to put her arms around him. He fought against her hold, staring at her as if she was attacking him, as if she was slowly and deliberately hurting him.

"Is there anything I can do to help you?"

Ten said, "Yes. I want to punish them. Bad people have to be punished. I know I'm a—a source. And you're a sorcerer, aren't you?"

Something about the little boy's eyes, his lost mother's eyes, made Holly feel as if that was an accusation.

"Yeah," she said. "I'm not very good yet."

For no reason Holly could see, news of her enormous incompetence seemed to reassure Ten. The terrible tension of his back eased slightly under her hand, though he was still straining away from her, not letting her really hold him.

"That's okay. You'll be good, once you have a source. If you promise to guard everyone, I'll be your source," Ten said between gritted teeth.

Holly's stomach sank. The idea of it, being so close to anyone the way she'd seen Kami struggle with, was horrible. Worse was how Ten looked, trembling and ashen, like a child being dragged to a stake to be burned.

"I can't do that," Holly said, hushed. "You'd hate it."

"But if someone else is going to die otherwise," Ten said, "it doesn't matter if I hate it. Rusty is dead. And my mum is dead. They are never coming back."

Tomo gave a sudden wail like a siren. "Mum's not!" he said. "She's not! Dad said she would be all right."

"You're a baby and you don't understand," Ten snapped. "But I do! My dad and Angela don't have any magic! Someone might kill them. And that lady, that Lynburn lady, she likes my dad but she doesn't like Angela. You don't want anything bad to happen to Angela, do you?"

His eyes made Holly feel not just accused but invaded. They saw too much. His eyes looked too old. Kami had always talked about Ten as shy, as quiet and sweet. Holly didn't know how he had been, before people started dying and the whole world had changed around him, but he was not sweet now. He might be a child shaking in her arms, but he was clear-eyed and cold.

"No," Holly whispered. "I'm sorry. I still can't do it. Not now."

"Will you do it?" Ten asked, his voice inflexible. "If it looks like we really need to. If there doesn't seem like any other way, will you swear to me you'll do it?"

Holly swallowed. "I swear."

"All right," said Ten.

Maybe he was relieved to be spared the necessity of having to hand his soul over immediately. He did not show it. He slipped out of Holly's arms entirely and lay down on his bed, motionless and facing the wall.

"Sorry, but I don't wanna be your source," Tomo said, kicking his chair legs. He seemed calm, now that Ten had not directly contradicted him about his mother. "I like you okay and all."

"Thanks," said Holly. "I get it. Sometimes you're just not feeling it."

She found herself able to grin at him, though it was a rueful grin. Rejected by an eight-year-old. It seemed in keeping with the rest of Holly's day.

"Ash could be my sorcerer if he wanted. He's my favorite." Tomo looked thoughtful. "But I guess he's Kami's sorcerer, as well as the other one with the—you know, the messed-up face."

"Don't talk about Jared that way!" Holly yelped.

Tomo rolled his eyes and shrugged, seeming to accept this. "Kami seems awful worried about sort of having two. She's responsible and stuff because she's the oldest, and it means she doesn't really enjoy herself. Not like me. I think it would be brilliant fun."

"I don't think anything about sorcerers is fun," Ten said in a low voice.

There was a long silence.

"Are you sure Rusty isn't coming back?" Tomo asked. "Are you really sure? I think maybe someone made a mistake."

When he turned the pages of his comic book, his hands shook and he crumpled the pages. But his face stayed smooth. He saw Holly looking at him, and he grinned again.

Holly really hadn't thought she had any special fondness for children. But she looked at Tomo, so determinedly blithe, and she looked at cold, wounded Ten curled like a comma on his bed and ready to do something that terrified him. She knew suddenly why someone would do anything to protect them. She knew why Rusty had given up everything.

* * *

Kami had gone to bed and even slept a little, wrung out after all her tears until misery and exhaustion seemed like the same thing. She was still lying in bed when she felt the shell in her pocket pulse into life.

She called for Ash in her mind.

Come quickly, she said. *Get Jared. It's your mother.*

Kami threw herself onto her knees at the foot of the bed, placed the shell on the white bedspread, and waited. Ash and Jared came in and knelt down on the floor at either side of her. Rob Lynburn's voice, calm and reasonable and reassuring, the voice of a good-old-boy politician, filtered from the shell and echoed around the room.

"I can understand how you must have doubted me," said Rob. "There was Rosalind and Claire Glass. I know you must have been jealous."

"Of you?" Lillian demanded, sounding almost amused.

"Perhaps not of your sister," said Rob. "You have always had such a touching loyalty to your family. But—"

"But Jon's wife?" Lillian asked, her skepticism as vast as space. "Why would she ever look at *you*? Did you two even know each other? I would never have noticed. I would never have cared. I have no interest in your behavior or in hers. I suppose you thought it was your due to have every beautiful girl in town at your feet, as the lord of the manor."

"She *was* very beautiful," said Rob. "Far more beautiful than you."

Lillian laughed.

"I'm sure she makes a very pretty ornament for the town square," she said, and Kami felt sick at her casual cruelty, hated Lillian for a moment. "The idea that I would care about her beauty is almost as ridiculous as the idea that I would be jealous of your affections. Feel free to bestow them on any unfortunate who passes by you in the street. I never wanted them. I never wanted you."

"Come, Lillian," said Rob.

Something about his voice was warm, almost welcoming. If Kami had been asked to guess, she would have guessed that he was holding out his hands to her.

"The game is almost over now. I won and you lost, but I will share my victory with you. It's true that you never came cringing and smiling to me like other women, as if I would love them if they could apologize enough. You've never humbly begged for anything in this world. You just walked through it and demanded all it could give you as a right. I suppose that is why I wanted you, as I wanted no one else. I suppose that is why, stubborn as stone and inflexible as steel though you are, I've never loved any other woman."

"Is this how you love?" Lillian asked slowly. She sounded vaguely surprised, more surprised than she was interested in the answer.

"What other way is there to love, except all-consumingly?" Rob asked. "You are everything to me, and I did everything to possess you."

"I am not a creature to be owned. No—I do a disservice to creatures. The dog will come to his master's call, the falcon return to kind hands and a hood, the caged bird will burst into song at the sound of a certain step in the hall. Love is essential for every one. You speak as if I am a jewel, to be tossed from hand to hand. That is insulting."

"To do anything for you? To consider you of such great value that you were worth any sin?"

"Yes!" said Lillian.

There was a pause.

"Ah well," said Rob indulgently. "Women can never say they are happy, can they? Of course no compliment is good enough."

"Go away and leave my town and my sons safe," said Lillian. "I will even go with you if you want. I would consider that a compliment worth having."

"Don't worry, Lillian. Our sons will be safe with us," Rob assured her. "I think it is a very good sign for peace that you are able to accept my boy Jared as yours too. It shows that you love me, despite what you might think, despite your injured pride, despite yourself."

Lillian said, "I know very well who I love."

"No woman has ever been loved by a man as I love you. I gave you a thousand proofs of my love. I gave up years of my life, let my plans for revenge wait, all for you. Not only so I could recover our knives, but for you, because you wanted to find your sister. I spurned your sister for you. I killed Edmund Prescott for you."

Rob did not sound like a politician now. He sounded like someone from Shakespeare, someone who lived in violently bright colors, a creature of red and gold. The normal person he had pretended to be was a mask. And though Kami had known that for some time, she hadn't quite realized what the mask was hiding. Delusions of grandeur, she thought: not the least mad of the Lynburns, but the most.

"Very flattering," said Lillian, dry as bones bleaching in

the desert. "I suppose wanting me had nothing to do with wanting Aurimere."

"Not a thing," said Rob. "You were what I wanted. Have you not realized yet, my dearest love? I hate Aurimere. I hate Sorry-in-the-Vale. I am going to destroy it all."

There was a long silence. Kami looked up at Jared. He had been right when he said Rob was planning something. He had been right when he said they were not ready.

Kami did not know what the others were thinking, but she felt as if she was following the steps to an inevitable conclusion: how Lillian had spoken of immortality as something you would have to kill hundreds for, Sorry-in-the-Vale as a source of power for generations of sorcerers, how Rob got his power and how Rob wanted revenge. Real revenge was not taking Aurimere House: real revenge did not end in a Lynburn in the manor, overlooking the town, time without end. Rob Lynburn did not want to carry on the legacy of the Lynburns. He wanted to walk away laughing.

One more sacrifice. Then I promise you on my word as the Lynburn of Aurimere, there will be peace for Sorry-in-the-Vale.

How he must have laughed, thinking about how he would keep that promise.

He was not laughing now. He sounded very solemn. "Your parents were my bitter enemies, and you have always been determined to follow their example, to walk the same tired path your parents walked, in narrow-minded blindness. It has been a dark irony and a torment to me that I should love you above all others."

"Very romantic," said Lillian, her voice now like the

sound of snapping dry bones in her bare hands. "A middle-aged Romeo, and a Juliet who wants a divorce."

"The time has come to stop tearing at each other. We are made of the same stuff, Lillian, if you would only see it. It is simply that my vision is grander than yours. I see a greater future for both of us, for our children, than you have ever been able to imagine in all your narrow dreams of this cold house and this pathetic town. We do not have to waste our lives in this backwater. There are a few other sorcerers in London, in Hong Kong, in Berlin—not the desperate strays hardly worthy to be called sorcerers that we are most familiar with—these are true magical aristocrats, with true power. They know how to take the power from sources, rather than letting sources control them. They know that those without magic are cattle to be used and disposed of, not pets to be cosseted. We could join them, be part of the true elite rather than moldering here in this medieval old house, pretending to rule over a rabble who grow more disrespectful every year and who do not deserve any of the benefits we have showered upon them or the mercy we have shown them. We could be immortal. We could be glorious."

"And how is all this glory to be attained?"

"The townspeople have given me their tokens of submission," said Rob. "I have had my equinox sacrifice, delivered willingly into my hands. The moon of the new year is coming, and soon I will have enough power to encompass the whole town in my mind, as Elinor and Anne Lynburn once did. I will hold it in the palm of my hand, and then I will crush it. The death of a whole town, the end of an old way of life, will give me enough power to live on for a golden age."

"I see," said Lillian. "And I am supposed to believe this is all for our good, and has nothing to do with the fact that you hated my parents for stopping your parents from killing? I am expected to pretend this has nothing to do with revenge?"

"Do not talk as if it was something noble. Your parents killed my parents, turned against their own kind, stole my life and told me that they had shown me mercy," Rob murmured. "Yes, I hate this town for being more important to your parents than their own blood. I hated your family, and I want the shining legacy of the Lynburns they held so dear to end. This has *everything* to do with revenge."

It was so simple, and they hadn't seen it. They had known Rob's story, of how his parents and he had killed for power, how Lillian's parents had come down from Aurimere and battled their own cousins but spared the child. Rob had told them nobody had any idea of what his end game was. They had almost guessed it, speculating about Rob's motives and his ultimate plan, his hatred of Sorry-in-the-Vale, but Kami supposed they had always had a picture of an evil overlord in their head, bent on ruling. But the power to rule meant the power to destroy—that was the darkness at the heart of ruling. It meant you had the power of life and death over people, and because you had the power, you thought that meant you had the right.

Lillian had said nothing in response to Rob's passionate speech of hatred and vengeance. Rob spoke again, his voice low and eager, coaxing now. Kami realized he was the type who found a woman's silence encouraging.

"Do you see how I love you now, my darling? I hate as lesser men could never dream of hating, with fire that will burn when the sun is ashes in the sky. My enemies are dust, and as dust I despise them still. Every one of their dreams will be dust, or my vengeance will not be complete. There is no force in the world as strong as my hate, except my love. I could have had my vengeance and put you in the ground with your family and the rest of their precious town, but I cannot do other than want you by my side. My love spared your life. My love will lift you up in glory, because glory is my destiny and I will have you share it. Glory is not complete to me without you. No woman is real to me but you."

"Rosalind was real to me!" Lillian snapped. "Why do you think I would be interested in your point of view, when you are so blatantly uninterested in mine? Your love, your grievances—why do only yours matter?"

The situation was obviously desperate: Lillian Lynburn was actually arguing for someone to feel more empathy.

"I think I have made clear why my claims are preeminent," Rob said coldly. "I have made clear that I am preeminent. The time of me catering to your whims is over. All I have done, I have done for your good. The time has come for you to accept it, and accept me as your master. The time has come for you to submit."

"And I shall," Lillian said unexpectedly.

Even Rob seemed to find that surprising. He did not speak.

Lillian continued, "What choice do I have? I said I know

who I love. I love my sons. You said that I care for power, and you were right. I'm not a fool. I can see that you have all the power. I can see that there is nothing I can do to stop you, and all I can hope from you is that you will spare my life and the lives of those I love."

Rob whispered, "I will give you more than that. We will live forever with our sons. I will crown you with power. I will make you a goddess among women."

"I'm curious," said Lillian slowly.

Kami heard the clear, sharp sound of her boot heels hitting stone. She heard Rob's indrawn breath.

"Suppose I said this to you: 'I never loved you. I never will love you. That I trusted you enough to think you were worthy of a place at my side, that you could be left alone with my sister or my sons, is my greatest regret. I will never forgive you for the deaths you have already caused, and I will hate you until the seas are deserts if you destroy my town. I will never willingly touch you, and I will hate every moment when you touch me. But I will stay with you, and keep faith with you, because my sons are hostages for my good behavior.' What would you say to me? Would you let me go, as I wish? Or would you keep me close?"

"I would have you with me," said Rob. "Always."

Kami heard the soft sound of a kiss. She felt Jared at her shoulder, turning violently away as if he could somehow make it stop by not listening to it. She felt Ash's helpless misery thrumming through her, and she reached out and caught Ash's hand.

"And so," Lillian whispered, "I see there is not one drop of mercy in all your love."

There was a crack then, a sound as if the whole faraway room had been made of china and abruptly dropped. Kami realized that Lillian had crushed the shell in her pocket before they could hear any more.

They knew Rob's plan. They had heard enough.

They knew that they had to do whatever they could to stop him.

Chapter Twenty-One
Girl Reporter

The last day before the spring equinox, they hid in the Prescott farmhouse like rabbits in a burrow. Even the boys were quiet, either from fear or with hushed solicitude for Angela.

Of them all, Jon was the one who was most active, the most obviously worried, pacing the floor with restless helplessness. Kami wished she could make him feel better. She knew that being the last adult, he thought he should be able to fix everything. She knew he blamed himself for her mother's fate and for Rusty's. She knew he would solve it all for her if he could.

Her dad had always been a young dad, a fun dad. She'd never looked to him with the perfect faith that the boys had. She understood now better than ever that you could want to do the right thing, try as hard as you possibly could, and fail. She looked at him pacing, looked at his tired face with lines on it that had not been there before this winter, and loved him better than she ever had before.

The bells in the river were ringing again, marking the hours, the sounds flooding to them over the fields. The bells tolled for the town, and Kami's head felt filled with the din, hammered with despair. There was no other sound in the night until there was a knock on the door, and Dad seized Tomo and pulled him close.

The door of the sitting room was open. They could see all the way down the long hall. The front door swung wide. Lillian Lynburn stood framed in the doorway.

"I came as soon as he was asleep," she said.

Jared and Ash were suddenly on their feet and running toward her. Ash grabbed her at once, the first of them to reach her. Jared hung back, hesitating. Lillian had to reach out to him. She put one arm around each of them, drew their heads down to her shoulders.

"I went with Rob so that I could learn his plans and spare all your lives," Lillian explained. "But I had to come back. I feared you would not hear the communication I sent you, and think I had turned to his side."

"We didn't think that," Jon said. "It might have escaped your attention, Lavinia, but you are not a terribly subtle person."

"And we heard," Kami added. "Thank you. It was good to know."

"It was good to know that creature is planning to destroy our town?" asked Lillian.

Kami was mildly surprised—she would have expected Lillian to say "my town."

"Yes," said Kami. "If he's planning to do it, better to know. I always think that it's better to know."

Even if what you knew meant that you had to stop someone, or die trying.

It was why she had first wanted to be a journalist, be

like the splendid figures of the past who had found power through words. She'd wanted to be like Nellie Bly, who had pretended to be mad and exposed the truth of what went on inside asylums more than a hundred years ago, or Gloria Steinem or Nancy Wake. She had looked up to such women, been so happy when she found a picture of a woman called Komako Kimura marching for women's suffrage and read about how she started a magazine called *New Real Woman*. She had loved the idea of spreading truth like a fire, like touching a lit candle to another candle and watching its flame come to life, until the whole world was bright and you saw everything clear.

Do you know how you want to spend tonight? Ash asked, and their link meant that Kami saw both the question he had meant to ask and the question that lay beneath it: *Do you know how you want to spend your last night?*

Kami looked from Ash, to Angela, to Jared, to Lillian, to her family.

"Yes," she said aloud, even though none of them knew what Ash had asked. "I think I do."

THE FALL OF THE HOUSE OF AURIMERE
by Kami Glass

I know the story of Sorry-in-the-Vale now.

Everybody knows that the Lynburns came to this place and created this town because it was a perfect place for magic. They called the other sorcerers to them, and the other sorcerers and their families served them. More people came, those without magic, drawn to the Lynburns' power and the prosperity of the town. They wanted to live in peace and happiness, on the wealth of the land. They believed that one sacrifice chosen from among the townspeople was a fair exchange for the protection and the plenty that the Lynburns offered. Even when the Lynburns left, we spoke of "when the Lynburns return" as though life without them was impossible, as if they and their power over us were as inevitable as the seasons.

From that day to this, the Lynburns have ruled us all. I worked so hard to find out the truth hidden at the heart of the town, and this is what I found. Magic and masters. What I want to ask you now is this: Do you believe their story? Do you believe that your town was a creation of the Lynburns, that you are the Lynburns' creature, that you and your home were never anything more than that?

Nicola Prendergast died first, and Rusty Montgomery died last. Chris Fairchild, the Hope brothers, Ms. Dollard, Ingrid Thompson. So many have died for the Lynburns. They used to write in their books that our sacrifices would not be forgotten, but every sacrifice has been forgotten, was taken for granted, was taken as their due.

Our lives are worth more than that.

Rob Lynburn murdered Rusty Montgomery the day before the spring equinox, and he has more power now than any Lynburn has had for a century. He is going to use his power to destroy this town, because he believes that your lives were always due to him.

The whole town knew Rusty. He died to defend children. He taught women to defend themselves. Was he worth nothing because he had no magic, because his family was new to this town? Remember him.

Remember something else. Perhaps you stood by, when blood was spilled, when battles were fought. Perhaps you were scared for a moment and felt you had missed your chance. Perhaps you feel as if you are committed to a course of weakness; perhaps you blame yourself for blood already spilled.

Do not remember you were afraid before. Remember something else about yourself. Remember the best and brightest thing about yourself: the memory in your life that makes you the happiest, the action you took that makes you the most proud. If you lost someone, the day before yesterday or twenty years ago, remember what you loved about them and what they loved about you.

You do not have to believe in me. You do not have to believe in the Lynburns either. I am asking you to believe in the best part of yourself. Believe nobody else has any right to that, or ever did.

This is the real secret at the heart of Sorry-in-the-Vale: the stories whispered behind closed doors are lies. The Lynburns are not protecting us by terrorizing us and demanding our loyalty. If someone has the power and desire to protect you, they should do it and not ask for any exchange. You owe them nothing. Anyone who ever told you that it was the Lynburns' right to rule was spreading a lie the Lynburns made up. They made up an excuse to take what they want, a lie because they did not want to give up power over you. They had to lie. They could not afford for you to know the truth. You were not born in their power. You lost nothing when they left. You lived without them, and you can live without them again.

You do not have to follow Rob Lynburn. You do not have to follow Lillian Lynburn either. It does not matter if your masters are kind or cruel, because either way they are trying to master you, and they have no right. If you were free, what would you choose to do? Do it. You are free.

This is true inside and outside our town. Other people will try to steal power that is yours. Never let them. Always fight. I do not believe that our power can be taken away from us forever.

Every town in England has a story, and our story can change.

Kami read the article aloud to her family and friends as they stood all together in Room 31B, Kami's newspaper office. They had magically broken into the school.

"My baby girl has a way with words," said Jon. "You're wasting your talent on journalism, though. You should write the text for video games."

"I don't like the title," said Lillian, and implicit in the words was her feeling Kami should change it, that a Lynburn still gave the orders around here.

Kami would take Lillian's suggestions sometimes, but she was not taking any orders, and she was not letting Lillian influence her writing. It was the one thing that was all her own.

She wheeled on Lillian, looked her in the eye, and said calmly, "I don't care if you like it."

"I like it," said Jared, kneeling on the ground and photocopying as others talked over his head.

His aunt sniffed. "You like everything that suggests chaos and the lower classes."

Jared grinned up at her, heedless of his scar, his eyes pale and wild. "I *am* chaos and the lower classes."

Lillian did not argue. She ruffled his hair and her fingers lingered for a moment, playing with the ends of his hair, her touch light and loving.

They had all agreed to spend the night putting a photocopy on every door in the town. Kami knew that Lillian was only doing it to please her boys, that the whole group was not arguing with Kami because of what might happen tomorrow. If she was going to die for them in the morning, they would do this for her tonight.

They went in groups. Lillian insisted that Ash and Jared would stay with her. Kami had asked her father to go with Holly, so she could stay with Angela. She didn't want to leave Angela too, not until she absolutely had to. Almost the worst thought about dying was how alone Angela would be.

But at least Kami could try to do what Angela wanted. She could try to punish the people who had taken Rusty away from her.

Kami and Angela went around the town affixing Kami's article to every door. Angela started complaining two doors in, and did not stop until they were done. Once they were done, though, once they were walking in the dark past the last house on Shadowchurch Lane, Angela said, "Remember the time you asked me to set up the school newspaper with you?"

"As I recall," Kami said, a little rueful, "I didn't so much ask you."

"I could've said no," said Angela. "I'm actually rather expert at it. 'Do you want to go out with me?' guys say, and I say, 'Why, no, I'd rather spend an evening marinating my own eyeballs in a lemon sauce.' 'Do you feel like getting up before three p.m.?' *No.* 'Can you give me a smile?' *No.* 'Could you be less of a bitch?' *No.* If you didn't hear it from me a lot, there was a reason for it. I wanted to say no to the whole world, until you. The stupid sorcerers would have come without the newspaper, would have—would have done what they did, but because of your newspaper we made friends with Holly, and we won over Ash. And we got to yell at people. I like doing that."

Angela stared across the square, up Shadowchurch Lane. The moon was low among the branches as if it was a softly glowing lantern hung from one of the boughs, and it had caught the cobblestones and made the normally dark street blaze like the path the moon sometimes painted across water.

"I guess I'm trying to say, thanks for making me do your dumb newspaper with you."

"Thanks for doing it with me," said Kami, tucking her chin against Angela's shoulder. "Every step of the way."

"Yes, well, I know how easily you get into trouble. I didn't want you to do it alone."

There was one thing Kami did have to do alone, though. She told Angela that she would meet her back at the inn, and she crossed the square.

Kami touched her mother's outstretched stone hand as she went, not sure if it was in benediction or in the hope of getting a blessing for herself. She walked up the two stone steps and she wove through the gravestones, the wind-worn words and the tufts of grass, the angels and the shadows, until she reached the gravestone of the person who had belonged to her.

The stone was simple, as was the kanji inscribed on it. Kami had seen her father weeping and raging here this winter. There were snowdrops fringing the side of the grave now, and it was so quiet that rage seemed impossible. Kami looked at the gravestone as if it was a window her grandmother might appear in if she waited and watched long enough. Her Sobo had been small with dark hair and direct eyes, confident and impatient, always sure Kami was going to get into trouble and always sure she could handle it. Kami had been her grandmother's favorite, as Ten was her dad's and Tomo was her mother's. She remembered telling Rusty that her every thought had been different because she shared thoughts with Jared, but Jared did not define her, had not been all that made who she was. She had been shaped by someone else, though her grandmother had never known what she was shaping her for. Kami hoped that she would have been proud.

She closed her eyes and tried to summon strength from the place that had made her.

"Obaasan," she whispered, and laid her hand on the moonlight-cool stone. "Wish me luck."

PART VII
SORCERY IN THE VALE

Do not stand at my grave and weep,
I am not there; I do not sleep.
I am a thousand winds that blow,
I am the diamond glints on snow,
I am the sunlight on ripened grain,
I am the gentle autumn rain.
When you awaken in the morning's hush
I am the swift uplifting rush
Of quiet birds in circled flight.
I am the soft stars that shine at night.
Do not stand at my grave and cry,
I am not there; I did not die.
—*Mary Elizabeth Frye*

Chapter Twenty-Two
Three That I Loved

Kami woke on the dawn of their last day with Elinor's bells ringing, a chorus and a warning. The sky outside was cloudy, as it had been for both the days and nights since Rusty died. Through the windows, the sky shone like a gray pearl.

She had not been expecting to, but she had slept a little.

Kami, Jared, and Ash had to do the ceremony on the very day of the equinox. It would kill two of them. Elinor Lynburn had said it would.

Now the day of the equinox had come. It was as simple as that.

Kami remembered how clear Rusty's eyes had been, how calm his voice, how steady and sure his hands. She wanted to say her goodbyes as well as he had.

Angela would not let her say a word. Angela just hugged her, her grip fiercely tight, and Kami closed her mouth and dipped her face down into Angela's shoulder, and wished Angela would not let go. But they had to let go of each other eventually.

Holly hugged her next, her arms warm and enveloping.

"Look after Angela," Kami said in her ear. "And— thank you."

Holly smiled. Her eyes were bright with tears, but her smile was always brighter. "For what?"

"For being my friend," said Kami. "Just that. You were fantastic at that."

She pulled away from Holly, and saw Holly turn to Jared and give him a big hug and heard Angela drawl, "I'm just going with a friendly nod for both of you" to Ash.

Dad stood with Ten and Tomo on either side of him. She stooped and hugged Tomo, who looked bewildered but hugged her readily back.

"Good luck," he said, blinking up at her. She thought he was still waiting for Rusty to come back. She swallowed a lump in her throat at the thought of him waiting for her.

"Thanks, kiddo," she said.

Her dad leaned down and wiped away a tear from her cheek that she did not know had fallen. She saw it all in his face, that he wanted to tell her not to do it, that he wanted to lie and promise there was another way.

"I love you so much," he said. "I could never let you go if it wasn't that I trust you just as much."

"I couldn't go now if you hadn't always trusted me," Kami said.

When she tried to hug Ten, he moved away. She wanted to say, *I'll come back,* but she did not want him to remember her last words as lies. She kissed his cheek, though his face was turned away, then straightened up and turned away. There was so very little time.

Kami began to walk through the fields and down toward the woods, her Lynburn boys on either side of her. She heard the drumming of small feet behind her, running desperately fast as if he thought she would not stop for him.

She did stop for him. She turned and went onto her knees in the long meadow grass and Ten came crashing into her arms. He buried his face against her neck and she felt the press of his glasses under her chin.

"I'm sorry," he whispered.

"You have nothing to be sorry for," Kami whispered back. "Nothing in the world."

It was a little thing, a sweet small benediction before what was to come, before she did what she had to do.

Kami could not think of death as all there was to be done. She could not die until she had saved the town.

Holly knew that Kami and the boys had one part to play, and they had another. They had dropped Kami's brothers off at the Water Rising, and now all that Jon and Angela needed was a ride. Holly knew exactly what had to be done.

The sorcerers might come out, on this last day. Rob might want to see his triumph, and Rob triumphing meant other people being hurt. They had to stop that, as far as they could, but the sorcerers were not only stronger but faster than they were.

Holly understood all that. She still felt the paddock had far too many horses in it.

"That's sort of the idea," Angie said.

Jon Glass had vaulted over the fence and was now approaching a horse chosen by some sort of weird horse-knowledge method, or possibly because it was shiny. Angie had noticed the way Holly was standing a careful distance away from the animals, though, and had stopped with her feet on the first plank that made up the fence to look at her quizzically.

"I thought you were a farm girl."

Her dad did not have any horses on his farm. Holly had heard people talking about horses, of course, and how such and such a horse was a good goer, or had a temper, or was a spirited beast, but that was only talk. Holly had fed chickens, milked cows, and gathered wool. No cow or sheep was a spirited beast. You were not supposed to ride them. Holly had not realized until this moment what a deep and profound affection she had for cows and sheep.

"I *am* a farm girl," said Holly. "Horses stopped being used on all farms about the time they replaced carts and horse-drawn plows with these newfangled things called cars and tractors. And I didn't get any fancy riding lessons."

Holly saw the moment of awkwardness and unease flicker across Angie's face, the rare way that Angie sometimes looked when she'd been inconsiderate of someone's feelings and she hadn't meant to be. She had only seen Angie ever look that way about three people in the world, and one of the three was gone. She loved Angie so much, for still caring about Holly's feelings, in the midst of all this chaos and all that Angie had been through.

"Well," Angie said after a pause. "If you want, I'll teach you, once all this is over. And you don't need to get on a horse today. So there's no reason to be afraid of anything. Don't be."

Angela didn't smile at her. Angela's smiles had always

come seldom, and now her face looked stern and somehow fixed—older and less open to happiness and hope, but no less beautiful. She had the air of a warrior, someone who had been through fire and would no longer be touched by fire. For Angie, maybe it was easy not to fear. With Angie, not being afraid seemed possible.

"Wait," said Holly. "Wait, I'm sorry, there's something I want to say."

Angie stilled.

Holly felt sick, in the same way she had when she was a kid so desperate to get out of school that she convinced herself she was terribly ill and then could not make the pain stop. She had to wrench the words out, because she could not put it off anymore, because this could be her very last chance.

"I know you think I was just feeling sorry for you, but that wasn't it at all," Holly said. She saw Angela flinch but did not let herself stop. "When we were first getting to know each other, I thought you were so great, and I wanted to be with you all the time, and I didn't know what those feelings meant. It took me a long time to understand, and to catch up with you, and once I did, I still didn't know what to do. I know that the whole offering-you-a-massage thing was weird and borderline creepy. I didn't know how to do it, when it was with a girl, or when it felt important. I know I did it all wrong, and I'm sorry. If that's wrecked any chance for us, I understand. I wish I could make up for it all. Or if too much has happened for that to be possible, I want, just once, to tell you the whole truth about myself and about what you mean to me. I've made so many mistakes and I've said so many dumb hurtful things, but I want you to know what it all meant. I want you to know that everything I've done lately, I've done because I wanted to be with you."

"You mean it?" Angela asked. "You r-really do?"

Her voice wobbled, and Holly stood stricken with a painful mingling of hope and fear.

"I mean it," she said. "I don't always know what to say, like you and Kami. I don't know how else to tell you that I mean it, but if things work out and if you were willing—I could keep thinking of how to prove it to you. I could keep trying different ways to tell you, until you believe me. That is, if you want to hear it."

"I do," said Angie, and the words tumbled out eagerly, in a way Holly had never heard her speak. "I do, I do."

"Yeah?" Holly asked. She heard her own voice come out shy, and thrilled. It was a little embarrassing, but it was how she felt. She wanted Angie to know.

She stepped up, one foot on the fence, so Angie was only a tiny bit taller than she was. She remembered how Angie had leaned in once before, and how Holly had shoved her back, how easy it had been to repel her in a moment of shock. Nothing was easy now, but it was so sweet.

It was strange, to taste someone else's lipstick. Angela's was slightly dry, with an edge of dark chocolate, mingled with the slick bubble-gum slide of Holly's own lip gloss. Angie had never been kissed before, which Holly had known but now really knew, because of the slight hesitation that Angie would never have betrayed if she could've hidden it, the hovering of Angie's hands like butterflies not daring to land on Holly's hair. Holly was surprised by the rush of protectiveness and satisfaction that washed over her: she had kissed and been kissed a lot, if never quite like this. She slid her hands from Angela's narrow back to Angela's small waist, drew her in so close against her body that their hips pressed together in a tiny jolt of contact, and deepened the kiss. Angie had always been one of the quickest studies in school. The kiss transformed into something world-changing, warming the air, slowing time. The sun shimmered behind Holly's closed eyelids, and above their heads the wind whispered promises to the leaves.

"Angela, are you ever going to pick a hor—Oh," said Jon Glass.

Holly looked over at him, in sudden guilty terror. Her fingers closed on Angie's hand, clutching too tight. Her heart was pounding. She didn't want to be separated.

For a moment, she could not see him clearly through her blur of panic, and then she could.

"Well, I must say this is a great relief to me," Jon said, with wicked eyes and infinite tenderness. "I was starting to think that nobody would ever be willing to take on Angela, homely as she is."

Holly giggled, the sound surprised out of her, like a hiccup of happiness. "Mr. Glass!"

"Oh, I know other people say she's all right looking, but I just don't see it," Jon continued. "Also, bad tempered as a camel in a shipwreck. You might have noticed that. But she has a good heart, and I think of her as a grouchy, overly tall daughter."

He reached out and touched, with absent affection, the ends of Angela's long dark hair, streaming in the warm breeze. For a moment, the wind whipped a few locks around his wrist, curling around like a bracelet, like a caress. Holly would have thought it was magic if either of them had been a sorcerer. Instead it was a happy accident of nature, and the simple fact of love: love tucked in the small upward curve of Angela's mouth, love in the gleam in Jon Glass's eyes.

Jon wheeled his horse away, handling the reins with casual expertise.

"He's kind of hot, for a dad," Holly said thoughtfully, and squeaked when Angela poked her in the ribs with her manicured fingernails.

"So it's like that, is it?"

"Yes," said Holly, and glanced at Angie through her eyelashes. "But that doesn't mean—I don't want you to think . . . I can find a lot of people hot, and I know how it might seem, but I don't want to be with anybody but you."

"I don't think anything," Angela said. "It doesn't seem any way. Hot though I am, I'd be waiting a long time before I found someone who thought I was the only hot person in the universe. If I did find someone who thought that, it'd seem like a lot of pressure." Her voice softened, brightened, like sun hitting water and turning it from something cold to something made of living, dancing brightness. "And I believe you. I believe everything you tell me."

Holly leaned forward and stole one more kiss before Angela climbed over the fence and walked toward the horse that was glowing gold in the sunlight, which took a few nervous prancing steps back but calmed when Angie put a hand on its arched neck.

She swung herself onto the horse's bare back, light and easy as a dandelion seed caught in the breeze, and followed Jon's lead as he opened the gate and trotted his horse through.

Soon the bright horse was chasing the dark horse, across the fields, over streams and hedges, so fast it looked as if they were flying, toward the town.

"Just you and me, girl," Holly whispered to her bike, and kicked it into purring life. She was still scared, scared to die or to hurt anyone else, but the sun was shining and she had said all she had wanted to say. She had been as brave as she knew how, and she was loved in return. She was as ready as she would ever be.

They went through the woods walking softly. Even the ringing of the bells seemed muffled by the leaves, becoming a steady sound as soft as their footsteps.

The Crying Pools were two silver coins laid out at their feet.

Ash was pale. Kami could feel his fear, so different from her own it was not like the same emotion. His was tangled with panic, with self-doubt, with desperate fear he would let them all down.

I'm not worried, said Kami.

I've let you down before.

You've changed, said Kami. *I know you better than anyone by now. I know you never will again.*

She felt his love pouring through her. She felt his faith, as she had once felt Jared's belief in her, and it helped her believe in herself.

"I want to go in the sinister pool," Jared said. Ash and he looked at each other.

Lillian had said the Crying Pool on the left was deeper and colder.

"Come on," Ash said. "No. Kami and I are the ones who are linked—"

"I'm the one who went in the pools last time."

"And that went so well," Ash sneered.

"We don't have time to fight!" Kami cried.

She could imagine her brothers hidden away at the Water Rising, with the sound of the bells shaking the windows.

"Come on," Jared said. "Let me do this. Am I your big brother or not?"

"I don't think so," said Ash, and managed a pale imitation of his usual sunny smile. "Actually, I think of you as my brother who's just a shade shorter than me."

Ash looked at Kami now, the faint glitter of almost-lost sunlight in his hair. Kami remembered her first sight of him, in the safety of her newsroom at school, when she had thought they would all be safe forever, when she had taken safety so perfectly for granted. All she had known about him was that he was beautiful, that he wanted to take beautiful pictures, and that he was at his most beautiful when he smiled at her. The first negative thing she had ever learned about him was that he did not like the boy he thought was his cousin.

You go get him first, Ash told her. *Promise me.*

Kami said, *I promise.*

Ash took a step into the lake, and then another, and another. He did it slowly, wincing at the cold, making things worse for himself by hesitating, but Kami thought he was all the braver for doing it when he was so afraid. She felt how cold he was, and how afraid.

He did not even think of turning back.

Soon all Kami could see of him was his golden head in

the gray waters, shining like a helm. He seemed like a knight emerging from a lake instead of a sword.

Then he was gone.

Kami looked over at Jared. He was already sitting on the edge of the sinister pool, one hand in water up to the wrist.

"I know there isn't much time," he said. "But I wanted to say something first."

Kami went and sat opposite him on the other side of the sinister pool, on the crumbling edge of the earth. There was a shimmering circle of water between them, and Ash's fear as he fell, still with her.

There was always something between them.

"My entire life, all I ever wanted was for you to be real. Then I came here, and I found out that you were. That first day I found out you were real, the first time I saw your face and heard your voice, it was all I could have ever asked for. Everything else after that has been a gift I could never dream of deserving, would never have even thought of asking you. Learning to know you, for real, being with you every day . . . I want you to know that I never thought I could be so happy. Being with you is the only definition of happiness I have."

Kami nodded, silently. She understood what he meant: that if he died, he wanted her to remember that he had been happy.

"I want you to know something else. I would have died for this, but I have other things to live for: Ash, my aunt Lillian, Martha Wright, my home, my town. I'm going to try to live."

He was facing his own worst nightmare, and he was taking the time to give her a gift to go down into the dark with. Sunlight was escaping from the clouds and being sifted through the leaves. It was almost as if it was raining, little sparkling drops of light rather than water. She had always thought of him—he had always thought of himself—as standing in the shadow, but now at the last he was touched with a hundred points of light.

"I want you to know something," said Kami. "I don't love Ash."

"No?" asked Jared, and smiled his small, crooked twist of a smile. "I do."

"You said that death means people are changed but not lost," Kami said. "Here's something that won't change. You will always be my favorite person in the world."

Jared looked at her. He stood up, and Kami thought he was going to come to her, but he did not. Even now, he did not. He dived into the pool, his body one long strong arch, scything through the air and plunging into the water. The surface of the water changed from gray to green, with a ring of rippling gold where he had been. They were both lost to her sight.

Lillian had taken Kami aside and told her everything she knew about the ceremony.

"They go down to the pools, as deep as they can go, and then deeper," Lillian had said. "They bring power up. You go into each pool, you claim it for your own. You have to claim both pools. You have to claim them both. You have to summon them from the deep."

Chapter Twenty-Three
The Source of Everything

The sound of the bells was coming without cease now, peal after peal, shaking the whole world. There was water trickling down the streets as if it had rained too hard, but it had not been raining at all.

Lillian had been right. Rob had not been able to resist the temptation to come down from Aurimere and into the streets.

But it was not only Rob's sorcerers walking through Sorry-in-the-Vale. Holly saw other people in the streets instead of hiding in their houses. She saw one woman with a piece of paper crumpled in her fist. Kami's article, she thought, and was as proud as she had been to see Kami walking toward the woods this morning. They were wandering, watching, looking uneasy. They weren't doing anything more, but they had come out.

The other sorcerers seemed disconcerted by the townsfolk, as if they had expected a victorious parade through empty streets. Rob looked around at them, laughed and pointed, held out an open hand to a boy walking beside his mother and sent the boy spinning into a wall. The boy fell on his hands and knees in the water. Holly recognized him: it was Raj Singh.

The other sorcerers started to laugh. Some of them.

"Leave him be," said Lillian.

Rob glanced at her, amused. "It hardly matters."

"It matters," Lillian said shortly. She shoved past her husband, knocking him roughly aside, and strode toward the child. She stuck out her hand. "Grab my hand," she said, and when he looked up, she added, "Take it. I won't let any harm come to you."

"Won't you?" asked Rob. There was a world of meaning in his voice.

Lillian swung on him, her hair flying from her shoulders like a silver cloak. "No," she said. "You cannot possibly have thought I would. And if you did, if you know me so little, what does that say about all your love?"

She turned back to Raj. "Take my hand," she repeated.

Raj hesitated, then grabbed hold of Lillian's hand. Lillian lifted him to his feet and walked him across the street to his mother.

"If you're not with me, you're against me," said Rob. The wind rose as his voice rose.

There was a sound like thunder in the streets, and more water came pouring down over the golden cobblestones, in every direction.

"Thank you," said Mrs. Singh. She looked at Lillian and did not glance toward Rob or show any fear.

"Go now," Lillian told Mrs. Singh and her son calmly. The path on which the two were walking home stayed dry.

Water rushed toward Lillian, higher than before, like a

wave crashing in from some strange sea. Lillian stood tall and straight as a spar of rock about to be engulfed in that sea, and Holly caught her breath, realizing that Lillian could not stop it. She tried to summon up magic enough to combat it, to save Lillian, and knew that whatever magic she had would be about as much use as a straw in a hurricane.

A black horse leaped over the low wall of the churchyard, into the square and up the High Street. Jon Glass snatched Lillian up onto his saddle and rode through the raging waters up the way the Singhs had gone.

There were more and more people coming outside or looking out of their windows. Rob's own group was looking apprehensive.

"Come on," said Rob. "Let us leave them to their fate. Let us return to Aurimere."

He turned, and Holly looked in the same direction.

"You think so?" Angela asked, at the top of the street on her golden horse, blocking the way to Aurimere. She was holding a chain in her hands: a chain Rob Lynburn had bound her with once. She smiled brilliantly at them.

The bells sounded like giants fighting with clashing weapons, the deaths of gods imminent. Holly saw Jon turn his horse around, back to Angela, back to join the battle. She saw Martha Wright step out of the door of the Water Rising.

Holly could not stay. She coaxed her motorbike into sputtering life, felt its wheels spinning in the water and thought that it might not go, until she remembered that she had magic. She let her desire to escape from her home, to help her friends, travel down her fingertips, and the motorcycle began to move.

* * *

Kami drew in a deep breath and jumped in the pool after Jared. This was the sinister pool, the coldest, deepest pool, and she knew no matter how deep a breath she took, it would not be enough, but she had to try.

The water was cool, cooler than it should have been, but it was not the bleak midwinter chill she had felt once before. The year had turned in her favor. She could bear this.

She took a swallow of the water. It could be air, she told herself. Sorcery came from the elements: she was a source. Every element could nourish her if she willed them to.

It felt like swallowing water, but she was still alive. She opened her eyes and all she saw was painted in green and gold: the lake bed below her, her feet about to touch it, and Jared nowhere in sight.

But she knew he was there. She knew, she knew.

She reached out. She was not falling. She was diving for treasure, diving for what was hers. She had chosen to jump and she was going to accomplish her purpose.

She knew Jared, better than anyone, inside and out.

She closed her eyes once more and stretched out her hand again, not clawing but calm and sure, reached through water and touched his face. She ran her fingertips over the sharp line of his cheekbone, the curve of his jaw, the slight irregular roughness that was his scar on water-slick skin. She felt as if she might be creating him anew. She believed she could do that: she knew him so well. She felt the curling tendrils of his hair against her fingers. She felt his hand reach out and take her hand. She could trust herself to always know him. She could trust him to always reach for her.

When she opened her eyes, for a moment it seemed as if she was in one pool and he in another, or as if one of them was in a looking glass and the other in the real world, as if they were reaching each other across a great distance. But water moved differently than air: water could draw two people together. Jared opened his eyes, and his lips shaped her name.

Their hands met, and between their linked hands shone a fierce and sudden gold.

They rose to the surface of the pool as if they were a bubble racing toward the surface, and emerged from it wet and gasping, the sun sparkling in every drop that fell from their clothes and hair. Kami gasped at the glory of it, but could not stop to marvel. She had to claim both of them. She had to get Ash.

Jared would not let go of her hand.

I have you again at last, he said, and she felt her own heart in rhythm with his, in agreement with his, echoing at last, at last. *Did you think I would let you go?*

They jumped again, jumped together, into the green and gold below the surface of the water, the writhing shadows and dancing lights at the very depths of the pool. She did not know Ash as well as she knew Jared, enough to create his image out of air or water, but she could feel him. She could feel him more strongly than she ever had before, with more power than she had ever had before.

She could feel Ash's loneliness and uncertainty. She could feel his fading hope.

We're here, she told him. *We're coming to find you.*

There was no answer from Ash. She could not even feel

a flicker of response, could not tell if he had heard her. She felt something else: she felt Jared reaching out to Ash as well.

She put out searching hands, and found them empty again, and again, and again once more. She tried to float in the water toward the direction of Ash's thoughts, tried to follow where Jared went. She did not know if she could have reached Ash without Jared, but she did reach him. The tips of her fingers touched the floating ends of his golden hair. They both reached out with their free arms and drew him in toward them.

They both had him. She was holding Jared, and she was holding Ash. Jared was holding Ash, and the circle was complete.

And she knew how Anne Lynburn and Matthew Cooper died.

The power was like water, like darkness, like fire, like all those things at once, overwhelming and assailing her, dragging her under and consuming her.

She felt how it was for Ash, felt how completely overwhelmed he was, felt all that was Ash being washed away like glittering grains of sand scattered and obliterated by the sea. The power came through her. She was the source. She was the conduit, she was the wellspring, she felt oblivion coming for her as well as for Ash.

The power could burn all the way through her, save the town and destroy her. She could see it coming, the darkness and the light, coming to blot out and burn away the fragile boundaries that set her apart, made her who she was.

Except that she had worried about her own control so much that she knew that her boundaries and barriers, the way she kept hold of herself, might feel fragile but were strong. She had already been tested like this, a hundred times before, and she knew she did not have to be isolated to be herself.

Except that she felt Jared too.

She was used to being part of something and still knowing who she was—so was he.

Jared was here, able to shape her out of any element. She could feel his belief in her, carrying her through the tide of power when she could not carry herself. She might feel lost, but he had not lost her. She could not be lost, when she was so well known.

They had been preparing for this moment all their lives.

They struggled upward, through power and awe, through drowning and darkness, fire and light, until they surfaced. Until they managed to struggle and scramble out of the Crying Pools and into the light and air of Sorry-in-the-Vale.

Until Kami, Jared, and Ash sat by the side of the pool. Ash was lying on the bank, his face still lost in dreams, his golden hair mingling with the tender blades of grass. Kami felt she should be much more worried, but she could feel the life pulsing strong through him. She could feel the life in everything.

I'll wake him, said Jared. *I won't let him go.*

Kami stood, and felt her legs tremble beneath her as if she was a fawn newly born. She felt light tremble under her fingertips, as if she could play the rays of the sun like harp strings. She felt newborn and ancient. She knew all the secrets of the forest and was waiting to be told a great truth.

She looked down at Jared and saw herself the way she liked herself best, reflected in his eyes. They stopped for a moment, rapt with each other, her hand on his shoulder, the white material of his shirt soaked through and the skin of his shoulder warm beneath the clinging fabric. She closed her fist on his wet shirt, bent down and kissed him on his open mouth, felt the springtime and the sunshine and the sorcery rushing back and forth between them. She wanted more, but she had a task to fulfill.

She let go of his shirt but she kept him with her, warm in her mind, as she walked through the woods. Flowers opened as she passed; fox fire danced in the trees. The woods woke to her footsteps; the leaves sighed with her breath. Once there was a glimpse of bright pearl and ivory: once Kami would have sworn she saw a unicorn.

Kami smiled, stepped out onto the road, and waited for the motorcycle to come purring down the lane.

"Remember you told me you had an imaginary friend once too?" Kami asked.

"Yeah," said Holly.

"I think I saw Princess Zelda," Kami told her.

"You think you saw a unicorn?" asked Holly, and then laughed without mockery, without Kami having to answer her, laughed with sheer delight. "Do you want a lift? I'm afraid there isn't any room for Princess Zelda."

Kami climbed on, and the motorbike roared to life beneath her. With her friend in front of her and her arms spread, the whole world hers.

Jared could feel Kami's elated triumph thrumming through him. He could feel her and knew that she was with Holly, knew that she was going all around Sorry-in-the-Vale and soaking up every drop of magic there was to be had.

And he knew his place in this—he knew who he had to save. He forced himself to focus on his own body, his own surroundings.

He could feel Ash, in a way he hadn't felt anybody but Kami: thoughts as well as feelings. He knew the shape of his soul, and knew that every soul was made of different stuff, shone a thousand different colors.

He sat on the earth, legs still in the cool deep water, one hand in the deep spring-soft grass and one set against his brother's heart.

Come back, he said. *Come on. Come home.*

Home. Not to Aurimere, but to him and to Aunt Lillian. Jared thought about Ash, reaching out to Jared no matter how many times Jared turned him away, of all the good about Ash that he had ever been jealous of.

Ash's eyes opened, the same color as the sky, which was now washed clean of clouds.

"We need to get there now," Ash said, starting up. "We're going to be too late."

"Come on," said Jared. "Aunt Lillian did it. Amber and Ross did it. We're Lynburns, aren't we? Don't tell me there's anything we can't do. Let's not get there. Let's be there already."

He was still holding Ash's hand when they wished themselves from the soft grass and the calm waters to the heart of their town, and found themselves on the High Street of Sorry-in-the-Vale.

Jared looked up at his father's shocked face and saw the moment when he realized what they must have done—saw his father raise his hand to strike him down. Jared felt the catch of his scar twisting his smile out of shape, and he only smiled wider.

"Don't you touch him!"

Martha Wright stooped in the swirling water and debris, then stood with one of the cobblestones clutched in her fist. She drew her arm back and hurled it with all her might.

The people of Sorry-in-the-Vale watched as the lord of Aurimere staggered backward, blood streaming down his face.

Jared dropped Ash's hand, bolted across the street to stand in front of Martha with power gathering in both his hands. It streamed to him out of the air.

"Don't touch her," he said.

Angela was circling Ruth Sherman, spinning her chain over her head. He could see his aunt Lillian, with Kami's dad. Her hands were full of light, and the light was shed on every soul she could see, protecting, blessing, keeping no power for herself. People were turning their faces toward the light, toward her.

Then there was sudden unrest in the group of sorcerers behind Rob.

"Did you kill my brother?" Hugh Prescott asked suddenly, loudly, as if the words had been waiting in his mouth for days and had to come out now.

"What?" snapped Rob, waving his hand as if the question was an irritating fly. "Why are you bothering about this now? That was twenty years ago!"

"He did it," Jared called out. "He killed him. I saw him. He's been walled up dead in Aurimere for twenty years. This whole town will be dead with him if Rob has his way."

Rob turned on Jared, furious, but he did not even have a chance to lift his hand. Holly's father gave a great bellow like a wounded animal and plowed directly into Rob's back.

Ross Phillips lifted a hand to help his leader, but Amber Green caught it and forced it down. Alison Prescott ran to help her husband. And Dorothy, the town librarian, a woman with no magic at all, ran through the water and dived at a sorcerer who was going for Alison Prescott.

Sergeant Kenn punched Jared in the face: Jared felt his lip break. He tasted blood as he laughed, and punched him back.

"What do you people think you're doing?" Ruth Sherman demanded. "What do you think you can do?"

Angela stopped twirling her chain and kicked Ruth Sherman in the kneecaps.

"We're fighting," she said. "My brother taught me that."

It was some of Rob's sorcerers, but not all, rising up against him. It was some of the townspeople, though not all, flooding into the street to fight sorcerers with whatever they could find.

It was chaos, but Jared felt like it was a bright hopeful chaos, the sound of fighting ringing with the bells. They were all together, sorcerers and ordinary mortals, the guilty and the innocent. They were different but united in sudden determination. They were not giving up their town without a fight.

* * *

Kami and Holly raced to the farthest outskirts of town, to the fields and hills, and they chased the clouds away. Everywhere they went, gold followed. They passed the house where Rob Lynburn and his parents had killed, Monkshood Abbey, and Kami felt it as a blot on the landscape: bloodstained and unredeemed. It was no part of the town she believed in, no part of the home she loved.

Kami held on tight to Holly, felt Holly's laugh go all the way through her, and raised her free hand.

A ray of light from the sun went rogue, streaked down from the sky like a falling star and hit that low dark dwelling. A crack appeared in the roof and spread in a wild, jagged zigzag down the gray façade of the house. The fissure widened and the winds blew in wild, and the house shattered like a mirror, into nothing but dust.

Kami thought she heard a tumult of sound, like shouting underwater. She thought of Rob's victims, the victims of all the Lynburns.

No more of the Lynburns' stories, Kami thought. *My story now, just as real as theirs.* More real, because the story was hers. She was not going to let anyone tell her that her story was less important than anyone else's. She was going to believe in it with all her heart.

Jared had said Rusty was not gone, and he had been more right than he knew. Kami should have realized that, all this time.

If the Lynburns had drawn power from death as well as life, she could too. If the power was here, some part of the people it had come from must be here too.

Those the Lynburns had killed would not want to help

them. They would want to help her, to save the people they loved and to protect the town that was their home. If there had been power in their deaths, there had been more power in their lives. Kami thought of Rusty and how he had chosen to give his life, a sacrifice offered not out of fear but from the desire to shield and preserve, a sacrifice offered without being asked. She thought of her grandmother who had lived for decades in this town and would never have borne any of this, thought of Lillian's poor lost sorcerers, thought of the stranger Henry Thornton's kindness.

She had thought they were lost, but if some part of them had been made into magic, then it was not Rob Lynburn's magic. Then they were not lost at all. She could not be lost, either. She did not know why she had ever feared it.

Why be broken, when you can be gold?

They drove around Aurimere itself, and Kami felt the mellow gold of the stones seep into her, knew the wild glory of the growing garden, the memories kept in paint and stone. The Lynburns did not get to be the only ones who told the stories anymore, but the Lynburns were part of the story too. Elinor Lynburn had put her golden bells under the water, but they had not been lost. They had only been waiting to be woken to life, to warn and to protect. Every Lynburn who had loved their town, she took them all with her.

The murmuring that had started in her ears when Monkshood Abbey fell came to her louder and louder, a glad tide washing up on her shores. She could feel the sunlight laid on her like a blanket by her grandmother's loving hands, she could feel wind rushing and leaves whispering like Rusty's low laugh. She could feel Ash, and most of all Jared.

Her friends were in the streets below, in the rising waters, struggling and never surrendering. She saw Angela swinging her chain against Ruth the sorceress.

She came down from the golden house and into the High Street, and she carried the town with her as an army that could not be defeated. Never sorry, never stopping, a world within a world. She was the world. She was sorcery in the vale.

Rob Lynburn was in her way.

He turned and looked at her, his arrogant head held high. He looked surprised and offended, his lips parted as if he was going to ask what she was doing there.

The very stones cried out against him. This town was too big for him. He had never understood that.

Water came to drown him, earth to bury him, fire to burn him, and air to carry every particle of the dust that had been him away from their town.

The supernova of the elements, the whirl of air and light, was too much to look at. But Kami kept looking. She did not see any of what they told her later had happened, how Jared and Angela chased off Sergeant Kenn and Ruth, how the other sorcerers left Rob at the last. The only thing she saw was Rob Lynburn vanishing, a stain of red and gold being wiped from her town.

When it was done, Kami could not look at any of them. She turned, chasing the last of the magic, the last bright dizzying moments of exhilaration and strength that felt like the strength of stone and mountains, of the hatred turned to dust and the love that had lasted.

She went wading through the water, stumbling on the

tumbled cobblestones as if they were the stones on the bottom of a riverbed. There was a blockage in the middle of the High Street, where it was the narrowest before it opened up into the town square. A fallen street sign and a tree trunk had formed a dam there, choked with leaves and branches, the water foaming and gurgling.

Kami did not dare waste a drop of magic. She tried to scramble over it, and then Jared was at her side. He stooped and slid an arm around her, put his other arm under her legs, and lifted her against his chest for a moment. Then he helped her over the obstacle in her path.

She ran down into the town square, laid her warm hand in her mother's cool stone palm, and held her breath. All she felt was stone against flesh, her heart sinking and her blood pounding under her skin; all this magic and life, and yet she could not help her.

Nobody had ever gained anything by despair. She pressed her mother's hands, so hard that her own hands hurt. Then she felt, so gently at first that she thought it might be her imagination and then with a stronger pressure, her mother trying to hold her hands back.

From an enchanted faraway place, she called her mother back, from stone to flesh, from grave to embrace. Kami felt her mother's hands clinging, and slid her hands up her mother's arm, cupped her mother's face, as her mother's hair turned from dead white to warm chestnut. Her skin flushed, and the light washed along the suddenly bright curl of her eyelashes as they fluttered open.

Her mother took her first breath in over a month, a gasping sob, and fell into Kami's arms.

The sun blazed in the sky. The links between them all were strong and shining, forming a line that bound them each to each like jewels on a chain. Kami looked to Ash, and nodded.

The link snapped. The feeling of being so bound you might blend together faded. Kami put her arms around her mother and knelt with her in the water and the debris, in the center of their wrecked and saved town. The river-soaked gold of Sorry-in-the-Vale glowed in the sunlight like treasure discovered underwater and lifted out into the light.

They had lived. Beyond all hope, they had lived.

EPILOGUE

And wilt thou have me fashion into speech
The love I bear thee, finding words enough,
And hold the torch out, while the winds are rough,
Between our faces, to catch light on each?
—*Elizabeth Barrett Browning*

Chapter Twenty-Four
Written in Gold

Sometimes Kami looked back on the day Sorry-in-the-Vale had been saved, and it felt as if she was thinking of a story that had happened to someone else. Everything that had happened still felt important and vital, felt like real things that had happened to those she really loved. She did not forget a moment of it. She knew the value of all she had won, and all she had lost.

She simply could not recapture the shining certainty of it all.

She did not know if the power had fooled her into feeling love in the sun, or hearing whispers in the wind. Kami did not know if it had been spirits or simply the memory of those loved and lost, giving her strength. Kami liked to think that it had been something real, so she could feel as if Jared had been right: that nothing was lost, only changed into what was strange to her.

Rusty and Angela's parents had come down from London, distressed at the terrible accident they believed had occurred, but Angela had not stood with them in the graveyard. She had stood between Kami and Holly, holding both their hands. She had stood with her family.

They had buried Rusty in a sunny corner of the grave-yard, the kind of nook he would have liked to stretch out and nap in. His gravestone was inscribed with gold letters.

RUSSELL MONTGOMERY III
Warm summer sun shine kindly here
Warm south wind blow kindly here
Still and always burns your light
Good night, dear heart, good night, good night.

Kami had woken too often in the nights that followed and cried for missing him. She did not know how much more often Angela had woken and wept. She had to remember that there was power and magic in life: that when the sun laid a ray as warm as a hand on her head as they left the graveyard, it could be an unseen hand, reaching out to her with love. Only changed, and not strange forever.

Kami did not look to the churchyard as she rushed into the town square. She was looking to the living. She was late.

As she passed the great glass window of Claire's, the reflection of her dress looked like a blur of gold and red. It was one of the new dresses that her dad had let her order online, with a pattern of golden pears and red cherries. Through the window, she saw her family, and waved to them through it, and waved again as she walked in.

"Ash!" she exclaimed, surprised. He was the one person she had not expected.

She had not seen him since the night last week when they

had gone down to the woods, to the Crying Pools, with Ash and Jared both bearing a golden burden. Jared had drawn his arm back and taken aim, and Ash had mirrored the action. With two silver splashes, the twin golden knives of the Lynburns were gone forever.

"How was the Royal College of Art?"

Ash was sitting on one of the stools at the counter, Tomo sitting at his feet. His hair was mussed and he had somehow acquired an air of glamorous travel, despite having only been a few hours away.

"Good," he said. "I think I will like it there. Lots of girls offering themselves as excellent models for photography, which is very welcoming of them and I appreciate it."

He smiled, and Kami knew it was meant to be reassuring. She smiled back. It wasn't that she didn't see romantic potential in Ash. She'd always been able to see that. Looking at him was like looking at a beautiful stretch of land and imagining the towers that could have been, if they had chosen to build them. The land was still beautiful without them.

Ash regarded her affectionately, and his eyes were free of the burning intensity and the unhappiness she had seen in them once. They had been clear as summer skies ever since the day the town was saved.

"I hear the London girls are terribly interesting models," said Kami. "Also, if I may use an artistic term, babelicious."

Ash shrugged. "Well, since Jared is going to help Mom handle things at Aurimere, this is my chance to live life with no responsibilities and lots of artistic models."

Jared and Ash had agreed that they would not talk about,

or listen to Lillian's proclamations about, a single heir of Auri-mere. The Lynburn legacy could be changed with the story of the town, could be whatever they decided they wanted it to be.

"We're very happy for you and we very much don't want to hear any of the details," said Holly, laughing. She was sitting on one of the workbenches at the far wall.

Nobody looked like they were being much help with the painting, but Angela looked like she was being the least help of anybody. She was lying on the bench, her head in Holly's lap and her eyes firmly closed. Kami could tell she wasn't asleep, though. When Holly carelessly stroked the dark hair spread over her knees, Kami caught the fleeting curve of Angela's smile.

"I thought we were going to help Dad painting," she said. "Not lie around discussing nude models."

"Nobody is helping me, because none of you have true artistic vision. And you're the one who just brought up nudes," said Jon Glass.

"I thought 'artistic' was cunning code for 'nude,'" said Kami. "Is that not true? Have I been lied to? Do I have a tragically perverted mind? Oh well, I guess that's a shame."

Jon had decided that he wanted to paint a mural on the wall of Claire's. Kami had thought Dad and Mum would be reunited, as simply and beautifully as the sun coming out, but her mother was living above Claire's, and the rest of the family were living at the Water Rising while the house was rebuilt. Yet Jon was painting this, making something beautiful for his wife. Kami did not know what would happen with them next. It was their decision. She knew that much.

The mural unfolding on the wall was beautiful. Kami saw her mother peep out of the kitchen and admire it. Kami went over to kiss her cheek.

"Nice to have a piece of art here that won't get eaten," Claire said, pressing Kami's hand. She still wore her wedding ring. Dad was still not wearing his, but Kami knew he carried it around in his pocket.

"Thank you for bringing up eating," Kami said. "We were promised cookies if we came to help. I intended to come and help, and as it's the thought that counts, I feel I'm still owed cookies."

"I'll see what I can do," said Mum.

Kami was going to be milking this "changed you back from stone" business for baked goods for a solid decade. That was the kind of person she was. She accepted this truth about herself.

"Are you people still not done?" asked Lillian Lynburn from the door.

Ten looked warily up from his book, but when he saw her doing nothing more than pulling off her black leather gloves, he returned to the story. Jared had given him the book, and promised him there would be explosions. Kami was not sure how many explosions Edgar Allan Poe would really provide, but Ten seemed to be enjoying it.

In the meantime, Lillian was looking speculatively at the mural. Kami saw her lift her hand. With sorcery, the mural could be done in ten minutes.

"I see you, Linnaea," Jon called over his shoulder. "Don't even think it. I have eyes in the back of my head, and all my eyes have artistic vision."

"'Linnaea' is not a name," grumbled Lillian, but she lowered her hand.

"It is a name," said Jon. "I looked it up."

Linnaea was the name of a flower, also called the twinflower. Kami knew it because she had seen pictures of all the flowers Jon was painting: call-me-to-you, daisies, goldeneye, wild daffodils, Lazarus bells, honeysuckle, and burnt orchids in the deep woods and by the shining lakes, nestled into the hollows of tree roots and trim gardens alike. Twinflowers were pearl-pale bells with lilac hearts, two flowers growing from a single fragile stem.

The woods in the heart of town. Kami thought it was a lovely idea for a mural.

Lillian walked over to Ash, who caught her hand as she went by. Lillian smiled and let him keep it, pulling herself up on a stool and regarding the mural with a critical eye. Kami was prepared to bet that either criticisms or more offers of magical help would be along in less than five minutes. She was prepared to bet a lot, if she could find any sucker who would take it.

She never found out.

There was another tap on the door.

"Oh, good," said Mum, disappearing into the kitchen. "Another Lynburn."

"Hi, Mrs. Glass," Jared called after her.

"That is how I shall always greet you from now on," Angela informed Jared, without opening her eyes.

Jared stayed standing in the doorway, hands on either side of the doorframe. It was almost summer, almost too warm for his battered leather jacket. There was something about the set of his shoulders that she thought looked tense.

"Kami," he said. "I came to ask if I could talk to you outside."

Kami looked around at her friends, at her family, for a hint as to what she should do. Her treacherous friends and family stared innocently and unhelpfully back. "Yes," she said at last. "All right."

They had not been alone in weeks. Kami had thought that it was because there was so much to be done, to be rebuilt, to be arranged, and then she had started to wonder if Jared had been avoiding being alone with her.

Now they were alone, and Jared did not seem to have much to say to her. There was no statue in the square any longer, her mother revived, Matthew Cooper and all his history gone. Jared paced silently in the sunlit square that was left.

Kami watched him. Jared looked up, and visibly nerved himself.

"Here's the thing," said Jared. "I thought it was obvious. I thought it was embarrassingly obvious, but—when we did the ceremony I saw your mind, and I saw the way you've seen the past few months. When you told me we were going out, I went along with it. You were calling me silly names, it was clear you weren't as serious about it as I was. I figured you could see that I would have taken anything you would give me, and you thought I was kind of ridiculous and desperate. But you didn't, did you?"

"No," said Kami. "I felt like I had to bully you into going out with me. So no. I did not think you were the pathetic one in that scenario."

Jared bit his lip. "Then I've been messing up everything, the whole time. Well. That shouldn't be a surprise, but it is. I didn't realize how I must have seemed, to you. I'm sure I'm going to mess this up too, but there is one thing I thought was more obvious than anything else. There is one thing I thought you knew, and if you don't I have to tell you. I am utterly in love with you. I've been in love with you my whole life. I've been in love with you *your* whole life. I don't know how to live without being in love with you, and I don't want to know."

He held her gaze for that long, then looked down at the cobblestones.

"I don't want to sound like my father. Like either of my fathers. My feelings aren't more important than yours. I don't want to act as if they are."

"You never thought they were, not really. You didn't think anything about yourself was important at all."

He had thought his life was worth so much less than hers, so much less than Ash's. But he had decided to live without them if he had to. She was so glad they had all lived, but she was glad to think of his decision, even now. She was reassured and warmed by it, by how far he had come.

"It's cool," said Jared. "I think I'm awesome now. So awesome. You should definitely go out with me."

Kami laughed and hesitated, leaning against the wall and watching him, his Lynburn profile outlined against gold stone and a summer sky. She was not sure if now was the time to act.

"I always thought that you could never love me," said Jared, and his voice was stark, not self-pitying, just stating facts. "Not really. Nobody ever did but you, for so long, and you weren't real. I thought nobody real could love me, and then you were real, and I still thought that. I resented you for not loving me, and I tried to accept you not loving me, and I am so sorry I hurt you. I hardly even believed I could. I don't ever want to hurt you again. And I can accept you not loving me, but I had to tell you how I felt. I want to love you, and I want you to love me back. I came to find out if that could ever be possible."

Jared hesitated, as if hoping for an answer, but when he did not get one he plunged desperately on.

"I said once that my idea of happiness is to always be with you, and it is. I'm always going to think of you as the source of everything. To me, the sun rises and sets on you. You make all things true. I am in love with you, and I cannot imagine being in love with anyone else. It would be like becoming someone else. Your name was the first word for love I ever knew." He broke off, and set his jaw, looking frustrated. "I don't want to talk like Rob, saying that you owe me something because I love you, or that other women are worthless because I'm not in love with them. Love isn't some kind of debt. That's not what I mean."

"I know," said Kami. "You always thought Holly was great."

"She is great," said Jared. "And beautiful. She's like a star to me, something bright and lovely seen from another world. She's someone else's sun. That's how all other girls are to me. You're my sun."

It was a nice recovery.

"Your courtship method of arrogance, self-loathing, and then telling me how beautiful other girls are is pretty unique," said Kami. "I like it. I don't know what that says about me."

"You like it?" Jared asked, with a shy glance up at her.

"I'm glad you told me the truth."

"That's all I intended to do," Jared said hastily. "I don't expect anything from you. That was what I've been trying to tell you. I want you, but I don't need you to give me anything you don't want to give. You existing in the world is all I need."

"I'm glad you told me the truth," Kami repeated. "Because I have something to tell you now."

Kami straightened up from the wall and looked into his eyes, those pale clear eyes, like mirrors, like pools.

She had not only worried that he did not love her the way she wanted him to. She had not only loved and longed. She had spent so much time worrying that accepting love, becoming part of all the love stories, would trap her in some way, change her into someone weak, someone she did not want to be. But she realized now that she had been narrow-minded, considering a love story as a lesser story, a story that might make her lesser to be part of. She had always thought she needed to be in control, but now she found she did not want to put any limits on herself at all. She wanted to be the person she was, and not the person anyone, including herself, had ever thought she should be. She had thought a lot lately about making all the love stories her own, of telling them her own way.

He had told her everything she had been hoping to hear.

She hadn't been sure how Jared felt, though she had hoped, because Ash had loved her when he was bound to Jared and not before or after. But what was between them was complicated and often painful and priceless, terrifying to risk. She had not known what to call it, for so long.

She had not been sure, but she had hoped, and planned. She had planned this. She had asked Ash to help her spend the last of their linked magic to build a barrier, the highest, strongest barrier she had ever built. To hide the link that Kami had not broken.

She brought the last barrier between them crashing down. She felt the link between them flicker and wake to life, like waking the woods except that it was just them, being marvels to each other.

The sky turned upside down for a moment, so they were falling into vivid blue. The gold of Cotswold stone blazed and embraced them, and Kami turned as Jared turned, moved with his movements. She felt his joy running through her like a river through parched lands, bringing everything to life. She felt her waist beneath her hands as he did, at the same time as she savored the sensation of his hands resting above her hips, moving to slide up her back. He bent down and kissed her and she knew his hunger and his longing, and knew he could feel hers. She knew which was her, and which was him, and being linked meant they could share, meant they had forged a blazing path and could meet in the middle, close, close as other people did not wish or dare to be, as close as they could get.

"So you do . . ." Still, after all this, Jared hesitated, hardly daring to believe. "Do you love me?"

Kami tipped back her head and laughed at him, felt her laugh running along his bones, delight mirrored back to her and back again. The sun hung above them like a silent shining bell in the sky. She opened up her thoughts and let him see it all, the story of her love laid out before him as though written in scarlet and gold.

She said: *Read my mind.*

Acknowledgments

Many thanks to my lovely editor, Mallory Loehr, and to Chelsea Eberly and Jenna Lettice; my wonderful copy editor, Deborah Dwyer; Jan Gerardi; and the whole great team at Random House Children's Books.

Thank you very much to Kristin Nelson and everyone at NLA for everything, forever.

And thank you to Ginger Clark: so sorry to torment you like I have!

Thank you to Venetia Gosling and Ellie Willis and Gail Hallett and the team at Simon & Schuster UK, for every stage of the Lynburn Legacy series! And to Kathryn McKenna and Sophie Stott for combining their publicity powers.

Thank you to Robin Wasserman, Maureen Johnson, Malinda Lo, Delia Sherman, Cindy Pon, Paolo Bacigalupi, Josh Lewis, Ally Carter, Jen Lynn Barnes, Leigh Bardugo, Karen Healey, R. J. Anderson, Saundra Mitchell, Kelly Link, Cassandra Clare, and Holly Black. Thank you for your support and your excellent faces. Especial thanks to Holly for the poem. She knows the one. (The suggestion that I should say "Thanks to all the jerks who got me through this!" was, as you can see, noted.)

Thank you to my Irish friends—I love you and by the

time you read this will be missing you. Hello to my UK and American and Australian friends!

Thank you to Chiara for Con Dau, where I got the edits for this book, but more importantly where we were friends for twenty-two years. Here's to twenty-two more, bestie.

Thank you to my family. Sorry for making fun of you on Twitter all the time.

I never knew, until this series, that I could torment people I did not know, lay waste to their dreams, blow holes in their ships, and drink their tears.

I regret nothing.

I hope you feel the same!

About the Author

SARAH REES BRENNAN grew up in Ireland and then moved to New York and London, where she wrote her first book, *The Demon's Lexicon.* She never had an imaginary friend as a child, but she returned to Ireland to write about all the imaginary friends she has now and hopes you like them. Visit her at sarahreesbrennan.com or follow her on Twitter at @sarahreesbrenna, where they cruelly stole her last "n" and she *will* have vengeance.